Time Will Tell

Time Will Tell

Trevy A. McDonald

May "time tell" of peace, joy, happiness, love, wonderful experiences and rich blessings

Sisterly

Trevy A. McDonald

Reyomi Publishing

Chicago, IL

Renew Your Mind

Published by Reyomi Publishing
P.O. Box 43255, Chicago, IL 60643
Phone: 877-473-9664, Fax: 888-739-6648

Library of Congress Card Catalog No: 99-90200

ISBN 0-9670712-0-8

Cover art and design: Erica Ramsey

http://www.reyomi.com
E-mail: timewyltel@aol.com

Printed in the United States of America
Second Printing

This novel is dedicated to my parents,
Juanita and Thomas McDonald.

Acknowledgments

And He who gave you a good work will be faithful to complete it.
—Philippians 1:6

Glory and Honor to God for inspiring me with Time Will Tell and for blessing me with many talents. To my parents, Thomas and Juanita McDonald, I thank you for your love, support and encouragement and for pushing me to bring this project to completion. To my brother, Lenny, thank you for believing in me and for sharing your knowledge with me. To my cousin Kaye Hill Lumpkins, thank you for helping me get past writer's block and for being there for me. I can't wait to read your book.

To my artist and friend, Erica Ramsey, thank you for your friendship, your artistic talent and your creative suggestions..

To my support team: Tisha M. Kelley, Rubin L. Whitmore, II, Shirley Hamilton, Beverly Mahone, Dr. Deborah Austin, Burmadeane George, Regina Ford-Patterson, Nikol Strong, MarinaWoods, Malaika Mayfield, Juanita Strong, Doug Heil, Lee West, James Tracy Tulloss, Rena Ramsey-Caldwell, Dr. Mark Orbe, and Ava Haskins Alston thank you for your comments, criticism and inspiration which helped me make *Time Will Tell* a better book than I ever imagined.

To my editor, Teresa Fowler-Walker, thank you for eliminating my qualifiers, making certain every comma was placed properly and for making *Time Will Tell the best it could be.*

To Tim Colton, and Kathy Kay, thank you for your advice, direction and support.

Special thanks to Jesse Rogers of WSCR-AM, David Greenbaum of WMVP-AM, Dr. James Tulloss, Rev. Trevon D. Gross, George Newell, and Rev. Javid Jenkins for sharing your expertise with me and for critiquing respective sections of the book. Your insight made *Time Will Tell* more authentic.

To the booksellers and readers, thank you for believing in me enough to buy my first novel. I hope that you will enjoy reading it as much as I enjoyed writing it.

Holding Back the Years

1

*T*homasine took one long look around the office of her River Run Estates home to make certain she had not forgotten any important papers, journal articles or books. She didn't know how difficult it would be to get these materials in Sydney or Cairns, where she was to spend the next two years of her life. A two-year Study Abroad Research Grant to explore the experiences and culture of Aboriginal women in Australia would be the answer to the prayers of many young academicians, and though ambivalent about going so far away, she felt the experience was what she needed.

The last ten years of her life had been like the "Screaming Eagle" at Six Flags Great America Theme Park. Still, Thomasine certainly had a lot to be proud of. Her road had been long and circuitous—beginning as a member of Piney Hill High School's Class of 1987 and coming to a junction as Assistant Professor of Anthropology and Women's Studies at the internationally known Steeplechase University in the Research Triangle Park, North Carolina. Before receiving the grant, her most important accomplishment was *US Women of Color*—a long overdue volume for Women's Studies curricula across the country.

When she thought about all she had accomplished in the last ten years and what the next two years would mean, she knew that going abroad was the right thing to do. After all, the prestigious grant guaranteed her a tenure award and promotion—to Associate Professor—all before her thirtieth birthday. Thomasine had made it, at least professionally. The last ten years had been a series of emotional, spiritual, physical and intellectual peaks and valleys. She may not have graduated the valedictorian of Piney Hill's Class of '87, that achievement went to her close friend Hope, but she truly had a lot to be proud of.

She was looking forward to going home to the South Side of Chicago; seeing her aging parents, Thomas & Crystal Mintor, her older brother Tommy and her friends Rachel and Hope. Rev. Mintor used to call them

the "Three Musketeers." If they weren't together in school, they were together at Front Street African Christian Church.

The girls met in 1981 in Mrs. Anderson's Sunday School class when
Rev. Mintor was appointed Pastor of Front Street. They had been best
friends ever since. During their senior year of high school, they team
taught a Sunday School class of eight-year-olds. Then there was Junior
Church, the youth group that had activities with other African Christian
churches on Chicago's South side. Hope was particularly fond of these
events, especially after high school, because they gave her an opportunity
to see Jason, now her husband. And of course there was the choir. Thomasine, with a vocal range from soprano to tenor, was the official soloist for
the Youth Choir, so the chemistry between her, and Rachel—the musician—
seemed natural.

Thomasine, or Sina, as she's affectionately called by her close friends
and relatives, was beginning to wonder if she were more in love with the
idea of spending a few weeks at home than with going abroad. She was really looking forward to the "Princess" treatment she would receive from
her father. Rev. Mintor, a tall, distinguished man with cocoa brown skin
and salt and pepper hair, dropped off her dry cleaning, washed her car,
shined her shoes, washed and ironed her clothes, cooked her breakfast,
and gave her anything she wanted. Crystal Mintor, petite with skin the
color of a walnut and a collection of the flyest wigs that she never wore in
the house, did not want her daughter to expect too much from men. While
the royal treatment was Thomasine's reality, her mother had preached to
Sina from the time she was six years old, "Don't sit around spending half
your life waiting for Prince Charming or some other knight in shining
armor, because he ain't coming." Thomasine listened, but still savored her
dad's royal treatment. Both she and Tommy were named after their father.
Tommy, tall with caramel colored skin and lips described as kissable by
many women, was ten years older than Sina, and most of her childhood
memories were of Tommy's taunting and teasing, but Sina always stood up
to her big brother. From the time she was in her walker, until the time she
dated a guy in college he did not like, Thomasine always spoke her mind
to Tommy, one of Chicago's finest.

Sina always thought he was jealous. After all, he had been an only child
for ten years and then his forty-something mom told him he would soon
have a brother or sister. Tommy prayed for a little brother. He thought,
"How neat, a little brother I can teach to play baseball, take fishing, and
train to take my place as an altar boy." And then Thomasine arrived.

Sina was Thomas and Crystal's miracle baby. After they had Tommy, they wanted another child. Crystal had given up hope. She was forty-two years old and had noticed stranges changes but blamed it on menopause. Crystal knew what the signs were because so many women had come into the gynecology clinic at South Side Hospital where she was a registered nurse with these same symptoms and it was always the beginning of "The Change." Crystal gave up hope because she knew the beginning of menopause meant she could have no more children. Thomas encouraged her to have more tests and much to their surprise and dismay, Crystal was pregnant at 42! For a couple of months one of the neighbors thought Sina was Crystal's growing fibroid tumor.

Thinking of her parents made Thomasine remember something very important. She walked over to the wall and removed the cherry frame that held her Ph.D. from The University of North Carolina. The day she received her Ph.D in Anthropology was almost as important to her family as the day Thomas first laid eyes on his "Princess," who had her eyes closed and her hands folded as if in prayer. That was the day Sina's father fell in love with her and the day she wrapped Rev. Mintor around her little finger. And at five pounds twelve ounces, that finger was little.

For ten years Thomasine had set a goal and then achieved it, the most important being her Ph.D. before her 26th birthday, and that she did. Many of her friends, not close ones of course, accused Thomasine of being just too full of herself. Hanging that diploma in her home office. Those in academe understood and supported her choice. Some had had their framed diplomas stolen from their offices at various universities across the country.

She surveyed the room one last time, and remembered her eight o'-clock hair appointment, She rushed upstairs, found her purse, and slapped on some of her Flori Roberts Dangerously Red lipstick, grabbed a button with pictures of her, Rachel and Hope taken during their senior year Spirit Week, and rushed to the hairdresser.

Thomasine had been going to Regina for four years now. It was inconvenient to go to the country to get her hair done and she was often accused of passing up several good hairdressers to save a few dollars, but Sina liked Regina. She was great with hair, personable, and relatively inexpensive. Thomasine's hair was so much healthier than it had been since she went to Monique in Chicago. As Sina drove into the gravel parking lot of the shop, she wondered what she would do with her hair once she went to Australia. When she was there last, she heard from Aboriginal Women that a touch-up was expensive.

"Good morning Gina," Thomasine said, smiling, as she sat down in Regina's chair in the shop with teal and peach decor.

"It's so good to be greeted by the smiling face of one of my preferred clients," Regina responded. "Now Sina, have you been scratching?"

"Oh you know the answer to that."

"One day you will learn," Regina pulled out the Sensitive Scalp Relaxer. "So what's new Sina?"

"Make sure you get my hair good and straight, because I'll be gone for two years."

"Is it already time for you to go to Australia?"

"I actually leave in a few weeks, but I'm heading home today. I got this early appointment so that I could hit the road fairly early."

"I knew this was not your usual day or time to come," Regina said as she worked the relaxer into Sina's hair. "Wait a minute, you mean you are driving to Chicago today?"

"Yes, I want to be there in time for my birthday tomorrow and my parents are looking after Sparky so I have to drive. He is the closest thing they have to a grandchild," Thomasine said of her five year old Golden Retriever. "With him there, maybe Mama and Daddy won't have to worry about anyone stealing their garbage can from the alley behind the house."

"You've got to be kidding," Regina replied. "The garbage can?"

"As in the one the city issues."

"If you want another can here, all you have to do is call the county and ask for one."

"It's the same way at home, but I guess they'd rather take someone else's than get their own. But you haven't heard all of it," Thomasine went on. "Mama and Daddy used to have two cans, now they have one. One of the neighbors down the alley who used to have two, now has three. When they fill up their now three cans, they put their trash in Mama and Daddy's can."

"The ways of city folk never cease to amaze me." Regina said. "But I'm sure Sparky will break that up."

"By the way Regina, I am burning."

"I declare, you will come in here for a touch up and tell me you haven't scratched. Now let's get you rinsed."

"I've got one on fire!" Regina exclaimed as she and Thomasine approached the shampoo bowls finding all of them occupied. Two other clients immediately jumped up from the shampoo bowl. They'd been there before.

When Regina finished rinsing, shampooing and conditioning Thomasine's hair, they returned to her station. Regina immediately took out her blow dryer and a brush. "Hold up, wait a minute," Thomasine said. "I'm not getting a blow-dry today."

"You mean to tell me you aren't getting your usual part on the right side, curled under, conservative hairdo?"

"No, I want a French roll in the back, swoop the front and put cup curls up top."

"What's the occasion? You must have a hot date when you get to Chicago."

"No, I'm also attending my class reunion, and since I was the Prez. I *have* to look good. Well, I always look good, but I have to look especially good because I never know who I'll run into," Regina poured the wrap lotion on Sina's hair.

Captain of Her Heart

2

I need to change this lightbulb, Rachel thought as she pulled the chain connected to the closet light. "I guess Hank can get me some bulbs from Commonwealth Edison when I get home," she said in a near silent whisper. She took her evening gown out of her closet and held it up to her. The hem of the dress fell just above her ankles, and as she looked in the mirror attached to the inside of her closet door, she was sure the dress would still hug the curves she had in all the right places, even after two babies. She placed it and a Sunday dress in the garment bag stretched out on her full-sized bed.

"Mommy, where we going?" five year-old Martin asked, with his upper lip curled, when he saw the packed bags.

"We are going to Chicago."

"To see Uncle Hank and Grandma?" asked bright-eyed Malcolm.

"And you boys will see Grandma and Grandpa Mintor and your T-Sina and T-Hope too."

"I want to see my T-Sina," the boys shouted with excitement.

"Mommy, how we gone get there? The car's broke," asked inquisitive four-year-old Malcolm.

"It's how are we going to get there?" Rachel replied. "We're flying honey." Rachel continued packing the boys' play clothes.

"But we don't have wings," replied Malcolm.

"No Malcolm, we fly in a airplane," explained his older brother Martin.

"Is it scary?"

"No. You will enjoy it. You can look down at all of the houses and see all of Nashville, Opryland, and when we get to Chicago, you can see over the Sears Tower." Rachel said as she sat on her bed with young Malcolm on her lap.

"Ooh, we go flying." Malcolm shouted.

"Do we have to go see Brothaman? Because I don't want to!"

"I want you boys to spend a little time with your father. And of course, I expect you to spend time with T-sina because she is getting ready to go far, far away for a long time. But she will be back."

"Will she take us to the beach?" Martin asked.

"Just maybe, if you're good boys."

"Yeah Malcolm, we get to go to the beach." Martin said jumping up and down with jubilation. "But I don't want to go to Brothaman's house."

"He's Daddy to you Martin Brown." Despite her sons' feelings, Rachel insisted that they spend "quality time" with Brothaman. It was important for Martin and Malcolm to see their father whenever they were in the same city, with supervision that is. Although she and Brothaman were separated she wanted the boys to form a special bond with their father.

Rachel wanted her young boys to have the things she and Hank had missed. Their father had been reported Missing-in-Action in Vietnam when Rachel was two and Hank was an infant. As a matter of fact, Henry Curtis, Sr. never even saw young Hank. He simply vanished. Shortly after Henry was reported missing, Rachel's 21-year old mother, Rebecca, unable to cope with the pressures of the disturbing news in the midst of caring for two young children, suffered severe depression and had a mental breakdown. Young Rachel and Hank were sent to live with their maternal great-aunt and uncle, Mary and Charles Anderson. Mary served as a Sunday School teacher and Minister of Music of Front Street African Christian Church until her death in 1991, and music teacher of several children including Rachel and Thomasine. Rachel followed in Aunt Mary's footsteps by serving as organist at Well of Salvation African Christian Church in Nashville.

Mary and Charles would be very proud of Rachel and Hank. Rachel realized her dream of becoming a Special Education teacher and the musical background was helpful, as she minored in Music Therapy.

Hank was quite successful too, having recently completed medical school at Duncan University. Henry Sr.'s MIA status did not have the same impact on Hank as it had on Rachel. Uncle Charlie was the only father Hank had ever known, but Rachel always felt that she had missed out on her father's love. The reassurance, affection, and encouragement from Uncle Charlie, her stepfather Sherman, and Rev. Mintor just didn't seem to fill the empty spaces. She didn't want her boys to have that same empty feeling.

They were once a very happy family. But that was when Malcolm was a baby and Brothaman had a cushy job at an advertising agency in Nashville. That job was the only reason Rachel ever left Chicago. But then

Brothaman had another lover, not another woman, not at first anyway, but that white pony, which quickly became that white rock likely to be cut with absolutely anything—even household cleanser. Just when Rachel thought they would be one happy family again like before her father was reported MIA, "Satan reared its ugly head once again," Rachel told Sina. She and the boys were back to square one.

When she decided to let the boys spend the night with their father who had been banned from the Anderson residence, Brothaman messed up again. Hank had just told Rachel to forget about that house in Beverly Hills, unless she planned to win the lottery or get the life insurance policy on her husband that Hope had so encouraged.

Rachel stormed in the bedroom as Brothaman scrambled to a sitting position in his bed. Seeing that women with flourescent colored hair and airbrushed acrylic nails had shocked Rachel so that she didn't see the crack pipe Brothaman inadvertently kicked under the bed. For Rachel, this was it. She could take no more.

"Just what on earth are you doing? And who the hell is this? Do you realize your children almost set this building on fire, because you are too trifling to get your lazy butt out of bed and fix them something to eat?"

"And just who is this bitch walking up in here Brothaman?"

"I'm his damn wife. Or I was," Rachel said slinging her wedding band across the room.

"I'm Shaniqua, bitch."

"I got your bitch," Rachel said as she directed her attention to the safety of her children. "And I need to have a word or two with you." Rachel said pointing directly at Brothaman as she walked out of the bedroom.

Rachel and Brothaman went out into the hallway of his apartment building and as much as Rachel wanted to start slinging cast iron skillets up in there, she knew she was on Brothaman's turf, and Shaniqua's irritating voice reminded her that she was outnumbered. Plus they were both probably high and Rachel did not want to mess with that. "Brothaman Brown, this is the last straw. Just what on earth were you trying to do? You must be back on that stuff. You were too knee deep in that skeezer to even take care of your responsibility. I don't believe this! Just what were you trying to prove?"

"I, I," Brothaman started.

"I nothing. Hank and Hope were right about you. I just wish I had listened. Sina said to give you a chance, but you have run out of chances. You do absolutely nothing for the boys. Do you honestly believe I want them to grow up like you? No good, can't keep a job, womanizing, crack head!

I'm calling the police on this one." But she really didn't need to do anything because her soon-to-be ex-husband was killing himself.

Brothaman knew that Rachel was telling the truth, and sometimes the truth hurts so much that he showed Rachel a new side of himself. "You skank ass bitch! Don't you ever call me a name like that again," Brothaman shouted, as he knocked Rachel against the wall, went into his apartment, and slammed the door.

"Brothaman Brown, you take one good, long, hard look at those boys because it will be the last time you see them," Rachel said as she took that stainless steel watch with the pink, yellow and white gold on the band and slammed it toward the door.

"Yeah, I've heard that one before. And I'm sure I'll hear it again." Brothaman shouted from the inside of his apartment.

Within minutes, Martin and Malcolm had left the apartment carrying their sloppily packed overnight bag. "What happened Mommy?" Martin asked.

"Mommy just fell down, that's all honey. But you know what? And I want both of you to remember this all of your life. You can't keep a good woman down."

Rachel took one last look around her room as she heard the horn of Rev. Hermann's car and carried the bags down for the ride to the airport.

Touch & Go

3

*T*hat will be $10.50," said the gas station attendant as Thomasine handed him her check card. As she walked back to her car, she slowly panned the Carolina blue sky zooming in on a sign she would not see again for two years, *Krisp & Tasty Donut Shop*. Popular in the Southeast, they are known worldwide for having the best pineapple frosted yeast donuts, Thomasine's favorite.

As she drove across the street and waited for a parking space, Thomasine knew if she left with a few dozen donuts for herself and Hope ever found out, her life would be over. *Well, I could always say Sparky ate them.*

Krisp & Tasty was one of Hope's favorite restaurants, if there is such a thing for Hope, when she was at Harrington College in Savannah. She was a fourth generation Harrington woman. Her mother had attended Harrington in the early 60s and her mother in the 40s and her mother in the 20s. Being a fourth generation Harrington woman meant a lot to Hope. For Harrington women represented the true essence of Black womanhood. They had style, class and prosperous futures. Hope was proud to be a fourth generation Harrington woman and live in the same dorm as her mother and grandmother. At first she was upset about going so far away from her high school sweetheart Jason, but family tradition and the prestige of Harrington soon won her over. After all, she could always call Jason or hop on a plane and see him in a few hours.

Hope was even prouder when she graduated Summa Cum Laude from the first Black women's college in the U.S., completing her course work in three years! Hope was always classy, courteous and kind. That is, except when it came to food.

As Thomasine ordered three pineapple donuts for herself and thought about what she would get for Hope, she was reminded of a time when Hope did not display her alma mater's motto.

Two years ago, when Thomasine graduated, Hope and Rachel had come early to celebrate. Hope insisted that Sina drive all the way to the other side of Burlington, at least forty miles from her South Durham home for *Krisp & Tasty* donuts. Rachel could not believe that Hope had asked Sina to drive that distance for donuts when there were several local bakeries.

Seeing the *Krisp & Tasty* sign from I-85, her mouth began to think out loud to herself. "Will I have powdered or chocolate cake with chocolate frosting or maybe I'll have French Crullers?"

With her 5 feet by 5 feet frame, she should choose none of the above, thought Thomasine.

"Humph, Sina should make Hope walk back to Durham and then she could eat all of whatever kind of donut she wants," Rachel said under her breath while she sat in the back seat with her boys.

"Good morning Ma'am, may I take your order?" said the thin blue-eyed teenager behind the counter of the busy restaurant.

"Yes, I'll have a baker's dozen."

"Okay ma'am, what wouldja like?"

"Three powdered, three chocolate cake with chocolate frosting, three sour cream, and four French crullers."

Sina and Rachel could never understand Hope's obsession with those stupid French Crullers or why she always spoke as if everyone around her was hard of hearing. Secretly, Sina and Rachel called her cruller because when they graduated from eighth grade, she was just a cruller away from 150 lbs. and not even five feet tall.

"Ma'am, you can only have three French Crullers," said Misty.

"No, you don't seem to understand me," Hope said impatiently as she shifted her weight from right to left. "I will have four French Crullers."

"Well then ma'am, wouldja like two powdered, two cake or two sour cream?"

"I will have three powdered, three chocolate cake, three sour cream, and four French crullers." Hope insisted.

"Oh, than ya want the dozen in the box and the French Cruller in a bag to eat now?"

"No, I want them all on the plate."

"All right ma'am, that will be $4.50." Misty said as she rang up Hope's order.

"You've overcharged me young lady. I ordered a baker's dozen." Hope was greedy, but when it came to her money, she balanced her accounts to the penny.

"But 3 + 3 + 3 + 4 is thirteen and a dozen is twelve."

"I ordered a baker's dozen, and I want my thirteen donuts on a plate. If I have any left over then I will ask for a bag."

"But you want a dozen which is 12 and there will be an extra charge for that fourth French Cruller."

"Hey, hurry up, I'm late for work," shouted a middle-aged man in a suit.

"You don't seem to understand me," Hope said sternly. "I am ordering a Baker's Dozen. I want my thirteen donuts and I have come all the way from Kalamazoo, Michigan for these donuts. Now give me my donuts!"

"Well, a dozen ain't 13 here ma'am. It is 12 and 3 + 3 + 3 + 4 is not 12 here in North Carolina, it is 13. If you want 13 donuts then you will have to pay for a dozen plus one," replied Misty, somewhat annoyed by now.

"I am a Certified Public Accountant and I graduated summa cum laude from Harrington College in Savannah, Georgia. I am a fourth generation Harrington woman and I CAN COUNT! I have eaten *Krisp and Tasty* Donuts since I was a little girl and a Baker's Dozen is 13. Now give me my 13 donuts."

"Mommy," three-year-old Martin began. "Why is T-Hope mad at that lady?"

"Been eatin' those donuts all your life and it shows," grunted another impatient customer. "Right now you 'bout a donut away from a heart attack."

Sina nodded at Rachel and approached the register. "Misty, please forgive my friend for the inconvenience," Sina said as she and Rachel dragged an enraged Hope kicking and screaming away from *Krisp and Tasty*.

That was Hope's problem. She was always right, even though she was in this case, and she never backed down. That's because she always got her way, and more so than most other only children. Her parents, Phyllis and Steven Jones gave her everything she wanted, especially food. Steven Jones, who felt guilty about all of his traveling as a corporate salesman for a pharmaceutical company, made sure that every Saturday was special for Hope. Since he was either traveling or working long hours during the week, Mr. Jones tried to make up the lost time on Saturday afternoons. It was a routine that Hope loved.

At about 11 each Saturday morning Steven and Hope got in their Sedan de Ville, left their Pill Hill home and headed for none other than Maxwell Street. They always went to the Polish stand where they got free fries. It wasn't long before Hope was eating two Polishes with mustard, piccalilli, fried onions and hot sport peppers and washing them down with a grape pop. They then headed down to the Loop to a museum or a theater and afterwards to the ice cream parlor for dessert.

When Steven and Hope got in the car to head South, Hope would ask what was for dinner. His wife was very busy on Saturdays preparing Sunday supper, so Steven knew he had to stop and get Hope a stuffed pizza or another Maxwell Street polish. Although her favorite Polish stand had been torn down a few years ago to expand the university, whenever Hope approached 13th and Halsted, she could still smell the fried onions. The thought of it all gave Thomasine instant indigestion.

And just what was Phyllis at home preparing all day Saturday? Being a true Southern woman, she was busy preparing Sunday supper with all of the trimmings: smothered chicken or steak, candied yams, collard greens, string beans, turkey wings, rice and gravy, and whipping cream biscuits made from scratch, oozing with butter for starters. She also fried corn and okra (not together), baked beans, made oyster dressing, macaroni and cheese and baked caramel cake, bread pudding, fruit cobbler and pecan pie. She did this religiously every Sunday, whether it was Easter Sunday or just the third Sunday in July.

Hope couldn't wait to get out of church, and she hated first and third Sundays. First Sunday at Front Street African Christian Church was always full at the 11:00 A.M. service because everyone came for their thirty-day booster shot of bread and wine. Third Sunday was a different story.

Third Sundays were special to Hope because the youth sang and participated in the worship service, and her father's steward board and her mother's missionary unit met immediately after the 11 A.M. worship service. Perhaps all of that singing, slightly off key, and reading the scripture or the decalogue worked Hope's appetite.

When the Joneses got home, Phyllis had but to warm the food and slice the onions, tomatoes, and cucumbers. It's a wonder Hope survived before the invention of the microwave oven. By the end of the evening she had sampled all of the desserts.

Thomasine like first Sundays, she got to go to Hope's house for dinner while her parents delivered communion to the sick and shut-in church members. When Sina went to Hope's house she was reminded that she was among friends and could eat all she wanted. One Sunday she left with a platter big enough to feed her entire family through the middle of the week and a tummy ache that screamed for antacids. She decided to leave the biscuits alone. "After all," Crystal told her young daughter, "That food is

just too rich for your system and you don't need all of that fat and choles-
terol."

"Would ya like anything else ma'am?" the lady behind the counter
asked Thomasine.

"Yes, I'd like a baker's dozen, three powdered, three chocolate cake,
three sour cream and four French cruller." Thomasine replied, smiling.
"And do you have any day olds?"

Thomasine knew she had to give Sparky something to keep him out
of Hope's donuts. She left the restaurant with the box, feeling a little guilty
because these donuts would put Hope even closer to a stroke, Thomasine
hoped she'd share them with her husband Jason or with Rachel's boys.

"NOT!" Thomasine said as she turned the key in the lock of her car.

Always

4

$\mathcal{Y}$ou're tuned to WQMG-Greensboro-Winston-Salem," said the radio announcer. "Hot off our Quiet Storm Request Line, going out to Natasha from Jeffrey in Reidsville, Greensboro's very own Barbara Weathers with Atlantic Starr and *Always.*"

"What a great way to start off this trip," Thomasine said to Sparky.

As she listened to the sweet melody, she was reminded of her Senior prom. As class president, she had served on the prom committee and came up with a theme, *Always*, from Atlantic Starr, one of her favorite groups. That was ages ago. So much time had passed since Hope mapped out her wedding to Jason; Conrad took Thomasine to the prom; and Rachel met Jamal.

Always. That was certainly the best word to describe Hope and Jason who had been together since Cain slew Abel. Well not quite that long, but they had been an item since October 1983 when they were all 14 year old high school freshmen. Jason was on the J-V football team and had asked Hope to the homecoming dance. Judging from her reaction, it was as if Todd Bridges or Michael Jackson had asked her out. She was on cloud nine. And her parents let her stay out until eleven.

Thomasine and Rachel weren't as fortunate. Thomasine knew better than to even ask. "No dating until you're sixteen," Crystal Mintor often told Sina.

"Princess, if you start these activities at fourteen, just what will you have to look forward to when you're 17 and 18?" Rev. Mintor would ask.

Rachel knew Aunt Mary and Uncle Charlie would let her go to the dance, but only if she took her brother Hank who was still in grammar school. "Be home by 9:30," Uncle Charlie would say. Since the party started at 8:00, and the commute was an hour on public transportation, she figured it wasn't worth the bother.

Hope, on the other hand, had a chauffeur. Phyllis Jones hoped that dating would take Hope's mind off eating, so she suggested that Steven carry Jason and Hope to the dance. Only Phyllis did not realize they would

follow the dance with a trip to the ice cream parlor across the street from
the school where Hope indulged in a Banana Split and Jason had juice because he didn't want to break training by eating so late. It was that night
over a Banana Split with extra hot fudge and an orange juice, that Hope fell
in love with Jason.

Jason's mother, a missionary at another A.C.Church had met Phyllis
Jones at an area meeting during the summer and discovered that young
Hope and Jason would be attending the same high school. She told her son
to look up that Jones girl when he got to Piney Hill. "She's a bit on the
plump side, but she has a pretty face and her Daddy's rich. They have that
nice house in Pill Hill. She'll make a good woman for you."

Unbeknownst to Mrs. McCoy, Jason and Hope were in the same division. Division 797. After hearing his mother constantly ask him who he
was planning to take to the dance, because after all, a future varsity star
needed to be seen at the Homecoming dance with pretty girl on his arm,
Jason finally did it. One early October morning during Division, he passed
Hope a note.

> Hope Jones, would you give me the honor of taking you to the
> Homecoming Dance?
>
>   Jason
> P.S. Would you go with me?

He knew the second question would really please his mother.

As Hope opened the note, a smile lit her face. She shook her head up
and down as she heard the end of division bell ring and headed to her
fourth period class.

Hope and Jason dated regularly and exclusively during most of their
high school days. Hope often bragged to Rachel and Sina about how much
Jason loved her and how she would be the first in the group to get married.
She never let Rachel and Sina forget Valentine's Day or Sweetest Day,
flaunting the carnations Jason sent her each year.

One April afternoon during their senior year, the girls went looking at
prom dresses for Rachel. After leaving the mall, they stopped by Hope's to
see her prom attire. When they got to Hope's immaculate bedroom with
its French Provincial furniture and pale yellow walls with a crown mold-
ing at the ceiling, Sina noticed a bridal bouquet.

"Where did you get that?" Thomasine asked.

"I caught the bouquet at my cousin Charity's wedding. And Jason and
I are getting married. This makes it definite."

"Oh Hope, don't believe that," Rachel said as she sat on the edge of Hope's bed. "It's just a silly old wives' tale."

"But we're getting married," Hope took a bridal magazine out of her night stand drawer and opened it to a page with the corner neatly folded. "And don't sit on the bed."

"Are you pregnant?" Rachel asked as she quickly got up. "Because I can't see any other reason for you to marry at seventeen."

"No, I am not pregnant!" Hope began in a tone that said 'No you didn't go there.' "Good girls don't get pregnant and good girls wait until they're married. Isn't that right Sina?"

"I suppose so," Thomasine replied nonchalantly. "When did he propose? Have you set a date?" Sina asked excitedly.

"Well, he hasn't officially proposed yet but we're going to get married after college. Now Rachel, you're going to play the organ and Sina, you're going to sing *Ave Maria*, the *Lord's Prayer* and *Always*."

"Don't you think that just maybe you're counting your chickens before they hatch?" Sina asked.

"And this will be my bridesmaid dress," Hope said as she ignored her friend's concerns and pointed to the picture of a fuchsia dress in the bridal magazine. "And here is a picture of my gown. The colors will be fuchsia and teal. Cousin Faith will be my maid of honor, and cousin Charity will be my matron of honor. And—"

"Stop it Hope!" Rachel demanded. "Let's put this thing in perspective. First of all, Jason hasn't asked you to marry him. Second of all, you aren't going to the same college. You're going to Harrington and he's going to Duncan. A whole lot of water will go under the bridge before you all finish college. I mean, what if you meet someone else? You haven't even finished high school yet, so just why are you so ready to plan the rest of your life?"

"Jason and I are in love." Hope said harshly. "But neither of you would understand that. We have been going together for almost four years now. Sina, you're just jealous because Rodney dumped you for Sophronia and Conrad is a bum. His best friend even said so. And Rachel, when was the last time you went on a date? Oh, that's right, you've never been on a date. Your little brother Hank had to set you up with one of his friends so you could go to the prom. You're jealous because no one wants to marry you and you don't have what Jason and I have."

The truth was neither Sina nor Rachel had whatever it was Hope thought she and Jason had. The year before, they had organized the *Sina and Rachel Desperation Club*. The President was Rodney Harris and the

C.E.O. was Maximillian Tate. There had been a few other members, some only having special guest appearances.

"If you and Jason have so much, why did I see him out with Sandra while you were at your cousin's wedding in Savannah?" asked Rachel.

"Oh Rachel, I can't believe you would use such a cheap shot to try to destroy my happiness. Sandra just happens to be Jason's godsister's cousin. What's that famous saying about envy? Envy is—"—

"Rachel, I think it's time to go," Thomasine said, grabbing the hand of her simmering friend.

Thomasine sat on the edge of her bed the evening before the prom with her TV turned to music videos and her head pressed to her shoulder to hold the phone in place as she filed her nails. "Now come on Rachel, I think you and Hope should make peace and you should sit at the table with us at the prom. You all have been friends since she moved from Savannah when you were three."

"I'm just sick and tired of her little self-righteous, holier-than-thou attitude."

"That's just part of what makes Hope Hope. Now forget about it. Remember my motto, 'time will tell.' We're going to have fun tomorrow night. That's if I have a dress." Thomasine said. "I wonder who Rodney's taking to the prom?"

"I heard he was taking Sophronia Lucas and her pom pons. But she doesn't look half as good as you. They're on shaky ground anyway. Thomasine Mintor, he will take one look at you on Conrad's arm and be so sorry he blew his chances."

"I hear he signed a letter of intent with Illinois. They are actually frantic about having him on the team."

"Yeah, Hank says the Illini could use a good point guard."

"Sina, let's go see about your dress," her brother Tommy called from the hallway. It was the night before the prom and her dress wasn't finished yet.

"Well girl, I gotta go. Talk to you tomorrow."

"Sina, after the prom, I want you to drop Conrad because he's too dependent. You don't need him, he's bad news. I can feel it," Crystal said as Thomasine drove down tree lined 95th street with boxes in the median which held dying tulips. "I mean, his mother's nice and all. But that son of hers is a different story. Do you know he called me four times last night practically demanding that I take him to rent his tux. He probably expected me to pay for it too after we paid the prom bid."

"Mama, you know they are having hard times, with the divorce and his father getting laid off."

"Think about it Sina. He can't even take you out. You take him out all of the time. And he doesn't even have his driver's license yet."

"Mama, you know how expensive insurance is in the city and their car is on the blink. I'm sure things will get better for them," Sina said as she turned in front of the hospital.

"Just remember what I said," Crystal told Thomasine as they stopped in front of the hospital where Crystal works. "I'll call this afternoon when I want you to pick me up."

"Yes Mama." Sina said as she kissed her mother on the cheek.

Chez Monique's Beauty Palace was busier than usual for so early on a Friday. There were three times a year people who believed firmly in home hair care went to beauty shops—Easter, Christmas, and Prom. The once white floor tiles were now a gray dinge from all of the traffic. "So Rachel, will you sit with us?" Sina asked her friend who was getting a relaxer.

"Yes. After I got off the phone with you last night I called Hope and made peace. We've been friends most of our lives and this is a night we've all looked forward to for a long time. Now I hope your dress is all the way live to match that fly hairdo. R.H. will be so sorry you aren't on his arm and Conrad will be so lucky." Sina formed a soft, sultry smile in reply.

"I'm headed to the Plaza. Do you need anything?"

"No, I can't think of anything.

"I'll see you at about six tonight then," Thomasine said just before she walked out the front door.

When Sina got to Evergreen Plaza, she could have sworn it was Good Friday rather than the first Friday in June. Cars were everywhere but she was lucky enough to find a parking space. Once she got into the mall she thought, *this is going to be an adventure*, wall-to-wall Black folk in the Plaza that day. And it wasn't Christmas, Easter or Mother's Day.

"I also need a pair of ivory stockings with gold accents," Thomasine told the store clerk. "And I'd like a size A with control top."

"You don't look to me like you need control top," said a male voice behind her." You have *the* perfect figure," Conrad said as he gently kissed Thomasine on the back of her neck. "You look beautiful. Gotchyo butter whipped and all."

"What are you doing here?" Sina turned to face him. "I mean, have you picked up your tux yet?"

"Well no, you see, I was here with my crew and I was gonna make my way over to Ford City to get my tux."

"Miss, will these do?" the cashier interrupted.

"These are perfect."

"Your total comes to $12.15."

"Thank you and have a nice day," Thomasine told the cashier as she paid her and took her package.

"You're always so cheery," Conrad said as they walked out of the store.

"I can take you to get your tux." Thomasine said as they walked hand-in-hand out of Evergreen Plaza.

"Well, there's a small problem. I have to get a check from mom."

"It doesn't sound like a problem at all to me."

Conrad and Thomasine's afternoon was spent traveling in a maze from the Plaza to Conrad's, to her house, over east to Conrad's mom's friend's house, back to Conrad's, then to the hospital to get her mom. Home, over west to Ford City, and back to Conrad's house was enough to exhaust the average person, but for a seventeen-year-old high school senior awaiting the biggest night of her life, all that movement was like a shot of adrenaline.

"I'm gonna bum a ride to your house with Rachel and her date. I'll be there no later than six."

"Remember what I told you." Thomasine insisted.

"I know. If I smoke at the table you're going to drive my ass somewhere and leave me. If I come to your prom drunk, you're going to drive my ass somewhere and leave me, and if I come to your prom high you're going to drive my ass somewhere and leave me."

"It's not that I'm trying to be square or anything. This is such a special night for me, and, well, I want it to be perfect. Besides, we're sitting with Hope and Jason, and Hope doesn't think you're, how should I put it—quite the guy for me."

"I understand perfectly well." Conrad said as he kissed Thomasine on the cheek. "I'll see you at six."

"No later than."

"Go and make yourself more beautiful and please, please, be ready. I know how long it can take some of you women to get dressed."

Truth be told, Conrad was bad news for Thomasine, Rev. Mintor's little princess. He partied late on weekends, smoked, drank beer and gin and juice, and even chain-smoked reefer. Sina did not know that he had been arrested for underage drinking. He and Sina had little in common. Ms.

Thompson tried so hard to support Conrad and his little sister, Tina and keep them both out of trouble. Rumor had it, that his sister, a sophomore at Piney Hill, started her freshman year pregnant. It was a scandalous deal. The guy she was going with was twenty-one and had two other children. Ms. Thompson thought that by leaving Detroit and heading back to Chicago, she could give Tina a fresh start after she suffered a miscarriage. It was quite a struggle, but as Ms. Thompson told her children daily, "All things are possible through Christ who strengthens me."

Thomasine was surprised when Conrad expressed an interest in her. She knew he was not the boy next door, nor the Prince Rev. Mintor envisioned for his princess. He was 5'10", nice looking with his box haircut, and had the prettiest teeth. He was what Sina and Rachel called a "slim." One afternoon in late March at choir rehearsal, Thomasine saw a side of Conrad she had never seen at Piney Hill or from the pew. They were rehearsing *We Are Not Ashamed* and Hope volunteered to sing lead. Since she was having vocal dysfunctions that day, as always, the director asked Thomasine to fill in, just until Hope could get it. Thomasine was a natural. Immediately, Conrad volunteered to sing the male lead. It was the tightest harmony that had been heard in the youth choir in a long time. "We'll do this one tomorrow," the director said as they were finishing the rehearsal.

That Sunday morning just before the 11:00 service, Conrad walked up to Sina and said, "I almost didn't recognize you. I've never seen you with lipstick on before . . . let's talk after the service."

When they sang the duet just before the sermon, folks were shouting up in Front Street A.C. Church. African Christian Churches, especially those up North, were known for having a very straightforward and sterile service. The Baptists and Methodists thought the African Christians were a bit saditty. But on that third Sunday in March, something special happened in Front Street, and something special happened for Sina. The Conrad who sang with her was not the Conrad who gave substitute teachers a hard time and cut class with his crew. There was something different about him that day.

"Maybe we can get together sometime and you can sing with my band." Conrad said to Thomasine after the service.

"Wow, you're in a band!"

"Yeah, and I'm the lead singer."

"Don't believe a thing he says," his best friend Jimmy said. "Don't trust him, he's just a bum."

"Aw, man, chill out."

"Well here is my number. Call me later about it. Maybe we can hook up on a couple of songs."

"Cool." Thomasine said as she put the number in her purse.

"Conrad Thompson, 555-7982," Thomasine read while she sat on her bed Sunday evening after dinner. She picked up her phone only to quickly hang it back up. She went through this ritual for about ten minutes until she got the nerve to make the call.

"Hello, Conrad. This is Sina, I mean Thomasine. I'm calling about getting together with you—and your band. I thought we could practice *All Cried Out* and *Always*. When do you all practice?"

"We're short a few members. We're looking for a bass player, a keyboardist, a guitarist and a drummer. But maybe in the mean time, you will let me take you to the prom, that is, if I can afford it."

Thomasine was thrilled. The prayers of some of her sister Sunday School teachers had been answered—at least for Sina. She had a prom date that wasn't a square. He wasn't quite a church boy either, but they had met in the church and he was in the church. But was the church in him? Sina's cousin Kelsey in Virginia always told her to get her a church boy or a square. They make the best boyfriends. Kelsey was very wise for her twenty-two years.

Thomasine found herself stopping by Conrad's house one afternoon just before spring break. "Sina, you don't mind if I call you Sina do you? Why don't you have a boyfriend? Is it because you haven't found Mr. Right? Have you just had rejections or are you even interested?"

After casually mentioning the Rodney situation, Sina said, "I guess I just haven't found Mr. Right yet."

"Well, I have Mr. Right's number right here and I'm giving it to you," he said smiling down at her. "Can I put it in your bra so that you can hold it close to your heart."

"Conrad, Dave is here." Mrs. Thompson called from the kitchen.

"Would you excuse me for a moment?" He went out at the side door.

Just wait til I tell Rachel, thought Thomasine. How cute and romantic.

Conrad returned ten minutes later and when he leaned over to kiss Sina his smell reminded her of the time she visited cousins in Tennessee for the Fourth of July. When they ran out of fireworks, they burned whatever they could find, including leaves. Thomasine wanted to ask Conrad about it, but she didn't want to destroy the mood. She had a funny feeling about his ten minute disappearance and this strange aroma. She knew she would have to ask her older brother Tommy about the smell.

"Sina, your date is here," Crystal Mintor called out.

"Just let me put the finishing touches on your makeup and you'll be all ready to go," said Patricia, Tommy's current girlfriend.

"You look stunning!" Conrad exclaimed as he laid eyes on Sina in her ivory and gold asymmetric gown with a gold lamé bow on the right shoulder. The tight fitting bodice had gold netting and a full ankle length skirt.

"You are so beautiful, Thomasine," Ms. Thompson, Conrad's mother insisted.

"Where are Rachel and this mystery man?" asked Sina.

"They're on their way," replied Conrad.

"We better go outside and start taking pictures because I don't have a flash," Tommy said. He was the family photographer, cuing his subjects on the count of three. Just as they began posing, Rachel and her date drove up.

"I just love your dress, Rachel," Thomasine said of the black and white, backless, A-line dress with a sweetheart neckline. "Show those legs girl. I'm glad you're here."

"You are so beautiful. Watch out Hollywood, here comes Sina." Rachel said. "And you know who is going to be sorry," Rachel whispered in Sina's ear as she hugged her.

They were both beautiful, Sina in her ivory and gold and Rachel in her black and white. Neither looked like Sunday School teachers nor youth choir members tonight. And though Thomasine did look like a princess, she did not look like the little preacher's daughter she was. Although Conrad had been excited and enthusiastic about this evening, Thomasine was so fine tonight that he was afraid to touch her.

"When can I expect you home?" Crystal Mintor asked the young couple.

"Well, the prom ends at 12:00 and there are a few after-sets."

"Be in by five."

As they drove down Lake Shore Drive in Tommy's classic 1967 Mustang, Sina looked down at her corsageless wrist.

"Conrad. How come I don't have a corsage?" She knew she had to produce a corsage or some sort of flower, and not the one Rachel wore, to keep her mother from using this as further evidence to kick Conrad to the curb.

"Honk the horn," Conrad said when they came to a red light, and a woman selling roses walked up to the car, now stopped in traffic. She had a big cardboard box strapped to her chest with a sign 1 for $3, 2 for $5.

"I'd like one," Conrad said as he handed the woman a wrinkled five dollar bill. As he handed the red American Beauty rose to Sina, he tenderly kissed the back of her hand. Sina was so caught in the moment that she didn't hear the blaring car horns telling her the light had changed.

They rode up and down Michigan Avenue, past the Buckingham Fountain and the Art Institute, taking in the evening. Thomasine was determined to arrive fashionably late, for she had to make a grand entrance. After all, it was in her Leo nature to be a ham.

"I wonder what's taking Sina so long. I bet that Conrad was late."

"Here she comes now," Rachel said as she looked in the direction of the doorway. Thomasine pranced so gracefully across the floor to table number 58 in the Royal Ballroom at the Hyatt Regency Hotel. She wore her ivory and gold gown with style. And Conrad was by her side, holding her corsageless wrist.

"For you my dear," he said as he pulled out her chair. Thomasine flashed a broad smile as Conrad pushed her chair in.

"What took you all so long?" Hope asked. "I thought you'd never get here."

"We had a little bit of a detour. We went for a carriage ride and took our portraits. Is there a problem?" Conrad answered with a half-truth as the waiter brought the salads to the table. They ate their dinner of roast beef, steamed carrots and rice in silence.

"Would you please excuse me?" Sina glared at Conrad.

"Sina, let's go to the ladies' room." Rachel whispered.

"Please excuse us." Thomasine said as they left the table.

"Excuse me." Rodney said as he nearly bumped into the duo. "Thomasine, you look lovely tonight." Now Rodney was stunning in his tux with tails, but Sina was not about to be drawn to his magnetism tonight. She felt she had something to prove—a point to make.

"Thank you Rodney." She and Rachel didn't stop until they made their way into the restroom.

"What did I tell you? Didn't I say he'd be sorry?" Rachel told Sina while looking directly at Sophronia. "You are just too sharp and look too good. Isn't that right Sophronia?"

"Humph," Sophronia said as she rolled her eyes and stormed out of the ladies room.

The duo erupted with laughter as they inspected themselves in the larger mirror.

"My girl knows how to handle herself well under pressure," Rachel said as she gave Sina a high five.

"It was hard though, brother was looking good tonight."

"But remember, you and Conrad look better."

"Enough for me and Conrad, What'sup with you and Jamal? Are y'all talking or are you just kickin' it cuz he is the definition of a slim."

"Like you always say Sina, 'time will tell.'"

"I heard that. We have beautified ourselves enough. Now let's get back to the party."

When they reentered the ballroom, the prom-goers were all seated and light dinner chatter filled the room. "Did I miss anything?" Sina asked Conrad as he pushed in her chair.

"They are about to announce the Prom Court."

"Remember our discussion about what I heard from that little birdie," Thomasine said wearing a sly smile.

"I remember Sina."

"We'd like to take this time to present the Piney Hill High School Prom Court 1987. Our attendants are Sophronia Lucas and Conrad Thompson," Mr. Attaway, the class advisor announced from the center of the dance floor.

"Congratulations baby." Thomasine said as Conrad walked to the wooden parquet dance floor.

"The prince and princess are Jason McCoy and Rachel Curtis. Give them a round of applause," Mr. Attaway said.

"And now, the envelope please. Your prom queen and king are Thomasine Mintor and Rodney Harris."

Sophronia took one look at Thomasine being crowned and nearly burst in tears.

"Piney Hill High School's 1987 Senior Prom court will now take to the dance floor while our band for this evening, Dreamweaver, performs this year's song, *Always*."

"Sophronia, don't be a damn baby about it just because my lady, with her fine self, happens to be dancing with your tired man," Conrad said. "I mean, I'm not exactly thrilled about sharing this dance with you. You know I'd rather have my arms around Thomasine's sleek body."

"You don't think Hope will be mad do you?" Rachel asked Jason. "This is your song, isn't it?"

"Hope knows this is just a dance and she knows how I feel about her. Besides, I have the rest of the night to make up these few minutes to Hope."

Thomasine put her arms around the waist of 6'2" Rodney. He gently put his arms on Thomasine's shoulders as they swayed slowly and fluidly to the tender beat, "Girl...," Rodney began singing in Thomasine's ear as he pulled her close and leaned downward. Casually and tactfully Thomasine took one giant step backward, remaining silent during the entire dance. As they posed for Prom Court pictures, Rodney asked Thomasine what she was doing later.

"Look down there, you know, where the attendants are. Do you see that slim standing down there? I think he's standing next to your date. Well, he just happens to be my man and we've got plans." She smiled for the picture and left the raised platform.

Don't Disturb This Groove

5

Conrad gave the parking attendant the ticket, ripped off his cummerbund and inhaled deeply to take in the June evening air. It was a perfect night. A gentle breeze blew from the shores of Lake Michigan making everything just right. He had been on his best behavior all night and now had his own design in mind. "Now I'll call the shots," he said with a grin as the parking attendant drove up in the candy apple red Mustang. "Open the trunk Sina, I need to get my bag."

Conrad tipped the parking attendant, grabbed his duffle bag and got in the car. As they headed south on Michigan Avenue, Thomasine tried to capture all of the sights of the evening from the fashion parade of prom dresses and tuxedos to the bright lights adorning the buildings.

"Conrad, look over there." She turned to Conrad. "Just what are you doing?"

"I'm taking off this monkey suit, or would you rather take it off for me?"

"You're doing mighty fine by yourself." She avoided looking at him. "Where to?"

"Let's go down to the Hilton. I need to hook up with my crew. Jimmy got a room. You can change there and we can chill."

"Let's get something to eat," Hope said as she and Jason rode in the white stretch limo with the sunroof open, absorbing the early June air. "There's a McDonald's between Randolph and Adams that's open late."

"I thought we'd get something later. I have a very special night planned and I thought we'd end it with breakfast."

"But I'm hungry now, Jason. That little piece of Roast Beef and that handful of carrots at the prom just teased me," Hope frowned.

"Okay," Jason sighed, "To McDonald's."

Thomasine sat in the car and thought about the night's events while

Conrad went into the hotel to hunt down his crew. "It can best be summed up in two words—overrated experience. But I did get to dance with fine ass Rodney. And right in front of Sophronia's face. I guess the look on her face was worth it all. They say a picture is worth a thousand words."

"Who were you talking to?" Conrad asked as he grabbed his tux jacket from the back seat and got back into the car.

"What's the deal? Where do I park?"

"Just pull off. Those bums dogged me. I couldn't find any of them. But that's okay." He pulled a small manilla envelope from his jacket pocket.

"What's that?" Thomasine asked, wondering what the surprise was. *How nice of you to bring me something.*

"Just a little herb." Conrad knew Sina wasn't down for that, but felt he should do some of the things he wanted. After all, it was his prom night too.

"Oh no. You cannot smoke that in here."

"But the windows are down. The car will air out."

"No way! If you light that thing I will stop the car and make you get out. I don't even like you having that stuff in my brother's car. You know he's a cop and this could get him in hot water."

"I'm sorry baby. Can I smoke a square in here then?" Conrad leaned over and kissed Sina quickly, grazing against her lips while they were stopped at a red light.

"Why do you have to smoke at all? But I guess that beats the alternative."

"Okay, Okay," Conrad said as he lit the cigarette. "We need to find somewhere for you to change and I'll just save the bud until then."

"Rachel," Jamal said in his most formal voice as they walked hand-in-hand out of the Hyatt Regency. "I've had a great time this evening. I'm so glad Hank introduced us."

"It's been a slice." Rachel giggled, finding herself getting giddy.

"Well, what do you want to do now? I mean, the prom is over and everything. And it is a beautiful evening."

"Hmm, I don't know. Why don't you surprise me?" Rachel glanced at the stars in the clear sky which promised a beautiful tomorrow. "It's a little chilly out here."

Without saying a word, Jamal took off his jacket and draped it around Rachel's shoulders. He put his arm around her shoulder to give her extra warmth. "Congratulations on being crowned Prom Princess." Jamal said as they walked down Wacker Drive and stopped at a horse drawn carriage. He took Rachel's hand and helped her climb aboard.

"Here's your Big Mac combo and cookies," Jason said as he got back into the stretch limo.

"You didn't get anything?" Hope asked, reaching into the bag.

"No, I'm not hungry," Hope tore into the bag, opened the styrofoam container with her Big Mac and poured her fries into the empty side of the container. "Hope, why don't you wait until we get settled. You don't want to get anything on that pretty dress you're wearing, do you?"

"I'm hungry now and I need to eat the food while it's hot," Hope retorted as she stuffed a fistful of french fries from her gloved hand into her mouth. "You know this stuff is no good cold."

"Park over here Sina," Conrad said as they approached an abandoned lot. The weeds had grown knee high and broken bottles adorned the ground. Only the Ryan traffic from the overpass reminded Sina that she was not entirely deserted. "You can change your clothes while I get out and smoke this joint. I promise not to peek."

Thomasine walked to the trunk of the car and sent up a quick prayer. "Father, protect me." These were the places Tommy had warned her about. She didn't know who could pop out of where and do who knows what to her and Conrad. Especially since the classic car always drew attention.

Thomasine grabbed the overnight bag from the trunk, removed her hose, stepped into the bottoms of the white cotton jumpsuit and slid them on underneath the full skirt of her gown. She then sat in the car and pulled the jumpsuit onto her hips and unzipped the side of her dress, slid the strap of her jumpsuit onto her bare shoulder and wiggled the other strap onto the right shoulder, then got out of the car, pulled the dress over her head, placed it neatly on the hanger and covered it with plastic. She took a light sweater from her overnight bag and closed the trunk.

"All finished," Sina said as Conrad finished his smoke. "What's next?" They pulled off, with a quickness.

"Jamal, this is really nice." Rachel said as they rode down the Magnificent Mile. "I've never been on a carriage ride before."

"I'll let you in on a little secret," Jamal responded, smiling. "This is also a first for me."

"This is so neat, I've shared so many firsts with you." Rachel said, getting even more giddy. "My first prom, my first date, my first carriage ride—"

"And your first kiss?" Jamal said as he embraced Rachel and kissed her for three passion-filled minutes on her lips, first lightly brushing his lips with hers and then gently opening and caressing her mouth with his tongue. "And I'm sure these aren't all the firsts we'll share." Jamal pulled her close.

The hotel room overlooking Michigan Avenue and Grant Park was not the typical cheap, fleabag hotel most prom attendees managed to secure. From the paintings on the wall to the complementary patterns on the bedspread, this room spoke of elegance. Jason had gone all out. This was a special night for him and he wanted to make it a night Hope would remember—Always. "Hope, you may not have been crowned in the prom court tonight, but you are truly a Queen." His attraction for Hope had become more than a fleeting passion. It had developed into a fondness, a kinship. "You have been a very important part of my life during a very important time in my life. And I love you. Over the past 3½ years you have taught me so much about love, so much about life, and so much about myself."

"I love you too, Jason."

"And these are for you," Jason said as he walked over to the dresser and pulled out a dozen long-stemmed red roses.

"This one is for caring," Jason said as he handed Hope a single rose and kissed her deeply, passionately, and needful. "This one is for your smile." Jason stared into Hope's eyes and kissed her again. "This third one is for the three plus years you've been in my life.

"And this one is for your grace." He kissed Hope softly on the lips. "This one is for your kind heart. And this one is for just being you."

"Oh Jason. This is so sweet of you."

"Oh, baby, I'm just getting started." He swept her up in his arms and ran his hands through her softly feathered hair. "Tonight will be unforgettable—I promise."

"Park in the next block," Conrad said as they passed the Power Plant thumping to the beat of House music. Sina felt as if the reverberations were bouncing off her being as she searched earnestly for a parking space. After settling on a space two and a half blocks away, Thomasine parked the Mustang on a hill and tried to remember which way to cut the wheels. "Up, up and away," Conrad said, reminding her. "Hey, I may not have my driver's license, but I do know the rules of the road."

Sina looked over her shoulder to make sure no cars were coming before she got out of the car. When she joined Conrad on the sidewalk, he put his arm around her shoulder. His quick peck on her cheek set her into a contented moment. "Conrad, you don't have to do that again," Sina pleaded, watching Conrad put a joint in his mouth.

"Come on Sina, take a hit? You know it's no fun getting high by yourself."

"No thank you. I just want to dance."

If It Isn't Love

6

*G*irl, I haven't talked to you since the prom," Sina told Rachel as they rode the Lake/Dan Ryan L train home from graduation rehearsal. It was midday, so the train wasn't crowded and they were happy to have a seat for a change. "What'sup with you and Jamal? Are y'all talkin' or what?"

"Well, we did go to Great America Saturday and we had the time of our lives. Where were you and Conrad? I didn't run into you."

"Conrad had to work Saturday afternoon. And let's just say I was tired. Girl, we hit three dance clubs and I got carded at each one," Thomasine said of the seventeen and older clubs. "But you know I had a slammin' jammin' time. Tell me what you and Jamal did after the prom."

Rachel recapped her first evening out to her friend, not missing a detail.

"I'm jealous. That is sooo romantic. And to think, you two just met."

"By the looks of things, I think it's later for the Sina and Rachel Desperation Club."

"I know that's right," Sina said as she gave her friend a high five.

"Next stop-87th," sang the voice of the conductor.

"I wonder what the two lovebirds over there did," Thomasine commented as an entrepreneur ambled down the aisle past them shouting "One dollar wallet wit' a Phone Book in it."

"Well, between you and me, Jason told me he had special plans for Hope Friday night. Since I saw them stuck together like a peanut butter and jelly sandwich at Great America and she wouldn't even go into the candy shop with me, just maybe he did propose. Or maybe she isn't such a good little girl anymore," Rachel said smiling.

"Next stop-95th — End of the line."

"Say, why wasn't Conrad at rehearsal?"

"You know he transferred from that high school in Detroit this year and his credits are all mixed up and stuff, so he has to go to summer school to meet the Chicago requirements."

"That's crucial. I think they should let him march. I mean, none of us get our diplomas when we go across the stage anyway. It's like they're cheating him out of his high school graduation."

"I agree. It's not like they are going to give us diplomas on Saturday."

"Well I know he better not try. Jamal told me that his cousin's friend got pulled out of line by Mr. Attaway last year because she failed the last quarter of Senior English and was determined to march anyway."

"I'll be sure and let him know that," Sina said as the train halted. "I don't think it's that important to him to march with our class. He spent his first three years at that school in Detroit and he hadn't even planned to participate in any activities. That is, until he decided to take me to prom."

"I'll catch you later Sina." As usual, the escalator was broken so the girls climbed the stairs in the station.

"No, I'm going your way. Conrad asked me to stop by after rehearsal. Do you wanna walk, or catch a bus?"

"Let's catch a bus," Rachel answered as she began rifling through her purse. "Oh shoot, I lost my transfer."

"Let's walk then. Four blocks won't kill us." Sina looked into the sky and saw gray storm clouds just west of them. "We'd better hurry. It looks like rain."

"It was such a nice day, and I didn't hear the weatherman say anything about rain today."

As they turned the corner of tree-lined Avery Street, Rachel began to fumble through her purse again. "Oh no, I hope Aunt Mary's home because I forgot my key. But I don't see her car."

"I'm sure Conrad won't mind if you chilled at his crib for a while," Thomasine said as she and Rachel walked past the Anderson house.

"Is that Conrad on the porch smoking? It must be because he's the only one on this end of the street who plays that doggone house music this loud," Rachel said as they approached the family's two-story Georgian.

"I've been waiting on you. Come give me a kiss," he said, pulling Sina close.

"Oh, whasup Rachel?"

"Nothin' much." She was very uncomfortable now because she was certain that Conrad was smoking weed. She knew that Thomasine Mintor didn't smoke and wondered why she would be so quick to run over his house knowing that he was into drugs. She thought Hank had told her that Conrad and his crew were involved in drug activity, but she didn't believe it. His mother was so active in the church. She was the president of the Missionary Society and he and his sister were in the choir. It hadn't been that long since he and Sina turned the church out when they sang *We Are Not Ashamed.* Rachel knew she would have to have a long talk with Sina about this.

"I've missed you." Sina said as she kissed Conrad quickly.

"Let's make up for lost time." Conrad took one last hit.

"Shoot, it's starting to rain," Rachel said.

"Then let's go inside."

"Conrad, Rachel is locked out. Can she come in and chill with us?"

"Damn," Conrad mumbled under his breath. "I guess so."

When they entered the recreation room in the basement of the Thompson home, Conrad turned the floor model TV to MV 50, and played around with the antenna to get a clear picture. The three spent the afternoon singing, dancing and watching music videos.

"What time is it?" Sina asked in a panic looking around the room for a clock. "It's almost four. I better get home. Mama will be home from work soon."

Rachel was walking Thomasine to the bus stop when she noticed that Aunt Mary had returned from whatever journey or volunteer activity had called her. "I better go in and let Aunt Mary know where I am Sina. I'll get the car and take you home."

When the girls entered the side door of the bungalow, Aunt Mary was in the kitchen cooking Fried chicken, green peas and rice. "Is that you Rachel?" she called out.

"Yes Aunt Mary. How was your day?"

"It was nice. I had to carry Sister Sims to the doctor and then to pick up her prescriptions. By the way, Jamal called."

"He did!" Her full lips smiled in delight. "Aunt Mary, may I use the car to take Sina home?"

"Sure. Take five dollars out of my purse and get some gas too while you're out."

The girls got in the 1985 Delta 88, put on their seat belts and Rachel checked her mirrors and looked over her left shoulder just before she drove off. "You'll beat your mother home now."

"Yeah. But even if I don't, I'll be all right since I'm with you."

Rachel sat in the car, trying to break the silence by turning on the radio, but when she couldn't find a song she liked, she decided that now was the time for her to have a talk with Sina about her concerns. "Sina, just maybe Conrad isn't the man for you. I mean, he's bold enough to sit on his front porch in the middle of the day smoking herb. There's no telling what else he will do," she said facing Sina once they reached a stop sign. "Besides, you know you can do better than that."

"I know Conrad smokes a little reefer every now and then, but does that mean he's an awful person? I think not. He's probably just giving in to peer pressure. He's had a lot of pressure on him lately with the divorce, the move and the fact that he's not graduating with us Saturday."

"What would your brother Tommy say?"

"Probably the same thing I do. He's just a soul in need of salvation. Have you stopped to think that just maybe he might change through my example? None of us are in any position to judge anyone else. My daddy has always told me to 'never judge a man until you've walked ten miles in his moccasins.'"

"Don't be so defensive Thomasine. You know that goes against everything your parents and Tommy have taught you." After a pregnant pause, Rachel continued. "Wait a minute. You haven't fallen in love with him, have you? Because that's the only thing that I could think would make you be so determined to associate with him."

"Well, I do care a lot about him and I think I can change him for the better."

"But Sina, you're not a potter and he is not a lump of clay. Promise me you'll give it some serious thought," Rachel said as she pulled into Thomasine's driveway.

"I promise I'll think about it. You have to tell me everything you and Jamal talk about."

"Okay. Catch ya later."

"It's been a slice," Thomasine shouted as she ran up the front steps and Rachel backed out of the driveway.

"Tell us all about what you and Jason did after the prom," Rachel said as she, Hope and Thomasine rode in Tommy's car from their class luncheon.

Hope recounted the evening, from the pit stop at McDonald's to the hotel room and the roses. "Number seven was for my beauty both inside and out. Number eight was for the times we'd shared. Nine was for our love, because it runs deep. Number ten was because I'm his Queen. Eleven was for that night. And twelve was for our future. He gave me each one individually and kissed me."

"Ooh, girl. So what happened next? Did he propose?"

"Well not exactly. He said he was ready to take this relationship to a higher level."

"What happened next? What happened next?"

"Calm down Rachel. Then he put his arms around me, drew me real close, kissed me, and declared his love over and over."

"Is that when he sort of popped the question?" Sina asked.

"No. He led me to the bed, gazed into my eyes and took something out his pocket and put it on the night stand."

"What was it? What happened next? Because inquiring minds need to know."

The Auditorium Theater was packed with Piney Hill graduates in their red and white caps and gowns. They were surrounded by parents, grandparents, aunts, uncles, and friends who had assembled to take snapshots immediately following the graduation ceremony. "It was so sweet of Jamal to bring you flowers today," Thomasine said as she met up with Rachel after the graduation ceremony.

"He picked me up this morning and took me to breakfast too."

"That is so nice. I haven't seen hide nor hair of Conrad today, but he has to work," Sina said as she looked through the sea of red and white for one of her friends. "Where's Hope? You know Tommy wants to take a picture of us together in our caps and gowns."

"I'm so proud of you Jason," said his Uncle Leroy. "It seems like just yesterday your mama was bringing you home from the hospital. And look. Now you're all grown up with your high school diploma and football scholarship to Duncan. I know your Daddy is just smiling down from heaven," he said as he hugged Jason. "By the way, how did things go last Friday? Did you get those roses? You'll have to tell me about it."

"Well Uncle Leroy. I just think there are some things that should remain between a man and a woman. I gave her the roses and told her why I love her and everything, just like you said."

"Well what happened?"

"I'll just put it this way. We ended with breakfast."

Divas Need Love Too

7

G irls night out! Girls night out!" Rachel said as she and Hope went to pick up Sina for an evening of fun. As Thomasine got into the car, the trio decided to kick off their evening at their favorite Mexican restaurant. It was a pleasant July evening, not too breezy or too muggy. The girls drove west on 95th Street and captured the South side atmosphere from the church parking lot full of revival attenders, to the hordes of people at the bus stop making their way home on Friday evening, to the now empty boxes in the median which, a few months ago, held tulips once they entered Beverly Hills.

"So Hope, how do you like your job?" Thomasine asked.

"It's all right I guess." Hope said, referring to her part-time receptionist position.

"I'd trade places with you anytime. I'm tired of saying 'Welcome to White Castle, may I take your order,'" Sina replied. "It's like I dream about making french fries and setting grills every night."

"Well at least you two don't have to wait tables. People can really be a trip sometimes." Rachel said. "It makes me cautious of how I treat people when I go out and eat."

"Let's hear some sounds." As Rachel turned on the radio in Aunt Mary's maroon Delta 88, Thomasine began to move to the beat of house music. "Um, Um, Um-Um-Um-Um," Sina hummed. "Rachel, why did you change the station? I was getting ready to get my groove on."

"You know I can't stand that music."

"I hope you aren't turning to that tired old country station. I just can't bear that on such a nice Friday summer evening on the South side of Chicago."

"You two need to quit," Hope said. "Rachel, why don't you just leave it here?" Hope said of the station called the 'Soft Touch.' " I think everyone will be happy."

"It doesn't matter anyway, because we're almost there."

Pepe's was more crowded than usual, even for a Friday evening. The restaurant had been one of their favorite Friday night hangouts since Sina got her driver's license. They were quite familiar with the menu and had sampled virtually every item. While some people found the dirty paneled walls and dingy orange decor a bore, Rachel, Sina, and Hope were able to look past that to what mattered most—the food. And it was good. "How many?" asked the hostess wearing a white blouse with a ruffled collar and sleeve cuffs and an orange ruffled skirt.

"Three"

"Smoking, non, or first available."

"By all means, non-smoking," Hope said curtly. As much as Hope loved to eat, she could not stand being surrounded by smoke while she tried to enjoy her meal. "It takes away from it," she always told her friends.

"Hope, we should have taken first available," Thomasine said as the three girls sat down on a bench in the lobby of the restaurant. "You know this is my favorite restaurant, right Rachel?"

"Yeah, this is my favorite too. But it's probably worth the wait."

"Well, I don't like cigarette smoke," Hope replied. "I just can't seem to enjoy my food as much."

"Boy am I starving," Sina said. " I worked 10-6 today and I haven't eaten since breakfast. I had just enough time to shower and change."

"Don't you all get to eat free at work?" Hope asked.

"Quite frankly, I'm tired of White Castles. I could eat before and after my shift and during my break. Some people do. But a little bit of that goes a long way," Thomasine replied. "Let me go wash my hands while we're waiting."

Sina returned just in time to hear the hostess shout "Jones, party of three." She then showed the trio to their booth in the dimly lit restaurant. Rachel and Sina sat on one side and Hope sat on the other. "Your server will be Maria. Enjoy your meal."

"I know exactly what I want," Thomasine said placing the menu on the table. "So Hope, have you and Jason gone shopping for rings yet?"

"I'll tell you once I've decided what I will eat," Hope said as she studied the menu.

"Good evening ladies, I'm Maria, your server this evening. What would you like to drink?"

"I'll have a white pop and I think we're all ready to order," Thomasine said. "I'll have two shredded beef tacos on soft flour shells an order of fries and tuna peppers."

"I'll have a coke and the stuffed nachos," Rachel said.

"And you Senorita?"

"I'll have the Mayan combination plate and a beef taco with a soft corn shell and an order of fries." Hope responded. "Oh, and a diet coke." Isn't it amazing how people always gorge themselves with food and think they can cut down on calories by ordering a Diet Coke?

"Could we also have a pitcher of water?" Thomasine asked.

"So Rachel, how are you and Jamal doing?" Hope asked.

"Well, he's been gone for two weeks to Basic Training and he'll be gone for another four weeks."

"Oh, I didn't know he was going into the service," Hope said. "I thought you told me he was going to Grambling. So which branch of the service is he in?"

"He is in the Air Force Reserves," Rachel replied. "He took ROTC instead of gym in high school just like Hank and he's going to college on the G.I. bill."

"So Jamal's gone, huh Rachel?" Sina inquired.

"Yeah. I miss him."

"No wonder you suggested this girls night out," Sina replied. "But I'm glad you did because our days here are numbered."

"We definitely have to make plans," Hope interrupted.

"So what did you do before he left?"

"He invited me over to watch movies. His parents really seem to like me."

"So what happened? Give us details, we need details. I mean, you told us about the carriage ride, the breakfast before graduation and we saw the flowers." Thomasine said in an excited tone. "Cuz, I know you didn't just watch movies."

"I actually didn't see much of the movie because, how shall I put it, Jamal and I were engaged in alternative activities."

"My girl. Ain't even got to Duncan yet and already you're using those college words—alternative activities."

"First we got pizza at Michelangelo's and then we went to his crib to watch movies."

"You already told us about the movies."

"Then, he told me he was going to give me a little something to remember him by."

"You didn't sleep with him did you?" Hope asked in a motherly tone.

"Of course not. It's too soon. Jamal and I haven't been together as long as you and Jason," Rachel said, smiling.

"We sat on the living room sofa and just messed around."

"Been there, done that, bought a T-shirt and came home," Sina said. "What did he leave you?"

"He gave me a hickey on my left breast. So that Aunt Mary or Uncle Charlie wouldn't see it."

"Weren't you afraid of getting caught?" Hope asked.

"No. By the sounds of things, his parents were busy upstairs and we would have heard them coming down the stairs," Rachel said. " So much for me and Jamal, how are you and Conrad doing Sina?"

"Things are going as well as can be expected. We've been hanging out with his friends lately most of the time. Since he's in summer school and I'm working I really only get to see him on my off days. It can put a strain on our relationship, but I think we'll make it through."

"How far have you two gone?"

"Well we haven't gone all the way. To be honest, I'm scared. I'm not ready for motherhood yet, or a broken heart," Thomasine explained. "But you know there are other things we can do. So what's up with you and Jason, Hope?"

"Here comes our food, I'll tell you after we eat," Hope said to Sina who seemed puzzled. "Well you said you were starving, didn't you?" Hope nearly gobbled her food and then ordered fried ice cream and sopapillas. By the time they were through, the 'Three Musketeers' found they had to rush off to the show to finish their girls night out.

I Feel Good

8

It had been a perfect day for Thomasine even though she had to work at White Castle on her 18th birthday. When she left work early, she found birthday gifts from Aunt Carla and Uncle Sandifer and her cousins Kelsey and Trevaughn. She even saw a cake in the fridge. When she took a peek at it, she knew that Tommy, as always, had gotten Sina *his* favorite cake for her birthday.

"Daddy, can I use mom's car? Rachel, Hope and I want to go out and Hank's using the car. You know how Hope hates to drive." Since Sina had started dating Conrad, lying to her parents had become easy.

"I suppose so, Princess," Rev. Mintor replied. "Where are you going?"

"I know we're going to get something to eat."

"Why doesn't that surprise me?" Rev. Mintor said chuckling.

"They've made plans for afterward," Sina explained. "I promise I'll be in at a decent hour."

Thomasine wondered what the evening had in store for her as she drove north on the Ryan to Conrad's job.

"Hey baby." Conrad said as he got in the car and lightly kissed Sina on her lips. "That is one sexy dress you have on."

"Thank you Conrad."

"I've got something for you. Happy Birthday." He handed Sina a small, thin bag.

"Conrad, this is so — nice." Sina said of the jet black thigh high stockings.

"And I want to see you in them. Tonight," Conrad said grinning devilishly. "Let's go to the Seafood Spot and get some shrimp and oysters. You can put the stockings on then."

The Seafood Spot was crowded for a Thursday night. The place smelled of fish, grease, and onions. "I just want shrimp," Thomasine said "What will we have to drink?"

"I'll take care of that. You just go in the little girls' room and take care of that," Conrad said, looking at the small thin plastic bag she held and then up at Sina with a straightfoward stare.

Sina walked down the long narrow hall to the ladies room. She had a fleeting vision of her grandmother but dismissed it as her disappointment at not celebrating her birthday with her mom who was taking care of Grandma. She knocked lightly on the door. When she went into the bathroom, she was so glad she was only changing; the place was filthy. She quickly and carefully pulled her hose down to her knees, stepped out of one shoe and put one of the thigh highs on while balancing on the other foot. She did not want her bare feet to touch the dirty floor. Doing the same with the other foot she threw her hose in the trash. She knew she could always say she ran her stockings and all that she could find were the thigh highs if the question arose.

"Thompson," the short, stout man behind the counter called as Thomasine returned.

"Right here," Conrad said, handing the man his ticket and grabbing the greasy brown paper bag.

When Conrad and Sina walked outside, an older man handed Conrad another big paper bag. "Hold this, Sina," Conrad said as he took the bag from the strange looking man. "Thanks bro."

"What's in that bag?"

"Just a little drink."

"Conrad, you shouldn't have had that man cop that liquor for us. He could have been an undercover officer or he could have just walked off with your money."

"But he didn't. And you should be happy about that because two of those coolers have your name on them."

"I don't know Conrad, I'm driving." Sina said as she drove off.

"You'll be all right baby. We're gonna chill at the lake for a few hours; there will be enough time for you to get your buzz on and off before we leave. Have a shrimp," he said, trying to put one in Thomasine's mouth.

"I'm not hungry right now."

"I guess I can save you some. But you know they're only good when they're hot." And they wouldn't have long to get cold because it was a short drive from the Seafood Spot to The Point where lovers often met.

"Let's just sit here and enjoy the view," Conrad said of the setting sun. "Have a cooler."

"I suppose," Thomasine said of the berry flavored wine cooler.

"Thomasine. We've been together for how long now?"

"About four months."

"One, two, three, four," Conrad said as he counted his kisses to Thomasine.

"That's for the four months we've been together. What do I get for the eighteen years I've been here?" she asked, expecting more of a birthday present.

Conrad took her left hand in his and pulled her close with his right hand and gently kissed her on her forehead. "One." Conrad then looked into Sina's eyes and took her left hand and said, "Two." He moved up to the tip of her nose, "Three." Down to her lips, "Four. And I'll come back here for more."

She felt warm inside. She had come to truly love Conrad over the months. She enjoyed being with him, even if it meant his friends had to tag along. She loved seeing a smile brighten his face whenever she walked into a room. She had come to love that intense burning she felt inside whenever Conrad touched her, even if it was just to hold her hand. He was the first boy she had ever kissed, the first date she ever had and the first man she ever loved.

She heard Crystal Mintor's stern voice. "You watch out. All they care about is that little piece of meat between their legs. And once they take all you got you'll be in a heap of trouble and they'll be nowhere to be found." Conrad would never do that to me, Sina thought.

"Your first time should be special Boo," Sina recalled her cousin Kelsey telling her at the family reunion last summer. Kelsey and cousin Trevaughn knew that Thomas and Crystal Mintor were overprotective and were concerned about Sina entering the real world sheltered and naive. After the family talent show they pulled Sina off to the side to have a heart to heart talk with her.

"That's right," Trevaughn said. "Make sure he loves you and you love him."

"No make sure he cherishes you," Kelsey interrupted. "And make him spend some money on you."

"That's right, don't be doin' it in no car or alley. Make him take you to a hotel," Trevaughn said. "And I don't mean one where you pay by the hour either."

"Remember you will be offering the most precious gift you can offer any man."

"Make sure he deserves you. Because if he don't, I just might have to come up to Chicago and steal on his ass."

"We're your cousins and we love you," Kelsey said. "You're special and you need to be treated like you're special."

"That's right," Trevaughn insisted. "And by all means, make sure he cares enough about you to take care of you and make sure you don't get pregnant."

"Tonight you become a woman. My woman," Conrad said as his tongue sweetly circled the nipple of Sina's right breast. By the time he got to eighteen, the sun had finally set and Thomasine found her wrap around dress open. Conrad had nuzzled her ear, brushed bare spots of her hot body with the cold and wet wine cooler bottle, and placed her hand at the center of his manhood. As Conrad softly swept his hand to the top of Sina's jet black thigh highs, the mood was suddenly broken.

"Wait Conrad. It's that time of the month. Besides, I'm not ready."

"Thomasine. We've been together over four months now," Conrad insisted.

"I know. But it's just—"

"I know you're probably a little bit scared of getting pregnant and all, but I'll take care of that," Conrad said as he pulled a condom from his wallet and held it between his fingers. "You can go on the pill too. Then what will we have to worry about?"

"It's not that. It's just that I want my first time to be special. I don't want it to be in the back seat of a car."

"I understand baby. Can you come by Wednesday afternoon?"

"It's not just the car. I don't want to have to worry about anybody walking in on us either. Please be patient with me."

"Four months is a long time."

"I have something to ask you. And I want you to answer honestly."

"What is it Thomasine?"

"Do you love me?"

"You know how I feel about you. If I didn't love you, would I be here celebrating your birthday with you?"

Thomasine fixed her dress and Conrad took a basket out of the back seat of the car. He put his left arm around Sina's waist and they walked across the cement bridge over the outer drive. Once they reached their destination, Conrad found a spot and laid out the blanket.

"What would you do if a wave came here and took me away?" Thomasine asked.

"I'd take off all my clothes and jump in the lake and save you."

"I could drown in the length of time it would take for you to take off all of your clothes.

"What's that?" Thomasine asked of the plastic bag Conrad took out of the basket.

"Just a little herb, that's all," Conrad said as he lighted the pre-rolled joint and sat next to Sina. "Come here baby, give me a kiss." Sina wrapped her arms around his head and gave him a firm, steady kiss. "Now that doesn't taste so bad, does it? Just inhale." Conrad put the joint in his mouth backwards and blew the smoke into Sina's mouth. "How do you feel?"

"I feel good."

"Wanna take a hit? Just suck on it. And don't go and get it all wet."

"Whew!" Thomasine said.

"Are you hungry now?"

Sina and Conrad spent the rest of the evening eating the seafood, lying on the beach and dancing with each other. When they got back to the car Thomasine took a bottle of perfume out of the glove compartment and sprayed it on. "What's that for?" Conrad asked.

"So Rev. Mintor won't have any idea what went on here tonight."

The couple drove west to the Dan Ryan and headed south. When Sina drove quickly past her Aunt Carla's house, she noticed both her father's and Tommy's cars parked out front. As she turned the corner of Avery Street, she saw Rachel out front. When she pulled in a vacant spot in front of the Thompson home, she saw Rachel was running down the street. *Oh shit, I'm busted.*

"Thomasine, your father has called my house three times tonight. Aunt Mary told him I wasn't back yet. Your grandmother died tonight. They're all at your Aunt Carla's house and he left a message for you to go there."

Grandma Stephens was Sina's only living grandparent. Her father's parents and her mother's father had all died before she was even a twinkle in her parents' eyes. She had just been to West Virginia two years ago to see her 90-year-old grandmother and she was in great shape. She lived in her own house, cooked her own food, did her own hair, planted her own garden and canned her own vegetables. She was one strong woman. She did everything except drive. That was the first time in years Thomasine had seen her grandmother. She didn't feel as fortunate as Tommy. When Tommy was young, the Mintors often sent him to West Virginia for two weeks each summer. By the time Sina came along, Grandma Stephens was in her mid seventies and Crystal didn't want to burden her mother. Sina always felt that she never really got to know her grandmother. Not the way Tommy did. "Oh no," Thomasine said, crying hysterically as Conrad put his arms around her to comfort her.

"I'll drive you over there. Since, according to what your father knows, we went out tonight," Rachel said.

As Rachel started the car, she noticed the overwhelmingly sweet smell. "What's that smell?" she asked, "did you and Conrad rob a perfume store?"

"No," Thomasine said, still crying.

"Oh," Rachel said slowly holding the vowel sound for as long as she could. "Do you want to run home and take a shower first? No wonder Conrad wanted to come along."

"No, it's not what you think," Sina answered. "Do you have a peppermint."

"I think so, look in my purse."

Thomasine fumbled around, still teary eyed, until she found a peppermint. When Rachel got to her aunt's house, she had to drive down the street to find the nearest parking space. They got out of the car, Rachel walked alongside Sina with her arm on her shoulder until they got inside.

"I see you've found out Princess," Rev. Mintor said. "Thank you Rachel, for driving Sina over here."

"Thomasine was very upset and I felt uncomfortable about her driving," Rachel replied.

"I know you're sad, Princess. But you need to realize that your Grandma is in a better place now. She lived nearly 92 years, raised 12 children, and saw them all graduate from college. She lived a very full life."

I Don't Want Your Freedom

9

I can't believe the summer's almost over," Rachel said as she walked over to the sofa. "It seems like just yesterday we were going to prom and graduating." The trio had assembled in Thomasine's basement to kick it real hard one last time before going off to college. They had just finished a stuffed pizza from Michelangelo's, drunk their favorite pops and dished up three bowls of Daiquiri Ice.

"And now it's almost time for Hope to head South." Thomasine said, licking her spoon. "Are you excited?"

"No. I'm not thrilled about going, but I don't want to burst Mother's bubble. All my life she has talked about me going to Harrington."

"You should be more excited. You get to go to Harrington in sunny Savannah and I have to go to some no name school in wintry Wisconsin. I'd trade places with you any day."

"Yeah, at least you don't have to stay here," Rachel said. "I mean, Duncan is a good school and all, but it's here in Chicago."

"But you get to live in the dorm. You don't have to commute." Sina said. "You two don't know when you have it good. Hope down in Savannah with the water and warm sun and Rachel here with perpetual house music and all the slims."

"Who's that?" Hope asked as the girls heard a noise at the side door located at the top of the steps.

"It must be Tommy," Sina answered as she heard the familiar rhythm of Tommy barreling down the stairs to the basement carrying his laundry.

"Hey Rachel and Hope," Tommy greeted the girls. "Oh, I forgot tonight was your sleep-over. Sina, would you please wash this load for me?"

"Sure, Tommy. You better enjoy this now because my days of doing your laundry are numbered."

"That's right. I can't believe you all are going off to college in a few weeks. It seems like just yesterday you all were just little freshies, dodging the pennies. You all are making me feel so old," Tommy said.

"But before you go I just have one thing to say. Although Sina is my only sister, each of you is like a little sister to me. And I'm going to tell you the same thing I planned to tell Sina right before she leaves for Wisconsin. I want each of you to think long and hard about what I am going to say. And always remember it."

"Would you cut to the chase?" Sina said, wishing her brother would get to the point.

"You all are going off to school. Remember why you are there. You aren't there for a modeling career, although you should always make it a point to look good. Study hard. Have fun. Enjoy these years. Say no to drugs. And by all means, don't listen to those sweet talking, trifling ass, big men on campus. Don't let them fool you and knock you up," he said glancing at each of them. "Because I don't want to have to make any unplanned trips to Wisconsin, the north side or Savannah to straighten out a sticky situation. I expect each of you to return with your degrees. Within four years. Don't come home without it," Tommy told the girls. "Now always remember what I just told you."

"Thank you for your words of wisdom big brother, but aren't you running late for work?"

"Yeah, I better run. Now give me a hug. Enjoy this time." Tommy hugged Hope. "Say no to drugs," he said as he hugged his sister. "And please. By all means, please. Stay away from those 'big men on campus,'" he said hugging Rachel. "And I do expect each of you to keep in touch. You can get my address from Sina." He barreled up the steps and out the side door while Rachel and Sina rolled their eyes at him.

"Please excuse my big brother. He gets a little sentimental at times."

"Oh, that's all right," Hope replied. "What he said was very true."

"Once he got it out."

"In a few weeks, we will have all parted our paths. We will be saying so long to our men and catch ya later to each other."

"I've already said so long to Jamal," Rachel said. "We've decided to have an open relationship since he's going to Louisiana and I'll be here. I mean, it's not like I can hop on a Greyhound and be there in a few hours."

"When did he leave?" Hope asked.

"Two days ago."

"You all hit it off pretty well for him to just be a hook-up," Sina stated. "What did you all do before he left?"

"He came by last Saturday and picked me up and took me to dinner."

"That was nice, but I know you all didn't just say so long over a plate of cold pasta."

"I wasn't finished," Rachel replied. "After dinner we went back to his house. He swept me up in his arms as he closed the front door, then kissed me and carried me up to his bedroom."

"Then what happened?" Thomasine asked wide-eyed.

"We did it!"

"No you didn't," Hope said in a school-mom prim and proper tone.

"Girl, tell me all about it," Sina interrupted. "And don't leave anything out."

"He stretched me out across the bed, we French kissed and then he turned on the lamp."

"Turned on the lamp!" Sina said with even more excitement.

"Yes, and a stream of red light gently flooded from the lamp. He turned on the radio to the 'Soft Touch' and came back over to the bed. We kissed again and he pulled my shirt over my head and told me I was so beautiful. He said he was happy that he met me and that we shared so many of our firsts together. Then I said it's time for us to share another first."

"My girl!" Sina said.

"Then he climbed in the bed on top of me and rubbed his body against mine. He went to kiss me and I turned my head and he asked me what was wrong. I told him I was a little nervous because I had never done it before."

"How did he respond?" Sina asked.

"He said for me to just do what was natural. It was his first time too. So I lay back and tried to relax as he felt around my back to unhook my bra. I told him it was in the front. You know, I didn't' want him to take any scissors to my bra or anything."

"Then what happened?" Thomasine interrupted, now sitting on the edge of her chair.

"He took off his clothes, and I'll just say he was ready and rarin' to go. He went to the night stand drawer and pulled out a box of condoms and said he was taking good care of me. I took one long look at him and just tensed up," Rachel said as Hope and Sina looked at her like children being told a ghost story. "He went downstairs, got some wine and gave me a glass and told me to just relax, when I finished drinking the wine, it happened. The next thing I knew I was hollering at the top of my lungs."

"Weren't you afraid of getting caught?" Hope asked condescendingly.

"No, he told me his parents weren't home. But we almost got caught. I had just come downstairs when they came home."

"Did it hurt? What did it feel like?" Sina asked.

"There were actually two feelings. I felt all warm, actually hot inside my body. My skin felt like it was on fire. Then, there was that feeling. It wasn't really painful. It was more like pressure for a little while. Then I felt warm again."

"How did you know what to do?"

"I just followed his lead and did what came to me naturally."

"Ooh girl, what did you do afterwards?"

"He put his arms around me and we just lay there looking at each other. Then he asked me how I felt, I guess because I was so quiet. I told him I felt wonderful. Then he asked me if I wanted anything to eat, so we dressed and went to the kitchen. He gave me one of his shirts to put on, but I thought I better put on my own clothes and I'm glad I did because when we got downstairs, his parents walked in the door."

"How was he dressed?"

"He just had on his pants but, since it was 90 degrees and the air conditioning was broken, his parents didn't ask any questions."

"I don't believe this. You just met this guy and you've already slept with him. Jason and I have been together almost four years and we haven't even slept together yet."

"It doesn't take forever and a day for you to feel close enough to a person that you want to share your personal space with them," Rachel replied.

"That was Saturday. What did you do before he left on Wednesday?" Thomasine asked, trying to divert any potential altercation between the two.

"He came by Monday evening and we went to the Point and had a long talk. He said he really cared about me but we were going to be a long ways from each other in school and everything. He gave me this speech about long distance relationships and our being so young and all," she said, pausing for a spoonful of Daiquiri Ice. "So we agreed to have an open relationship."

"How do you feel about that?"

"Well, it makes perfect sense. I mean, he's eighteen and I'm seventeen. We're both young and we have our whole lives ahead of us. It's like Tommy just told us. Enjoy life."

"Do you regret sleeping with him now that he doesn't seem to want to have anything to do with you?" Hope asked.

"First of all, we didn't sleep together; we made love. And he never said he didn't want to have anything to do with me. We will still see each other on holidays and breaks."

"Things will be all the much better too when you see each other again. What's that saying? Absence makes the heart grow fonder," Sina reassured.

"But after you slept, I mean made love with him it's like he just cast you off to the side. The last time you saw him he was just kicking you to the curb."

"That wasn't the last time we saw each other." Rachel said. "Since we were at the Point and all we took advantage of the atmosphere."

"No you didn't do it in the car." Sina said.

"Yes we did, and it was better than the first time."

"I can't believe you fell for that. He planned it all along didn't he," Hope replied. "He came prepared to break it off with you and then have sex with you one more time."

"No he didn't. It just happened. Haven't you ever heard of spontaneity?"

"So you mean, it just happened?" Sina questioned. "He didn't come with protection?"

"No."

"I can't believe you had unprotected sex with him. What if you get pregnant or some disease?"

"I'm not worried about getting any disease from him because I'm the only one he's been with," Rachel retorted. "And I'm not worried about getting pregnant because we took other precautions. Hope, you just worry too much. I went over his house to see him off early Wednesday morning. I'm certain we'll be in touch."

"Well Conrad and I are going to try this long distance thing. I mean he can come up and see me on weekends since it's only three hours away and I can come home."

"Have you all done it yet?" Rachel asked.

"No, but when I get my single, he's going to come up one weekend with a bag and we'll spend some quality time together," Thomasine responded, realizing she just mentioned him bringing some herb.

"What types of things will he have in his bag?" Hope asked.

"Maybe something a little sexy for me to wear and some protection and maybe a gift." Thomasine responded, silently sighing relief for that close call. "What about you and Jason?"

"Well, he's into this long distance discussion too, but I'm not having it. He says we should see other people and that he understands if I want to date someone else when I'm in Savannah."

"What did you tell him?"

"Quite honestly, I told him 'I don't want your freedom.' And that I was not ready to give up on our love."

"He told me he still loves me and he always will. Did Jamal tell you that Rachel?"

"I'm going to miss you two," Sina said as she quickly changed the subject in order to avoid a fight between Rachel and Hope. "It's funny. Neither of us has any biological sisters, but we are like sisters."

"You will always be my sisters," Rachel said. "Because God knows, putting up with your worrying and your habits is something only a sister would do."

"I'm really going to miss you two," Hope said teary eyed. "But I'm going to write once a week and call twice a month."

"Hey it would be neat if one of us had a three way and then we could all talk at the same time." Sina said.

"If we can't do it this semester, we will be able to do it one day," Rachel said as the girls separated.

"I've got dibs on the sleeper sofa." Rachel and Hope shouted in unison.

"That leaves me with the sleeping bag." Sina turned off the lights.

Breakout

10

I'm gonna miss you two," Hope said, teary-eyed as she hugged her friends Rachel and Sina goodbye at the airport. O'Hare was busy as usual with vacation travelers revealing their destinations with golf clubs, surf boards, and other attire suited for exotic locations. Sina and Rachel had managed to bogarde their way through the crowd just in time to see Hope off.

"We'll miss you too," Thomasine said quickly. "I expect a letter from you shortly and you have my address at school, don't you?"

"Eastern Airlines now boarding flight 1873 with nonstop service to Atlanta, continuing to Savannah. We are now boarding all first class passengers, families traveling with small children or anyone else who may need extra time boarding," said the voice over the intercom.

"It's time for us to go honey," Phyllis Jones told her sad daughter. "It was so nice of you girls to come to the airport to see Hope off. These girls are good people to have as friends." Tears continued to well up in Hope's eyes. "Now stop that crying. You're acting as if you're going to China or somewhere very far away. You'll get to see your friends at Thanksgiving and Christmas and before you even know it you will have graduated," Mrs. Jones said to Hope as they walked down the jetway.

In the midst of her tears and sobs, Hope didn't hear a word her mother was saying.

"Well, Hope's gone," Rachel said as she and Sina headed south on the Kennedy expressway.

"You might as well get used to it, Rachel. My days here are numbered. You know I leave on Monday after next."

"First Jamal, then Hope, and soon you."

"But we'll keep in touch. You can always come up on the weekend and see me and you know how I like to write. I'm going to write you each week. After all, I have to find some time to study and as Tommy said, enjoy life."

"I guess you're right," Rachel replied. "Besides, I'm going to have fun keeping an eye on Jason for Hope."

"What about all of that trust and love and that special bond Hope says they have? Why does she have to have someone spy on him if they have all of that?"

"I guess she's concerned because he wants an open relationship and she refused."

"Quite frankly Rachel, I think you should stay out of it. I mean, if she had gone on with the open relationship thing, at least she would know what he was doing, but since she gave him an ultimatum, it will hurt her more when she finds out he's seeing someone else. Rachel, promise me you won't say anything to her. Tell her you only see him at the games or in a class and that the athletes live on another part of the campus. I mean, she'll buy it. With 25,000 students at Duncan, you all will probably rarely see each other."

"I suppose you're right."

Savannah was a beautiful place. Warm, sunny, lined with palm trees and near the ocean. Anyone would just love it. But not Hope. Although she had spent her first few years in Savannah and had relatives nearby, she hated Savannah. She hated the South. She knew she would have to get a perm because her hair wouldn't hold a press in the hot and humid weather. Sticky was the best word Hope could find to describe how she was feeling as she and her mother stepped outside the baggage claim area and looked for her cousin Charity.

Charity, like all of the other women in Hope's family, was a Harrington Alumna. She was so proud of her alma mater and even more excited when she found out that Hope would have her old room in Truth Hall, the freshman dorm named after Sojourner Truth. "Hope, you haven't hardly said a word," Charity said as they turned into the parking lot of Truth Hall.

"She's a little upset because she's going to miss her friends and her boyfriend Jason."

"You'll make new friends," Charity reassured her. "And you'll keep in touch with your close friends from Chicago. Maybe they can come down for Spring Break. Schools in the North usually don't have break at the same time we do. You'll have a lot of fun." Charity parked the car. "And as for that boyfriend, if things don't work out between you two, there's always the men of Savannah State. There's plenty of them over there, Kappas, Alphas, Omegas, Sigmas and even Omicrons, if you want to go there. That's where I met my husband.

"You just don't understand," Hope said. "No one seems to."

"She's head over heels in love with that Jason," Phyllis said as they walked up the stairs of the red brick building to the main entrance of Truth Hall. "Even plans to marry him when they finish college."

"Hey Soror!" called a fortyish woman who looked like a Clair Huxtable with salt and pepper feathered hair.

"Hattie, it's been years. I haven't seen you since our ten-year anniversary."

"I know, it has been ages. I'm bringing my oldest daughter here for her freshman year."

"Me too, this is my daughter, Hope. Hope, this is my line sister Hattie Johnson."

"It's Wilson now. It's so nice to meet you Hope. I had to keep your mother in line when we pledged."

"Oh, it was the other way around. If I remember correctly, your line name was—Treacherous."

"Those were the days," Hattie said laughing. "We had so much fun. Now Hope, I know you know that AKA is the only way."

"You better run along honey and get your room assignment," Mrs. Jones told Hope.

As Hope walked up to the table, she looked at the cinder block walls painted yellow. *They've tried to make this place more cheery I suppose*, Hope thought. *But I still don't like it.* "Your name please?" the girl with a bob hair cut sitting on the other side of the table said.

"Hope McCoy. I mean Hope Jones."

"Hope Jones from Chicago. I'm from Gary, Indiana. Let's see. You're in room 203. Hey that's on my floor, I'm your R.A. Anyway, your roommate is Nia Wilson from Cleveland. Here is your room key. If you get locked out go to the front desk across the way and someone will let you borrow a key to the room. If you lose your key there is a $20.00 fee. You can sign up for the tea tomorrow afternoon, but if you do, they will take your lunch away tomorrow; I promise you, the food at the tea will be better."

"Yes, I think I want to go to the tea."

"Make sure you wear your white dress and gloves with flesh colored stockings and black leather pumps. If you have any other questions, I'm in Room 215."

"Now Thomasine, don't cry," Rachel said. "Just the other week you were telling me to get used to you and Hope not being here. I know you're going to miss me and Hope and your family and of course Conrad. But what did you just tell me a few weeks ago. You'll be home in a few weeks and things will be all the much better between you two."

"I know," Thomasine said, sobbing.

"This is for you," Rachel said as she handed Sina an envelope.

"Should I open it now?"

"It's up to you."

Sina opened the envelope to find a beautiful Hallmark card from the "Between You and Me." collection. "Our friendship has meant so much," Thomasine read the outside and opened the card.

> *Sina, you have been the only sister I'll ever know. You are patient, caring, honest, and just. You have always accepted me as I am and you are very slow to judge. These qualities are the reason I love you as both a friend and a sister. I'll miss you when you're in Wisconsin but boy will we have a ball when you come home. Keep in touch,*
>
>   *Love always,*
>   *Rachel*

"Now you've got me all misty eyed," Rachel said as Sina hugged her. "We can just look at it like this. You're coming home in two weeks and I can come see you on some of the weekends you don't come home. Let's think of it this way. You aren't going off to some old college in Wisconsin. You're going on vacation. Just like you used to do in the summers. And you'll be back in two weeks but then you have to go on another vacation, so that way you really aren't leaving."

"Sina, it's almost five. Time for us to leave," her mother called from the hallway. Sina felt that her parents were getting rid of her. They had packed the car before they went to bed. Sina wondered what the rush was. She had all day to make the three hour drive and move into her room. And even if she wanted to wait a day or so, the dorm would still be there. Then there was that element of mystery that surrounds a change, something new. This was Sina's first time away from home and while she knew she was going away to get an education, she really didn't know what to expect.

"Good morning, Rachel," Rev. Mintor said. "If Sina wasn't taking so much junk, you could ride up with us, but we can barely get the three of us in the car."

"Thank you Rev. Mintor."

"Well maybe you can ride up one weekend when we take her back to school."

"That would be nice. Well, I better be going now." Rachel turned to hug Sina. "I'll give you a call later."

"Thomas, did you turn everything off?" Crystal asked her husband.

"Everything is off, and besides, we'll be back this afternoon."

"Well, let's hit it then," Crystal said as they opened the gate to the backyard. At that moment, Rex began what would become an annual ritual. Each time Sina got ready to go back to school, he ran away and always ended up in a bush covered with sticker bugs in his long coat. He had his head down and was trying to pull the sticker bugs out from underneath his neck. Once Rex was safely locked away in the back of the basement with enough food and water to last a day, they were ready to roll.

"Yes, indeed," Crystal said. "That Rachel will be your friend for a long time. Anyone who cares enough about you to get up at that ungodly hour just to bring you a card. You better make sure you keep in touch with her." Sina was unresponsive. She just sat silently while her eyes shined with a film of water.

"What's wrong Princess?" Rev. Mintor asked his sobbing daughter. "I know this school isn't your first choice, but we aren't sending you there as a punishment. We think it's best for you. And you got a four-year, full tuition scholarship. You have a lot to be proud of and we're proud of you. Go up there and study hard."

It wasn't going away to college that had Sina so upset, it was going to this school in Wisconsin. Sina had applied to Illinois, Purdue, U of Miami and this school in Wisconsin. By early April she had been accepted at Illinois and U of Miami and was all set to go to sunny Coral Gables, thousands of miles away from Chicago and its fierce winter winds. Then came the four-year full tuition scholarship. When she read the words, she cried. Tommy was at the house so she called him in the room. "Tommy, I have something to show you. But you have to promise not to say anything to Mama and Daddy about it."

"Okay."

Sina handed the letter to Tommy who immediately ambled out of her bedroom, "Mama, look at this. Sina got a four-year full tuition scholarship to this school in Wisconsin."

Thomasine began to cry hysterically. She knew she would have to accept it. She wouldn't be able to go to Miami and major in Broadcast Journalism at their School of Communication. She would have to put away her shades by mid-September and buy another pair of those Sporto boots she and her friends called Rubber Duckies. She wouldn't be near the ocean or the palm trees. And she wouldn't be that far away from home.

After Tommy tried to convince his parents to buy Sina a car because after all, she would be saving them a whole lot of money by accepting this offer, Sina stopped crying and began to think about it more logically. "It just don't make sense for you to go into debt getting a Bachelor's degree when someone is offering you a free ride," Crystal said. "If you still feel strongly about Miami, you can go there for graduate school. Besides, I don't really want you down there anyway, with all that drug trafficking and those riots last year and stuff. They say people go into the Everglades and they're never seen again. It's best for you to take this scholarship and go to Wisconsin. If you want to go into debt to get a graduate degree, then fine. They say a Bachelor's today is just like a high school diploma in my time. To make it in this world, honey you're probably going to have to get at least a Master's. Then it'll be worth it to go into debt."

Thomasine finally agreed to accept the scholarship and actually got excited when she looked at the course catalog. "I can take Art History of India, China and Japan for my Non-Western Culture course," she said to the counselor helping her choose her classes when she visited the campus in early July.

"That hasn't been offered in a long time," the counselor replied. "I think right now we just better try to find some classes for you. Since this is the last day of pre-registration, just about everything is full. All of the Speech, English, Biology and all of the interim classes are full."

"But I'm a Radio/TV/Film major. Fundamentals of Speech is required for me."

"You can try to see if a teacher will sign you in when school starts. Let's see. You placed out of Math, but you didn't pass your German placement test so you will have to take German I. And it looks like there are some openings in Intro to Radio/TV. Now you will need to take at least one Honors class a year because you are a University Scholar. Also, since you're a University Scholar, you get to register on the first day of registration so you can get all of the classes you want in the future. As for that interim class, try back during the semester. All that's open now is Nordic Skiing which would meet part of your P.E. requirement. Some students go home and end up working during January so it should be really easy for you to get an interim course."

"Thank you," Sina said politely to the counselor as she went to take her ID picture. *This is just great,* she thought as she smiled for the picture. *I'm really going to hate this place. I get stuck with the classes that nobody else wanted. The only black person I saw had a white woman on his arm. And to top it all off, the girl at the fast food restaurant acted like she was scared of us when Mom asked for a bag to carry half of her sandwich back to the hotel.*

As the Mintors approached the Edens expressway leading them to Wisconsin, Thomasine was still crying. She looked in her purse to make sure she had her mirror. When she told Tommy about her visit, he told her he could relate. He went to college in northwestern Iowa. He told Sina that days would go by and she wouldn't see another black person and advised her to keep a mirror with her at all times, so she wouldn't forget what black people looked like. "Wake up, Princess, we're here," Rev. Mintor said to Sina, who had fallen asleep before they even made it to the Wisconsin border, as he parked the car.

"Where is everybody?" Crystal Mintor asked. "I just know we can't be the first ones here. They said the dorms opened at 8:00 and it's five after." Crystal grabbed Sina's suitcase out of the trunk of the car. "You run on in Sina and get your room key. It's room 354, right?"

"Yes Mama." She walked into the brown brick high-rise building.

"Welcome to Zimmerman Hall," said a portly, mousy, blonde woman. "I'm Sandra Miller, your Resident Hall Director and you are?"

"I'm Thomasine Mintor."

"Let's see, Room 354. Do you know you are the first person to move in today. Your parents were really smart getting here early. Now you don't have to compete for the elevators. Here's the key to your room. Will Kirchner is your C.A. We call them Community Advisors here because we don't think of this place as a dorm. Dorm is a bad word around here. It is a residence hall, a community. He is in room 370 and if you need anything he will be happy to assist you."

"Thank you."

"Oh, I almost forgot, we're having a cookout on Saturday. There will be volleyball, burgers and hotdogs, and chips. If you're interested, you need to sign up and give me your ID. This cookout replaces your dinner on Saturday."

"Sign up for it princess, it will be an opportunity for you to meet people."

"These are my parents, Rev. and Mrs. Mintor. Mom and Dad, this is Sandra Miller. She's the dorm, I mean residence hall director."

"Nice to meet you."

"Let's get going so we can take you to get something to eat and get back on the road. You know your father has to get back," Crystal said. "And we aren't going back to that same restaurant either."

"Oh, you must be Thomasine!" A middle aged, tall, thin, strawberry blonde woman said as a younger woman put a six pack of Budweiser in the fridge. The fridge sat on top of one of the side by side dressers. Two desks were across the room with built in bookcases just above them. The beds on either side of the dresser formed a backward L. "Amy dear, come meet your roommate."

"It's so nice to meet you finally. I feel like I already know you from all of your letters this summer. These must be your parents, Rev. and Mrs. Mintor."

"It's so nice to meet you."

"This is my Mom, Jennifer Mueller and my dad is carrying some things up."

Once the parents met, the Mintors had to head back to Chicago. Annual Conference started the next day and everyone knew Annual Conferences in the African Christian Church could be grueling, so Rev. Mintor needed to get his rest.

"Thomasine, we're going out to eat; do you want to come along?"

"Thank you Mrs. Mueller. I'll have to pass. We just came from a restaurant and I think I want to catch up on some sleep. My parents woke me up at three this morning and we were the first ones here."

"I understand. You get some rest."

Before Sina caught up on her sleep, she checked her mail, just for the heck of it and to familiarize herself with the residence hall. When she placed her room key into the box numbered 354 and slowly opened the metal door, she saw a letter. It was from Hope. She was so excited that she quickly shut the box and nearly bumped into another student on her way back to her room.

"Excuse me," Sina said, looking up from the letter.

"That's all right," responded the petite, brown skinned girl. "I'm Stephanie Lewis from Milwaukee. You must be new here because if you were here last semester, I certainly would have known. What room are you in?"

"I'm in 354. Oh, and by the way, my name is Thomasine Mintor, but my friends just call me Sina. I'm from Chicago."

"I'm in 357, two doors down and across the hall from you," Stephanie replied. "I was named after my aunt and my family calls me Gwen, my middle name. I will answer to either. What are you getting ready to do?"

"I was going to my room and take a nap. I was the first one to move in the dorm, I mean residence hall today. My parents got me up at three this morning. Let me give you my phone number, it's 0958."

"You sound like you need some rest. I'll call you later. My sisters and I are having a wop party at her house off campus. She's from the south side of Chicago, her name is Measha. It starts at nine and if you want to come along and help us set up you're welcome."

"What sorority are you in?"

"There are no black sororities up here; we're both Alpha Roses," Gwen said as she walked away. "I'll call you around six."

Tommy was wrong.

Sina's nap had been so peaceful that when her sleep was interrupted by the telephone, she woke up, completely forgetting the events of the morning. Familiarizing herself with her new surroundings, she reached for the phone. "I'll get it. Hello."

"Hello Sina. I just called to see how you were doing, you were pretty sad this morning."

"Rachel. I'm so glad to hear your voice. So what did you do today?"

"Hank and I went to our mother's house for a cookout. She wanted to give me a party before I leave for school next week, but I declined because my closest friends can't come. We talked about having one for my 18th birthday either before, at Thanksgiving or when you and Hope come home for Christmas."

"That will be so cool. Oh, I got a letter from Hope today. She seems miserable, she hates Harrington and as usual, she's judging her roommate whose mother, it turns out, was Mrs. Jones line sister. She said she went to this tea her second day there and didn't like the people too much. It seems her roommate and some other girls on the floor snuck out one night and went to a party at Savannah State, but that she wasn't into the Greek scene and she hoped her mother wouldn't be mad if she decided not to pledge AKA. She said her roommate is fast and smokes, but she doesn't let her smoke in the room. The food is great there and they have fried chicken every day for lunch and dinner. And of course, she misses Jason."

"I'm sure she has written him a zillion times since she got down there," Rachel said "And she has plenty of time to think about pledging."

"I don't have much to think about. It's Delta or nothing for me. My mother and Kelsey would probably kill me if I came home wearing some pink and green or any colors besides red and white. But since there are no black sororities here, I don't have to worry about that."

"So have you met any other black students?"

"Yes. I met Stephanie Gwen Lewis who lives down the hall. She's an Alpha Rose and invited me to a wop party tonight. It's only a dollar to get in."

"I know you're going, because you can really do the wop."

"You got that right. I'll write you and tell you about the party tomorrow. Classes don't start until Wednesday. I think tomorrow, my roommate Amy and I will walk around the campus so we can find our classes easily later in the week."

"Look, I better get off this phone."

"Someone's at the door, I'll catchya later."

"It's been a slice." Thomasine hung up the phone and walked across the small room to the door. "Hey Stephanie. Amy, this is Stephanie, she lives down the hall. Stephanie, this is my roommate Amy."

"Nice to meet you."

"Well, I called a few minutes ago and the line was busy."

"Yeah, we've got to get call waiting," Amy said.

"I was talking to my good friend and sister, Rachel."

"I just came to tell you I'm going to leave to go to the party at about 7:30, a quarter to eight. The dress is casual, and I'll stop back by to pick you up," Gwen said as she left the room.

"What are your plans for tonight?" Sina asked her roommate.

"Some people from my hometown are having a beer and brat party."

"Sounds fun. I think I'll jump in the shower before I head to the party. Will you be in the room?"

"Yes." Sina undressed and put on her bathrobe.

As she walked down the hallway in what seemed like an obstacle course of students' belongings strategically placed in the hall as they were moving in, Thomasine felt uncomfortable. Here she was, walking along, in front of all of these strange people she didn't know, in her bathrobe. She finally reached the bathroom and was surprised that there was only a shower curtain between each shower. She had thought there would be shower stalls with doors and walls so that she could have more privacy. Sina put her shower cap on, hung her robe on the hook in the tiled area of the bathroom with the benches, and grabbed her towel.

She opened a new package of Caress soap, turned on the hot water and hummed Anita Baker's *No One in the World* as she showered. Sina turned off the hot water, wrapped the towel around her and went to get her robe, but it was gone. She looked around the bathroom and in the trash, but it seemed to have disappeared. She just could not bear to walk down the hall with a towel wrapped around her in front of all of those strange people, so she waited and waited, trying to muster up the courage to walk back to her room when Gwen walked in.

"You aren't going to believe this, but someone stole my robe."

"I'll go down and get mine so you can get back to your room. It's probably just a prank. They are always doing stuff like that. Saran wrapping the toilets and penny jamming the doors. I'll be right back."

"Thank you so much," Thomasine said as she put on Gwen's big, fluffy pink terry cloth robe.

"If I were you, I wouldn't take showers at night again. These fools are always trying to pull some prank."

"Sine, telephone," Amy said as Sina walked into the room.

"Thank you."

"Sina baby, what's up?"

"Conrad."

"I told you I'd call."

"You will not believe what just happened. I was taking a shower and somebody stole my robe. I almost had to walk down the hall with a towel around me with all those people around."

"I wish I had been there to see you wearing just a towel."

"This is not funny."

"Okay, then, if I were there, I'd find whoever did this to you and give them a Windy City Butt Whuppin," he said, still laughing. "On to happier things, have you met any other black people?"

"Yeah, I met this girl named Stephanie Lewis from Milwaukee. They have enough blacks up here to have an Alpha chapter and Alpha Roses. They invited me to a wop party tonight and that's what I'm getting ready for."

"I wish I was there to watch you shake your groove thing and wop your butt off," Conrad said. "I won't keep you. Have fun, and don't say out too late."

September 23, 1987

Dear Rachel,

Thank you for covering for me last weekend when I was home. I owe you one. It's not that my parents don't like Conrad, it's just that my mother thinks I spend too much time with him, and she did find those thigh high stockings he bought me. This place isn't as bad as I thought it would be, that is, once I got over the initial shock of my bathrobe being stolen. Well, my C.A. found it in the men's room that same night. Other than the pranks and practical jokes, this place is okay.

Classes are fine. I know I will make an A in German. I got a perfect score on the first quiz and I fell asleep on it. Music Apprec. is easy too. I've met a few other black students. I attended the first

Black Student Union meeting and there were only a handful of us there. I got the notice about an hour before the meeting and I could hear my mother telling me I needed to attend, that I needed to meet people and connect. They said they sent the letters out a week ago, but campus mail is just so slow. Anyway, I've joined the BSU Gospel Ensemble, we don't have enough black folk to have a choir.

The wop party was fun, but it was not about the dance the "wop." If you want to know more about it you will have to come up here one weekend and go to one with me. Weekend before last the BSU had a party and I had this Alpha on my left trying to bet me to become a Rose and then there was this B.A.I. (Brothers, Acquaintances and Independents more commonly known as Black Ass Individuals) on my right whispering in my ear that "Greece is dead and so are Greeks." He said, "You go to Greece and you don't see nothing but ruins." The Alpha then whispered in my ear, "Ask him why he only dates white girls?" At that point I walked away from both of them.

Other than the Alphas there's this other black frat called Omicron Xi Mu. Their little sisters are the Omicron Opals. Most of them are seniors so they're looking for new members. A little birdie told me that to get in the Opals, the Omicrons give you a condom and tell you to bring it back used. Now is that nasty or what? But then I guess they didn't say how you were to use it. I guess it's just part of that mind game you have to play in order to get in.

I trust that all of your classes are going well and that you've adjusted to Duncan. Have you seen Jason? Have you heard from Hope? I haven't, since that first letter, but I'm sure she is busy as all of us are. I've been having the weirdest dreams lately. I keep dreaming about fish. I'm fishing, I'm cleaning fish and in one dream I was even a fish. Somebody is definitely pregnant or will be soon. I know it's not me, and if you and Jamal always used protection it shouldn't be you either. We both know it's not Hope. Maybe it's my cousin Kelsey. She and her husband are trying to have a baby. She says if it happens now she'll be happy, but if it doesn't then it will happen one day, but I know she really wants a child now.

Well, I have to run off to my 12:40 Music Appreciation class. I'm going to stop at the mailbox and drop this letter off on my way to class.

It's been a slice.

Sina

Pump Up the Volume

11

*I*ndian Summer had set in and Duncan students were enjoying the last chance of warmth the fall afternoons had to offer before the onset of November's windy, pre-winter blast. Bright hues of red, orange, and brown leaves decorated the red brick sidewalk. Rachel had adjusted, and Sina had been right, Rachel rarely saw Jason, except at parties. Rachel and her roommate Candace were getting along quite well. Candace was a violin major from a small town in Oregon, so she and Rachel had something in common. It was now October, the mid-semester stretch; Rachel had nearly depleted her summer savings on late night pizzas and other social activities, so she found herself in the Office of Scholarships and Student Aid.

"Miss Curtis, we have reviewed your application," said the woman sitting behind the desk, wearing her glasses low on her nose. "And we have found a position for you in the Black Cultural Center."

"Do you know where that's located?"

"Yes, I've been there a few times." *A-duh.*

"When you go there ask for Mrs. Washington. She is the Administrative Assistant and she will be your supervisor. Here are a few time sheets, you will be paid biweekly but you won't get your first check for a month. Do you have any other questions?"

"No," Rachel said as she stood up, shook the woman's hand and found her way out of the maze of cubicles which made up the scholarship and student aid office.

"I thought I'd get paid sooner," Rachel said to herself as she walked down the steps of Hargett Hall. She was actually excited about her job and all of the people she would get to meet and talk to. She was friendly, outgoing, easily adaptable and possessed a gift for gab. She always seemed to fit in easily in most places and could talk to just about anybody. She enjoyed the long walk across campus from Hargett to the Black Cultural Center located in the Multicultural Village. The powers to be at Duncan University had strategically placed this village on the complete opposite end of campus from the major administrative buildings and the dorms. "Maybe I should hop on a bus," Rachel thought. But being a native Chicagoan, enjoying the outdoors, and knowing that these warm, sunny days were certainly numbered, she decided to enjoy the walk.

At the Commons, she was surprised so many students were hovering in that vicinity since lunch had ended almost an hour ago. As she bobbed and weaved her way through the labyrinth of students wearing shorts and T-shirts for the last time, she caught a glimpse of Jason walking along with someone who looked familiar. "Oh, shoot," Rachel said as she tried to quickly head in the opposite direction.

"Hey Rachel," Jason called. He walked briskly in her direction. "I haven't seen you all semester." He reached out to hug her. "Have you met Naomi?"

"Yes we've met," Naomi replied. "Little Sister Square Rock. Just how are you doing today?"

"Greetings Big Sister Nicety Nacre Naomi. It's like a jungle sometimes, it makes me wonder how I keep from going under," Rachel replied *narcissistic, narrow-minded, nauseating Naomi is more like it.*

"Where are your other Little Silicas? And why the glamorous look?"

"Number one, three, and five are in class and number two is at work, Big Sister Nicety Nacre Naomi, one beautiful, brainy embodiment of a Black woman," Rachel replied. "And as for the look, I report to my Student Aid job for the first time, and as a future Omicron Opal I feel that it is important for me to make a good first impression, because you'll never have a second chance to make a first impression and when people, especially other black students on this campus look at me, some will judge the Opals."

"So where is your job?"

"In the Black Cultural Center."

"Carry on Little Silica."

Rachel was ecstatic that she only had a few more days to go. She wondered why she ever considered screening for this little sister group, but with Sina and Hope so far away, she thought it would be a great chance to find sisterhood at Duncan. Besides, her roommate Candace had become a Sigma Phi Frigg and she seemed to have a ball socially. Rachel enjoyed the bonding she did with her sisters, but breakfast, lunch, dinner, study time and sessions with them had been enough. Staying up half the night with them practicing for their probate show and then getting up early to walk number two to her morning job in the Commons had taken its toll. She would also be glad to get her freedom back. She knew by now that both

Jamal and Sina were outdone with her. Jamal sent her flowers for Sweetest Day which Candace graciously said were hers when Big Sister Queensland Boulder inquired. Sina had written her twice and she hadn't responded. In her first letter she talked about the Opals and the rite of passage. Rachel was thankful for Sina's wisdom and insight, with Jamal being down South and everything. In her second letter she had a new address—she moved into a single. Sina said she got tired of coming to her dorm room to find her roommate Amy and nine of her closest friends: Polly, Becky, Molly, Stacy, Wendy, Tracy, Jenny, Susy and Jill sprawled out in her room watching *The Brady Bunch* on Sina's TV. And *The Brady Bunch* came on at the same time as *Good Times*. Some of the girls had the nerve to be sitting on Sina's bed, that was, until she came into the room. When Sina walked into the room, they quickly got up. As much as Sina wanted to just take the remote and change the channel, because after all it was her TV, she didn't. She just walked down to Gwen's room and watched her program on Gwen's black and white TV. Gwen's Rose sister, Deborah always said, "Let's go down there and bum-rush the boob tube." But Sina was content just chilling in Gwen's room.

Rachel had a feeling that Sina was going to become an Alpha Rose whenever they had screening. She would have become an Alpha Rose, but after two of the Roses got into a knock-down, drag-out fight at the interest meeting, the Alphas decided they needed to get their household in order before they let anyone else in.

Finally here, Rachel reached the Multicultural Village. As she walked past the Center for Native American Study and the Center for Latino Culture, she realized just how happy she was about her job. She had planned to become involved at the BCC as soon as the Opal screening was over. While she would just be answering the phone and greeting people as a receptionist, she knew she would be able to get on some of the different committees for planning events like the Multicultural Film Festival and the Ethnic Food Fair and Unity—the Anti-Discrimination Workshop.

"Is Mrs. Washington here?" Rachel asked as she entered the reception area of the BCC, finding no one there who she thought could possibly be Mrs. Washington.

"Mrs. Washington had an emergency and had to leave early. I'm Calvin Hardy, Assistant Director of the Black Cultural Center. May I help you?"

"I'm Rachel Curtis, the new student aide. The lady in Scholarships and Student Aid told me Mrs. Washington would be my supervisor." Rachel shook Calvin's hand.

"Yes she will. Would you like to get started right now? We could really use you to man the phones," he showed her to the desk. "Dr. Foster, the Director is away at a conference. Normally I would give you a tour, but I'm sure I can do this tomorrow when Mrs. Washington returns."

"Yes, Mr. Hardy. I would like to start right now," Rachel replied.

"Well here is the message pad, and the extensions are right here on the desk," Calvin said pointing the items out. "To transfer a call, just press the hold button, and then the number of the extension," he said looking down from Rachel's face. "And by the way, does that ribbon you're wearing mean anything to you?"

"Yes it does, Mr. Hardy."

"Please, cut the formalities. It's Calvin. And I'm an Omicron. Been an Omicron man for 13 years now. Pledged up in Wisconsin Fall of 74. I can tell already you're smart, you're making an excellent choice," Calvin walked toward the door. "By the way, please hold all of my calls. I have an important report to finish. I'm so glad you came today."

"I like this already," Rachel thought. I can just sit here and answer the phone, do my Analytic Geometry homework. Rachel found herself in the midst of a cardioid polar graph when she was interrupted by the shrill ringing of the phone. "Good afternoon, Black Cultural Center this is Rachel Curtis speaking, how may I help you." Rachel thought she was good at this already. Aunt Mary would be so proud.

"May I speak to Calvin?"

"Mr. Hardy is in a meeting. I'd be happy to take your message."

"This is Charleen. Would you please buzz his office."

"I'm sorry, he's in a meeting. But I would be happy to take a message ma'am."

"Buzz his office."

"Ms. Charleen. He left strict orders not to be disturbed. But I would be very happy to take your message."

"Buzz his office."

"Is there a message ma'am? He doesn't want to be disturbed and I feel I must honor his request."

"No message." Click was the sound of Ms. Charleen, whomever she was, slamming the receiver down. The afternoon waned on and the bright orange globe in the sky began to lower, promising a beautiful tomorrow. Rachel found herself exhausted. The late nights and early mornings had finally caught up with her. As Calvin walked down the steps with his jacket in his right hand and briefcase and car keys in left, he heard a buzzing sound. He approached the entryway and turned to face the reception area, finding the source of the noise. He casually walked over to Rachel and tapped her lightly on the front of her shoulder.

"Wake up sleepy head," Calvin said softly.

"Oh no. I'm so embarrassed."

"No need for anyone who is as cute as you are to be embarrassed when you're sleeping."

Rachel wanted to roll her eyes. She did not find it appealing at all to be told she was cute by someone as old as Calvin. He had to be at least 32. That was if he had pledged Omicron as a sophomore. "In the future, we won't pay you for sleeping on the job," Calvin said, smiling at Rachel. "Can I give you a lift, because I think you need to be in the commons in about five minutes? And there's no way you can walk or run or even hop on a bus over there in that time."

"Yes, thank you."

"Anything for my little sister."

Rachel was silent as they rode in Calvin's IROC. He slowed his car to a stop in front of the Commons and Rachel began to wonder how she would explain this to the Omicrons or Opals. But it was as if Calvin was reading her mind. "Don't worry about what anyone will have to say. I'm the faculty advisor for the Omicrons. After all, you just have two more days and then we won't have to worry about you falling asleep on the job. At least until finals."

"Thank you, Calvin."

"I'll see you tomorrow, Rachel."

October 26, 1987

Dear Sina,

I'm so sorry for not returning your letters. I've been busy the past few weeks. I'm now an Omicron Opal. My line name is Iridescent. I was number four and there were five of us. I had a blast that weekend I came up which seems like a century ago. The wop party was great, that is until the morning after. I was so hungover. You know I'm not used to drinking alcohol. About the only high I had ever gotten was from Daiquiri Ice from that ice cream shop. Remember how we used to go and get a quart, eat it and then act like we thought people acted when they were drunk. You all need to send them the recipe so they can make some wop ice. Then we wouldn't need to act. I think the next time I come up I'll pass on the wop. You all got some fine Alphas up there. Some real slims.

I'm glad the screening is over. Our probate show was great. We came out with tunes and then said "Sigma Sweets must be sick,

Omicron Opals don't need to step with no damn sticks." And then
we threw the sticks at them. Now I get to do the call Ooohm-
mmm. Sounds like moo backwards. You can't know what that
means unless you become an Opal._ We get to walk at all of the
parties. Also, every Wednesday we wear red and green. But I'm
most glad that the screening is over because I get to finally return
your letter. I really miss you. When are you coming home again?
We have to kick it. I hope you're coming home soon.

I've decided to have my birthday party early, at Thanksgiving.
Hope's coming home and so is Jamal. And you'll get to meet my
roommate, Candace from Oregon. She's staying with me over the
holiday. Jamal sent me a bouquet for Sweetest Day. What did you
and Conrad do? Since you got your single I know he came up to
see you, with his bag. I hope that Clayton wasn't around. I think
he's sweet on you, but if you want my opinion, he's too old. And
remember what Tommy said about the Big Men on Campus.
Clayton's graduating in December, he told me. You'll have to tell
me all about it. As you told me, inquiring minds need to know.

I got a letter from Hope. She is in the Accounting Club and the
Chicago Club. She said her roommate Nia screened for Alpha
Rose at Savannah State and may be your sister if you decide to go
that way. She asked me all about what Jason was doing, and if he
was seeing anyone. Would you believe I've only seen him a few
times since school started? I ran into him with Naomi, one of my
Opal sisters. I really feel like I'm stuck between a rock and a hard
place. I mean, I don't know anything about the relationship, but
I do know that Naomi is crazy about him and like Hope she always gets what she wants. Everything.

Anyway, I'm going to have to close this letter. I'm at work. I'm
a Student Aide at the Black Cultural Center. It is so cool because
I get to meet so many of the multicultural students. The Assistant
Director, Calvin is also cool. He's an Omicron and would you be-
lieve he wears red and green every Wednesday. My supervisor,
Mrs. Washington is at lunch right now and she will be back soon.
I want to get this in the afternoon mail so I'll end now.

Always your sister,
Rachel

P.S. About those dreams you keep having about fish. It's not me.
I'm on my period right now.

Sina smiled as she read Rachel's letter. *An Omicron Opal. Hmm. I don't think I'll go that way. Maybe we can be Delta sisters, if they ever get a chapter up here.* Sina had decided not to join any of the little sister groups. Especially since she often heard her Alpha Rose friends talk about the big Alpha ball and pageant in the spring. Sina knew, the diva she was, that she could win. She had often heard Gwen and Deborah say the Alphas really liked to hear old church songs sung in the Miss Alpha Sweetheart pageant. Miss Sweetheart was an honorary Rose. She was considered part of the family even though she didn't learn the call or get to step. The women had really welcomed Sina and helped her adjust to her new surroundings. When she moved next door, into her single, Gwen, Deborah and Measha helped her out. Measha and Deborah took the bolster off the wall and pushed her dressers together. They were strong women. Although Sina grew up fighting Tommy, she knew she never wanted to get into a fight with them. They even hoisted her bolster onto the railing above her mirror and balanced it on empty soda cans. In Wisconsin it was soda and not pop; rap and not house; and a bubbler and not a drinking fountain. Sina really felt she had made some close friends. They watched out for her and were almost overprotective. She was sweet and they wanted her to stay that way. They didn't want any of those pompous men to turn her out. And she and Amy were still friendly. They were both Radio/TV/Film majors and sat together in Intro. Gwen was a business major so she quizzed Sina for her Honors Micro-Econ tests. Deborah was a junior nursing major. The three of them always joked about starting their own sorority, since there were no Black sororities at the university. "We'll call it Tau Gamma Delta." Thomasine said.

"The history would be easy to learn," Gwen said.

"Yeah, how old were the founders?" Deborah asked.

"Eighteen, Nineteen, Twenty," Gwen and Sina answered in unison.

"Where were they from?" Gwen questioned.

"Chicago, Milwaukee, St. Louis."

But since they each wanted to pledge Delta, they decided to put their revolutionary idea to rest.

"Hey girl, do you want to do breakfast in the morning?" Gwen asked.

"Yes, I'll meet you at the Commons at 7:30," Sina replied. "Oh, is that my call waiting signal?" she asked jokingly.

"I'll let you go, I've got some more studying to do."

"See you in the morning," Sina said as she moved the receiver from her ear and pressed the switch hook just below the earpiece on her trim line style telephone.

"Hello."

"Sina darling. This is Clayton. Can you do a favor for me? Yes or no?"

"It depends on what that favor is."

"I need a paper typed. It's due tomorrow at 8:00 and I just finished it."

"How many pages?"

"Five."

"Bring it on over."

"Meet me downstairs."

Sina just hated doing this but her father always told her that you receive blessings by helping others. She walked down the long hallway to the elevator and pressed the down button. When the doors opened she absorbed the mean stares from the other passengers. "Yeah, I wish I just lived on the third floor. I'd walk down the stairs all the time," said a white guy wearing a Bon Jovi T-shirt.

When Thomasine got to the lobby the long folding table was already set up and it was only 9:55. She knew that by the time Clayton arrived from his off campus apartment and found a parking space, it would be well after ten. Before she knew it, Clayton had arrived. He was a tall, pecan-colored guy with a box haircut and pretty teeth, Thomasine's weakness. But he was a fifth year senior and would be graduating in December so even if Conrad wasn't in the picture, there would be no sense in getting anything started. Thomasine handed the C.A. on duty her ID card and signed Clayton in. As they got off the elevator, once again, Sina had to listen to the snide comments about her riding to the third floor.

"I lived here my freshman year," Clayton said as they took that long journey down the hall to Sina's room. Room 352. All the way at the end of the hall and right next to the stairway and fire alarm. Although that alarm was right outside her room, Sina managed to nearly sleep through every fire drill. A discomforting thought! As for the elevator, Sina would have gladly walked down the stairs, but the stairwells were locked at night and while she could have gone down or up a floor or more, she couldn't get out of the stairwell on the first floor, unless she broke the glass on the fire pull station.

Clayton removed his Troop jacket and casually tossed it on Sina's large bed. Since she had the room to herself, she pushed her beds together, for when Conrad came up to see her. "Clayton, could you please set my typewriter up?" *It was the least he could do.*

"Sure." He slid the Brother typewriter out from under the desk and placed it on the top of her desk. Sina watched from a distance as she went to her other desk to get her typing paper and thesaurus. Crystal had insisted that her daughter and son take typing in high school so they would-n't be a burden to anyone in college. Clayton's mother should have given him the same advice.

Clayton had quite a physique. He went to the gym every day and it showed. He encouraged Sina to go too, after all, she had already paid for it in her student fees. Sina watched as he bent down in his tight blue jeans to lift the typewriter on her desk, with his biceps and triceps bulging on his bent arm. "Let's get started. I have an 8:00 tomorrow," Sina said.

"So do I."

"The Role of the Quakers in the Abolition Movement." Thomasine typed.

"Just how do you plan to pay me? My services aren't free and they don't come cheap." Tommy would be proud of her. He always told her not to let anyone walk over her.

"With this," Clayton said, removing a fifth of Beverage Store Vodka from his bag. "Make sure you hide it because I don't want you to get writ-ten up."

"What's this word?"

"Let's see, proselytizing."

"Well, what does it mean?" she asked.

"Converting from one religion to another." He opened the window. "A little stuffy in here, don't you think?"

"Yes, it does get hot in here. I don't even have my heat turned on, yet it's coming on full blast," Sina said as she continued typing. Clayton walked across the room, removed a towel from the rack just beside the door, and stuffed it under the door. He then sat down on Sina's bed and rummaged through his backpack until he found a bag of marijuana. "Got any matches? Cuz I know you girls keep them for your eyeliner." Sina reached up for her cosmetic bag and tossed Clayton a book of matches and con-tinued typing. "Time for you to take a break," He walked over to the win-dow and lit the joint.

"Here, Sina darling, take a hit. It'll help you sleep better."

Thomasine took the joint from Clayton and sucked lightly, careful not to get it wet like Conrad told her. "Have you ever done an airplane?"

"No."

"Squat down," Clayton said as he put the joint in his mouth back-wards. "Now put your hands on my shoulders." Clayton gently blew the smoke into Sina's mouth as they slowly rose to their feet. "Now if you want a real high, you should try some coke."

"You must be crazy. That stuff causes heart attacks," Sina said as she walked back toward her desk. "I guess, I'd better get back to your paper. It's almost 12."

Clayton sat down on Sina's bed and picked up her phone as if he were at home. Sina looked over her shoulder at him; he was wearing out his welcome. She was high and was not in the mood for any confrontation. *The sooner I finish typing this the sooner I can get rid of him.*

"Hey Shorty. Did anybody call me?" Clayton asked his roommate. "By the sounds of things, you're having a party and you didn't invite me. (Pause) Yeah, yeah. Look, hold on for a minute." Clayton said and then pressed the switch hook. "Hello," Clayton said to silence followed by a dial tone. "Whoever it was must have hung up." Clayton told Sina. "But like I was saying earlier man—wait a second." Clayton depressed the switch hook again. "Hello." They hung up again he told Sina.

"It's probably just somebody playing on the phone. The people at this university need to grow up. Somebody's always making a prank call to this room. One of the girls who lived here before me was named Barbara Doll. Someone is always calling me late at night and asking me if I know where Ken is. I guess since they heard a man's voice they must have hung up."

"Well look man," Clayton said to his roommate. "I'ma let you get back to your party."

"Ciao."

"I'm almost finished. I just have to type the cover page."

"You know what Sina darling?" Clayton said as he stood behind Sina and began to massage her shoulders and blow into her ear.

"What?"

"Everybody's been talking about you lately."

"Really, why?"

"Because you haven't slept with anybody up here this semester," he said as he kissed her neck. "And they're talking about me because I haven't slept with anybody black."

You Used to Hold Me

12

$\mathcal{A}$s Thomasine made her way through the mountains of Asheville, North Carolina, she thought of how she always wanted to drive up in the fall. From the time she first moved to North Carolina, everybody in Durham told her about the beautiful array of vibrant colors the changing of seasons had to offer. After she gassed up, walked Sparky and proceeded west on I-40, she wondered why Fall was her least favorite time of year. Since her first year of college she always became depressed as the days grew shorter. Her grades weren't as good and she wasn't as productive in the fall as she was in the spring. Friends had always told her that she had that seasonal disorder syndrome disease and needed to fill her home and office with bright lights. That hadn't quite worked. *When I return from the Land Downunder I'll have to make it a point to drive over to Asheville,* Sina thought that just maybe the burst of colorful leaves was what she needed to get her out of her annual autumn rut.

Thanksgiving, 1987 was a first reunion for the Three Musketeers. They had all longed for that time when they would all be together again. Rachel's pre-birthday blast was what was needed as the silver lining to the dark cloud cast by the untimely death of Mayor Harold Washington. Just five months earlier he was the speaker at the Piney Hill High graduation.

Sina was happy because Rachel was gracious enough to invite Conrad. She still didn't agree with Conrad's drug use, especially since Hank told her that Conrad now mixed cocaine with his marijuana. "Good thing Sina doesn't smoke that stuff," Rachel told her brother. "But since it's his birthday too, I can at least invite him." As Rachel called her friends to remind them of her party, she told each of them it would be an excellent way to work off some of those Thanksgiving Day pounds.

"Sina baby," Conrad said. "I've got my driver's license now and insurance and I'm taking you out. I'll be by at seven-thirty to get you. Oh yeah, and wear something sexy."

Sina was ecstatic. Now her mother could get off her back about her taking Conrad out all of the time. She dressed in her black miniskirt, and looked frantically for those thigh-high stockings Conrad had given her on her birthday. "Aha," she said as she put each one on. *Good thing I gained a couple of pounds. Now when I dance I won't look down and find these things around my ankles.* She grabbed her silk blazer and put it on over the gold camisole that fit her so nicely.

"Just where do you think you are you going young lady?" Crystal questioned her daughter.

"Rachel's mom is giving her an early birthday party at her house in Evanston. Oh yeah, and Conrad got his driver's license so he's driving and today is his birthday so I'm taking him to dinner."

"I suppose that's all right. Just don't act so gung-ho. And be careful honey." From the living room window, she saw Conrad open the door for Sina and then back slowly out of the driveway and head toward the end of the street.

"Happy Birthday baby," Sina said as she sneaked a quick kiss while they were stopped at a traffic light. "I want to take you to dinner. What are you hungry for?"

"You. Let's get a room."

"It's early. I thought we'd start out with dinner and then go to Rachel's party. I mean, if we're going to get our drink on we better do it early and we do need to eat first so that we don't get sick. Rachel's been talking about this party all semester. Besides, now that you're driving maybe you can come up one weekend. You know I've got my own room. I don't want to feel rushed or anything."

The two rocked in their seats to the thumping beat of house music as they headed to a quaint little restaurant in the South Loop. When Conrad parked the pre-owned Ford Escort he had managed to scrape up enough money to buy, he pushed in the cigarette lighter and performed his usual ritual.

At the dinner table they hardly exchanged words as they waited with bated breath for their meals to be served. "I hope you enjoyed your birthday dinner," Thomasine said as she and Conrad walked back to the car. Thomasine stood at the passenger's door waiting, but Conrad unlocked it from the inside. As Sina sat in the bucket seat, Conrad was leaned over from unlocking the door and planted a short, stiff kiss on Sina's lips.

"Sina, it's my birthday and I'm driving. And I want to stop at AKAs first. I mean, Rachel's party won't be jumping until at least 11. By then, your boring friend Hope is sure to be gone."

"I guess you're right. Knowing Rachel, there won't be any house music. And I want to hear some house. Up in Wisconsin it's that rap mess. Dana Dane with Fame and Eric B. I want to hear Farley or Armando. Let's go dancing. But how are we going to get in?"

"No problem. I have connections. Jimmy's cousin is a bouncer. I get in there all the time."

"Well all right now," Thomasine said as she pulled a mirror out of her purse and retouched her makeup.

"Will you do the honors?" Conrad asked as he handed Sina a primo.

"Thanks mom," Rachel said. "I am having so much fun." The basement was decorated with red and light green streamers. Rachel had really gotten into this Omicron thing. Good thing Naomi had to go home to Peoria for Thanksgiving. She hated to think of what would have happened with Hope and Jason there. Rachel's mom had even hired a DJ who had a strobe light and could really mix. The Omicrons were there in full force and two of her line sisters, Luminous and Lustrous had tired of walking the floor. Mrs. Thorne had a huge house with a basement big enough to throw one slammin' jammin party.

"I'm glad sweetie. I hope that we get to spend more time together. And I'm so glad to meet so many of your friends," Mrs. Thorne said as she surveyed the basement floor as streams of youth danced to Keith Sweat's *I Want Her*. "Now, I met your friend Hope, but where is this Sina I always hear so much about."

"I'm sure she's on her way. Today is her boyfriend's birthday and they went out to dinner first. She'll be here shortly," Rachel said as Jamal grabbed her hand and led her to the dance floor.

"You danced your ass off baby. Had that miniskirt swingin' here and there. Oh, and then baby, you took that jacket off and showed much skin. Woppin and Cabbage Patchin' your butt off," Conrad said as they walked back to the car.

"I had so much fun. And now we can head to Rachel's mom's house. You have the directions don't you?"

"Yeah, baby," Conrad turned to the Hot Mix 5 on WBMX and hit the outer drive. "Let's stop off at the lake. I got some coolers in the back." Sina reached in the back of the car and grabbed a bottle.

"What about me?" Conrad asked.

"You know you have no business drinking and driving."

Conrad took the next exit and drove along the blacktopped lot. There wasn't a soul around. He found a dark, secluded spot and parked the car.

He stopped the motor, but left the key in the ignition's utility position so that he and Sina could enjoy the house music. Other than the music, all they could hear was an occasional droning sound of a car passing on Lake Shore Drive. Conrad pulled his last cocaine-laced joint out of his pocket. "Let's smoke some herb before we go to Rachel's." He lit the joint with his right hand and held his cooler in the left. "You'll be really mellow, real chill."

December 10, 1987

Dear Rachel,

Please forgive me for missing your party. I really wanted to come and see you and Hope. I also wanted to meet your room-mate, Candace. She sounds really cool. I guess you're expecting an explanation. Conrad picked me up, we went to dinner and then we went dancing at AKAs. He had some coolers and we stopped at the lake and then I got sick. I sat on the stool with my head over the sink all night. I must have had food poisoning or something. We also had an argument. He's not speaking to me right now. All of this has me feeling so crazy. It's like I'm sick or something. Maybe I should have gone to the doctor when I had that food poisoning. I was even too sick to come to church that Sunday.

It's really weird. I can't pinpoint what it is. I have been to Student Health at least half a dozen times. Sometimes I think it might be a sinus infection, then I think it might be a bladder infection. I make sure I drink plenty of cranberry juice but nothing seems to help. Maybe it's anxiety about finals and Conrad being mad at me. I mean, I really hope we can work things out. I wanted him to come up here last weekend, but when I call him he just hangs up on me. And boy does that hurt. I love him so much. Well, since all of these crazy things are happening to me I have decided not to go to any wop parties for a while. Until my system gets back to normal. I'm sure things will be better at Christmas. I'm riding home with Measha on the 18th. She doesn't live that far from me. I guess I'll see you in choir rehearsal on Saturday. I promise to make it up to you.

Right now all I can say is study hard for those finals and I'll see you soon.

Am I still your sister?

Sina

P.S. I finally stopped having those dreams about fish. My cousin Kelsey said she was late so just maybe she's pregnant. I sure am glad it's not you or me.

"She owes me," Rachel said as she read Sina's letter while sitting at her desk at the BCC. It was now December in Chicago and the green lawns and once colorful trees were now a winter wonderland of snow lined lawns and trees decorated with icicles.

"Rachel, are you interested in serving on the Black History Month Activity Committee?" Calvin asked as he walked into the reception area of the Black Cultural Center.

"Yes. I'd love to. By the way, Charleen called."

"Oh yeah, she's an ex-girlfriend who constantly bothers me. If she calls again, make sure you put the call through to me. Maybe I can clear this up once and for all. As for the Black History Month Activity Committee, we are meeting over dinner at the Trattoria. Since that's off campus, I'd be happy to give you a lift."

"That sounds great," Rachel answered as she heard the phone ring. "Please excuse me.

"Good afternoon, Black Cultural Center, this is Rachel Curtis speaking."

"May I speak to Calvin?" said the lady on the phone.

"Just a moment," Rachel said, pressing the hold button. "I think it's Charleen."

"I'll take it up in my office."

"Hey baby," he said as he picked up the phone, knowing that Rachel had transferred the call.

"Ask me what my future husband is doing for dinner."

"What is your future husband doing?"

"I've got a romantic candlelight dinner for two planned at a restaurant overlooking the north harbor of the lake."

"Oh honey, that sounds great, but I've got a meeting with this committee at six. I tell you what, why don't you see if you can change the reservations to 9:00. You see, I haven't forgotten that I met you five years ago today."

"I'll see you at nine."

"How 'bout I pick you up at 8:30. And I want to see you wearing that red dress I got you for your birthday."

"I'll see you then."

As Rachel sat in the bucket seat of Calvin's sports car, she felt a little uncomfortable. He had the radio tuned to the Soft Touch and he came close to placing his hand on Rachel's thigh. She was so happy when they finally reached the Trattoria. She was actually surprised that he wanted to hold a committee meeting there. She had heard from Candace that the

Tratt, as it is affectionately called, was a very romantic spot, ideal for a first date. Peter and Candace went there for their first date. Rachel was even more surprised when she and Calvin sat at the table for nearly an hour before she realized no one else was coming.

"Rachel, you are a beautiful woman."

"Well, thank you Calvin, but I don't see what that has to do with planning events for Black History Month."

"It looks like no one else is coming for this meeting. I guess we should order."

"Calvin, would you mind if I passed on dinner. Suddenly I'm not very hungry." She was suddenly annoyed with this old man's advances. He was older than Tommy. "And I need to study. I have a final tomorrow morning."

"That's just fine. I understand. I have to run myself, you see, I've got another appointment tonight," Calvin said as he stood up to help Rachel with her coat.

There were now two shopping days, well actually one and a few hours left until Christmas. The Three Musketeers met up at church Sunday but didn't really have much time to spend together. With Hank and Rachel having to shop for Aunt Mary, Uncle Charlie and their mother and stepfather, and Tommy and Sina having to shop for their parents, the short days went by very quickly.

"I don't see why you're not mad with her," Hope said as she and Rachel parked in front of Sina's house on Wednesday afternoon. "I mean, she would clearly rather spend time with that Conrad than with you. And she has known you longer."

"You know I'm not the type to hold grudges. Anyway, I got a letter from her last week and she had a very good reason for not showing up. She was sick. Had food poisoning or something. Besides, if Jason didn't have practice for that bowl game, we both know where you'd be."

"You're better than me. If Sina had just come to your party and not taken Conrad to dinner for his birthday, she would have never gotten food poisoning." They climbed the snowy steps of the parsonage.

"Sina, why aren't you dressed?" Hope asked.

"What's wrong?" Rachel noticed Sina's swollen eyes.

"It's over between me and Conrad."

"Now aren't you glad you didn't sleep with him?" Hope asked.

"I know one thing, girlfriend," Rachel said. "I am not about to let you sit around and wallow in misery over this. Just who does he think he is? To argue with you on his birthday, nearly a month ago, not speak to you, hang up on you and then to have the nerve to break up with you on the day before Christmas eve. Oh, and by the way, that is one fly haircut you got, with the back tapered and all."

"Monique had to cut it. My hair had broken down to the new growth in the back. I guess it's just from stress. Maybe if Conrad saw my new haircut, he'd give me another chance. He always wanted me to cut my hair."

"Why did he break up with you?"

"He just said that since we have nothing in common, it's best that we go our separate ways."

"I think he's just trying to get out of getting you a present," Hope said, adding her two-cents. "I mean, did he even get you a birthday present? I never saw it."

"I want you to go and wash your face. Put on some clothes and we're going out. We can get something to eat and then go to the show. Now you go in the bathroom and clean yourself up. I've got a good mind to call that Conrad and give him a piece of my mind. Trying to mess up your holiday and all. I'm going to pick out something for you to wear and you are going to look good. After the show we can go to the mall and scout you up a new man. Because there's plenty fish in the sea."

Sina found herself hungrier than ever when they ordered. She hadn't eaten all day long. But after a few bites she was full. When they got in the car to head to the movie theater to see Eddie Murphy's new movie *Raw* Sina tore into her doggie bag, almost licking the styrofoam container. The girls had just gotten into the theater good when Sina had to run to the bathroom. She still smelled that peculiar smell when she went to the bathroom. This time, it nauseated her so that she lost the meal she just gorged.

Eddie Murphy was hilarious, but Thomasine felt sad. She looked around the theater and all she thought about was where she and Conrad sat when they saw different movies there. The last one they saw together was *Fatal Attraction*. That was the time when Rachel covered for her. It was raining cats and dogs and Conrad slipped and fell as he tried to run down the stairs to the car. He hurt his back, but when Thomasine rubbed her loving hands on his bare back, he said he suddenly felt better. Every now and then, Thomasine would laugh when she heard the rest of the audience laugh. But deep down inside she was crying. She was hurt by Conrad's rejection of her love, hurt by the memories of her surroundings, and hurt that her sisters thought coming to a silly movie would somehow make it all better. Before she knew it, she was crying outside too. "Now girl, aren't you having a good time," Rachel said, sitting a seat away from her. "You're laughing so hard, you're crying."

Trapped

13

The holiday had come and gone with lightning speed. Duncan University's football team won the Soup Bowl and boy did they beat the soup out of Lake Effect State University in Kalamazoo. Jason, Hope, Rachel and Jamal celebrated the New Year in style. Sina had gotten into an interim class, Old Testament, so she headed back to Wisconsin. She just knew that being a preacher's daughter would guarantee her an A in that intense course. It was now 1988. The last year had been so eventful and this year had more to offer. Hope returned for her second semester. Being able to find a haven from Chicago's arctic blast almost made Harrington and Savannah likable to Hope.

Community service was an important part of Harrington's mission. Each student had to complete 120 hours of community service as a requirement for graduation. Being on the fast track and nearly having sophomore standing, thanks to her Advanced Placement credits, Hope knew she had to start tallying the hours. The more hours she got, as she saw it, the sooner she'd be able to leave this Southern part of hell and be with Jason. Having a knack for numbers, Hope decided to offer her services as a tutor for the basic Statistics course to students at Savannah State. For many students across this world, Stats was like a grizzly bear standing on its hind legs. But not for Hope, who preferred crunching her numbers on pencil and paper over the calculator or a computer.

As Hope sat in the study lounge on her floor in Truth Hall, she thought that just maybe being at Harrington wasn't so bad. At least here she didn't have to worry about falling on the ice.

"Are you Hope?" asked the student who walked into the lounge.

"Yes, but I'm sort of busy right now. I'm waiting for Dana, a student I'm tutoring."

"I'm Dana," said the male student of average height with a muscular build.

"Oh, I'm sorry, it's just that I thought Dana was a girl."

"Well, I'm sorry to disappoint you, but I do really need your help. I failed my first quiz and I just seem to get these terms and formulas mixed up. You know median and mode and all. Let's not even talk about skewness and kurtosis."

Hope was surprised. She wondered what Jason would have to say about her tutoring a male student. He couldn't really say much, because his study partner was that Naomi from Peoria. But she didn't want to give Jason any reason to think that she may be interested in somebody else. "Have a seat." She motioned toward the chair beside her at the table. "I'm here to help you with all of that." Dana pulled his textbook and notebook out of his bag and began. "The mode is the most frequent score in the distribution. Say for instance that you're a teacher and you give your class an exam. The mode would be the score that the largest number of your students made."

"Oh, okay I see."

"And the median is the point on the scale below which half of the scores fall. Say there were seven students in your class and they all made different scores. Here you would write n=7," Hope said pointing to his paper. "Now let's say that the scores were 56, 63, 72, 78, 80, 87, and 95. Which score would be the median?"

"Hmm."

"Remember it is the point on the scale below which half of the scores fall."

"Okay, if there are seven numbers, the fourth number would be the median. So the answer is 78."

"Very good."

"You probably think that I'm just totally dumb or something. But I've always had a problem with numbers."

"A lot of people are intimidated by numbers, but you don't have to be. Let's do some other problems. On your stats test the questions aren't going to be this easy. You'll have median problems that deal with much larger numbers of sets so you will need to learn these formulas. You need to know median and mode before you can get to multiple regression."

Hope wrote several problems and Dana spent the next hour and a half figuring them out on pencil and paper like Hope suggested. She reassured him that if he could do it with pencil and paper, he'd have no problem doing it on the exam with the help of a calculator. As long as he put the right numbers in, that is.

"Thank you so much for your help, Hope." Dana said as he looked out the window at the dark sky. It was only 5:30 and the sun had already set. "Now I feel like I have a handle on mode and median."

"Next time we'll get a handle on distribution polygons, skewness and kurtosis."

She walked down the hall back to her room, delighted to see that her roommate Nia hadn't gone to dinner yet. Hope hated eating alone, although she often did on Fridays. That was the day the Alpha Roses went to the Alpha house at Savannah State and had their weekly family dinner.

"Who was that guy you were with?" Nia asked. "He really had a body on him."

"That was the student I was tutoring."

"I thought you told me you were tutoring some girl named Dana. I even thought she was one of my Alpha Rose sisters. You know, Dana Riley."

"Well, I guess Savannah State has two Dana Rileys. And one of them happens to be male. The tutoring session went well though. I feel he is really making progress already. And he seems so interested in learning."

"All you're thinking about is the tutoring?" Nia asked, very matter-of-factly.

"Yes, that's why he came over here."

"I wish it were me girl. Cuz I'd be thinking about how I could get with him. Does he have a girlfriend back at home, or is he seeing anyone here or what?"

"I don't know."

"I bet you didn't even ask him where he was from."

"I sure didn't."

"Well girl, you've got to find out. If you don't want him, you can hook him up with me."

"But what about your boyfriend back in Cleveland?"

"What about him? He ain't put no ring on my finger yet. I can do whatever I want. Besides," Nia said as she opened the door, "I'm too young to be tied down."

"Hello Sina," Rachel said from her dorm room one wintry Saturday afternoon. "You would not believe what happened."

"What's up? You don't sound too good."

"I got a letter from Jamal. A Dear John."

"Oh, Rachel, I'm so sorry to hear that."

"Hope thinks he's just trying to get out of getting me a Valentine's Day gift."

"Please. With all those flowers and stuff he bought you for no special occasion. After all we both know better than that. Well how do you feel?"

"It hurts, but I'll get over it. I guess since I just got the letter today, I haven't gotten over the initial shock."

"What did he say in the letter?"

"He said that he really cared for me and that I would always have a special place in his heart. That I was his first love and he was so happy that he got to share such an important part of his life with me. He then dropped the bomb. He said that he's met somebody else. A girl from New Orleans. And that he's breaking things off with me because he doesn't want to hurt me. Isn't that funny?"

"They always say that they are doing things not to hurt you. But I guess that they probably think that it hurts less now, than it will in the future. By the looks of things we can restart the Sina and Rachel Desperation Club, this time with new officers. Conrad will be the president and Jamal will be the CEO."

"I've been talking so much about me, what about you?"

"Well, I'm tired of walking across this wintry campus with icicles on my eyelashes for one."

"No girl."

"And I got a C in that Old Testament class. I guess being a preacher's daughter and a former Sunday School teacher didn't have much clout in the eyes of that professor. Can you believe we had to read a whole book of the Bible every night in that three-week class?"

"At least it was the only class you had."

"But still. I mean all of Exodus in a night. A lot of stuff happened in that book. But I guess it's over. I took my C with pride. And 70% of the class got a C or lower. Daddy said that would be difficult and suggested I should take New Testament. So much for that. I'm working at the radio station. I've got a Jazz show on Monday evenings from six 'til nine. I'll have to send you a tape of the show."

"Have you heard from Conrad?"

"No. I heard that he went to Michigan to go to some school there. I saw him one Sunday and he didn't even say anything about my haircut. I guess he doesn't care."

"How are you doing, I mean your health?"

"It seems to be getting better for the most part. I missed my last period. But I think that was due to stress. And then I've put on a few pounds. But don't they say that most freshmen gain fifteen."

"Or something like that. When are you coming home again? You know we have a lot of events planned for Black History Month."

"I don't think I'll get home until Spring Break. We have a bunch of stuff planned here. The Gospel Ensemble is having a concert and then there's a talent show at the end of the month. And I'm the mistress of ceremonies."

"When is Hope having her break?" Rachel asked.

"I think it's the week before ours. Maybe we can go down and visit."

"That would be nice. Look, I've got to run. Thank you for making me feel better."

February 13 had finally arrived and Rachel just had to go to the BCC Valentine's Ball. Being on the Black History Month Planning Committee, it wouldn't look good if she wasn't there. Since Paul, the Black Student Association treasurer had asked her to the dance she decided to go. Paul was kind of nerdy. The kind of guy who had been attracted to her in high school. But Sina always said that her cousin Kelsey swore by squares. They made the best boyfriends and were real good in bed, according to Kelsey. *Just maybe I'll get lucky tonight* Rachel heard a light rap on the door. She was really glad that Candace was over at Peter's for the weekend.

"Let me help you with your coat, it's really cold out there," Paul said, in anticipation of the evening.

When he and Rachel walked outside, she was happy that he had a car and was driving her to the dance. She hated to think of what it would be like to have to walk the long journey across the campus with the wind howling like a wolf staring at the moon. Her mother had bought her this red satin dress with a sweetheart neckline. She borrowed a rhinestone necklace from her mother and some earrings from Candace to complete her outfit. She almost wished Jamal was here to see her in the dress, but then she thought that just maybe he was celebrating with his new lady.

Paul had been the perfect gentleman, that was until a medley of Rachel's favorite songs was played. When Miki Howard's *Baby Be Mine* came on, Rachel looked around the dance floor for Paul. "I mean, he brought me to this dance, the least he can do is dance with me, on a slow song." Finally, two songs later, Rachel spotted him. During the first chorus of her absolute favorite song, LeVert's *My Forever Love*, she spotted Jason and Naomi dancing closer than her friend Hope would have liked. Just to the right of Jason stood Paul with his hands on the butt of this girl named Persephone . He was closer to Persephone than Rachel wanted him to be to her. And she was his date. She watched as Paul smoothly let his hand flow up Persephone's back and she noticed this pink string hanging down on her shoulder. Rachel couldn't figure where this pink string came from, since Persephone was wearing a black dress. Rachel got her coat and walked outside. It was a long walk from the Multicultural Village to her dorm. And since it was so cold out, the more she walked, the further the dorm seemed to be. She knew it would take her forever to walk back. She was thankful that the campus was well lit and security telephones were placed every 15 or so feet. Everything was still and Rachel could hear only the faint sounds of the music coming from the BCC. There was no one or nothing moving in sight. As she stepped into the street, Rachel stepped on a piece of black ice and down she went. Startled by the fall, the first thing she did was look up to see if anyone had seen her. She was so embarrassed, and she had heard her dress rip. All of a sudden, she saw the headlights of a car approaching her. She tried to scramble up so she wouldn't get hit when she fell again.

"Excuse me Miss. Are you okay?" she heard the familiar voice ask.

"Calvin," Rachel said, figuring out who the owner of the voice was.

"What is a pretty girl like you doing out here alone on St. Valentine's Day eve?"

"My evening didn't go as planned."

"Well it looks like we have something in common," Calvin said as he helped Rachel to her feet. "Let me give you a lift."

It was fate that brought Calvin and Rachel together that night. Calvin had plans with Charleen. They were going to stop by the ball on their way to another dance. He had filled his bed with rose petals for them to end the evening and then planned to serve Charleen breakfast in bed on Valentine's morning. He had called her earlier to let her know he was on his way to pick her up but didn't get an answer. He figured she probably just ran out to get some hose or something. He headed over her house anyway and was surprised when he saw a 1985 black Mercury Cougar outside that he knew belonged to her ex-boyfriend who he had believed, wanted Charleen back. When Calvin saw the car, he didn't even bother to stop in front at Charleen's. She was otherwise occupied and obviously thought very little of their plans. He figured he'd just go on to the BCC and pass through the dance on his way home by himself.

Calvin drove around the campus at a snail's pace. The freshly fallen snow mixed with oil made the streets slick as owl's shit. "So just how did we end up together?" Calvin asked Rachel as they listened to the Soft Touch on his car stereo.

"Would you believe I lost my date to a bad hair weave?"

"Not that Persephone?"

"You guessed it."

"That girl was dancing at a party one night. Really woppin and stuff.

And her hair stood still. That's how you know it ain't real," Calvin said, smiling at Rachel, as he slowed to a stop. "Oh, and then there's that pink string. You would think that being in college and all the girl would have sense enough to not to sew her weave in with pink thread."

"I was wondering where that pink string came from." When Rachel smiled back, her eyes met Calvin's and they leaned toward each other.

"Well, here we are at your dorm."

"I guess you're right. But it would be a shame to end such a nice evening like this."

"Yes, you're too dressed up and too beautiful to go back to some cold, stale dorm room by yourself. Let's go back to my place for some cocoa. We can talk about the Ethnic Food Festival coming up next month."

"Why not?"

Calvin had a nice condo in Lincolnwood, just north of Chicago. As they rode up in the elevator of his high rise building, Rachel felt all warm and fuzzy inside. When they entered Calvin's condo, overlooking Lake Michigan, Rachel went to the window and inhaled the view.

"Let me take your coat. That is one beautiful dress you have on."

"Oh no, I must have ripped it when I fell," Rachel said looking down at the split that now came up to her hip. "You have a beautiful view," she said, looking through the glass patio doors.

"I don't believe this. I'm fresh out of milk. And I don't do instant cocoa. It just doesn't taste right. How about some sparkling cider?"

"That will be fine."

"A beautiful view, and a beautiful woman," Calvin handed her a champagne flute, kissed Rachel on the back of her neck and put his arm around her waist. She took a sip of cider and turned to face him. They kissed each other slowly and gently. "Would you excuse me for a moment?" He returned in a split second and joined Rachel on the leather sofa.

She took one look at him and knew what she wanted to happen, what she needed to happen. She gazed into his eyes as he leaned forward and gave in to the unleashed desires of his mouth against hers. Suddenly he wasn't so old and unflattering to her anymore. She felt his hand on her back as he unzipped her dress and the pit of her began to burn with his touch. She stood up and the dress fluidly fell from her body.

"Oh Rachel," he said as he grabbed her hand, picked her up and carried her to the bedroom. "You have something to be proud of."

"What's that?"

"You are one sensuous black woman."

The soft romantic light of scented candles flickered throughout

Calvin's bedroom. They somehow managed to leave a trail of clothing along the voyage from the living room to the bedroom. When Calvin gently placed Rachel on the bed of rose petals, she glanced over and noticed a wine cooler with a bottle of champagne. He kissed her again on the mouth and then planted hot kisses all over her chest. He walked across the room, picked up the bottle and poured it on the hottest spots of Rachel's body. He then leaned down and drank from her body. He told her that he "didn't need champagne because her mere presence was intoxicating."

"Our final act this evening is the Three Brothers Blues Band. Let's give it up." Sina said, emceeing the Talent Show.

"I was drunk," the singer sang. "And I was wasted." Doo-doo, doo-doo-doo, the riff of the guitar played. "And my lady left me. To this day I ain't seen her no more. And I got the blues."

The college-aged crowd looked in astonishment. They couldn't understand why this band hadn't considered the audience. They had no interest in the blues or this act. But they were gracious and didn't boo the act off the stage. "You did a fabulous job girlfriend," Deborah and Measha told Sina after the show.

"You were really great. You're a natural at it," Gwen said. "I can already see you in television."

"Thank you so much," Sina said as she hugged her friends.

"Well, we're going to run," Gwen said. "I'll see you back in Zimmerman."

"Congratulations," Dr. Olatidoye told Sina as her friends walked off.

"Thank you. I'm glad it's finally over. I was a little nervous and all."

"Oh, I'm not talking about the talent show," Sina's Myth and Mystery professor said. "You see, in my country when a woman is glowing like you are, everyone is happy. You have a lot to be proud of and happy about. With that new life inside your belly. And don't worry that you aren't married. Everything will be all right."

Sina stood still. What was he talking about, new life inside her? Then it all clicked. She couldn't believe it. She was pregnant. And she had to be at least three months along. Now that she thought about it, she hadn't had her period since November. But she couldn't be. Not Thomasine Mintor. The cop's sister. The preacher's daughter. Not after all of her mother's warnings and cousin Kelsey's advice. Now it all made sense. She stopped having those dreams about fish when her period in December was supposed to come.

Spring had sprung in Savannah and the dogwoods were beginning to bloom. Hope was packing to head home tomorrow for break when she heard a light rap at her door. "Just a minute." She closed her suitcase and sauntered over to the door, and when she slowly opened it she was surprised to see Dana wearing a big grin. "Thank you so much," he said as he quickly grabbed Hope and hugged her. "I owe it all to you." He held out a stapled set of papers. "I made an A on my stats midterm. And it's all because of you."

"Now Dana," Hope said unlocking herself from his embrace. "You have really worked hard and you earned this A."

"I'm so happy. Just think, a few weeks ago I couldn't figure out the difference between the mode and the median. Now I'm doing hypothesis sampling. Hope, you make stats lovable. And to celebrate, would you let me take you to dinner. It's just to Nate's Chicken and Neckbones, nothing special, but the food is real good."

Hope loved Nate's almost as much as she loved *Krisp & Tasty* and she had never been known to turn down a meal. "I'd love to go to dinner," she said deciding to give the cafeteria a rest for the evening.

As they sat at a table with a red and white checkered tablecloth and listened to the blues music, Hope sipped her sweet tea. "You don't know how much this means to me," Dana said. "Or how much your help has meant. In school I always thought that I was dumb in math, just dumb. I hated everything from pie charts to decimals. One day the teacher asked me if I would rather have a half of pie or a third of a pie and I just told her I like cake."

"I like cake too," Hope said, chuckling.

"But you have made numbers lovable. I thought I'd never succeed. I started to change my major from Psych when I found out I had to take stats. But then you came along and changed all of that."

"Who had the country fried steak with collards and black-eyed peas?" the waitress asked.

"That would be me," Hope replied as the waitress set Hope's plate in front of her and Dana's in front of him. "And I would like to see the dessert menu."

"Let's say some blessing," Dana said as he grabbed Hope's hands.

"Lord, I thank you for this day, and everything in it. I thank you for leading me to Hope who has shown me the light where numbers are concerned. Now Lord, I ask that you make us thankful for the food we're about to receive. May it nourish and strengthen our bodies. I also ask that you bless the hands that prepared it. Amen."

Hope was silent as she ate her home style dinner. *Preparing me for my break at home*, she thought as she ate the tender country-fried steak. She found the peach cobbler to be good, but not nearly as good as her mother's.

"Thank you for dinner," she said as Dana walked her up to her room and kissed her lightly on her right cheek. She went in her room and finished packing. She was excited about going home and staying with Rachel at Duncan tomorrow night. Since her parents were away celebrating their anniversary, Hope decided she didn't want to be in the house by herself. She looked forward to seeing Rachel and hoped they would be able to go up and visit Sina while she was there. She hated that Sina couldn't come down to Savannah during her break. But she had a University Scholars retreat to attend and she was working at the radio station. "I better finish packing," Hope said to herself, for she knew she had to get on a plane right after her 8:00 class.

The Duncan campus was beginning to thaw. It was always said in Chicago that March comes in like a lion and goes out like a lamb. Rachel was thankful to Calvin for driving to O'Hare to pick up Hope who couldn't wait to see Rachel, but first wanted to eat. The food on those planes wouldn't satisfy a church mouse. As Rachel and Hope walked down the stairs of the Commons, Rachel caught a glimpse of Jason and Naomi and hoped Hope didn't see him. Hope planned to surprise Jason and was going to call him as soon as they got back from lunch. Calvin had given Rachel the afternoon off so she could spend some time with her friend. Jason was in class when Hope first arrived and since Hope thought she knew where he was every minute of the day, she thought she'd just wait until later to surprise him.

Rachel was wondering how Hope would react if she had seen Jason when Hope said, "Is that Naomi?"

"Yes, I think so."

"Well Jason has told me all about her. She's his study partner and lab partner this semester in Chemistry. I guess they're on their way to the library or to the lab."

Love Is Stronger than Pride

14

"When we seek the ultimate origins, three things happen," Dr. Olatidoye told his Myth and Mystery class one beautiful April afternoon. Spring had finally sprung in central Wisconsin. "First, truth seems to recede into prehistory," he said facing his class and moving his head with each word starting at the right, moving to the center, to the left and back to center. "Second, truth is sometimes stranger than fiction," this time his students stopped and paused as in deep thought. "Finally, myth might be the creative fictionalization of events." The fifty students silently, diligently took notes.

"Before you leave," he said, while walking zig zag through the students' desks, "I want you to ponder the following questions over the weekend. First, does myth bespeak man's insatiability for drama and/or play? Does it exaggerate the nature and significance of ordinary events in order to build an extraordinary basis inspiring enough in transmission to motivate human beings and future actions? Finally, could there be a more dramatic dimension implicit or inherent in many human situations that is not visible or obvious to us at a given time? And for added measure, are the words accident and coincidence synonymous? Give these questions deep thought as you meditate during the remainder of the week and this weekend between parties. On Monday we will discuss these questions as well as Edgar Cayce and retrocognition. We will also begin our discussion on OOBE— Out of Body Experiences."

Deep was what Sina and Gwen thought as they walked back to Zimmermann Hall. They had heard that Dr. Olatidoye was intense, but had no idea what they were getting themselves into when Deborah and Measha recommended this class. Deborah said he was special. Had a special gift from God. She wasn't surprised at all when she overheard him congratulate Thomasine on her pregnancy. Last year, when she went into his office to talk with him about a Religion and Personal Ethics class he was teaching in the fall, the first thing he said was, "You don't need a man in your life right now," which shocked Deborah because her boyfriend had called it quits the previous night.

"Sina what are you doing this evening?"

"I have that scholarship banquet tonight. I get to meet my sponsors."

"I'll give Deborah a call, maybe you can give me your ID so Measha can come to dinner. You know it's steak night and this time they also have shrimp."

"Yeah, I'll do that," Sina said. "No one will pay attention. They think we all look the same anyway."

Sina had time to relax a little before she headed to the Student Union for the banquet. She flicked through the channels on her 13-inch color television and settled on catching the end of "Oprah." She listened to the discussion on rape survivors and ironed the new dress Measha had taken her to the mall to buy. She couldn't believe she had to buy the dress two sizes above her normal size six. But she had no problem filling it out about the bust and waist. She put her robe on and went to the bathroom to brush her teeth.

"Hi Sine," Amy washed her hands.

"How are you doing?"

"Fine. It's too bad that we don't have any classes together this semester."

"Yeah."

"Watch those donuts in the commons. I can see that you've gained a few pounds," Amy said as she walked toward the door.

Sina wondered who else had noticed her weight gain. She was happy she had only another six weeks before going home for the summer. But then she didn't know if she would be better off up there or in Chicago. Maybe she could go to Kelsey's. Kelsey was expecting and her baby was due in August. "Yeah," Sina thought. "I can tell Mom and Dad I'm going there to help Kelsey out with her new baby." Thomasine put on a loose-fitting dress and looked for her invitation. "The Odenwelders," she said. "That should be easy to remember."

The days were getting longer and in a week or so, they would turn their clocks ahead an hour. It was such a nice afternoon, Sina decided not to cut through the Commons as she usually did. She arrived at the Wau-nakee Room in the Union, looked around at the name cards and heard a man call her from across the room. She walked across the room and was pleased to meet Mr. and Mrs. Odenwelder.

"So Thomasine, what is your major?" Mr. Odenwelder, a balding white man with a pot belly and a plaid sports jacket, asked after Sina took her seat.

"I'm a Radio/TV/Film major. I do a jazz shift on Monday nights at the station."

"Isn't that nice?" Mrs. Odenwelder said. "I bet you want to be just like Oprah."

"Oh and you're a little bit on the plump side, like Oprah. Isn't that special?"

"Now being like Oprah wouldn't be bad at all. But I just want to be Thomasine."

That silenced the Odenwelders. "So what are your plans for the summer, hon?" Mrs. Odenwelder asked.

"I'm signed up for an interim. I have English II. I CLEPed out of English I. And I'm also taking Radio Workshop. That's just for starters."

"That's wonderful Thomasine," Mr. Odenwelder said assuringly.

It was mid-April and already eighty degrees in Savannah. Thursday afternoon Nia and Hope were walking back to Truth Hall from Nate's Chicken and Neckbones when they stopped at a corner. Across the street in the middle of the block was a large beige Victorian house with a huge magnolia tree in the front yard and a wrought iron fence. The house was two stories tall with bay windows on each floor. In the bay window on the first floor a sign read "Sistuh Miracle, Reader & Advisor, Astrologist. First Reading Free."

"Let's go have our palms read," Nia suggested fixing her eyes upon the sign.

"I don't know," Hope responded.

"Come on. It'll be fun." They walked up the steps and pressed the doorbell.

"Come on in sistuh girlfriends," Sistuh Miracle said. "Do ya want yo' palm read, future tole or star chart?"

"Well it's our first time here," Nia explained. "Maybe we can have our palms read."

"Bump yo' rump down on dis here bench. Now honey, what's yo' name?" Sistuh Miracle asked.

"Nia."

"As I look at yo' palm, I'm seeing a strong sense of purpose. Ya have a double head line. Ya independent, a free-will. Ya don't let nobody tell ya what to do and I can tell—"

"Ma' Shafeek took my doll," Sistuh Miracle's young daughter said.

"If ya don't get yo' hind quarters back in de kitchen, ya bedder. Now where be I at?"

"You were telling me about my independent free-will."

"Oh, yeah, And ya have a disjointed heart line. Yau'll never let no mon walk all over yo' heart," Sistuh Miracle said looking at Nia's facial expression.

"And on to ya, girlfriend," Sistuh Miracle said as Hope uneasily placed her palm on the table. "Very interesting." She looked at Hope's left palm.

"I feel a lot of—"

"Ma', Sharelle hit me."

"Now hush yo' mouth," Sistuh Miracle told her son Shafeek. "Ya'll know if ya keep runnin' back and fo'th in here you upset de spirits. I need quiet."

"Now let's see," Sistuh Miracle said once again placing her hand on Hope's. "Your name is T—."

"Ma, I'm, hungry," Sharelle ran into the parlor. "And I'm tired of beans and rice."

"I tell ya what, go and get dose food stamps off my dresser and ya go down to de corner store, and get me some neckbones. And I don't want ya spendin' de change on no candy eider."

"Now where was I? Focus, concentrate," she said looking at the ID bracelet on Hope's wrist.

"You were just starting, my name."

"Ya have an interesting name, I can tell it starts with a H."

"Hope."

"I'm looking at yo' love line and I see a phyne young broda' in yo' life." Love line? A quick perusal of any basic palmistry book would reveal that there is no such thing as a love line. The three major lines are life, head and heart.

"Tell me more."

"And I believe him name is Jason," she said peeking at the bracelet

"Yes," Hope said. "Are we going to get married?"

"Oh de energy is gedding weak, de spirits are leaving, ohn de free reading is finished."

"But you were so close to telling me my future."

"Let's see," Sistuh Miracle said. "It's faded. Ya must come back. And if ya really wants to know what de future holds for ya I need your birt'dates, birt'times, birt'places, and birt'order. And den I can do yo' star chart," Sistuh Miracle said smiling as she saw dollar signs. "But de star chart takes up a lot of time, I have to find yo' sun, moon, and planets. So it'll cost ya."

"I'll definitely be back."

Friday had finally come and Thomasine found herself sitting in the middle of her bed reviewing the notes from her Myth and Mystery class.

As she sat, cross-legged in the middle of her double bed with her eyes closed, she heard a loud knock at her door. "It's open," Sina said, figuring it was Gwen as they were study partners for Myth and Mystery.

It was Rachel. "I thought I'd surprise you this weekend. We're making some Opals here this weekend," walking over to the bed to hug Sina.

"Well, I sure am surprised to see you."

When they hugged Rachel felt that Thomasine seemed wider than she remembered; she was glowing, yet she didn't seem really happy. "Sina, are you pregnant? Why didn't you tell me?" Rachel looked at Sina's face. "This explains all those dreams and the health problems and everything. How far along are you and what are you going to do?" Rachel asked, as if she were playing 20 questions. "Have you been eating right? Taking prenatal vitamins? Is it a boy or a girl? How did Conrad react? Oh, I bet he doesn't even know since he is acting like a stubborn butthole. Did you even tell him? He needs to know."

Rachel looked as Thomasine gave her the surrogate mother spiel. "Now Sina. I'm your sister. We've shared too much. You know I'll be there for you," she said looking above Sina's desk at the card she had given her just before Sina left for school.

"Oh Rachel," Sina cried. "You can't tell anyone. Promise me it's our secret."

"I promise."

"I'm almost five months along; my last period was in the middle of November."

"How do you plan to support a baby?"

"Adoption." Sina said, still crying.

"Are you sure? Have you discussed this with your parents? What do they think?"

"Rachel, it's the only choice. This just may be a blessing in disguise for some childless couple. From Kelsey's experience, I know just how depressing infertility can be. As for my parents, they don't know yet, and I want to tell them in my own way."

"Sina, you need to tell them now," Rachel said, handing Sina the telephone.

"No," Sina said crying. "I can't do it over the phone."

"Have you thought this out? I mean how do you plan to keep it a secret if you have to go to mid-August?"

"I'll figure something out. I just don't want my business all over the church. You know how scandalous church folk can be."

"I know. And if you're going to have a happy, healthy baby, you have to get the proper nourishment. Let's go to dinner, and not to the Commons, my treat."

The weekend went by with lightning speed. Sina gave Rachel the key to her room so that she wouldn't have to go downstairs and sign her in. Rachel stumbled in late Friday night from a session and Saturday night from the probate show. The time she didn't spend with the Opals she spent comforting and consoling her friend.

On the two and a half hour drive back to Duncan, Rachel sat in the bucket seat of Calvin's red IROC. Some Omicron's had to be made that weekend. Since Rachel had been packed in the car on her way up with her Opal sisters and told them she wanted to spend a little more time with Sina, no one questioned when Calvin volunteered to drive her back. Rachel was pleased. Once the campus station where Sina did her weekly jazz show faded out, Calvin searched the dial for another station. Finding none, he turned to Rachel. "Things have changed since I graduated in 1977. This place has really grown, but then I guess they haven't really diversified. We won't get another black radio station until we get near Milwaukee."

Rachel didn't say a word. She stared out the window deep in thought. "Did you catch up with your friend? I'm sorry I didn't get to meet her. Is everything all right, because you're not the usual talkative Rachel I've come to know and love."

"Everything's all right, we hung out some this weekend. Mostly at restaurants."

"Did she come to the party last night?"

"No, she wasn't quite up to it."

"Wait a minute. I saw you going into a restaurant on Main Street with some pregnant woman. She was kind of cute. Was that your friend, Sina."

Rachel was still silent.

"It had to be because you don't know anybody else up here. My goodness, that's what took your voice away, isn't it? Well, I can understand if you don't want to talk about it. But let me tell you one thing. You don't have to worry about it happening to you. I'll make sure of that."

May brought swarms of lake flies to central Wisconsin and she made her way through them for the three weeks she took English II and worked at the radio station. Allison, the station manager for the next year, even offered her the position of Jazz Coordinator for the fall. By Friday, June 3, Sina's breasts and belly had blossomed to a full bloom. Mcasha offered to take her home, but there wasn't enough room in her car for the two of them and all of their belongings.

Thomasine sat on the bare bed trying to find the words to tell her parents she was six and a half months pregnant. They were not due for an hour so she unplugged the TV when she heard a knock at the door.

"Hello Princess."

"Thomasine, let's get a move on and try to get on the road as soon as possible," her mother said as she walked in the room. "Now come over here and give me a hug. I'm so happy you're going to be home all summer. I've really missed you. And talking on the phone just doesn't do the trick," Crystal opened her arms to hug her daughter. She hadn't seen Sina since the semester break at the end of January.

"Thomasine Mintor," Crystal said as she looked in amazement at Thomasine's stomach.

"I'm just a little pregnant, that's all," Sina said very matter-of-factly, unable to soften the shock.

"Oh Lord have mercy," Crystal said sitting down on Sina's bed. "Thomasine, I am hurt. I thought we could always talk about anything. I always told you when you felt you were ready for sex to come to me and we would talk. Now I come here and find you pregnant! You must be about six months."

"Six and a half."

"I just don't believe this. Why didn't you tell us? You didn't think we'd love you any less, did you? "

Sina just continued crying.

"Now, Princess," Rev. Mintor said walking over to his wife and daughter. "You have nothing to be ashamed of. This is a gift from God. And everything will work out all right. Just stop that crying. When we get back home, we'll just invite Mrs. Thompson and Conrad over. I'll marry the two of you and everything will be just fine. We love you and we're here for you. We want the best for our first grandchild."

"Daddy, it isn't Conrad's."

"Well, we'll just call whoever is responsible for this up and the two of you can get married."

"He doesn't want to have anything to do with this," Thomasine said as tears gently rolled from her face. "I've decided on adoption."

"You need to give this more thought," her father said.

"It's my life, and I've made my decision."

All the way back to Chicago there was complete silence in Rev. Mintor's Town Car. Crystal took her daughter to the Obstetrics Clinic at the hospital where she worked and was delighted that her daughter had taken good care of herself and the baby was healthy. Tommy was enraged when he found out and was ready to put a hurtin' on whoever had knocked up his baby sister. But his father convinced him to stay out of it, hoping that Sina would change her mind and decide to keep the child. Kelsey called her often. They had a lot to talk about since she was pregnant too. Rev. Mintor waited on his daughter hand and foot, letting her drive the Town Car to summer school, running to the store to buy whatever she wanted when she had cravings, and even cooking her breakfast and serving it to her in bed, then quizzing her for her biology class.

One afternoon Hope called to come over and chat.

"Today really isn't good," Sina said. "I'm a little under the weather."

"Well, I'm concerned about Rachel. I think she's sleeping with that Calvin guy. She's spending the night at his place sometimes and Aunt Mary thinks she's with her mother."

"Now Hope that is Rachel's business and she can do whatever she wants."

"But what if she gets pregnant?"

"If she gets pregnant, she gets pregnant. But I'm sure that she and Calvin have thought about that and are taking precautions." "Look, I've got to go," she told her friend.

The biggest problem that Rev. Mintor had with Sina's pregnancy was her unwillingness to go to church. He felt that her spirit needed to be fed. "I don't feel like being bothered with those hypoChristians," Sina said.

Crystal understood her daughter's concerns. On the third Sunday in July, she and Mrs. Thompson were walking down the center aisle after their missionary unit meeting when they came upon Phyllis Jones and Martha Mitchell.

"Yeah, my son's friend is taking a biology course over at CSU and he said there's this Mintor girl in his class. And you know Mintor ain't a common name. The girl look like she gon' pop that baby out anytime."

"Um um um," Phyllis said shaking her head. "That's why she ain't up here this morning trying to out sing my Hope. She thinks she's so good. Now that preacher ought to be ashamed of himself, up there trying to tell us how to live our lives as Christians and he ain't even got his own household in order."

"But wait until you hear this," Martha said. "She's goin' around tellin' folk up there in Wisconsin she's having the baby for some cousin of hers in Virginia. They say the father is a senior who's graduated and didn't even give Sina his phone number. He don't even know about the baby."

"She should be ashamed of herself," Phyllis said, shaking her head from right to left. "She's a bad influence on my Hope. She should try to be more like her."

"My daughter is fine just the way she is," Crystal said interrupting, "I would never want her to be more like your narrow-minded, self-righteous, afraid-to-live daughter."

"Well all I know is that my Hope would never bring shame on her family like your daughter has," Phyllis retorted. "She and Jason have been together for almost five years now. It just goes to show you that a girl ain't got to throw her legs open just to keep no man. Oh, and I heard the baby's daddy just sprouted wings like an eagle and flew as far away as he could. Your daughter spread her legs, and all it got her was pregnant and alone."

"My daughter will never be alone. And as for your daughter, she ain't gonna keep that Jason for long being a prude. Good thing she's smart. At least that will get her somewhere in life, because in the looks department she's lacking. And with all of that weight, she might as well be the one who's pregnant. She probably weighs more than Thomasine, and she's the one who is entitled to be young and big. Don't make no sense for anybody to be that young and that big. Oh, and the way you and your husband just spoiled that girl, she'll be lucky if anyone ever marries her, the bovine that she is."

"Sister Mintor, may the blood of Jesus be upon you," Martha said.

"You and Phyllis' bloods gon' be upon me if I ever hear you talking about my daughter again." Crystal said walking away.

Mrs. Thompson, shocked by it all, literally ran to her house around the corner from Front Street A.C.C. to talk to her son. "Well it's like this, Ma," Conrad said to his mother. "I used to call her late at night up at school in the fall, and some dude would answer the phone, I would call back, he'd answer it again. You know, I wanted to make sure I dialed the right number," Conrad added. "And I know there's only one reason some dude could be up in her single room after midnight. That's why I stopped talking to her and broke up with her at Christmas."

On Saturday, August 13, 1988, Thomasine gave birth to a 6 lb, 10 oz baby girl. She signed the papers releasing the baby to a black couple in their thirties. Thomasine wanted to get her life back in order. Her cousin Kelsey wasn't as fortunate. She delivered her baby a few days after Sina, but it died within an hour of birth. In a few weeks Sina would be going back to school ʼnd working at the radio station.

Give Me a Chance

15

*H*ope said her goodbyes to Rachel and Sina and actually apologized to Thomasine for her mother. She hated to say goodbye to Jason. With her working and him in football camp they didn't get to spend as much time together as she would have liked. She had saved her summer money and gotten most of the information she needed for Sistuh Miracle. "What time of day were you born Jason?" she asked him at the airport before she left.

"Why do you need to know that?"

"It's just that I need, I mean, want to know everything about you."

"I was born at 6 or 7 something in the evening," he responded.

"But I want to know the exact time," Hope insisted.

"I'll have to get back to you on that one." He hugged and kissed her when he heard the boarding call. As her flight took off, she thought of all the great things she planned to do this school year. She was excited about having her own room; Nia decided to room with one of her Alpha Rose sisters. Hope's mother had almost convinced her to pledge AKA but since there probably wouldn't be a line until the spring, she still had time to decide, but first, she had to see Sistuh Miracle.

She got her baggage from the claims area and nearly knocked down a fine young man. "Hope?"

"Hello Dana. How was your summer?"

"Great, thanks to you. I got an A in my stats class, so we have to celebrate."

"Sounds good," Hope said remembering the dinner at Nate's Chicken and Neckbones.

"Oh, by the way, do you have a ride back to campus? I was supposed to pick up my roommate but it looks like his flight from D.C. has been canceled due to fog."

As they drove through town, Hope was pleased to know that Sistuh Miracle was still in business. *Now I can really find out what the future holds for me,* she thought as she passed the Victorian structure. "I'm in Tubman Hall this year," Hope said once they reached the Harrington Campus. "That's just over to the right."

Dana helped Hope carry her bags up to her new room. She was glad that she didn't have to take a cab all the way in from the airport. She could use that money for her palm reading later. "I'll call you later about our celebration," Dana said. "Right now, I've got to figure out when and if my roommate is going to get back here."

The decor at Sam & Andy's in Knoxville reminded Thomasine of Ratch & Benzies. She looked forward to going back to that small town in Wisconsin for her second year of college and was anxious about the job at the radio station and getting back to the Gospel Ensemble. She was also looking forward to sharing a room with Gwen. They had written each other letters over the summer to coordinate who would bring what. Once Thomasine moved into her room her parents took her to lunch at a deli called Ratch & Benzies. As the Mintors sat in the booth to eat their lunch two black men in their early twenties walked in. Thomasine could tell by their dress that they weren't from the Midwest. Shorts and tank tops. She didn't think it ever got hot enough in central Wisconsin for such attire. The two young men walked by the booth, and cordially spoke. Sina figured they were probably just passing through, since they looked just a little bit too old to be starting school there and neither had attended the previous year.

"The Alpha's got it going on this year," Gwen said when she returned from the monthly breakfast at the Multicultural Education Center.

"Oh do they?"

"Yeah. They got this brother from Hampton named Scott. And he's a graduate student from Richmond, Virginia," Gwen said excitedly. "So you know we're gonna have it going on. We will be the flyest chapter in the state."

"I guess this means there will be a ball this year."

"Definitely. And then there are some junior tranfers interested, as well as some incoming freshmen. Our family is growing. We will probably screen for Alpha Rose this semester. Hint, hint."

"When is the first wop party?" Thomasine asked.

Hope finally gathered up the courage and funds to go back to Sistuh Miracle's and get a reading. She had heard rumors about Jason and his study partner, Naomi, but she didn't believe them because Jason would never cheat on her. People probably started rumors because they were jealous of what she and Jason had. She knew she could put all of this to rest with Sistuh Miracle's help.

"Come on in, sistuh girlfriend," Sistuh Miracle said. "And bump yo' rump in dis here chair. I remember ya. Yo' name is Hope."

"Yes," Hope said smiling.

"What can I do ya for today?"

"I would like to have my chart done and my boyfriend, Jason's."

"Now ya' know it'll cost ya'. Dat takes a lot of energy and communing wit da spirits. Ahn I need to know very specific information. Birtdates, birtplaces, birttimes. Down to da minute. If I don't have de exact numbers, da chart'll be off."

"Well, I have everything but Jason's time of birth."

"Can't do it. I mean it wouldn't be fair for ya to pay me for all dis work, an' da chart be off."

"I guess you're right. I'll have to get his time of birth. But for right now could you read my palm?"

"Okay, honey, let's see," Sistuh Miracle said, taking hold of Hope's palm. "I see dat phyne broda again. Oh, he's definitely in yo future. Wit a love line like yo's yau'll be real happy wit dis broda. Yau'll gone have some babies in yo' future. I can see it clear as day."

Rachel returned to Duncan destined to have some fun this year. Candace had moved off campus to try to establish residency and Rachel was now rooming with one of her Opal sisters. She had been creeping with Calvin since February and no one knew. He was secretive, probably because he was on the faculty. Hope thought he was bad news, but Sina was cool with it.

One Monday morning on her way from her Music Therapy class Rachel was walking behind Persephone and a new freshman, LaTonya. "Things are pretty cool here. You just have to watch out for that Calvin Hardy in the BCC"

"You mean the director?" LaTonya asked.

"No, he's the Assistant Director."

"What's the deal with him?"

"It's like this. He used to date, let's say, a friend of mine. Now he pursued her, they dated and she fell in love with him. Then all of a sudden he announced that he was engaged."

"No."

"Just watch out."

Rachel couldn't believe her ears. Not Calvin, who took her to all the finest restaurants. Not the one who made her feel like a woman. And certainly not the Calvin who made love to her as she had never imagined in her wildest dreams, atop a bed of rose petals. It couldn't be. He had told her everything about his past, about how he grew up on the north side of Milwaukee, graduated from the same school Sina attended in 1977, worked for a community group for five years before he decided to go back to school at Duncan and get a Master's in Higher Education. He had even told her about his ex-girlfriend Charleen and how she tipped out on him and then wanted him back so bad. "I'll just have to hear it from the horse's mouth," Rachel said as she marched across Duncan's campus on that gloomy Monday morning.

She walked up the stairs of the BCC to Calvin's office and ignored the hellos from Mrs. Washington and the other students. Turning the door knob with quick and strong force, Rachel heard Calvin's voice over the faint sounds of Lisa Lisa's *All Cried Out* from his boom box. He was turned around in his high-back leather executive style chair with his back to the door. "Charleen, you know I've missed you sweetheart. I'm so sorry I let a misunderstanding come in between us for so long. It's just that when I saw James' car that night and then you didn't answer the phone I just thought—I'm just so glad to have you back—" the line went dead.

"Charleen, Charleen," he said as he turned around in his chair to face a very irate Rachel.

"If you think I'm gonna sit back and let you walk all over me, you are wrong. Because I will never, do you hear me? Never be second choice. And to think, I actually believed all of the silly little promises you made me."

"Now calm down Rachel."

"Don't tell me what to do! I'll do whatever I damn well please. Oh Charleen is just my ex-girlfriend who keeps bothering me. Since when did ex-girlfriend and fiancee' become synonymous?"

"Let me explain."

"Explain my ass! Oh, Rachel we can't go to this function together tonight, it just won't look right if we're together on the campus. I've got a date to cover, but she doesn't mean anything to me. Just meet me behind the Bell Tower and we'll make up for lost time. Oh, and to think I thought I actually meant something to you. All those nights I gave you all of me. I really thought you cared. You even cooked me breakfast. But I guess that was the least you could do."

"Rachel, lower your voice."

"Calvin Hardy. You are not a man!" Rachel said staring him down in his eyes. "Men have backbone and you don't. You're nothin' but a liar, a cheat and a weak-minded fool. And you're out of my life. Do you understand? Out of my life!" Rachel said as she waved her right hand in sync with the words while the left was glued to her hip.

"Now Rachel, when you calm down, we can talk about this like two logical adults."

"The discussion is over." She walked out and slammed the door.

She walked across the campus in tears. Everybody was staring. Did the whole campus know she had let some ole ass two bit hustler play her like a church organ—with both hands and feet? No one said anything, but by the way she was feeling, the look on her face probably said to them, "You better not." Hope had been right about Calvin. When she got to her dorm room, she looked in the mirror just above her dresser. She couldn't believe she let herself be used like that. Working in the BCC, she felt she should have known that Charleen was more than just an ex-girlfriend. Sina would know what to do.

"Hello Sina."

"Just a minute," Gwen said. "Sina, telephone. "

"Hello."

"I'm so glad you're in," Rachel said.

"To what do I owe a call from you in the middle of the day on a Monday?"

"I need to talk to you."

"What's the matter?"

"You know Calvin, the one I thought was my man?"

"Oh Rachel, he didn't break up with you did he?"

"I found out, from somebody else, that he is engaged."

"No."

"Sina. I did things with him, for him," Rachel said crying.

"I know you're hurting right now. But he's not worth it," Sina said. "Oh, could you hold on just a minute," Sina said setting the phone down on her bed. "Hold up Gwen, I need you to get me something from the store. Here's five dollars, get me a fifth of vodka."

"You better watch it girl. You don't want to become a lush," Gwen said as she walked out of the door.

"Rachel, you still there?"

"Yes."

"Just like you told me, actually not that long ago. There's other fish in the sea. Calvin Hardy didn't deserve you. Girl, you need a man who deserves you. You're too good for him."

"I guess you're right."

"And I'm coming down this weekend for that Players' Ball so we can go scouting. Slims will definitely be in the house. Look, I gotta run. Gotta practice my karate before I go to the station."

"Karate?"

"Yeah, you should consider taking it up."

It was a beautiful Wednesday evening in early fall in Savannah. Most of the humidity from the summer had moved out and the mild temperatures Hope loved had returned. She and Dana walked down Vidalia Avenue from *Cinema I & II*, past *Nate's Chicken, Neckbones and now Catfish*, past outdoor cafes with umbrellaed tables, and fancy antique shops. Savannah had a charm of its own.

"I'm so glad we were finally able to get together," Dana said as they approached the Harrington Campus. "I've been so busy in the psych lab doing experiments and stuff that I was lucky to find a free minute."

"You've really come a long way, and I was happy to be a part of it," Hope said. "Dinner was great."

"Yeah, good thing Nate's finally added catfish to the menu. For the last two years I've been trying to get them to do it. I even got a petition circulated around Savannah State and Harrington."

"Now if they only had spaghetti and cole slaw to go with that fish, I'd be in there every Friday," Hope said smiling.

"I could get another petition going, you know," Dana said chuckling as they walked toward Truth Hall.

"Let's just let them get used to the catfish first." She looked at the full moon. "And the movie was really funny."

"I'm sorry there wasn't more of a variety."

"No, I was planning to see *Who Framed Roger Rabbit.*"

"Well good, I'm glad we got to see it together."

"Here we are," Hope said. "Tubman Hall."

"Well Miss Hope. Thank you for all of your help and thank you for an enjoyable evening." He leaned down, embraced Hope and gave her a quick peck on the lips. "I'd like to spend some more time with you. Maybe we can do brunch at Nate's Sunday and then go to church."

Hope was caught completely off guard. He had a muscular build like Jason's and when he kissed her, she thought of Jason. When he asked her out again, she even heard Jason's voice. "Sure." When she opened her eyes and realized who she was with, she looked down at her watch. "Look, I must be going, I have a 9:00 in the morning."

Sina and Rachel, decked out in their scouting gowns, walked into Hunam's upper level banquet room. Round dinner tables surrounded most of the room with the exception of the bar and minuscule dance floor. It looked like Christmas in October. Red and green balloons and streamers covered most of the walls from the contestants' box to the wooden dance floor. Rachel was delighted Sina needed to do some last minute shopping before the ball, it saved her from having to clean up the banquet room earlier that afternoon. When the buffet was set up, everyone was surprised that they were expected to eat from paper plates and plastic forks despite all of the money they had paid for their tickets and their attire. But their protests were heard, and china and flatware were put out. Sina piled her plate with sweet and sour chicken and shrimp egg foo young. Rachel loved the strange flavored chicken, but Sina thought the drumsticks looked too small to come off any chicken she had ever seen. The waitress came to refill their drinks. "That will be 25¢ please," she said. As they went into their small beaded evening bags for the change one of Rachel's Opal sisters, Luminous, jumped up from the table as the waitress slammed her hand down on the table faster than the speed of light.

"Dag, you got all six legs," Luminous said.

"We just sprayed Thursday," the waitress said. Rachel and Sina lost their appetites.

"Good evening ladies and gentleman," said the announcer, "And welcome to the 1988 Omicron Xi Mu Players' Ball." Shouts of Ooohhmmm and Oh-Xi from the Omicron men and Opal women filled the air.

"He sure is a slim," Sina said of Sam as he crowned the 1988 Omicron Xi Mu Player of the Year. "Oh, and he has the prettiest teeth."

"I can hook ya'll up you know. He's my big brother, and he's available. He just dumped that Persephone and I know he'll be glad to meet a woman who wears her real hair and nails. Your hair may be short, but you sho do got that butter whipped."

"It looks like he's coming over here anyway," Thomasine said.

"Hello Rachel, my sweet little sister," Sam said giving Rachel an innocent kiss on the cheek. "And who is this lovely young lady?"

"This is one of my best friends, Thomasine Mintor."

"It's a pleasure to meet you Thomasine." He kissed the back of her hand.

"My good friends call me Sina. And you are?"

"Samuel Connor, but my good friends call me Sam," he said sitting across from her.

"Well, I'm going to leave you two here, to get to know each other," Rachel headed for the dance floor.

Sina found Sam charming despite his red bow tie and green cummerbund. "You look radiant in your red dress tonight. Are you an Opal?"

"No, but I do love red," Thomasine said smiling. "And you look good in your tux."

"Tell me about yourself. I want to hear more of that sexy voice of yours," Sam said flashing his million-dollar smile.

"What do you want to know?" Sina asked in her best Quiet Storm voice.

"Hmm, I want to know what makes Thomasine tick. What do you like to do, where do you like to go, that kind of stuff?"

"Well, let's see. I'm a Chicago native, South side."

"Me too," Sam said interrupting.

"I'm a sophomore, Radio/TV/Film major."

"How did I guess?" Sam asked. "You go to school in Wisconsin, right?"

"And if you want to know what makes me tick, you'll have to get to know me better," Sina said remembering what her cousin Kelsey had told her about men. — Don't talk too much. Men like to talk about themselves. "How about Sam? Tell me why I should want to get to know Sam better."

"I'm a junior, pre-med major. An Omicron man. I pledged solo last spring. I'm the oldest of four he said smiling. "And if you give me a chance, I can show you why you will want to get to know me better." He took her hand and gently kissed it. "Why don't you stop by later? I'm having an afterset at my crib and I have to go get it ready. Rachel will bring you."

The party at Hunam's didn't last much longer. Once the Omicrons started walking the floor in a line and the Opals started stepping, the owners pulled the plug on the power. Insulted, everyone left.

"Do I look all right?" Sina asked Rachel in her Used jeans.

"You're just fine. I mean, this is really no big deal."

"I know one thing, I was glad to get that girdle off. I haven't completely gotten my shape back since the pregnancy."

That was the first time Rachel had heard Sina even mention her pregnancy. "Well you sure looked good tonight." The moon was full and the wind brisk. Indian summer had somehow overlooked Chicago this year. It was no big deal to Sina though, who learned very quickly, how to walk fast during her first winter in Wisconsin. "Not much further," Rachel said as they turned the corner on to High Street. Sina was hoping they had something to drink there, and she didn't mean Kool-Aid, unless it had some vodka in it. Or better yet, maybe she could slip outside and fire up the joint she had stashed away in her purse. She really needed to be relaxed. She hadn't been interested in anybody since Conrad dumped her nearly a year earlier.

"The party must be jumpin," Sina said as they got within an earshot of Sam's duplex apartment.

"His parties usually are. And I'm sure they have plenty of Obsession."

"Obsession?"

"Yeah, Omicron Obsession. It's kinda like wop."

Sina smiled knowing she would not have to bother anybody for a match. They entered Sam's basement apartment, as anticipated, it was packed with Omicrons, Opals and other Greeks. Furniture had been moved around the walls and stacked to make room for dancing.

"Come on in Rachel and Sina," Sam said, taking their coats. "Let me get you some Obsession." He returned with two clear plastic cups of this green stuff. While Thomasine liked Green River pop, this did not look good. It had stuff in it that looked like algae.

"That's just the pulp from the lemonade," Rachel said as Sina downed hers. "My girl. You ain't gonna let Obsession obsess you." Rachel and Sina stood on the wall moving their shoulders to the beat of a mix of Ten City's *Devotion* and *Right Back to You* when Rachel's Opal sisters began to walk the floor. "I'll be right back," she told her friend, as she got at the end of the line and synchronized her moves with her sisters.

As the house mix faded, Bobby Brown's *My Prerogative* came on. Sam walked over to Sina and flashed his smile. "Would you like to dance?" he said, taking hold of her hand and leading her to the dance area. "Wait a minute. I had to turn the heat up. That way people will take their coats off and stay."

"I'm having a great time. And this Obsession is really good," Sina said as if she were a connoisseur of college alcohol concoctions.

"You sure can dance Sina," Sam said as Inner City's *Good Life* came on. "Why don't we go outside for a minute and talk? I can hardly hear you down here." Sam took Sina's hand and led her up the stairs.

"Whew, what a relief."

"Sina, I know we just met, but I want to ask you a personal question?"

"What's that?"

"Now, we know a little about each other and I think I'd like to get to know more about you. So my first question is—Do you have a boyfriend?"

"How would you feel if I said I did?"

"I'd be very disappointed."

"Well, I don't. Now I wouldn't want to disappoint you," she said once again putting on her best Quiet Storm voice.

"Tell me why a very attractive and obviously intelligent young lady like yourself doesn't have a boyfriend."

"Why don't you tell me why?"

"Because I just met you."

"So I take all of this to mean, then that you don't have a girlfriend either. Tell me why?"

"Because I just met you," he said flashing his now billion-dollar smile.

"Sina," Rachel called from the doorway.

"Would you please excuse me for a moment?" Sina asked, still using her sweet, seductive voice.

"What is it Rachel?"

"Here's the key to my room. The same key will get you in the main door."

"Where are you going?" Sina asked taking note of the red Camaro IROC that just pulled up.

"I've got to go take care of some business."

"Not Calvin?"

"Sina, you don't understand. I have an acute case of dwd."

"Dwd?"

"Dick withdrawal," Rachel said, in a loud whisper.

"Rachel, I just know you aren't going to leave me here."

"I'm certainly not going to take you with me. I'm not that freaky. Besides I'm sure Sam would be happy to walk you back."

"Rachel," Sina said in a stage whisper as Rachel ran around the front of the car and opened the door.

"We'll talk in the morning."

"Now where were we?" Sina asked, walking back over to Sam.

"We were just about to go in and dance," Sam said as he heard the mellifluous strains of Phyllis Hyman's *Living All Alone*. When they returned to the basement, most of the guests had left for the evening. Sam put his arms around Sina's waist and pulled her close. They rocked from side to side and Sina began to gently sing along. "You have a great singing voice. But someone who speaks with such a sweet melody as you do should have no problem singing."

"Phyllis Hyman is my favorite."

"Let me ask you another personal question," he said as Sina smiled. "Do you mind if go and brush my teeth so I can kiss you?"

"I would like that very much," Sina said, now slightly intoxicated by the Obsession, the music and the mood. By the time he returned, the smooth reggae beat of Terence Trent D'Arby's *Sign Your Name* permeated the room. The crowd seemed even smaller and the more seasoned couples had probably left to get their grooves on. Sam once again put his hands around Sina's waist and pulled her close. He looked into her eyes as they continued to move to the music and leaned forward to kiss her. He started by lightly brushing his lips with hers, the whole time looking in her eyes. He then began to brush her lips with his tongue and then her tongue with his tongue. They stood there kissing and caressing until everything stopped. The music stopped, the other dancers left and it was as if time was standing still.

"Let me ask you another personal question," Sam said as he walked Sina back to Rachel's dorm, his arm around her shoulder.

"Haven't you asked me enough personal questions for the night?"

"But this one is really important."

"Okay, what is it that you really need to know?"

"Do you mind if your boyfriends have other girlfriends?"

Thinking about the situation with Hope, Jason, and Naomi, Sina looked Sam directly in the eye and said, "I don't care what he does as long as he is honest with me."

That's the Way Love Is

16

Another semester drew to an end for the Three Musketeers. Hope was disappointed that she had not spent much time with Jason during Thanksgiving. His team had conference playoffs, so he was busy with practice and studying. Thomasine looked forward to seeing Sam, (they had been in contact over the phone for the past month), but she dreaded going home to Rachel's Uncle Charlie's funeral. He was accidentally killed the Saturday before Thanksgiving when deer hunting with co-workers.

"I just can't believe he's gone," Rachel told Sina and Sam the day before Thanksgiving. "He called me on Friday and now he's gone."

"Everything's gonna be all right Rachel," Sam told Rachel as he embraced her. "It'll be all right."

"It seems so final," Rachel continued. "If I had known, I wouldn't have rushed him off the phone the way I did. I would have come home on Friday night instead of going to that dumb party. If I had known that I would never see him again, I would have told him how much I loved him and how thankful I was for all he did for me and Hank."

Uncle Charlie and his wife, Mary had raised Rachel and Hank since they were both in diapers. Almost all of Rebecca and Henry Sr.'s relatives were in Louisiana, so when state agencies threatened to place them in foster care, and possibly separate them, the Andersons adopted the children. Despite being in their late forties with no children of their own, they gladly accepted the challenge and responsibility

Uncle Charlie's funeral was the first time Thomasine had stepped foot in Front Street African Christian Church in nearly a year. Aunt Mary had asked her to sing "He Touched Me," at the funeral. When she walked out, with Sam's arm around her shoulder she got mean stares from Martha Mitchell and Phyllis Jones. She couldn't believe that two grown folk could act so petty at such a sad and tragic time.

"Rachel, if you need anything, I mean anything at all. Or if you just want to talk, please give me a call," Calvin said as he left the Anderson home after the burial.

"Honey, I know it's really rough," Rebecca Thorne said, with her arm around her daughter on her right and son on the left. "Uncle Charlie was a father to you ever since you can remember. Me and Sherman are here for you," she said of her husband.

"Rachel, you haven't eaten all day. Do you want me to fix you a plate?" Hope asked.

"Everything happens for a reason," Tommy said. "We experience losses so that we can become stronger."

All the while Rachel remained silent, still in shock over the tragic death of her uncle. Sina and Hope offered to take her out, to the show and shopping the day after Thanksgiving, but she decided to spend the time with Aunt Mary. Sina went out with Sam instead who had been right by Rachel's side before, during, and after the funeral. Sina admired him for that, and liked that he always talked about his family, who she looked forward to meeting. "How about lunch tomorrow?" Sam asked.

"I don't know why you are going out to eat with all of this food here," Crystal told her daughter. "It just don't make sense," she continued as she went to answer the door. "Sina, Sam is here."

"I'll be there in a minute," Sina said as she curled the last strand of straight hair with her curling iron, unplugged it and combed her hair in place.

"Do you have any money, Princess? You shouldn't leave home without any," he said handing her a twenty-dollar bill.

She greeted Sam in the living room and he helped her with her coat just before they walked out to his car.

"Don't expect me to open the door for you when your parents aren't looking out," Sam said, smiling, as he cranked the engine in his dark blue Chevette.

"It's as simple as this. What else could you do but open the door for a diva like me? By the way, where are we going?"

"Some place special. It's a surprise."

They spent the next 15 minutes discussing current events. How disgusted they both were that Dukakis had lost the Presidential race and what they expected for 1989. Sam got off at Garfield Boulevard, the same exit that Rev. Mintor took when he took the Three Musketeers to school on those bone-chilling winter mornings.

This seems familiar, Thomasine thought as they rode through Washington Park and came upon the campus of the University of Chicago. "I hope you like Italian," Sam said as he turned onto a side street and looked for a parking space. It was a good thing he had a small car because parking spaces in Hyde Park were about as difficult to come by as bread and milk during a snowstorm in the Southeast.

"Well, I didn't expect you to open the door for me," Thomasine said as she got out of Sam's car.

"I always treat a diva like a diva." He took her hand and they walked to Michelangelo's for the best pizza in Chicago. Their thick, stuffed pizza is better than that thin crust New York pizza or that so-called gourmet mess with chicken and goat cheese that California boasts about. When the girls were in high school, about once a month they made a special date to go to Michelangelo's for pizza and a pitcher of white pop.

"Reservations for Connor," Sam told the uniformed hostess.

"Right this way sir. A booth for two. Chandrinka will be your server." She handed them the menus. "Enjoy your meal."

Chandrinka took their order for a stuffed pizza with shrimp and a pitcher of white pop.

"Has anyone ever told you you have the most beautiful eyes?" Sam asked Sina.

"No."

"Well you do. They say you can tell a lot about a person by their eyes."

"What do my eyes tell you?"

"I'll have to look at them and study them under different situations and different light settings to really tell you. But from what I can see right now, I see a very ambitious young lady who overcomes any obstacle put in her way."

"Oh do you?" Sina responded as Chandrinka returned with two glasses with ice and a pitcher of 7-Up.

"Thank you," Sam said to Chandrinka as she once again exited."You know what Thomasine?"

"What Sam?"

"She didn't even ask me what size pizza I wanted."

"Well, it does say on the menu that a small serves one to two people. They will probably make a small."

"Well, whatever size she brings us, they will have to charge us for a small."

"Why don't you tell Chandrinka you want a small?"

"No, it's her fault. She should have asked us. Whatever she brings us I'm only paying for a small."

"Oh well," Sina said. "At least I tried."

"We have a little while to wait so let's talk about something more important. Rachel tells me you're Jazz Coordinator at a radio station."

"Yeah, I really love radio, but I think I want to work in TV. I've done a little bit at school and I'm going to apply for some internships at TV stations here for the summer. That way, I'll see if it's really for me," Sina said just before she took a sip of her 7-Up "So you're a pre-med major. What do you want to specialize in?" Thomasine asked.

"Probably pediatrics. I have wanted to be a doctor since I was a little boy. Either that or ob/gyn."

"Where do you see yourself in ten years?"

"In ten years I'll be 30. Let's see. I see myself out of school, and my loans paid off. Married, with one child and one on the way. To a beautiful woman with ambitious eyes. How about you? What does the future hold for you?"

"I'll be out of school definitely. Maybe by then I will have gone back for an MFA. I want to produce and direct so maybe I'll be working on a television show and perhaps I'll be married to an ambitious, successful man with beautiful teeth."

"Are you sure you don't want to be a dentist? You and Rachel seem to have this thing about teeth."

"One medium stuffed pizza with shrimp," Chandrinka said as she placed the hot pizza on the side of the table.

"But I didn't want a medium. I wanted a small."

"Then I'll bring you a small. It'll be another thirty minute wait," Chandrinka said as she placed the long-handled wooden plate under the hot pan and turned to leave.

"Can't you just take a couple of slices off? You know y'all ain't gonna do nothing but sit back there and eat it anyway," Sam said as Chandrinka stalked off.

Sina was a bit surprised at Sam's reaction. But Gwen could have told her what to expect from an Omicron man. After they were done and all Sina could manage was one slice, Sam asked for a container to take home his left over pizza. Sina could understand that, but she couldn't fathom why he asked for a styrofoam cup to take leftover 7-Up which after two hours in an open pitcher had to be flat. She was a little disappointed too when he refused to leave a tip. "I'll tip my hat. That's about the only tip she'll get from me." And it wasn't completely Chandrinka's fault. Sam was upset because things had not gone his way. After all that's what often happens when you try to take advantage of a situation. In spite of his tackiness, he was nice, seemed to want to do something with his life and flashed a pretty smile. So when Thomasine got a letter from him once she returned to school, she agreed to go out with him over the Christmas break.

December 3, 1988

Dear Sina,

It was good seeing you over the break. I really wanted to spend more time to get to know you better, but with Thanksgiving and Mr. Anderson's funeral, the break was over before I knew it.

I guess I'm writing to let you know that I've been thinking about you lately. I've even dreamt about you a few times. Can't tell you what you're doing.

I'm coming home for the break on the 16th and I hope we get to spend some time together. Maybe we'll even bring in the New Year. One thing's for sure though — thinking about me and you together over the holiday will definitely get me through finals.

Please write back and let me know when you're coming home.

Waiting,

Samuel X. Connor

P.S. You'll have to get to know me better to know what the X is for.

Thomasine smiled as she held the letter scented with Drakkar Noir and folded it. Conrad never wrote Sina. He always said he'd rather hear her voice than read a letter. Now a year had passed since she last saw or talked to him. But that was okay, because judging from the letter, Sam was very much interested.

Waiting was right, Sina thought as she put the letter back in the envelope. Sina had been named Program Director at the campus radio station for the Spring semester. Since the outgoing PDs carried the station over the summer, they were eager to hand programming duties over to Sina and her assistants ASAP. Sina reported on December 16 at 4 P.M. It was her responsibility to do all she could to keep the station on-the-air 24 hours a day, 7 days a week. Tommy told her not to spend her holiday up there, because after all, she wasn't being paid.

Sina had become quite active in her major, working as a segment producer for campus TV and Jazz Coordinator at the station. Considerable media exposure had awarded her a popularity she never anticipated. And her family had quickly tired of watching videotapes of her boring segments.

Sina was quite excited about her new position and all of the responsibility that came with it. She was surprised though one of the Assistant PDs had worked at the station longer than she, and was even preparing to graduate in the spring. But her first night on the job, Thomasine learned why she was the Program Director. Maggie was not only a senior, but had a part-time job at an area station, so Thomasine spent most of her afternoons and evenings at the station, doing the Contemporary Jazz show from 6-9 PM and even skipping dinner because she was at the station by 2PM. She'd order pizza when she got back to her residence hall. (You can eat and lie down like that when you're 19). She closed her show with Dianne Reeves' "Better Days." Liston, the Urban Rock jock, was on-time as usual and ready, as always, to do his show from 9-Midnight.

As Thomasine walked into the music library with a stack of albums in her hand, and could see that the music library staff had been slack over the past few days, she looked and saw a sign, "There is no music library staff as of 12-13-88. File your own records." Thomasine knew that if she didn't file the records herself none of the announcers would be able to find any good music for their shows.

Thomasine put Brenda Russell's *Piano in the Dark* album on the antiquated turntable and spent the next hour and a half sorting albums by genre, alphabetizing, and refiling them. And she got through the jazz, classical and folk albums. Since rock had a hefty playlist and all of the playlist albums were left in the control room, she decided to put that off until tomorrow.

As Thomasine made her way across the windy, snowy and icy campus, she was glad she had thought to call *Rocky Rococo's* before she left the station. This would give her plenty of time to get to her room, get the $6.45 cents and go back downstairs to the lobby of her residence hall.

Thomasine sprinkled crushed red pepper on her sausage and mushroom pizza and washed it down with Berry Blue Kool-Aid and vodka. Her residence hall was like a ghost town. The only students left in the building were Sina and a handful of graduating seniors who were out getting drunk. Since Sina was only 19 and the drinking age was 21, she decided to just stay in. With her belly full, nightcap dry and complete silence, she had no trouble falling asleep but the phone soon awakened her.

"Sine, this is Maggie. I need you to come to the station." It was 12:45.

"Is there an emergency?"

"I'm half in the bag and I need you to come to the station and do my show. I'm on until six."

Sina could not believe Maggie's nerve. There was no way she was going to do her show, and then turn around and do the Classical and Jazz I the next day, while calling volunteers to cover shifts after she left. "I'm sorry Maggie. I can't come in. I just left the station."

"Sine, I'm in no condition to even be on the air. If an FCC Commissioner came up here, I'd lose my license and the station would be fined."

"It's Sina. And that's not my problem. You volunteered over a week ago for this shift and you made the choice to go out drinking tonight and now you will have to make a choice about what you're going to do about your show tonight.

"Have a good evening," Sina continued. "I'll be in at about nine in the morning.

"Oh, and by the way, don't bother to call me again, because my phone will be off the hook. Goodnight."

Having to vacate the residence hall by 5 P.M. Saturday, Allison (the immediate past station manager) offered her hospitality and let Sina bunk at her apartment. Thomasine spent most of the next week at the station playing folk, jazz, classical and rock, while securing volunteers to cover Christmas week between her three hour naps. She was very pleased to see her father's Town Car pull up in the driveway of her friend Allison's house.

It was now the day before Christmas eve and Sina still had to pick up presents for Tommy, Rachel, Hope and Sam. Tommy had already done the shopping for their parents and had the presents safely tucked away in his condo. But all Sina could think about right now was sleeping.

The holidays went by with lightning speed. Hope managed to find out Jason's time of birth over Christmas while Rachel and Sina spent the holiday with their families. Sina saw Sam quite a bit and even ditched Hope's slumber party to bring in the new year with him.

Armed with her information about Jason, Hope went straight to Sistuh Miracle's establishment, suitcase in tow. "I've got that information on Jason." Hope said with jubilation in her voice. "And now you can do our charts."

"It be a long time for I kahn git ya two charts did," Sistuh Miracle told Hope. "I havta find de rising sign and de moon sign and where all de planets be housed at."

"I guess I can wait a little longer, I mean I've wanted this done for almost a year."

"Ohn since de chart take so much time I must have de payment up front."

"Well, I came prepared to pay you today."

"Let's see. Two charts. Dat be two-hunnert dollar."

"Two hundred. I only have one. I guess I'll just get Jason's chart done then."

"If ya want to know if him gon' marry ya ya need to get them done at de same time."

"I don't know. I have to buy books. This is cutting into my book money."

"I tell ya what. Since ya be here oh two-tree times a mont, I'll do ya two for da price of one."

"Thank you so much Sistuh Miracle," Hope said handing her two crisp $50 bills. "I was born September 24, 1969 at 9:58 A.M. And Jason was born February 14, 1969 at 7:02 P.M. in Chicago."

"Ya bot' be air signs. Interesting. Gut harmony be between ya two."

Since Thomasine had a week long break after her intensive three week interim she decided to pay a visit to the Duncan University campus. She had received another letter from Sam who said he couldn't have thought of a better way to start off his year than with Sina.

The gothic architecture of the Duncan University campus blanketed with snow and enveloped in a howling wind created an eerie, yet sublime scene. The cobblestone sidewalks, and century old buildings, were exactly what Thomasine always envisioned college life to be. Rachel didn't know how good she had it, Thomasine thought as she walked up the steps of Rachel's dorm. "And the food is better here than it is in Wisconsin." Sina thought. "At least here they have fried chicken."

She saw a girl whose skin was the color and texture of fried chicken, golden brown—greasy and bumpy—with hazel contacts, inch long finger nails and a very bad weave. *Must be Persephone.* Thomasine continued down the hall until she reached Room 304. As she lightly rapped on the door, she noticed the bulletin board across the hall from Rachel's room already decorated for Black History Month. *Impressive.*

"Sina," Rachel said as she opened the door with one hand and held the telephone in the other. "Look, I gotta go. My sister is here. I wasn't expecting you until tomorrow."

"Daddy dropped me off today. I thought I'd surprise you."

"Does Sam know you're here?"

"Probably not. He'd be here by now if he knew."

"I think he has a Chemistry lecture this afternoon, but he passes right by this building on his way home. Sometimes he even pops in to say hello, and I suppose, to warm up."

"Maybe he'll see me sooner than he thinks. By the way, how's your love life?"

"Well, Calvin still calls every now and then, but we just talk."

"What about your dwd?"

"It's really not worth it. I mean, knowing he's going to leave me to be with the woman he is going to marry."

"They're not married yet."

"I know, but I just don't think it's right. I do have some respect for Charleen. Somebody has to, because he obviously doesn't."

"I guess you're right."

"After I found out about his lies, it just wasn't the same between us— intimately. So right now, I'm just remaining friendly because I still work at the BCC."

"You decided to stay there?"

"I didn't go there because of Calvin Hardy and I'll be damned if I leave just because of him."

"I heard that."

"Besides, I just get to meet so many other people there. I'm the chair of the special projects committee for the BSA so I'll be busy putting together committees for special events."

"But what about that slim you told me about when we talked last week?"

"One day after children's lit. I asked him to serve on the committee for the Ethnic food festival."

"And?"

"And he told me he'd think about it."

"I like your strategy." Sina said as they heard a loud knock at Rachel's door.

"Get in the closet, Sina," Rachel whispered.

Rachel opened the door and Sam ran to the heat register. "It sure is cold today. I hope my landlord got the oil tank filled. Otherwise, I might have to find some prospective to let me crash in his room."

"Oh, I don't think you'll have any problem at all keeping warm tonight," Sina said popping out of Rachel's closet. "No problem at all."

"Sina! When did you get here?" He hugged her.

"You are cold," Thomasine commented as she quickly unlocked herself from his embrace. "But that won't last long."

"Well Rachel, I guess I'll see you later in the week," Sam said as he helped Sina with her coat, put his backpack on his back and grabbed Sina's overnight bag.

"I'll give you a call tomorrow," Sina said, "And if my father calls, I'm either sleep, or at the library or doing something college students do."

"Here we are," Sam said, turning the key in the doorknob. "My humble abode. And just as I expected, no heat."

"Are you sure the thermostat's on?"

"That's right, I turned it off because I wanted to save the little bit of oil I have left.

"Have you missed me?"

"Have you missed *me*?"

"You know I have," Sam said as he gave Sina a quick kiss on her ruby red lips. "I think maybe we better keep our coats on for a little while until it warms up. Can I get you anything to eat or drink?"

"Not right now," Sina said sat on the couch.

"Well, would you excuse me for a moment. I've got to call Quincy, one of my Omicron brothers, he's sick and I had to tape the lecture for him." Sam took his backpack and went into his bedroom. He sat on the side of the bed and placed the microcassette recorder on the night stand. He opened his Chemistry notebook and rewound the tape slightly to clarify a section of his notes. He then called Quincy, pulled back his sheets and sprinkled powder on them, took a condom out of his night stand drawer and placed it on top of the night stand, and put a red lightbulb in his lamp.

"Are you sure you want to do this?" Sam asked Sina for the third time before he pulled her close to him where he lay on his bed.

February 18, 1989

Dear Sina,

Gary and I went to the B.C.C. Valentine Ball last Saturday. We had a great time. I was glad too because Calvin and Charleen were there. He asked me to dance on (how appropriate) Bye Bye Love when Charleen's back was turned, but I just walked over to Gary. Charleen doesn't look bad for somebody over 30. I hope she's happy with him. Better her than me.

So you never told me about your night with Sam. I thought you had planned to stay two days and I was surprised when you went home the day after you came. I asked him if you all had a fight or something but he was wearing a big smile and he told me that the last thing y'all did was fight. He said you were too busy to fight. He also said something about not being able to find his tape recorder. He needs to get some notes to Quincy before the midterm in March. I saw him with Persephone at the Valentine Ball. He said that since you couldn't come down and she didn't have a date they just went together. He told me it was no big deal and not to mention it to you. (Oops, I guess I just mentioned it.) Anyway, I have a feeling she is trying to get her Press-On claws back into him. You better watch out. He doesn't stop by that much anymore on his way from Chemistry. But I guess it's warming up outside.

I got a letter from Hope last week. Said things between her and Jason were perfect. Said something about an astrology chart (I hope she didn't pay for it) and them getting married. Had to do with her being a Libra rising Scorpio with moon in Pisces and Jason being an Aquarius rising Virgo with moon in Aquarius. Something about a lot of air. I don't know. She said she is pledging so she probably won't be able to come home for Spring Break. She really doesn't know. She really regretted not being able to do anything for Jason's birthday or Valentine's Day. But I'm sure Naomi made up for it. Although I heard they just broke up. I guess I'll see if they're together weekend after next when we play Illinois. I hope you can come down. I mean that is like the grudge match—kind of like Kenwood and Whitney Young playing when we were in high school. The Omicrons are having a party after the game. And, from the way Sam talked, I'm sure he'll be glad to see you.

Hope to see you soon.

Your sister,
Rachel

"You're listening to the Voice of the University. We're gonna finish things off tonight with Bobby Lyle and *Tropical*," Thomasine said into the microphone as she turned its pot down and the pot for Turntable 1 up.

"Hey Sina," Gordon said as he pulled his playlist albums. "I'm surprised to see you here. I thought the Program Director didn't have to pull any shifts."

"That's what happens when your Jazz Jock makes a decision 10 minutes before his show to drop out of school."

"No shit!"

"And he was supposed to fill-in for somebody tomorrow. I don't know what I'm going to do now. I'm supposed to go home tomorrow and now it looks like I'll be here from 6-9," Thomasine said as she unplugged her headphones.

"Look Sina, I'll fill in. Besides, I need the hours," Gordon plugged in his headphones and cued up a record. "You just remember this when you give me my grade," he added as he pushed the button for the cart introducing the New Form Rock show.

Trudging through the slush, Thomasine began to think about how she was going to prepare her weather forecast. She signed up for Advanced Television Newsgathering this semester for two hours. When she found out she needed Friday mornings free in order to produce the show she wondered how she would make up that other hour, because she got credit for one hour for reporting. Allison suggested the weather segment because none of the anchors really wanted it. Thomasine had done quite a job with the weather. Every Friday morning, she and Allison went and got a *USA Today* and a *Chicago Tribune* to make her weather maps. She then ripped the weather off the radio station's UPI wire for the local forecast. But she couldn't answer the million-dollar question. Would spring ever arrive in Central Wisconsin?

Making her way to the Student Union, Sina went to the near empty Downunder Diner for a slice of pizza. She sprinkled her pizza with oregano, crushed red pepper and Parmesan cheese and filled her cup with coke. She nearly dropped her tray when she bumped into Scott. "Oh excuse me," Sina said. "It's been a long day."

"Tell me about it. Are you here by yourself?"

"Yes."

"Not anymore. If those white folk saw me at one table and you at another, they would figure there wasn't much union in the Black Student Union, especially on the heels of Black History Month."

"You're right," Sina said placing her tray on the table and slipping her backpack from her shoulder.

"Say what are you doing later, a few of us are going to Dalmatians at about 10:30. Wanna come?"

"I'll have to pass. I've got to get up early in the morning to edit my story. It seems the only time Allison and I have to get together and edit is Friday mornings."

"That's right, Miss Weatherlady. Your predictions are pretty accurate. How do you do it?"

"For one," Thomasine said as she paused to swallow a bite of her pizza, "I forecast only for Friday, Saturday and Sunday. With the show airing live on Friday and then throughout the weekend that's really all of the information they need."

"Have you had a lot of meteorology classes?"

"No. I guess I just have a knack for it. Basically all I need to know is that Low Pressure Systems bring precipitation and High Pressure Systems bring clearing skies." Thomasine took the last bite of her pizza and picked up her Coke.

"Well you do a great job."

"I better be going now. I've got to pack, I'm going home tomorrow."

"Chicago, right?"

"Yes."

"Lucky you. I'm so far away from home I'll be lucky to get there for Spring break."

"Well, I have to get my hair done and I figure if I'm going to go all the way to Milwaukee for a touch-up, I might as well go to Chicago to my own beautician."

"True dat. You know, I think it's a disgrace that I can't even get a hair-cut in this town. And they're always talking about Diversity."

"I think it's even a bigger disgrace that it's 1989 and they still have Curly Kits in the bookstore. I mean, if nobody's bought it in oh about seven years what makes them think that somehow somebody's going to buy it now."

"Curly Kit, that's really lame."

"Look, I've got to run."

"Oh, before you go, did I tell you that the Alphas are having a Sweet-heart Ball in April. I think I have an application in my bag," Scott said putting his black leather portfolio case in his lap and rumbling through it. "Let's see. Here it is."

"Thank you."

"Make sure you get it in on time, because it would be a disgrace if you didn't enter."

"Thanks Scott."

"Oh, could you pick up a few things for me while you're home?"

"Sure, what do you want?"

"Some grits—not the instant kind and some magic shave," Scott said handing her a five-dollar bill. "Keep the change."

It was funny to Thomasine that time was moving so slowly since she got on the Greyhound Bus. That morning had gone by like her night with Sam and unlike that night, it was action packed. Allison had picked her up at 7:00 AM and they went to the gas station for the newspapers and Sina's favorite Orange Cupcakes, then to the editing room to edit their story on Women's History Month. From there Sina went through the underground tunnel connecting the Arts and Communication Building and its annex, caught the elevator to the radio station, grabbed the weather pile from the newsroom, went back downstairs, through the tunnel into Master Control where she and the engineer prepared her Weather map. She finished this in time for her 9:10 Educational Telecommunications class and then took that long journey to Polk for her German class only to find out that her German professor wasn't there, again! She walked through the slush back to the TV studio and plugged in her curling iron. Ran back over to the station to see if there were any new weather developments and found time to do make up and touch up her hair before she went on live. She was pleased that her weather segment had gone off without a hitch today. Last Friday she lost audio when she began her segment and when she looked in the monitor as she prepared to point to her map, she saw herself standing there with Carol Burnett and Tom Selleck. The Technical Director hadn't taken Sina off line. She just casually turned to face them and nodded in response to whatever they were talking about. She figured she had to make the best of the situation. She finished the newscast in time for Allison to take her to the bus station for her 1:15 bus to Chicago. Good thing it was late too, otherwise Sina would have missed it and the game.

She never understood why it took Greyhound five hours to make it to the north side of Chicago when it only took Rev. Mintor three hours to get to the south side. And he didn't believe in speeding. With all the stops in Fond Du Lac, Kewaskum, West Bend, and Menominee Falls before they even got to Milwaukee and then the college stops at Parkside, Lake Forest, Northwestern and Duncan, it was really no mystery. Delighted when the driver called Northwestern, Sina pulled out her mirror fixed herself up in case she ran into Sam before she got to Rachel's room.

"My roommate went away for the weekend," Rachel said handing Sina a pale orange ticket. "But she said you can use her meal ticket. And we'd better hurry, because they stop serving dinner at 6:30. But first I have to run to the ladies room."

Thomasine walked over to Rachel's chair to get her coat when she was interrupted by the ringing of the telephone.

"Hello, this is Rachel and Natalie's room"

"Sina. I didn't know you were coming down this weekend," Sam said. "What a pleasant surprise."

"Rachel went down the hall for a few minutes, but I guess we can chat until she comes back. What's up.?"

"I was just calling to invite Rachel to a pre-game party at my place. At 7:00. And since you are here, you're invited too."

"Isn't that special?"

"Well, that was all I wanted. I guess I'll see you shortly."

"Yeah, we'll stop by when we come from dinner."

Sam's basement apartment was packed with men and women in red and green with green and white Duncan University banners and clear plastic tumblers with green Omicron Obsession in their hands. When Sina walked over to hug Sam, she noticed he pulled back and asked to be excused before she could kiss him. Surveying the room she noticed that Persephone was nowhere around. *It must not be true, then about Persephone trying to dig her claws into Sam,* Thomasine thought. *Because if she was, she would be here and probably up under him tonight.*

When Thomasine and Rachel got to the game, they were pleased to see Jason alone. "He and Naomi must have called it quits," Rachel whispered to Thomasine as they climbed up the bleachers. It was almost like old times. Rachel, Sina and Jason together. Only Hope was missing. But she probably had more than she could handle pledging down South. Rachel was glad that Sina was there. Now she had an excuse for not sitting with her Greek family. While she loved her sisters and brothers, she was tired of wearing red and green, especially before Thanksgiving and after Christmas.

"There's Rodney, Ring it up Rodney," Jason yelled as Rodney Harris hit a three.

"Just who are you rooting for? I thought you were loyal to Duncan."

"I am, but you know Rodney and I go way back. I want him to do well so he can get in the NBA. Thomasine, you used to have a thing for Rodney, didn't you?"

"What's past is past."

At the start of the second half, Duncan was down by ten. They rallied in the second half and with :05 left in the game they were down by two. Baker, the Duncan forward, inbounded the ball to Verdegan, the point guard, who dribbled down court and passed it to Griffin, the 2-guard. With one second left he threw up an air ball beyond the arc, but was fouled. At the line Griffin made two out of three of his free throws so the game went into overtime. The game was still tied with ten seconds left in the second overtime. Duncan had the ball. Baker called a time out when there were none left, turning the ball over to Illini. Cederholm, the Illini small forward, inbounded the ball to Davies, who passed it to Rodney Harris, who spotted up in the corner. Rodney sank a three pointer at the buzzer and the game was finally over.

"My boy is bad," Jason said as they began to leave the stands. "Hey Rodney," Jason called.

"Jason, my man. It's good to see you," Rodney said giving Jason some little secret handshake the athletes at Piney Hill High had.

"You remember Rachel and — "

"Thomasine," Rodney said slowly, yet enthusiastically.

"Hello Rodney. Since I don't have any allegiance to either team I guess it's safe for me to congratulate you. You played a great game."

"Thank you. I guess I better hit the shower. We're heading back to Champaign tonight. But maybe we can get together sometime when we're both in Chicago."

"Maybe we can."

"I'll catch you all later," Jason said as he walked away. "And by the way, Thomasine, I heard you have been making visits to Duncan. Stop by and say hi when you come here."

"So what are you and Sam doing next. Are you going to the party?"

"I guess if there is one. The Omicron section seemed dreary when Duncan lost." Thomasine said as she and Rachel walked over to Sam.

"Guess who," Sina said, standing behind Sam with her hands covering his eyes.

"Judging from the scent, I can tell it's somebody beautiful."

"Let's go party," Sina said, moving her body from side to side as long-faced Duncan fans left the gym in scattered droves.

"After this loss, there's not going to be much of a party," Sam responded. "Rachel, where is Gary?"

"He had to go home. His nephew is being baptized this weekend. And it's a long bus trip to Toledo." They walked out of the gymnasium.

"I'll give you a ride back to Dailey," Sam said as they approached his car on the brisk March evening.

"A full moon," Thomasine said. "I wonder what Hope would have to say about this."

Sam unlocked the passenger's door for Sina and Rachel and walked around to the driver's side. As Sina pulled up the seat for Rachel to get in the back, she told Rachel to wait up for her because she wouldn't be staying all night. With a 10:00 hair appointment on the South side she couldn't spend the night and had to settle for creeping. Sam dropped Rachel off and then went back to his apartment where they finished off the leftover Obsession.

"This stuff has me feeling funny. What's in it?"

"Ancient Omicron secret." He slowly led her to his bedroom and clicked on the switch of the red lamp. Sam planted kisses on Thomasine's forehead, nose, a tongue in the ear and mouth. Taking off his sweatshirt,

Thomasine began to work her way down his neck and chest when she was startled by Sam's pleas.

"Sina. Please don't give me a hickey."

"Oh Sam why not."

"Just stop. We need to have a talk."

"We can talk later."

"I'm serious." Thomasine sat straight up, beside him. "Now I have a personal question to ask you."

"Sam you can ask me anything."

"Do you know and love the Lord?"

"Of course I do, you know my Daddy is a preacher."

"Do you know that sometimes things happen and that they're blessings in disguise?"

"Yes Sam. What are you getting at?"

"Sina, you will always be special to me, do you understand that?"

"Sam, you will always have a special place in my heart too."

"It hurts me to do this, but I've got to come clean. Sina, there's another woman in my life. And she was in my life before I met you. You really caught me off guard when you answered Rachel's phone. And I had to invite you to the party," Sam said, now near tears. "So I talked Persephone out of coming to the pre-game party and the game. I told her her time would be better spent working on her big paper due next week. I even took all of her pictures down. But I just can't do this anymore. You are such a sweet, intelligent young lady and I just can't lie to you anymore."

"Sam, didn't I tell you in the beginning that I didn't care what you did as long as you were honest with me?"

"Now tell me the truth. If I had told you about Persephone wouldn't you have dumped me?"

"No. I just wanted you to be honest with me. That's all I ever wanted Sam. Because when you're dishonest with me you do not respect me."

"Sina I have a great deal of respect for you and I love you, which is why I have to do this," Sam said as he reached down to the bottom of his night stand. "I don't believe it," he said as he stood up with his microcassette recorder in his hand. "This has been missing for over a month, and here it was under my night stand."

"Getting back to what's important. I have my photo album here, And I have kept all of the pictures and letters you sent me. Thomasine, you are special, and you deserve someone who's going to treat you like you're special."

"I guess it's for the best," Thomasine said.

"And I have another confession to make. When I invited you to the party and that night you came over I took Persephone's picture down," Sam said as he walked over to his dresser drawer and took a glamorized shot of Persephone out. "But I have to put it back, because she is the woman I love."

"I think I better be going," Thomasine said as she slipped on her shoes and walked toward the door.

"Let me take you back to Rachel's," Sam said.

"No, I think I'll walk."

"But you shouldn't be out by yourself this late," Sam insisted.

"I'll be fine. I just got my yellow belt"

"Well can I have one final hug?" Sam asked.

"I guess it won't hurt."

"Thomasine, I wish you the best life has to offer, because you deserve it. And I'm sure you're going to knock them dead over the airwaves whether in radio or television," Sam said tearfully.

"And Samuel Xavier Connor, I'm certain you will make one hell of a doctor. I might even bring my kids to you. So long." Thomasine walked out of the door.

The snowy eeriness of the surrounding Duncan area had been replaced with a fierce howling wind. The saying in Chicago was "March comes in like a lion and goes out like a lamb." It was a good thing Thomasine had her coat with the hood. *I should have recognized the signs,* Thomasine thought as she left High Street. *Rachel told me in so many words in her letter. But I should have known before that, back when he asked me about him having other girlfriends. And to think he pulled out her picture to throw it up in my face. If that's what he likes, I guess I'm just too real for him. But I've faced bigger hurts and losses.* Thomasine thought, now at the front door of Dailey Hall. She pressed the little black button on the speaker phone and dialed Rachel's number. "Rachel, I'm downstairs." *But Mama and Daddy have always told that these losses and disappointments in life come to make us stronger.*

"I'm surprised you're back so soon," Rachel said. "I didn't know you worked that fast."

"You know what Rachel?" Thomasine said as they walked up the stairs. "We have something else in common."

"What's that?"

"Last year you lost your date to a bad hair weave. And tonight, or maybe even before tonight I lost my man to a bad hair weave. And it was the same one, pink string and all."

"No, I'm so sorry Sina. Sam should be ashamed of himself letting Persephone dig her press-on claws back into him."

"I'm fine with it though, because he served his purpose — to pass time."

More Than Physical

17

Spring's bright sun and mild breeze had finally cast a comforting shadow over Savannah. The dogwood and Bradford pear trees had blossomed to their fullness. Pink tulips adorned the AKA plot on the Harrington campus, and Hope was finally able to dress in season. She found the pledge period, although intense, valuable and even enjoyable. Knowing though, that if it hadn't been for her mother's urging, she would have never become a part of this network of Black women.

The morning after she and her 36 line sisters "went over" Hope felt compelled to call her other "sisters" in the Midwest. "Rachel, are you still there?" Hope asked after she dialed Sina's number on her three-way. "Sina?"

"I'm here. What could you be calling me about so early on a Saturday morning?"

"I went over last night. Now I'm an AKA."

"Just what has brought about this change?" Rachel asked. "You weren't so enthused at Christmas."

"I guess just the experience, and the fact that everything, I mean everything is falling into place in my life."

"I'm so happy for you Hope," Sina said with a hint of glee in her voice.

"The bonding with my Sorors was an experience I could have never imagined."

"What types of things did you have to do?" Sina inquired.

"You wouldn't even want to know," Rachel responded, curtly.

"My grades didn't even drop that much," Hope continued, ignoring Sina and Rachel's exchange. "I had an A average before and now I have an A- average with four weeks left to change that."

"Well you always were a gifted student," Sina responded, truthfully.

"And most of all, my love life couldn't be better. Dana and I went to church one Sunday before I went on-line and what the minister said was true. He said 'Them that wait upon the Lord shall renew their strength.

They shall mount up with wings as eagles, they shall run and not be weary and they shall walk and not faint.'"

"That comes from Isaiah," Sina interrupted.

"And it's like I've been patient. I've gone through these trials and—"

"Now you chose to go through that AKA trial," Rachel interrupted. "But for you and Dana. It sounds serious. You all going to church together and stuff—like it's—"

"More than physical," Sina said quickly, adding her two-cents.

"There's nothing going on between Dana and me. We're just friends," Hope explained. "But me and Jason. That's a different story. Things have never been better between us. He calls me all the time and even sent me a dozen pink and white roses this morning. You know pink and white means I love you still and always will."

"That's great," Sina said.

"There's even a future for us. It's in the charts. How's your love life?"

"Sina, speaking of your love life and I guess mine. I haven't talked to Gary or Sam much because of the Omicron's line, but one day when I was in the BCC, the pledges were there studying when Sam came in. And on cue they all stood up, Gary included, and they said in unison, "Greetings Big Brother Short Stroke."

"Oh no. That must have been so embarrassing," Sina said in a dead serious tone. "It's obvious that Persephone can't be trusted." Sina recounted to her friends that she had dealt with the breakup quite well and had sent Sam a card and wished him and Persephone well.

The girls giggled and shared details of their love lives until Hope changed the direction of the conversation.

"By the way Sina, I heard you were having racial problems?"

"It's nothing. Just some coward leaving some notes on my door. Not actually on my door, but on a newspaper clipping that was taped to my door and on the floor bulletin board. It happened right before I returned from Spring Break."

"What did the notes say?" Hope asked.

"It seems that someone's St. Patrick's Day wish was that that 'Nigger Bitch Thomasine would go home and get a man.'"

"Maybe you should transfer," Hope said.

"She's right you know," Rachel added. "You never know how far someone will go with that kind of hatred."

"I'm not going anywhere. I have junior standing, so I will probably graduate next May—that is if I can get in that summer school class at Chicago State. I'm doing well here in my major and I'm up for Station

Manager at the radio station. I will not let the idle threats of some coward keep me from achieving any goal I wish to set."

"Well that makes sense," Hope responded. "But you be careful up there."

"Yeah. Especially coming home from your night class. Oh, and don't go to the Radio Station late at night."

"You all are about as bad as Daddy. He wanted to hire a private detective and bodyguard. But I'm working toward my green belt in karate now."

"Okay Chuck Norris. But a bodyguard doesn't sound like such a bad idea."

"So you mean you came back and these notes were on your door, just like that?" asked Rachel.

"I actually didn't see all of the notes. Some of the other women on my floor took a black marker and covered up the notes on the bulletin board. I guess they were trying to spare my feelings, but they just made it difficult for the campus police to do a handwriting analysis. I do appreciate their thoughtfulness."

"How did it make you feel?" Hope asked.

"It didn't hurt my feelings or anything but if I could face the person who wrote it I would just ask why? Even though I work hard, why do I deserve less because I'm Black? It reminds me of the day Gwen and I went to the grocery store. We saw these people pulling out of a space close to the store and we sat there and waited. In the meantime, this white woman pulled around from the other end of the parking lane and tried to pull in the space. Once we were in the spot, she pulled right up to the rear of Gwen's car and accused us of taking her space. It didn't matter to her that we had been waiting longer than she had. She just felt that she was entitled to the space because she had her turn signal on. Even went as far as to say that if we had some education we would know what the turn signal meant."

"That is unbelievable," Hope asserted.

"That's not all. She followed us in the store, called us black bitches when we were getting the grocery cart. When I got to the deli counter, she had the audacity to get in my face bugging me about the parking space and even told me I needed to get some education."

"Oh, no. What did you do?"

"I politely looked her dead in the eye with my most serious look and said, ' That's what I came here for. An education. Now what can you say for yourself?"

"I bet she left you alone after that."

"I know that's right."

"And she is really lucky she ran into me and Gwen. Deborah and Measha, if she were still here, would have eaten her for breakfast. The days of separate bathrooms and drinking fountains, segregated schools and riding on the back of the bus are over. If I work hard and treat people fairly don't I deserve the same rewards as other people who work as hard and treat people as fair, no matter what their skin color is?"

"You're exactly right. I thought I had it bad here at Duncan. Shoot, Duncan's like a vacation compared to that."

"And just the general reaction we get from people in the stores—long stares. Would you believe that Deborah told me when I first came here that her first roommate told her she had never seen a Black person except on television? Can you imagine living eighteen years of your life without seeing people who looked different from you?"

"At least here in Savannah they've seen you before; they just may not like you, but they're always friendly."

"Let's move onto something else," Rachel said, with an upbeat timbre in her voice. They discussed Sina's upcoming competition for Miss Alpha Sweetheart. Hope suggested *His Eye is on the Sparrow* and Rachel suggested a more contemporary gospel song. Both regretted not being able to attend the pageant but resolved that they would share in other special events.

April flew by like summer or Christmas to a six-year-old. And that had really been Thomasine's month. She was named Station Manager. She would be the Assistant Station Manager in the fall and get the training she needed to run the station the following semester. She also got her Summer internship at Chicago's Superstation, in production. Now all she had to work on was getting in that class at Chicago State. When Thomasine climbed down from her bunk bed on the morning of April 29th; she was greeted by Gwen's big smile.

"What's got you grinning from ear to ear?" Sina asked.

"I know somebody who likes you, but I'm not gonna tell you," Gwen responded in a singsong tune.

"You're just trying to get me all happy and then you're gonna say 'psyche.' Right?"

"Not this time."

"I know somebody who likes you and I told him he needs to approach you himself."

"Who is it?"

"I'm not telling."

"It's one of those neophytes I bet."

"Not this time."

"Who is it?"

"Not telling."

"Come on Gwen, you always do this to me."

"He asked me if I thought you'd go out with him. He said he didn't want to ask you out and have you turn him down cold."

"Do I come across like that?"

"I guess to guys you do."

"Who is it Gwen?"

"I'm not telling."

"It's one of those neophyte Alpha brothers of yours."

"It is an Alpha, but he's not a neophyte."

"That eliminates half of them. Is it Charles?"

"No."

"Corey."

"No."

"Antoine?"

"No."

"Then it must be—Scott. Scott Lancaster likes *me*."

"Yes, and why shouldn't he like you? Sina, sometimes you don't give yourself enough credit."

"It's just that he's older, a grad student and all, and I'm not even twenty."

"Age ain't nothin' but a number."

"It's funny Gwen. Because I've sort of been looking at him since last semester."

"Really."

"Yeah, I always make it a point to talk to him when I see him around campus."

"Who knows what will happen between you two."

"I guess time will tell."

That evening, in her black strapless dress with a velvet bodice and a satin balloon skirt, Thomasine found herself juggling her time between the Alpha ball and the Radio/TV/Film banquet. Although she appeared confident, she was anxious and unable to eat. When Gwen peeped her head into the banquet at the Pioneer Inn, Sina knew it was time to make her exit and her grand entrance into the Alpha Ball at the Hilton. Shortly after she arrived, the contestants were asked to assemble in the contestant box. Each contestant was then introduced separately. Fate had it that Scott introduced Sina who happened to be the last contestant. As she was walking to the stage he whispered, "If you kiss me I'll be your good luck charm." Once Thomasine reached her spot on the stage, she turned and kissed Scott on the cheek. After her workout, she had gone to the BSU picnic where she got tanked. Slightly inebriated, Thomasine was bolder than ever. As each contestant was awarded, from Miss Personality, to Miss Talented and given some plaque or small trophy, Thomasine felt even more butterflies in her stomach. Suddenly, the contestant pool had dwindled from eight to three. Time stood still as her competition got even smaller, now down to two. As Thomasine stood there, with her feet firmly planted on the stage, she thought that it wouldn't be so bad to be second place. After all, all of the contestants were talented young women with bright and prosperous futures, but when the announcer said the first runner up, Miss Black and Gold was Vivian Gaines, Thomasine applauded and hugged Vivian. She was Miss Sweetheart. Scott presented her with a two and a half foot trophy and a dozen long stemmed roses, then escorted her to her throne where Gwen crowned her and put the Miss Sweetheart 1989 banner around her. Once seated on her throne, Sina was surrounded by men (from all across Wisconsin) in black tuxedos with gold accessories serenaded. "Frats will come, Sigma, K-O, Que. They won't do for you. Can you stand Alpha Love?" was the last thing Sina heard as she began to cry tears of joy. What a month!

The Vapors

18

Sina didn't think anything could top her action-packed month of April. Yet May brought the excitement of her new internship in production at Chicago's Superstation, a reunion with her "sisters," and the start of her summer school class in Management at Chicago State University. Two days after attending Allison's graduation in Wisconsin, Sina caught the Greyhound home for what she hoped would be the last time. Rev. Mintor had come earlier in the week to get her things. It amazed him just how much his young daughter had accumulated in a school year. She said her goodbyes to Gwen, Scott and Allison and was surprised that Scott hadn't asked her out yet, especially after what Gwen had told her. By the looks of things, 1989 had to be her year, and possibly, Hope's.

Hope waited as her plane began its initial descent into O'Hare International Airport. She knew Jason would be waiting and felt that he would pop the question. Sistuh Miracle had told her—in a roundabout way, so it just had to be so. And with the few pounds she had lost during the last semester, she knew she would be a sight for Jason's sore eyes. They hadn't seen each other in five months. *But what is that saying about absence—it makes the heart grow fonder,* Hope smiled as the plane touched down. *I wonder where we'll go to eat.* The plane taxied to the jetway. Hope grinned as she removed her backpack from the overhead storage bin and began her short journey from the plane to Jason's arms.

Rachel looked forward to the summer too. She hadn't seen Hank since Spring Break and looked forward to his coming home from the University of Iowa for the summer. She had lined up a summer job at a day care center and looked forward to working with the children. She hadn't really been around any small children since she was young herself—with Hank only being a year younger. She was happy about Sina's, Hope's and her job, but she knew that when she picked Sina up from the bus station, they would have to plan a night out.

"Mama, do you know what happened to my tote bag?" Thomasine called from her bedroom in the midst of rambling through her closet.

"You got so much stuff girl, there's no tellin' where it is," Crystal called from the kitchen where she was washing the breakfast dishes.

"Well, I need something to carry my shoes in. I can't run for the bus in these heels. Never mind, here it is," Thomasine put her polished black leather pumps in her tiny tote bag and walked down the hallway in her crisply pressed linen dress.

"I guess I better be going. I wouldn't want to be late on my first day."

"Honey, let me give you a ride to the el station," Mrs. Mintor said as she grabbed her purse and tote bag.

Thomasine waited for the El at Adams and Wabash for the Ravenswood train, and wondered what her summer would be like. What opportunities would she have? Who would she meet? How often would she be able to work in weather forecasting—which had become an interest of hers since working at the campus TV station? She hated the hour and a half commute to the North side, but knew that the experiences would be well worth the trip.

She got off the last bus and admired the tulips, gladiola, and small shrubbery that adorned the Superstation's entryway. She walked in, shoulders back, head high and said to the plump, red-haired receptionist behind the sliding glass window, "I'm Thomasine Mintor, a new summer production intern."

"You'll need to go to Human Resources first and they will take you to the Production office. Just go through the double doors on the left and at the end of the hallway, turn right. Human Resources is the third door on your right," The woman said as she buzzed Thomasine in.

Thomasine didn't see anyone she noticed, yet the people she saw smiled. *I'll enjoy working here this summer.* "Good morning, I'm Thomasine Mintor, the summer production intern."

"Yes Miss. Mintor, Mrs. Bradford is expecting you. Just go right through the door."

Thomasine gently pushed the door open. "Miss Mintor," a tall, middle-aged woman the color and texture of pure milk chocolate said, "it's nice to see you again." It seemed to Thomasine that Mrs. Bradford was taller than she remembered.

"It's a pleasure to see you again also," Thomasine said as she gave Mrs. Bradford a firm handshake. She had read in her AERho Newsletter that a handshake said a lot and that it was best, especially in employment situations, to have a firm handshake.

"I'd like for you to meet the sports production intern, Rodney Harris who attends the University of Illinois."

"Hello Thomasine," Rodney said smiling. He must have gotten braces since high school because his teeth were even prettier than Thomasine remembered.

"It's nice to see you again Rodney," Thomasine said with the same firm handshake.

"Since you're both here we can go over some preliminary items. First, you need to work at least three days a week. And Rodney, we can adjust that to include some weekends in order to meet your Basketball Camp schedule. Thomasine, you will be working with the Noon-time News until one and then you will assist in the production of the Public Affairs programs. Ordinarily you'd work with the Circles the Clown show but we are on summer hiatus. Rodney, you will be working with Mr. Drummond, our sports production manager. With a baseball game scheduled virtually every Saturday or Sunday—now that we're carrying all three Chicago teams you will be fairly busy. When you're here during the week, however I do expect you to assist in pre-production of the Noon-time News. Have you thought about your work schedule?"

"I can cover any Friday evening games, Saturdays, Sundays, and Mondays," Rodney responded.

"Mrs. Bradford, I will be here each Monday, Tuesday, and Thursday. What time should I report?"

"11:00 will be fine. By the way, you will get your biweekly stipend and your check from Mrs. Lopez on the first and third Monday mornings. Do you have any other questions?"

Rodney and Thomasine said "no" in unison.

"You both need to report to the production office. That was the first door on your left when you came through the double doors. If you should have any questions or concerns in the future, do not hesitate to call me. My extension is 2536."

"Thank you," the duo said once again in unison as Rodney held the door open for Sina.

"Funny meeting you here," Rodney said as he and Sina walked down the hall. "But then it really doesn't surprise me, after all, you put on one fantastic newscast when we took Speech at Piney Hill."

"I didn't realize you were a Communications major," Thomasine replied. "You always impressed me as someone who would go into business."

"I do plan to get my MBA after I graduate and my minor is business, but I've always been interested in how a television production is put together. It amazes me that someone over 1,000 miles away can watch a basketball or baseball game in Chicago."

"Well, it is fascinating."

"I also want to make sure I have plenty to fall back on in case I don't make it in the pros. I can always be a sportscaster."

"With a sportcaster's salary in a major market like Chicago, you will probably need an MBA just to manage it."

"You know what Thomasine."

"What?"

"I think it's going to be great working with you this summer," Rodney said as he stepped to the side so that Sina could enter the narrow doorway of the Production office first.

The crowd at the pancake house was fast paced as people walked in and out of the door carrying briefcases, with the exception of the retirees who sat in the far corner sipping coffee and reading their newspapers. The waitress, wearing a white oxford shirt, navy skirt, navy ascot, and navy apron with white pinstripes, escorted Jason and Hope to a booth upholstered with blue vinyl. A tray of syrups ranging from apricot to strawberry sat at the inner edge of the table and the center was adorned with a bud vase that held two pink carnations as if they could add beauty to the place. Just over the table was a Tiffany lamp hanging from a chain. Dusty silk spider plants had been strategically placed between every other light fixture and ceiling fans provided some air circulation in the hot restaurant.

"Are you excited about your first day of work?" Jason asked Hope as he scanned his menu. "You really look nice in your pink dress."

"Thank you Jason. I'm glad I finally get to put all of this accounting and statistics I've been studying the past two years into practice. How about you? Are you working with your uncle?"

"I just hope this summer is as hot as last summer," Jason responded. "Otherwise there won't be any need to repair and check air conditioners."

"May I take your order?"

"I'll have country fried steak, three eggs, hash browns, and three buttermilk pancakes. Oh, and orange juice," Hope responded.

"And I'll have a short stack of blueberry pancakes and a glass of whole milk."

"You can still drink whole milk? It cramps my stomach. I have to drink 1%."

"It doesn't bother me," Jason replied, smiling. "Now that we have a little moment to ourselves, I have something for you."

"Oh, how nice of you Jason." *I wonder if he's going to get on his knees in this restaurant. Or maybe he's going to announce it to the whole place. This is the moment I've been waiting for over two years now.* Jason took a small, velvet box from his pocket.

Hope extended her left hand across the table, Jason reached for the right. "Hope, it's been almost six years since we've been together and I know the last two years have been—sporadic, for lack of a better word. With both of us in school so far away from each other and all. Although we've stayed in touch as much as our schedules allowed, I feel that over the last year or so, especially the last six months, that we've lost the closeness we once had. And I hope that over the summer we can rediscover it. So as a symbol of our relationship and to congratulate you on becoming an AKA, I have this for you."

"So it isn't an engagement ring," Rachel told Hope as they headed up North for their girls' night out on a warm June night. "But it's still pretty."

"Rose Zircon isn't bad either. At least it's not that pink ice, or that ugly green birthstone of mine. Besides Hope, you all are still so young. He's twenty and you're nineteen. He is in school full-time and his football schedule doesn't leave much room for him to work. How do you expect him to be able to afford an engagement ring? They're expensive."

"And as long as you two have been going together, you better get an expensive ring."

"I know that's right," Sina retorted.

"Wait until after he graduates. He'll probably go pro and then you all can get married. It makes sense, doesn't it?"

"Yeah, girl, just wait. Then he can make a financial investment in an engagement ring closer to the emotional investment you've made in the relationship."

"I suppose you're right."

"So how's your internship going Sina?"

"You would never guess what I passed up to hang out with you two tonight."

"What?" Rachel and Hope asked at the same time.

"Rodney Harris."

"That's right, you did tell me he was a sports intern."

"I see him only on Mondays. But on Monday's he is on me. Always complimenting my clothes."

"No he isn't."

"He's probably just making conversation," Hope added.

"I don't know, Hope, Sina has kept the weight off. She keeps her butter whipped and does have a sharp wardrobe."

"Not only does he compliment me, but we sit together at lunch and he has offered to take me to lunch."

"You should go. It sounds like he likes you," Hope said.

"As much as I like to eat, and there is a Pepe's nearby, I can't go out to lunch on Mondays because we tape *Chicago People*, at 1:30 so I have only a half-hour."

"No, girl. Just two years ago he didn't even want to give you the time of day. And now that you lost that adolescent fat and slimmed down and are looking like a woman, he's all interested in you," Rachel said while changing lanes. "Girl, he's got the vapors. And he's got them bad. You can go out with him if you want but if I were you I'd make him wait until the end of the summer."

"I don't know Rachel. He got braces or something; he's got the prettiest teeth now."

"He probably got them bonded or something. You can do what you want to do but let me be the first to tell you I have no plans of re-chartering the Sina and Rachel Desperation Club. Remember he is the CEO."

"What about Scott?" Hope asked. "Didn't you tell me he asked you out?"

"He didn't ask me out."

"He didn't ask you out yet," Rachel interrupted. "You will be in Wisconsin at least another year."

"But I did get a letter from Gwen who is up there for interim. She told me he told her to tell me hi."

"Isn't that cute?"

"He really seems like a sweet person," Rachel responded. "And speaking of letters, I got a letter from Jamal a few weeks ago. We're going to lunch next week."

"I hope lunch is all you have," Hope retorted. "And have you heard from that Calvin Hardy?"

"Would you believe he invited me to his wedding—which happens to be tomorrow?"

"No girl. You have got to be kidding."

"Look in my purse," Rachel said as Sina reached on the floor of the car and grasped Rachel's purse. She unzipped the Coach look-a-like bag and pulled out a wrinkled wedding invitation.

"I don't believe he invited you to his wedding."

"I knew you wouldn't so I kept the invitation to show you."

"I hope you aren't planning to go."

"Shoot, forget that. I say let's go," Sina suggested. "Let's get drunk. Go to the Plaza and get makeovers, put on our finest dresses and go. I for one want to see. We can sit back and crack on them. It'll be a slice."

"I don't know Sina."

"Girl, put on your flyest dress and go. Let him see what he passed up. I mean Charleen must be at least 31 now and there's no way she could look as good as a 19-year-old. She's over the hill."

"But then so is he," Hope added. "I don't think it's a good idea for you to go to the wedding."

"But she was invited, and it says here Miss Rachel Curtis and guest. Call Jamal and see if he wants to come and I'm sure Rodney would be really glad to go with me. It's supposed to rain tomorrow, look up at all of the clouds. He's supposed to work at that Cubs game, but there's a 90 percent chance for thunderstorms. That's pretty certain. He'll be free tomorrow."

"You just want Sam and Persephone to see you."

"Now see, I didn't even think about them being there."

"It's a really bad idea," Hope said, struggling to add her two cents.

"Who knows Hope, you could possibly catch the bouquet."

"Well, I guess we could go, but I want you two to be on your best behavior," Hope said quickly changing her mind.

The girls entered the storefront church just east of Oak Park on that stormy afternoon. *What a way to start a marriage.* Rachel thought. The pews in the small sanctuary were decorated with green bows on one end and red velvet bows on the other, and it was June. "Aren't you glad you're through with Calvin?" Sina whispered in Rachel's ear.

"And aren't you glad Sam is not in your life?" Rachel said as she glanced a few pews forward and Sam and Persephone, fixating on that dangling pink string.

"Like I said, he served his purpose."

Hope had attended many weddings in her short life, and she was surprised there was no usher. But she was glad that Jason was with her. They sat at one end of the pew, holding hands. Rodney sat with Hope on his right and Sina on his left. Rachel sat next to Sina with Jamal on her left. Hope was even more surprised when Charleen, with red and green weave, came bopping down the aisle to the off beat of a drum machine and synthesizer, although there were an upright piano and an electric organ at the front of the sanctuary.

After a very weak rendition of *Endless Love* by the nuptials, one of the guests in front of Rachel and Sina commented, "That was good." Her friend shook her head from side to side and said, "Gurrlll, don't tell that lie." Rachel hung her head trying to smother one of her "please-God-not-in-church laughs." When the minister asked if anyone wanted to contest this marriage, a clap of thunder so loud that it nearly shook the church emitted snickers from Sina and Rachel. The couple exchanged their own vows and Charleen went on and on about Calvin—all from her heart, but Calvin had to rely on notes to tell Charleen that he loved her and that she was an important part of his life, now and always.

The reception was held in the Fellowship Hall; green and red cake, chicken wings, meatballs, fried chicken livers and "chitterling" ravioli, cornbread in the shape of petit fours and a big dish of collards... After Sina reluctantly vied for the bridal bouquet, and Rodney caught the garter, the Omicrons made their tribute to the bride. They were amazed with the un-rehearsed step show reminiscent of a minstrel show. And even Hope had to tell Rachel and Sina, "See what a mess you all almost got yourselves into."

A few weeks later, Sina and Rodney found themselves assisting in the pre-production of the Midday news, separating the 5 part carbonless scripts and distributing them to the appropriate people. "Rodney," the director said. "I want you to be the runner today. And Sina, grab your stop-watch, you're the A.D. today."

Sina walked into the studio and put her headset on so that she could communicate with the directors. *Now calm down, don't get so nervous that you mess up. This is live television and there is no room for retakes.* Sina waited for the start of the newscast and said a quick prayer. It always amazed her that the anchor could arrive on the set just 30 seconds before the start of the newscast and go on just as if he had been sitting there all day. Just as he put on his earpiece and clipped on his lav, Sina cued him into Camera 1. Shortly after the newscast began, Rodney came in with this hot story and set it on the edge of the anchor's desk.

"This just in," James Woods said as he looked down at the copy. "We'll be right back after a break."

Sina looked on the rundown sheet and did not see a scheduled break. "Young man I want you to confirm this story before I air it."

"It's true," the director said over the loudspeaker, "we have a crew in the area and we will go to a remote in a few minutes. Oh and Ron, we will need a very tight 3:30 on you weather segment."

Sina was fascinated by the number of exchanges that took place during the commercial break.

"Ten seconds," Sina said as she began to countdown and cue James.

"This just in. Despite a string of wonderful seasons and bowl championships, Duncan University's head football coach has just been fired. We have a crew en route to the scene and we hope to bring you live coverage of the press conference and reaction from the players." In spite of her shock and dismay Thomasine kept her cool. This was the first time she had been given an opportunity to prove herself on a live show. She certainly didn't want this to be the last. When she was finally able to give the wrap signal, Sina breathed a sigh of relief.

"I just can't get over it," Rodney said as he and Sina made their way through the cafeteria line. "This has been their best season ever. What's going to happen to Jason? He and Coach T had such a good rapport. When I first got the story I just looked at it and read it over because I just knew I was reading it wrong or something. Then the news director told me to take it in the studio and give it to James."

"It was surprising," Sina replied. "I got so nervous that I would mess up the show or something after that early commercial break. But I guess that's why my professor always told me I had to be adaptable."

"That's the truth. With news breaking every second, you never know what will be next. And every station wants to be the first to get it on," Rodney said as they stopped at a nearby table. "And there's no telling what else will happen in the next month or so before our internships are over."

"You're right," Rodney said, as he put dressing on his salad. "What are you doing this afternoon?"

"We're taping *Chicago People*, at 1:30."

"What's the topic? Who is the guest?"

"Some doctor or something. I don't know; why don't you sit in?"

"Thomasine, you did a wonderful job as A.D. on the news today. You want to give *Chicago People* a try?" the director asked as he passed her table.

"Yes I would, Mr. Peltzer."

"You go Thomasine. We will definitely have to go out to celebrate this," Rodney said, reaching across the table to pat her on her back.

"I've lost my appetite," Sina said, a little nervous about her newly-assigned task.

"You'll do fine."

When they entered Studio 2, Thomasine introduced herself and Rodney to the guest and let Fran, the host, know that she would be the A.D. *After that live show, this had to be a piece of cake.* "10 seconds," Sina shouted in the studio as she held the stopwatch that hung around her neck in her left hand. "Five, four, three, two, one," Thomasine said as she cued the host.

"Good morning, I'm Fran Kidd and this is Chicago People. Today we have a very special guest from Duncan University Medical Center. Dr. Janet Gray, an obstetrician who has started a program called *Fresh Start*. Dr. Gray, could you tell our viewing audience a little bit about *Fresh Start?*"

"Yes Fran, *Fresh Start*, is a program designed to give drug-addicted babies a good start in life. You see Fran," she said turning to face the host, "In the first six months of this year over 1,000 babies were born addicted to cocaine in Cook County alone. We have a major problem on our hands. It would be wonderful if we could prevent these innocent babies from being born addicted to drugs, but we can't. So *Fresh Start* is designed to help them once they get here. This program provides nurturing, love and care for these babies during their first days of life with the help of volunteers . . ."

Thomasine got the second shock of her day in this message. *How could someone sell drugs to a pregnant woman?* It happened every day, but this was something Thomasine never thought much about. *How? That is just so cruel. Ruining the life of someone before it even started. If the woman decides that's what she wants to do to her body that's one thing, but to harm your child like that is just awful.* It was then that Thomasine decided she would never smoke marijuana again. She would not support anyone who would sell drugs to pregnant women.

A Piece of My Love

19

Thomasine was very happy to start her senior year and to finally have a car on campus. That made it easier for her due to her Midnight to 3 A.M. show. She hit the shower after *Diff'rent World* and tried to take a catnap before heading to the station at 11:00. She thought she might have some peace and quiet because Gwen was always out. Thursday was the big party night at her college. Somehow her rest was often disrupted by the telephone. Everyone called because they knew she was home getting ready for her show.

She agreed to do the show when Tyson asked her so that they could keep the hours. Previously urban music had been allotted only three hours a week in the program schedule. Sina spoke to the previous Station Manager about expanding it. After all, it was the program with the most underwriters, but the manager didn't agree. Tyson was able to talk the new student manager into allotting 18 hours a week, from 9 P.M. to 3 A.M. on Thursday and Friday nights. She agreed to these hours with one concern. "Will you be able to find announcers to fill these shifts and will you have enough music for eighteen hours a week?" Tyson told her that it would be no problem, especially since the Assistant Station Manager would do one of the six three-hour shifts.

"You're tuned to the Voice of the University, I'm Lady Essence and I'll be your host for the next three hours of the best in urban slow jams. We're gonna kick things off tonight with Christopher Max and *I Burrrrnnnn For You*," Thomasine said as she turned the pot for turntable one up and potted down and turned off her microphone.

She loved playing the music she wanted to hear, but the late-night shift left her a little harried for her early class in Radio-TV advertising. Still she managed both.

The semester was well underway and Scott finally asked Sina out. In Scott's black Cavalier Z24, she absorbed a perfect late summer evening and the smooth jazz of *Dreamin'* from the George Benson/Earl Klugh Collab-

147

oration album from the campus station. The bright orange just over the horizon promised a beautimous tomorrow; with gentle breeze, just enough to blow Thomasine's hair lightly, they headed down New York Avenue to Botticelli's.

"Reservations for Lancaster," Scott told the host as he entered the dimly lit restaurant.

"Right this way," the tall, dark-haired waiter escorted the two to their table. Scott pulled out the chair for Sina and sat across from her. Scott wore dark pants and a sports jacket with a white mock turtleneck. *It wasn't like the jeans and sweaters Sam and Conrad considered to be proper attire.*

"I caught your show last night, you were good."

"You were up at that time?"

"It wasn't that late, besides I was reading for my Psycho class."

"Psycho?" Sina asked, puzzled.

"Psychotherapy. I want to become a therapist."

"At that time?"

"Sure, I study different types of material at different times of the day, I have to do the stats during the day, cognition in the evening and this psychotherapy class in the middle of the night. Once I get a system in place I stick to it. But let's not talk about this, I want to know about you."

"What do you want to know?"

"Let's see, I know you're from Chicago and I've always envisioned you as someone who was probably the oldest in your family with two or three younger siblings."

"Well, I'm from a small family. It's just my brother Tommy and me. He'll be thirty next week and he's a police officer in Chicago. How about you? Tell me about your family."

"I'm from a pretty big family. I have two brothers and three sisters back in Richmond," Scott said, looking up from the wine menu at the waiter. "How's a white wine, a Chablis?"

"That will be just fine," Thomasine said.

"So what do your parents do?"

"My mother is a nurse and my father is a minister."

"I didn't make the connection," Scott said as his face broke freely into a smile. "Does he pastor Front Street?"

"Yes. Since 1981."

"No wonder I never see you out, at clubs."

"You don't see me out at clubs because there's a well-kept secret about me that I'm going to be nice enough to share with you tonight," she said beaming.

"What's that?"

Thomasine leaned across the table and whispered, "I'm underage."

"Get out of here. I thought you were at least 22."

"Nope."

"What will you do if the waiter comes back and asks for ID?"

"I have a fake, but I don't want to get put out of the club like Shaunda does every week. That's embarrassing."

"True dat."

"Well you've told me about what your family does in the community. What do your parents and siblings do?"

"My father works for state government and mom is a school teacher. Most of my younger siblings are in school. Rubin is a freshman at Hampton and two are in high school, Ella Marie and Miriam, and Keith is in fifth grade. My sister Almeda, the one just under me, went to Howard but got pregnant after her sophomore year so she is going to school part-time at Virginia State and working."

"Oh," Thomasine said very uneasily. The subject of pregnancy, especially unplanned pregnancy, made her uncomfortable.

"But it's worked out as best as can be expected. When I first met her boyfriend, I didn't like him. Well I can't actually say I didn't like him. It was just something about him. He seemed a bit fickle and flighty. But boy was I wrong. He has been so supportive, even adopted my niece when she was born."

"How old is she now, do you have any pictures?"

"Yes," Scott said as he raised up and removed his wallet from his back pocket. "Here is little Brittany. And I tell you, I love that child like she was my own."

"Are Almeda and Brittany's father still together?"

"Yes. He just graduated in May and they are even talking about getting married."

"That's nice."

"It's strange enough for Almeda to be a mother, I can't see her married. I guess I always thought I'd marry first since I'm the oldest."

"Sina, Sina. You would never guess what happened to me yesterday." Rachel said with a mild sort of excitement that didn't always mean good news was to come.

"I was going to call you. I had quite a day myself yesterday. And it ended in disaster."

"Yesterday I was at my Practicum, at Thom Elementary School, and one of my students, a first grader, just passed out. And I just freaked out. I didn't know what to do. I got so scared that he might just die on me that I nearly froze," Rachel said virtually ignoring Sina's mention of her wreck of a day. "So I went out into the hallway yelling help, help."

"The child wasn't choking was he?"

"No. I think he had an allergic reaction to something he ate or some medicine or something, and he even stopped breathing."

"Well what did you do?"

"I was out in the hallway and this counselor, Patrick came in and administered CPR and I went to the office and called the ambulance."

"It's a shame there aren't nurses in the schools around the clock like there used to be when we were in grammar school," Thomasine said adding her two cents. "And to think that you had to go all the way to the office to make the call. You should be able to make the contact from your classroom. By the way, how is the little boy?"

"He's fine now, thanks to Patrick. The paramedics said if he hadn't been given CPR when he did he may have died. They took him to the hospital and Patrick said they would probably give him a shot of Benadryl."

"Thank the Lord!"

"And as soon as I got back to my dorm, I called the Red Cross and organized a CPR class for my residence hall. I used to always put off learning CPR, thinking I had plenty of time and stuff, but I guess I learned the hard way, that I should have done it a long time ago."

"They should have offered it to us at Piney Hill in gym instead of having us draw diagrams of dashboards. I mean all of the cars are different anyway."

"You're right about that," Rachel said, now calm and pausing. "Now how is that karate class coming along?"

"Great. I hope to test for my brown belt in the early part of next year. Who knows maybe sooner."

"And how are you and Scott? Have you all gone out again?"

"Rachel, I think it's over between us. I mean, I would be very surprised if he ever called me again."

"What happened?"

"It was just horrible. A disaster," Sina said with that shaky uneasiness in her voice which often signaled upset and disappointment.

"Calm down. You know you can tell me anything. Just think of all we've been through together."

"Well last night I was over Scott's. He had a bunch of friends over. We were watching music videos and playing spades. Utilizing about all of the social outlets we have in this lily white town."

"Yes."

"And I had a few glasses of Asti."

"How many is a few?"

"I can't really even remember. But I wasn't guzzling it. I was sitting on the couch just chillin' and talking to some of the new junior transfers. This was definitely an upperclassmen party."

"And?"

"The next thing I knew people started leaving, mostly in pairs, but before I knew it everybody was gone except for me."

"Sounds to me like its getting good."

"Rachel!"

"I'm just kidding."

"So I thought that I would talk to him for a little while, since we were alone and all and maybe get to know him better."

"Okay, that makes perfectly good sense."

"But then I thought, I don't want to wear out my welcome."

"That's understandable too."

"So I told Scott I thought it was time for me to go home. It was at least 1:30. So he got up to walk me to the door. When he opened the door, it was raining torrentially. And it was a bit windy. And I didn't have an umbrella. He got his, but I would have gotten wet anyway because of the wind."

"Would have?"

"So he told me I could stay until the rain let up. And I thought, cool. Because those kinds of storms usually pass through really fast. So I took my coat off and sat down on his couch and he sat next to me and kissed me. Well he had kissed me at least four times already and I let him know that I liked him so I kissed him back. Was I too aggressive?"

"No. It sounds like perfect logic to me."

"And one thing led to another. The next thing I knew Scott had his head up under my shirt and my mind was saying 'Now Sina, you need to stop this right here before it goes too far,' but my body was saying, 'Sina you've never felt this way before and you've never felt this good before so you'd be a fool to stop now.' So I just leaned back and took in every moment. Maybe I was naive or something but when I agreed to ride out the storm, I really didn't think anything would happen. Then part of me was saying, Sina, here's this grown man. He's older than you and this is a very adult thing to do and there ain't nothin' to it but to do it."

"I can understand how you felt, I felt the same way the first time I was with Calvin."

"So I did it. He took my hand and led me to his bedroom. It was almost romantic, but not really because we haven't known each other that long."

"Did you use protection?"

"Of course. I don't intend to have any more children for a long time."

"How did you feel?"

"Like I never imagined. I was lying there thinking, here I am with this grown man in his apartment doing this very grown up thing and enjoying every second of it. But emotionally I got this very warm, almost intense feeling inside my chest, stomach and other places. And it just intensified with each kiss. It was like I wasn't there, or maybe I wasn't mentally. It was just an emotional and physical thing. It's like they had a fight with my mind and locked it up and said 'Sina, just do it.'"

"I know that's hard for you Sina, you have never been one to act on impulse."

"I just hope I wasn't another one night stand for him. But I did hear him say my name a few times."

"Well did you talk afterwards?"

"I fell asleep in his arms. And then when I woke up this morning I just looked around the room, not believing that I was butt naked in bed with a butt naked man in his home and had obviously done something. I mean I knew I had been drinking, but certainly not enough to not be aware of what I was doing, that had I been sober, I probably would have braved the rain and gone home."

"It's all right Sina. Did he say anything to you this morning?"

"I got dressed and woke him up and told him I was going home and that I had a lot of things to do today. He seemed to want me to stay. He said that he had a nice time, but I thought, *yeah, he's just telling me that to make me feel good, I know it was probably awful for him, being more experienced and all.*"

"I used to think that about Calvin but there is actually a lot you can both teach each other."

"I'll never get the opportunity because I blew it last night. I just blew it. I'd really be surprised if I ever heard from him again."

"He didn't call you all day?"

"No, he said he'd call me this evening but I haven't heard from him."

"It's only 8:30 girl. You've got to be more patient. The evening is just beginning."

"I suppose you're right. That's the thing I like about having you as a friend?"

"That I'm right. I was wrong about Calvin and Sam."

"No, that you're not judgmental and are always supportive. I'm so lucky to have you as a friend and I'm so glad you called."

"Since you just said that, let me give you a piece of advice."

"Okay."

"Talk to Scott. Tell him everything you just told me; I'm sure he'll understand. If he doesn't, then you know he's not worth it."

"I don't know about that Rachel, I don't want him to think I'm stupid or a nerd, or even worse—a child."

"He won't think that at all. Just be a little more trusting. And I know it's hard after everything that happened with Conrad and Sam but those are choices they made and you have no business whatsoever internalizing any of it. You can't compare Scott with them. It would be like comparing Filet Mignon with cube steak."

"I guess you're right. I'll think about it."

"Well, I better go. I've been on this phone long enough. Besides, I have another call."

Tuesday, October 10, 1989

Dear Sina,

I trust this letter finds you well with a load off your shoulders now that you and Scott have had your talk. I'm certain you've had it by now and I know it wasn't as bad as you thought it would be. I mean, it's been at least three weeks since we talked. If I remember correctly, this week is your homecoming week. Are you still running for homecoming queen? If you do, I know you'll win. My girl, Sina. You have a lot to be proud of.

The Practicum is going much better now that I've had my CPR training. And Patrick, the counselor is actually a graduate student at Duncan doing his Practicum. He seems really nice and gave me a ride back to my dorm last week when it was raining. He's from St. Louis and he's cool. A slim, but right now I'm not interested.

Look, I've got to run, but call me as soon as you know when you'll get crowned. I'm so excited for you.

Your sis,
Rachel

Thomasine smiled as she read Rachel's letter and heard a light rap on the door. "Come in," she called as she folded the letter and walked across the room to place the letter in her desk drawer. Scott Lancaster strutted in wearing his Hampton sweatshirt and jeans.

"Hey, where's your school spirit?"

"I'm wearing it."

"I mean for this university, the colors are black and gold."

"I just can't get into this Homecoming thing. Especially with this weekend being homecoming back at my alma mater and me in Wisconsin."

"Well I hope you find some spirit somewhere when they announce me and Corey Homecoming Queen and King tonight."

"Sina, I need to talk to you about something," Scott said walking over to the lower bunk and sitting beside Sina.

"Can't it wait?" Sina tied her shoes. "We have to be there for "yell like hell" in ten minutes. And I wonder where Gwen is, she's the one who came up with the Keep on Movin' yell," Sina added as she heard the doorknob turning.

"Hey Sina and Scott," Gwen said as she entered the room and tossed her backpack in her closet.

"That's what I have to talk to you about, Sina," Scott said holding Sina's right hand and looking into her eyes. "I just hope you're not too upset if you don't place in this homecoming queen contest."

"Yeah Sina, you have about the chance of a 90-degree day here in January of winning anything in this contest on this white campus. Don't let the outcome reflect on you as a person."

"I'll be fine. I don't really want to be homecoming queen. I just ran to see what would happen. Don't either of you worry. Believe me, I've faced many disappointments and I've only just begun."

"BSU just keeps on movin', BSU just keeps on movin'..." the members of the Black Student Union rhythmically chanted as they marched off the stage in front of the Fox River during the "yell like hell" competition. Homecoming on this predominantly white campus was an event very few of the Black students got even remotely excited about. Although they had the most innovative yell—the keeps on movin' chant under some inspirational words sung in unison by members of the Gospel Ensemble—they had less of a chance of winning than Thomasine. Some of the white fraternities were as large as the total number of Black students.

"Hey Corey, wait up," Sina yelled as she ran over to Kendall who had a bottle of vodka in his hand. "I just know you aren't leaving before they announce homecoming court," she said taking the bottle from him and drinking a swig.

"I have something to do. And besides we ain't gon' win. Sigma Phi swept the homecoming court for the last two years and they're going to do it again this year."

"You don't know that." The emcee summoned the candidates for Freshman attendant to come on stage.

"Look, I'm outta here," Kendall said taking his pint from Sina.

"I saw that," Scott said smiling at Sina. "Where is Kendall going?"

"Since he thinks we're not going to win he just jetted. Do you believe that?"

"I don't blame him."

"So I guess that means you aren't going to go up on the stage with me when they call Senior candidates."

"Not a chance."

"Can you at least give me a good luck kiss?" Thomasine asked as she heard the emcee call her slate.

"Come here," Scott said, embracing Sina; his kiss was extended, experienced. Thomasine walked over to the stage and grabbed Tyson, who just finished filling in for the missing Black male junior attendant.

"I guess I'm Mr. Fill-in tonight."

"You're so good at it," Thomasine smiled. She heard her name.

"Senior attendants for our 1989 Homecoming Court are Thomasine Mintor and Kendall Shaw."

"Now aren't you glad you came up here with me?" Thomasine said as Tyson gave her a big congratulatory hug. Of course the Homecoming Queen and King represented Sigma Phi Fraternity, but Sina and Kendall managed to beak the monopoly Sigma Phi held for so many years. "And you'll have to tell that trifling friend of yours that we won. He should have stayed."

"But he didn't," Tyson said as they walked off the stage.

"Congratulations," Scott said.

"Are you surprised?"

"Shocked is more like it, but I'm happy for you." He put his arm around Sina's shoulder and they walked toward her residence hall.

"We need to celebrate, tonight," Thomasine said giving him a sly smile.

"Well all right, but I don't have anything at home and well, let's just say that with midterms and all, my cleaning lady hasn't been by to straighten up, but my place is clean and fresh."

"The best celebrations are not planned. I just need to grab a few things and call my sisters,"

"I thought you told me it was just you and Tommy."

"I mean Rachel and Hope."

"Who are they?"

"We've been best friends since—wow, since my father went to Front Street. That was in 1981."

"Really?" Scott asked, surprised that after a month he had never heard of these women who were so close to Sina's heart that she called them sisters.

"Really," Thomasine said as she and Scott entered her room and she picked up the phone. After talking briefly to Rachel and Hope on her three-way, Sina put clean underwear, her curling iron and comb, and her fifth of Citrus Vodka into her backpack. She was going to do exactly what Rachel told her—Celebrate.

When Sina and Scott got to his apartment, books and papers, strewn about, decorated the living room. His kitchen table was covered with yellow legal paper and on the wall beside the table was some sort of chart on stages of relationships. Sina made her way over to the fridge and took her bottle out of her bag. "You got any lemonade?" Scott popped in a Jeffery Osborne tape.

"Look in the pitcher."

"Bingo," Sina said as she removed glasses from Scott's lower cabinet shelf and fixed cocktails for the two of them. By the time she had finished shaking the vodka, lemonade and crushed ice, Scott's living room was transformed into a neat yet lived-in room. "Here you go," Thomasine said handing Scott the drink. "Is it straight?"

"It's straight." Thomasine sat next to him.

"So you didn't think I'd win?"

"To be completely honest, I didn't. But that's not because I don't think you aren't talented enough to win or even popular enough. When you didn't call all of the Black students last week and tell them to vote, I just didn't think you had a chance. But you had to get some serious votes from white folk to win that. Maybe if you had called all of the Black students, you and Kendall would have been Queen and King. I don't know. It's just so different from the way they do it back at Hampton."

"How to they do it at Hampton?"

"Each organization, building, and anything else that matters just a little bit had a representative. There's a Miss Student Union and a Miss Gospel Choir. There must be dozens of them. Then there's a vote and Miss Hampton is elected. That comes after a week of events including debates, speeches, and a pageant. Just anybody can't run either. They have to have a certain GPA and a whole lot of public service. Miss Hampton is usually elected in the Spring and then we kick off Homecoming week with coronation of Miss Hampton."

"Coronation. Wow. You know they don't do anything like that here. I don't even know if they actually crown the homecoming queen. I would love to know what a coronation is like."

"You won't wonder for long," Scott said taking Sina's hand as the deep, rich tones of Jeffrey Osborne's *True Believers* permeated the room. "It won't be long at all," Scott continued as he first danced slowly with Thomasine before placing her on his throne in all her glory.

"Damn," Scott said reaching under his bed.

"What's wrong?"

"I'm out of rubbers."

"Damn," Sina said, turning on her side. "I guess the coronation's over."

"Not exactly. We can have coronation on a different level."

"Nothing too strange I hope."

"Not at all," Scott said pulling her closer. "We can have a heart to heart about our relationship and where it's headed."

Thomasine was amazed that Scott didn't make a midnight run to the drugstore or even just take a chance. Sam would have jumped at the chance of going to Walgreen's and Conrad definitely would have taken the chance. But Scott wanted to talk. *What's up with him?* Sina thought as she tried to further avoid the now inevitable.

"What's wrong? Cat got your tongue?"

"I'm a little shy," Sina replied. "Why don't you start?"

"You're a very interesting person Thomasine Mintor, intriguing yet sincere, friendly and there's this very gentle, yet assertive side of you. All of these qualities are the reasons why I like you. Not because you're a diva—just kidding, not because of the bright future you're sure to have, but because you're you. I guess it's been about a month now since we first went out and the relationship moved kind of fast. Certainly faster than any relationship I've ever been in. I've really been concerned about that but I really didn't know what to do. It's not like we can start over because we have already shared a special part of ourselves with each other. I really wasn't sure how to broach the subject. How do you feel about where we are and where we've been?"

"The relationship did move kind of fast and I too had some concerns, but then I wondered if it was normal. It seems that other relationships I've been in started kind of fast but I managed to slow things for a little while. I had actually been afraid of—I don't know, I guess because of where I've been."

"Where have you been?"

"Well my first boyfriend was Conrad. I guess I was sort of a late bloomer. We started dating right before the prom and I met him at church. I really loved Conrad. I would have done just about anything for him. But he was involved in the wrong scene. He had a little bit of a drug problem."

"What do you mean by a little bit?"

"He smoked a nickel bag every day and sometimes used cocaine. He even gave me a shotgun on my eighteenth birthday but I've put pot down. I never really got anything out of it. I never did the cocaine. I was always scared."

"Oh Sina, I bet that relationship must have been torture. People with addictions usually have inconsistent and addictive personalities."

"I really loved him; but didn't feel that he loved me. He would always tell me he loved me if he were trying to coax me into sleeping with him. That's why I never really wanted to go with him where I've gone with you. He broke up with me finally right before Christmas. Was that cold or what? He could have waited until after Christmas."

"I know how it feels to lose someone you really love. I was engaged to my high school sweetheart. She went to Virginia Union. We had set a date and everything. Then I got this fellowship to come here. And to make a long story short we parted our ways. Now she's married and Almeda tells me she has a baby due soon."

"Was it because you came here?"

"Not completely. We started to grow apart before I graduated and I guess my coming here was the test. And I didn't pass."

"I didn't pass either. My next boyfriend after Conrad lied to me from day one—he had another girlfriend the entire time. I later found out that he'd take me out for pizza in the afternoon and go out with her at night."

"Sina, that's awful. But that's in your past. You're in good hands now," Scott said as he pulled her even closer. "I would never do anything that I would not want done to my sisters."

Spread My Wings

20

As Hope pulled out of the parking lot of Savannah International Airport, she recognized a dull hue in the sky she had never seen in Savannah before. *A wasted trip,* she thought as she reached down with her right hand to turn on the radio and used her left hand to signal a left turn onto US Highway 80. When Jason called her and told her to expect a package he was sending on Eastern Airlines, she was overjoyed. She really regretted that she couldn't spend Valentine's Day with him, but since she expected to graduate in May, she would be able to spend all of her Valentine's Days with him. She was excited and thankful that he was sending her something special—with extra care and not trusting the postal system in Chicago.

Hope was dismayed that the arrival of her package had been delayed by a snowstorm in Chicago. She purposely waited until rush hour traffic thinned out before she mustered up the courage to head to the airport. Hope hated driving and once considered not even becoming licensed. Most Chicagoans can understand why. In fact Sina nor Rachel ever uttered a curse word until they began driving in Chicago. They started with "shit" and "damn" but quickly graduated to "asshole" and "shithead." To Hope, it seemed that Chicago drivers were always in a hurry, rarely going anywhere, just reckless and rude. As much as Hope was ready, willing and able to receive Jason's gifts, she definitely dreaded the drive to the airport. She tried to get several of her sorors to drive her but she knew her request fell on deaf ears.

Tonight was a big game at Savannah State against archrival Morehouse. And no one in Savannah ever dared to miss that game—that is, unless they were like Hope and plain didn't care. Just as she began to hum along with Luther Vandross' *Here and Now* the radio cut off. She fumbled with the dial thinking that perhaps she had temporarily tuned out the station, but then she noticed that she had no dashboard lights and her car was merely coasting. She automatically signaled, and with all her might, turned the steering wheel to the right until she was safely on the shoulder.

Naturally she examined her gas gauge although she had filled up on her way to the airport. *Thank goodness it's not dark yet.* She reached into the glove compartment for her manual, but tossed it back into her glove compartment. *What good will it do anyway? I can't fix cars.*

Thinking quickly, Hope got her sunshade from the trunk. "The dumb thing did have some good use after all," Hope said as she opened it up to the *Need Help — Please Call Police* side. When she closed her trunk and walked around to the passenger side of her car, she couldn't believe the giant snowflakes coming down all around her. *Only me,* she thought. She positioned the sign in her back window and sat in the front seat of her Hyundai Excel and locked the door.

"I can't believe it's snowing," as if someone else were in the car with her. "No one will ever stop now; everybody's rushing to get home."

The weatherman had predicted snow; Hope just refused to believe it. "What on earth could a thunderstorm nine days earlier have at all to do with the weather today?" she had asked her suitemate as she left Terrell Hall. *Now if Sistuh' Miracle said it would snow today then I'd believe it, — but then I haven't seen her in two weeks.* The temperature was dropping fast.

She was calm, but after about an hour, it was darker and the snow was deeper. She thought of Jason. She would have to call him if she ever got out of this mess. "Think, think," she said. The only brightness was the falling snow which broke up the overwhelming black beginning to envelope her.

"Lord, help me to hold out," she said as she saw headlights in the distance behind her. "And Lord, please don't let them be an ax murderer." The pickup truck slowed to a stop behind her and a dark, short man wearing a patched coat approached.

"'Ooman, you touble witcha car be haben."

"I'm hav-ing car trou-ble," Hope said in her usual loud voice, enunciating each syllable as if she were teaching the Gullah man to speak or as if he had hearing problems.

"Name me be Fradjuh. It be dainjus f'you here affa dayclean," the man said, walking toward the front of the car. "Lift de hood, ma'am." She released the lever. She was now thankful she had paid attention to Jason when he gave her her crash course in car maintenance. Thinking quickly, she reached in her glove compartment and got the flashlight her father always insisted she keep in her car. The man walked around the car, lifted the hood. While the stranger worked under the hood, Hope thought she'd better get his license plate number, just in case. She quickly returned to the car almost tripping in the dark, and jotted HP5 2649A.

A car approached. It was a state trooper. "Ya'll need help?" asked the tubby trooper with the name S. Bobstanobos on his name plate.

" 'stributo cap shot," the Gullah man yelled from behind the hood.

"We'll have to call a wrecker for you then ma'am," Trooper Bobstanobos said. "Why don't you go on and get in my car ma'am."

With that leather coat on, she did not need to be asked twice. She quickly pulled out the piece of paper she jotted the plate number on and compared with the plate as the Gullah man slowly drove off. She wondered how his raggedy vehicle even moved. Just then, she remembered she hadn't even thanked him. When she looked up again, the vehicle seemed to have disappeared, no red taillights or anything.

"The wrecker'll be here shortly ma'am and they will tow your car to the nearest service station," Trooper Bobstanobos said to Hope. "We'll wait here, but they should be here shortly.

"Ya musta had a crack in yo dis stributer cap. With it snowing now and the humidity up its no surprise you had problems."

"Let me thank you now for your help. I didn't get to thank the other man. He pulled off but I did get his plate number."

"Lemme have it, I'll call it in," Trooper Bobstanobos said.

"It is Georgia HP5 2649A."

"Hey, this is Saucy. I'm doing a plate check. Georgia Henry-Peter-5-2-6-4-9-Angel.

"It'll be just a second ma'am. These computers we got work real fast."

"That number was Henry-Peter-5-2-6-4-9-Angel," Saucy said into the radio once again only to hear the dispatcher tell him. "No such plate."

"Ma'am, are you sure they were Georgia plates?"

"I'm positive," Hope insisted. "I saw the peach myself."

"This is really weird," Saucy, his hand on his double chin. "The dispatcher said there was no such plate registered in Georgia."

"But I copied it down and then I compared it as he drove off. And I have a knack for numbers," Hope said as she saw the flashing lights of a tow truck behind her.

"You stay here and keep warm until he hooks up your car to the tow," Trooper Bobstanobos said as he got out of the patrol car and walked over to the truck.

"And the strangest thing of it all was that the Trooper told me there was no such plate registered in the state of Georgia," Hope told Sina and

Rachel from her three-way. "And it was like he disappeared into thin air. But he told the trooper exactly what was wrong with my car because the trooper looked like he couldn't believe it was that simple."

"Well I'm glad that man did stop and help you. You must have been frightened in the dark with the snow," Rachel said.

"I thought no one would ever stop. And just when I said Lord, help me to hold out. Remember when we used to sing that Sina back in youth choir—"

"Yeah, I remember. But you called on the Lord and then this man stopped and disappeared after the trooper came and now there is no trace of him."

"That may sound crazy, but that's exactly what happened."

"Hope, you encountered an Angel."

"What, Sina? That sounds crazy."

"From everything you've told me that's exactly what it sounds like. Raggedy car, patches upon patches on his clothing, he spoke in a Gullah dialect, and no trace of his plates. He was definitely an Angel. Daddy always told me to be careful of how I treat people because we will entertain angels unaware," Sina broke it on down to Hope. "And you called on the Lord in your time of need and he sent you an Angel." Both Hope and Rachel were silent.

"Well if you don't believe me, just think about it a little. By the way, how did you get back to the dorm?"

"I was able to catch up with Dana before he left to go to the game. The wrecker would only take me to the service station," Hope replied. "Dana even told me how much the repair should cost and said he'd take me to pick it up."

"So what's up with you and Dana," Rachel asked.

"Nothing. He calls me every now and then to ask me a question."

"I've got a feeling there's more going on than numbers," Sina said slyly.

"Honest. You both know that Jason's the love of my life."

"This is true. So what did Jason send you anyway?"

"A portrait of him and me. For Valentine's Day."

"Now that is nice."

"What did Scott get you, Sina?"

"Scott and I are no longer."

"What?" Hope replied. "I thought he was the one for you."

"You must not have gotten my letter yet. But basically he asked me for space and I backed off. He said he felt the relationship had been stagnant. Like he didn't really know that much about me and that my life was the radio station."

"Well you are the manager and aren't you supposed to eat, sleep, and breathe the radio station?" Rachel asked.

"This is true, but he feels that we should be further along than we are and says he is trying to make sense of it all. But it's all good. I really liked Scott and I miss him and the time we spent together, but to be completely honest with you, it wasn't a relationship, it was a sexship."

"No wonder it didn't work," Hope responded. "You should have held out so he would hold on."

"I'll have to remember that next time. Kelsey said she could see it coming when he gave me that watch for Christmas. She swore that was a sure-fire sign that time was running out.

"But I'm on to other things like getting ready for graduation, graduate school, and of course, managing that radio station."

"Where have you applied?"

"Just to two programs, U of I and UNC-Chapel Hill. Right now I'm waiting to hear. So is Gwen," Sina said of her roommate. "She applied to MBA programs at Penn and Duke. If I get into UNC and she gets into Duke, we can get an apartment together because I heard they are just down the road from each other. But you two know I'll let you know as soon as I hear something. How's your love life Rachel?"

"I can't complain. Patrick is the sweetest man I have ever met. He just has so much respect for me and he doesn't give me any reason not to trust him. Oh, and he's really religious—Pentecostal."

"That sounds serious," Sina said.

"It's interesting how we met. I guess you could say he's the Angel God sent to my rescue when that student was choking."

"But it looks like your angel didn't disappear."

"I still don't believe that man was an Angel, Sina," Hope interjected.

"Then you figure it out. Look, I'm going to have to run. I've got to go to the station to do my show."

"I thought the station manager didn't have to do a shift."

"Well I don't, but I produce and host a weekly program called *Diversity Magazine* that focuses on the culture and activities of the various Multicultural groups on this campus."

"Sounds interesting."

"It always is."

"Well, I'm going to have to go too because I'm expecting Patrick. We're going to dinner."

"Have fun and by all means, don't do anything I wouldn't do," Hope said to Rachel.

"I guess then I won't have any fun," Rachel said as she and Sina laughed.

"Bye ya'll. I guess I'll have to get my Southern drawl on just in case I move to the Carolinas."

"You're so crazy," Rachel said. "Bye now."

"Goodbye."

Thomasine looked out the window of her dorm room at the melting snow mid-March had left, with the phone cradled under her right ear while she waited for an answer. "Guess what?"

"I don't get a hello."

"I'm sorry Rachel. Hello, how are you doing?" Sina said. "And guess what?"

"I'm officially a Tarheel. I got into UNC. It's on paper. So it's official."

"Now Sina, did you honestly have any doubts?"

"Well, they did kind of hint at it when I was there last week, but it's official. I can now escape this great white North. No more trudging through snow for me. I'm headed South."

"Congratulations. Have you told Hope yet?"

"No, I called her, but she wasn't in."

"You know what? She has an interview in New York with that large Black-owned accounting firm, McDonald, Baker & Jackson."

"That's right."

"My girl, you're going on to even higher education. I'm scared of you," Rachel said, smiling and twirling the telephone cord with her fingers. "Tell me about your trip to NC. I'm so sorry I didn't get to spend anytime with you over your Spring Break."

"My trip was great. Let's see, where should I start? I got there Wednesday night and two graduate students in the Communications Department took me to dinner at this little restaurant on Franklin Street that had all kinds of books and stuff in it. It kind of reminded me of Lubin Blvd. near Duncan. Anyway, then they took me back to my hotel. They have a hotel right on the campus and it's real close to the Communication Building, called the Carolina Inn; and it's really nice. I called Mama who of course asked me what I had eaten. I guess that's a mother's job. I went to a grad school party. They have gatherings every Wednesday night. I think that's so cool. That's where I met the Director of Graduate Studies. And one of the grad students is a bartender so you know I got my drink on. Vodka and lemonade with ice, shaken, not stirred."

"My girl."

"I got to meet all of the grad students. Some of them are graduating in May. There weren't any black students but the group was really cool. You know I've found that among my white classmates, the Radio/TV/Film-Communications people seem to be pretty liberal and less racist."

"Really? We have all kinds among the future educators. It's almost scary."

"Anyway, the next morning I went to the Department and met the other professors. You know there are but two women in the department, one black and one white. They seem really cool. We went in one of their offices and they closed the door and told me I could ask them anything I wanted to about the department. Oh, and there is a black secretary from Southwestern Michigan. Both of the secretaries gave me their home numbers and told me to call them if I needed absolutely anything."

"They sound like really good people. They are not at all like we were always told Southerners are."

"Part of that may be because of the Research Triangle Park. Everyone is from somewhere else. I went to the Union and guess who was in the Black Cultural Center?"

"Who?"

"My favorite singer."

"No."

"She was promoting a movie that was just released last week."

"Wow."

"I sat in on a few classes too. There was one, Minorities and the Media and there were beaucoup black students in that class. I was invited to a Kappa Party and a talent show so I spent Friday evening at the talent show and then this student named Cedric picked me up to go to the party at Steeplechase U. I thought they were going to stand me up at first, but they finally called. So many people wanted to go to the party he had to try to get everyone there so finally he came and picked me up."

"How was the party?"

"Goin' on girl. I've never had so much fun. Everybody was so cool. Some slims even wanted my number, but of course I don't know what it will be because I will have to find an apartment."

"Did Gwen get into Duke?"

"She hasn't heard yet. But I'd be very surprised if she didn't get in. After the Steeplechase party, we went to a Steak and Egg off the beaten trail. It was packed. That may be because half the restaurant was closed. They told me someone had driven their car through half of the restaurant so they closed that half and went on about business as usual."

"No."

"You know, the restaurant was exactly like I've always pictured that Nate's Chicken and Neckbones Hope always talks about."

"You mean Nate's Chicken, Neckbones and now Catfish."

"That's right. Anyway, after that, we went to an after set and I think I got back to my hotel at about 6:00 and I had an 8:30 meeting with this guy at the radio station. They know how to party down there.

"And the campus was beautiful. The dogwoods and this other kind of pear tree were in full bloom. The brick sidewalks reminded me of Duncan. But they didn't have a Multicultural Village."

"I can't wait to visit you."

"I got my class schedule for the Fall too. I have two classes Monday and Wednesday afternoon and two Tuesday and Thursday afternoon. I start at one on Mondays and Wednesdays and two on Tuesdays and Thursdays and I end at five every day. I have Fridays off."

"That's straight."

"Oh, how are you and Patrick?"

"I don't know Sina. Patrick is different."

"You said he was very respectful. Judging from where I've been, with the exception of Scott, that is different."

"That's not what I mean though."

"What do you mean then?"

"Patrick is—a virgin."

"What?" Sina asked with a very puzzled look on her face.

"You heard me right. He is a twenty-two-year-old virgin. Last weekend when we went shopping for Luminous' bridal shower gift, he gravitated toward housewares and became uncomfortable in the lingerie section. I picked out a few things and just held them up to me and asked him what he thought and he wouldn't even look at me."

"Nooooo."

"Have I ever lied to you?"

"No. But you know Rachel, you have to respect his wishes. He really sounds like a gem. You know, Good Ebony Man. It makes me think back to me and Conrad and how he always tried to seduce me. But I didn't fall for that at all. Anyway I just think that you need to be patient with him."

"And what am I supposed to do in the meantime?"

"Do you honestly want me to answer that?" Sina asked as she heard her door opening. "Look Rachel, I'm going to have to go, Gwen's here and I have to tell her the good news."

"Bye."

"I'll catch ya later. It's been a slice."

"Guess what Gwen," Thomasine said as her roommate put her back-pack down on the floor near her desk and took off her coat.

"What?"

"I got accepted to UNC. I got accepted," Sina said jumping up and down.

"Congratulations Sina," Gwen said hugging her.

"Once you hear from Duke. And you will. And it will be a letter of ac-ceptance. We can go down and look for an apartment. I have a nice finan-cial package so we can get a decent crib."

"This calls for a celebration. You know, Tamika and Tarsha are having a party tonight. You've got to come."

"Oh yes," Sina said as she plugged in her curling iron. "I'm just so happy. My parents were glad, but I think Mom is concerned about me going so far away."

"You'll be all right. And once I get that letter from Duke we can start decorating our apartment."

"I know that's right. Let's see, we have all of the kitchen appliances and a VCR. Maybe we can go half on a bigger TV. You know it would be a shame to put a 13" store brand TV in the living room."

"That's right. And I guess I can put up with living with you for another two years or so."

"You weren't that bad. You just poot a lot when you drink. But that's not that often."

"That's not nearly as bad as the little relief sculpture of boogers you have under your desk," Gwen said laughing while ironing. "You know, I told my parents that you pick your boogers and put them on the bottom of the desk but they don't believe me. They said, 'Not Thomasine. Why, she would never do a thing like that.'"

"That just means you can't try to use that as blackmail in the future. No one who knows me—with the exception of Kelsey, Rachel, and Tommy would ever believe that. Hope wouldn't even believe it. But at least it's not gum. Boogers dry up and fall off eventually."

"That's true. What about that scarf you snatch off your head first thing every morning."

"Now you know that's a necessity. Let's make a deal," Thomasine said as she began curling her hair. "No more booger bas reliefs if you take Tums or something before you drink so that you don't come back here pooting all night."

"Deal," Gwen said as they shook hands and hugged.

"I'm so glad I met you," Sina said. "And to think, Tommy told me that I would have to carry a mirror around with me so I wouldn't forget what Black people looked like."

"No," Gwen said laughing.

"And you were the first Black person I met here," Sina said, now combing her hair. "And contrary to popular belief, we still get along."

"I think we'll be friends for a long time—kind of like you, Rachel and Hope."

"Exactly," Sina said, now surveying her closet. "Now what should I wear tonight."

"Your suede skirt. Definitely wear your suede skirt. It'll probably be the last time you get to wear it before the weather breaks."

"You're right. And there's nothing more I can't stand than seeing somebody in suede when it's hot. It's like it's a status symbol or something."

"True dat. My cousin Lee once brought this woman to a Fourth of July cookout and she was wearing a suede suit. And the skirt was long."

"Noooo," Sina said, putting on her pantyhose. She wouldn't trust her thigh-highs in a celebration like this. "In the middle of the summer."

"Yes."

"Now that's some crazy shit."

"So was she. She was one crazy, silly heifer. The type that sets women's liberation back at least a century. You know the 'What Have You Done for Me Lately' type. And she did not a thing for my cousin, but she expected him to pay all her bills and keep her car running."

"My Momma always told me self-preservation is the first law of nature," Sina said putting on her suede skirt.

"I know that's right. How can you expect somebody else to take care of you if you aren't taking care of yourself?"

"That is so true."

"Let's hit it," Sina said, grabbing her purse. "And promise me you won't come back here pooting all night."

"I promise," Gwen said. "And promise me you won't run all up under Scott. Let him come to you."

"Promise."

Tamika and Tarsha's apartment was clear across town, quite a trek for students, but good in a way. The local police didn't follow the Beverage Store van out this far. But then the Black students never bought kegs. They just picked up a bottle here and a bottle there and when they got enough to make a mean batch of wop; then they had a party.

The apartment was nicer than most of the undergraduates' apartments. The construction was much newer than the half-century old frame houses that bordered the university. Tamika and Tarsha had a nice little hook up for college students with lots of milk crates and plastic coffee and end tables and even an etagere. "Yeah Gwen, we're gon' hook our crib up," Sina said as she walked in dancing to Technotronic's *Pump up the Jam*.

As she surveyed the room, she saw a game of Spades going strong in the dining area and people standing around talking and dancing in the living room. T & T as they were called by the other Black students, had moved all of the furniture around the edges of the room. Or just maybe they had those strapping football players move it. Did they have bodies on them or what?

"Guess what you all," Gwen said getting a cup of wop. "Sina got in UNC."

"Rock on wit yo bad self," Corey told her.

"I'm scared of you, girlfriend" Tamika said.

"I think we should propose this toast to Sina and her next two years at UNC," Gwen said.

"To Sina," everyone said raising their styrofoam cups.

"Hey, Sina," Scott said walking up to her with his baritone voice. "Congratulations. I'll have to take you to dinner to celebrate or something."

"That would be nice," Sina replied, slightly smiling just as Milli Vanilli's *Blame it on the Rain* came on.

"Would you like to dance?" Scott asked, smiling.

"This was one of our songs, why not. For old times sake," Sina said as she placed her arms on his shoulders.

"And don't be so shy either," Scott said pulling her closer and rocking her body from side to side in time with the music.

"You know, I've been meaning to call you," he said. "I think we need to go out to dinner and talk."

"I'll have to check my calendar," Sina said, trying to be coy.

"You do that," Scott said, just as he began to massage Sina's lower back.

"Telephone Sina," Tarsha shouted from the bedroom.

"Excuse me a moment Scott."

Sina took the short journey from the living room to Tarsha's bedroom. "Look I told Tyson don't be calling you over here either. You don't live here."

"Thank you very much," Sina replied taking the phone and trying to find someplace to sit on the bed covered with coats.

"What's up Tyson?"

"I need you to do Midnight to three tonight. I've got an exam tomorrow and Ayesha can't come. She's got the flu and she can barely talk."

"I'll have to find a way to get to the station, but I'll be there. Oh, by the way, I got into UNC."

"Congratulations. You know, this place is not going to be the same when you're gone. We're really going to miss you."

"I'm not gone yet. And don't rush my time away either."

"See you soon."

Sina hung up the phone and picked up the coats that fell off the bed when she sat. She carefully searched through the pile of coats and found hers. When she walked back to the living room, she searched for Gwen. "Look, I'm going to have to run," she said when she bumped into Scott. "Station emergency."

"That figures."

"Just what does that mean?" Thomasine questioned Scott. "Look I don't have time for it anyway. Have you seen Gwen?"

"Look over at the spades table. She and Tamika just ran a Boston on Corey and James."

"Gwen," Sina said once she had made her way over to the dining area. "I've got a station emergency. I gotta do the 12 to 3 shift. Do you mind if I use your car?"

"How much have you had to drink?"

"Just one cup of wop. Honest."

"Okay, here are my keys. Oh, you see Mark over there?"

"Yeah."

"Tonight, he's mine."

"I'm scared of you girl."

"Don't worry about me getting back to the dorm. I probably won't be back until the morning anyway, just before class. That is, if what I've heard about him is true. I know with you doing the 12 to 3 I'll really be able to get a groove on—you know."

"I heard that," Thomasine said taking Gwen's car keys. "And thank you."

Thomasine walked back to the Music Library which now had a few shelves just below the Contemporary Jazz albums for the Urban Sounds music. She quickly pulled all of her favorites from last semester including Christopher Max, Troy Johnson, Ten City, Joyce "Fenderella" Irby, Tammy Holt, Tyler Collins and Vesta Williams. "That's right, I'm back, Ayesha's home with a bad case of the flu, but she'll be back next week. And since you have me for tonight, we're gonna kick tonight's Contemporary Urban Sounds off with Luther Vandross' *If Only for One Night*. Only, on the Voice of the University," Sina said as she potted down her mic and potted up the music. She turned the studio monitors up so she could really get into the groove. She would have put her cans on, but being in this big building, by herself—or at least she was supposed to be by herself—made her a little cautious. She didn't want to have to break out in a Kiba dachi up in there.

Her next three hours were spent answering the phone and running into the newsroom to rip the UPI wire in between playing Rhonda Clark's *Stay Here, Stay Near* and Troy Johnson's *Love Me*. Sina breathed a sigh of relief when London called to say he was on his way to do the House show from 3 to 6. "That's gonna do it for me tonight, until next time, I'm gonna leave you with some hot new music from a group of, let's see, one, two, three, four, sisters out of California. The group is En Vogue and the song is *Don't Go* only on the Voice of the University," Sina said now realizing she could get some much needed sleep. She parked Gwen's car in the book-store lot across from her dorm and was kind of pissed off that she would have to walk all the way to the main entrance when her room was right next to the stairs which placed the first door she passed the most conve-nient for her. As she climbed up to her top bunk, Sina looked in the lower bunk for Gwen. "She must have got her some," Sina said as she fell fast asleep in her bed, not even taking time to tie the infamous scarf around her head.

As the first few rays of sunlight made their way through the small crack in between the curtains Sina heard a loud knock on the door. "That's right, I have Gwen's keys," Sina said as she climbed down from her top bunk prepared to tease Gwen about her night of creeping. "Tell me all about it," Sina said as she opened the door expecting to find Gwen, but being surprised by a tall, slender officer.

"Is this the room of Stephanie Lewis?" the man with Whittaker on his name plate said.

"Yes it is, I'm her roommate, Thomasine Mintor."

"I think you need to sit down ma'am."

"What is it? Stephanie Gwen Lewis is a good, law-abiding citizen."

"I have some very bad news to tell you. I was able to contact her par-ents in Milwaukee earlier. You see, there was an accident last night. She was a passenger in a car."

"Is she all right? Is she at Mercy Medical Center?" Sina asked jumping up.

"I'm sorry to have to tell you this first thing in the morning and all. But you see, the car she was a passenger in collided with a train. There were no survivors."

"Noooo!!!" Sina yelled. "It can't be."

"It appears alcohol may have been involved."

"No." Sina was hysterical.

"Ma'am, I'm really sorry." Officer Whittaker left the room.

"I can't believe this. It can't be," Sina said shaking her head from side to side and still crying. She picked up the phone to call her parents but her mother was probably en route to work and her father was probably visiting some sick soul in the hospital. She tried Tommy, but he wasn't home either. Rachel was probably in the shower. Finally, on the fourth try, she was able to get in touch with Hope.

"What's the matter, Sina," Hope said. "You don't sound too good."

"Gwen was killed in a car accident last night," Sina said now hyperventilating. "And it's all my fault."

"Were you driving?"

"No."

"Then you can't blame yourself. Just calm down and tell me what happened."

"We were at this party off campus last night, I wasn't going to go at first, but Gwen insisted since I got into UNC."

"Congratulations."

"Anyway, we were at the party when I got a call about a station emergency so I had to leave. Well, I didn't drive and Gwen was playing cards so she told me to take her car and she would catch a ride later. She kinda had a date."

"Okay."

"And they drove into a train."

"Why are you blaming yourself? Sina it was not your fault."

"She would have been driving her own car if it weren't for me."

"Sina, it just happened that way. You can't blame yourself. You didn't drive into the train. It's not your fault."

"It's really ironic too. Gwen almost never drinks," Sina said, quickly reflecting on it. "I mean drank. Alcohol gave her a bad case of gas," Sina said, now sobbing more and more in a crescendo. "And the officer said alcohol was responsible for the accident."

"Thomasine, I'm so sorry. If there is anything I can do for you, let me know. I'm so far away, but this is awful. Just let me know if there is anything I can do. And I mean anything."

"I guess I have some phone calls to make. I need to call Deborah and Measha. And I'll have to call her parents. Could you let Rachel know for me please?"

"Certainly. I need to call her back too, you know I just got back in town. Just walked through the door."

"That's right. Your interview with McDonald, Baker & Jackson. How did it go."

"They made me an offer with full benefits and stock options."

"I know you accepted it."

"I don't know. I have to think about it."

"What's to think about? That's a fortune compared to what I'll be getting at UNC. This is a golden opportunity."

"I'll have to talk it over with Jason."

"You do that."

Thomasine was glad to see Deborah and Measha again, but was sad about the circumstances of their reunion. Mrs. Lewis had asked Sina and Scott to sing a duet of *His Eye is on the Sparrow* and that had to be the most emotional song she had ever sung. After some reassurance from her father, Sina became more accepting of Gwen's death. Following the memorial service, Sina found herself back in her dorm room going through some of Gwen's things. She sat at Gwen's desk and shuffled through the stack of mail that had accumulated over the past few days when she saw a letter from Duke University. Tears formed in her eyes when she picked up the phone to call Gwen's mother about it. Getting a busy signal and figuring Gwen would want Sina to know if she had gotten accepted, Sina ripped open the envelope. The water in her eyes made the print a little blurry, but the words were plain. "Stephanie G. Lewis, we are pleased to inform you that you have been accepted into the Fuqua School of Business Class of '92..." *She got in,* Sina thought as her sobs turned to cries and she heard a knock at the door. "Come in," she said to whomever was stopping by to pay their condolences.

"Sina," Scott said. "I just thought I'd stop by to check on you."

"She got in Scott. She got into Fuqua at Duke. And she'll never get an MBA. All because of me."

"Sina," Scott embraced her. "It's not your fault. If you had known, I bet you would have been in that car instead of Gwen. But it's going to be all right. Just let it all out. Let it all out baby," he said as he kissed her on her forehead. "I'll stay here as long as you need me."

"Scott," Sina cried. "I miss her so much. Already," she paused to wipe her face. "We were supposed to go down to North Carolina to find an apartment and we were going to be roommates."

"It's going to be all right," Scott said putting his arm around Sina's shoulder. "Just all right."

"And it seemed like we were just really getting closer. Kind of like me, Rachel and Hope," Sina said, as her soft whimpers stabbed at his heart. "Scott, will you just hold me. That's what I need right now."

"I'm here. Whatever you need, it's yours," Scott said as he locked Sina more tightly in his embrace. "Don't you worry about a thing," he said while kissing Sina on her mouth and then neck. "Just let it out."

"Scott," Thomasine uttered. "Make love to me. Please."

"It's all right," Scott said, unzipping the back of her dress and kissing her on her neck and chest. "Everything's going to be just all right. I've missed you so much," he said as she unbuttoned his shirt and he moved down to her now flat stomach. "So much," he said, temporarily ending all conversation.

Scott helped her to her feet and watched her dress slide from her body as he fell on his knees to place himself in a very strategic spot. Sina welcomed his strokes and found herself burning with intensity as soft coloratura soprano strains flowed from her voice. An overpowering flashover! Scott ran his tongue back up her body, slowly making his way to the nook of her navel and stopping to give each breast individual attention. Looking in his eyes, Sina held him tightly. Slowly taking him to the floor and stepping out of her hose, Sina found herself straddling him, sliding his pants off his hips, down his legs and facing his feet. With the clothing that once adorned his body now cast aside, Sina began to give him the same level of attention he gave her. She gently massaged him with her tender hands until the only sound she heard was Scott's muted moans which told her he wanted more, much, much more.

Sina rolled over on her back as Scott made his way once again to her mouth and nose and neck and breast. He entered her, slowly, but gently, savoring every moment and telling Sina, "I wish I could make this moment last forever." Their souls meshed and their bodies entwined as Scott moved deeper and deeper into her inner being. It was as if the world stood still and time stood still and nothing else mattered right now but Sina and Scott. Scott and Sina were the perfect match. On one accord. The beating of their hearts provided the rhythm as their bodies moved in time. They harmonized together as each moan came from deeper and deeper within and their muffled sighs furnished the lyrical melody which rounded out their sweet symphony. And the cadence was like a backdraft, smoldering down only to burn more intensely each final second. They held each other in a tight embrace with their clothing scattered across the room and Gwen's acceptance letter just beside them.

The lakeflies had made their triumphant return to Sina's college town. With nine days to go until graduation and the Three Musketeers in the midst of finals and semester projects, a three-way-call served as a welcome relief. "Are you excited about graduation?" Rachel asked her two friends during one of their three-way exchanges. "Because I know come this time next year, I'm gonna throw down."

"Yeah, I'm excited," Sina replied. "But I'm even more excited about going down to North Carolina and experiencing a little Southern Comfort."

"I heard that," Rachel said, now giggling. "So Hope, do you have any more job leads."

"No, but I'm sure something will come along," she said. "One of my professors said something to me about a friend of his who has a firm in Kalamazoo so I just may have to check into that."

"I can't believe you turned down the chance of a lifetime in the Big Apple," Sina replied.

"Yeah, really," Rachel said. "To go to someplace like Kalamazoo."

"New York is just so far away from my family."

"So was Savannah, but you lasted and did quite well there. I hear you're graduating summa cum laude."

"My girl," Rachel said. "Do it with distinction."

"That was just not the right job for me."

"Well, I guess you really had to go with your gut feeling," Sina said. "Always go with your gut."

"So how's your love life?"

"Me and Patrick are in the same place as before. It's like we're in a holding pattern just waiting to land."

"Don't be in such a big hurry to land," Hope said. "You just might crash and burn."

"I guess you're right," Rachel replied. "Have you seen Scott lately?"

"You know, it's like he's avoiding me or something. He used to come by from time to time right after Gwen's accident then the strangest thing happened the other day."

"What?"

"I was minding my own business, walking to class and I looked up and caught a glimpse of him and then he did the strangest thing. He ran into the math building."

"That's strange. Did you do something to him?"

"Nothing he didn't want."

"Interesting."

"Well I know one thing," Sina said matter-of-factly. "It is not my problem and he is not my problem. If he wants to run a marathon away from me, that's fine."

"I can't believe you said that."

"No, I'm sick and tired of all of his silly ass little bullshit games. First he wants space, then he wants to take me to dinner, then he tells me that he's missed me and he wants to be with me forever and then he's running away from me. I have too much to do and plan to be bothered with that."

"I heard that," Rachel replied. "Don't waste your time girl. Because if he loved you he would be right by your side, especially after all that you've been through."

"And he never took me to dinner either," Sina said picking up her calendar. "And it's been at least three, four, five, six, seven weeks since," she said turning her calendar back to March and noticing the red T she writes on the calendar to indicate the arrival of her monthly visitor. "Shit," she said scrutinizing the April calendar for that red T. "I have to go," Sina said with no explanation. She hung up the phone and went to her top dresser drawer for her pack of birth control pills.

It was dated March 9, 1990. She remembered having her period last when she was in North Carolina, and it appeared the last pill she took was on the first Thursday of the cycle. "No," she protested as if she were warding off an attacker. She sat and counted the weeks over and over. With the stress of Gwen's untimely death and her upcoming graduation, it hadn't even dawned on Sina that she hadn't taken her pills and that she might be pregnant. How would she tell Scott, when he was running away from her on campus? What would she do? Abortion was not an option for her. But she wasn't ready for motherhood. And Scott didn't seem to be that interested in her. She had to call him. And she had to call him now. Sina picked up the phone and frantically dialed his number. "Everything happens for a reason," boomed Scott's baritone voice from the answering machine. "And there's a reason you called this number. So tell it. At the beep. Peace."

"Damn, damn, damn," Sina said as she waited for the beep. Those few seconds seemed to last an eternity. "Look Scott, I have to talk to you. It's very important. Let's meet at Tortilla Flats tomorrow at 12. I have a test in my nine o'clock so I'll be finished by then. I'll see you there."

All the time Sina should have spent studying for her Weather and Climate final was spent worrying about her condition. Then she thought about Gwen and this baby, and the conception and how her father said someone dies and someone is born every minute. But she didn't know how she would face her family, or Front Street, or Hope and tell them she was pregnant with another man's child who wants nothing to do with her. The thought of it all made Sina tear up. "I am not going to cry. I am not going to cry. I am not going to cry," she sang as she fell asleep.

The next morning Sina rushed off to her exam, hoping and praying that she wouldn't fail it. That would put a damper in her graduation plans. She could repeat the course, in summer school. When Sina took the final all she could think about was babies and what her child would look like and if she would still be able to go to UNC in the fall and what Scott would say. After answering the only questions she could, Sina made her way to the station to give them her write-up in which she almost wrote she had a baby due in January. From the station she walked over to the parking lot and drove over to Planned Parenthood to get the real verdict. Again, that journey from her car in the parking lot to the receptionist's desk seemed like the longest.

"Miss, may I help you," the carrot-topped woman with freckles asked.

"I would like to have a pregnancy test."

"You're going to have to come back first thing Monday morning. We need the first urine sample of the day," she said making Thomasine even more edgy. "But we can take some information now. First your name, and have you been here before?"

"Thomasine Mintor."

"Let's see, Thomasine," the woman asked as she thumbed through the information cards. "When was your last menstrual period?"

"March 13."

"Have you had unprotected sex with more than one partner?"

"No, just one partner."

"When was your last HIV test?"

HIV Test, Thomasine thought. "I've never had one."

"How about your partner?" the woman asked. "When was his last test and what were the results?"

"I don't know."

The woman's questions just caused Thomasine's pregnancy scare to turn into a nightmare. Could that be why Scott avoided her so? Could he be afraid he had given Sina a deadly disease? *Not the Scott who told me last fall he would never do anything to a woman he didn't want done to his sis-*

ters. She said as she drove down Main Street and found a space in Tortilla Flats' lot.

"I'll have a Mexican Jade," Thomasine told the waitress hoping she wouldn't get carded. "I'm waiting for someone. I'll order when he gets here."

Pregnant. AIDS. AIDS/HIV. Pregnant. Words outside the realm of Sina's vocabulary for so long, but right now all she could think about. How would she make it through the weekend not knowing? *And how will I tell Scott?* He walked up to the table.

"Sina," Scott asked, cutting to the chase. " What could be so important?"

"I guess I'll just be direct. I have something to ask you and something to tell you," she said figuring why should she spend her weekend worrying alone. "And I'll start with the question," she said as the waitress walked up.

"I'll have a shredded beef cheese crisp," Sina said. "Oh, and another Mexican jade."

"Give me the chicken burrito platter," Scott said. "And I'll have a Margarita on the rocks."

"Now what is this you have to ask me and tell me," he said, appearing slightly irritated.

"First, when was your last HIV test?"

"HIV?" Scott said with a puzzled look on his face. "I don't have no HIV."

"When was your last test?" Sina asked, now insistent as the waitress put the drinks down on the table.

"Why are you asking me this?"

"Because we didn't use anything that afternoon in my room. And I mean absolutely nothing. And now I'm late Scott," Sina said as a shocked Scott spit his Margarita out in fast short spurts. "And don't you even try to think that this is some sick scheme to get you back," Sina added. "Because trust me. If it weren't for this, I surely wouldn't be talking to you right now. Especially after how you've treated me. Running away from me and stuff."

"It was a mistake Sina."

"My biggest ever. That is next to giving that damn Conrad Thompson my phone number. Look, particularly given the circumstances I'm really sorry it happened, but we are going to have to make some plans."

"Okay, let's look at this rationally. I don't have any HIV symptoms so I'm probably not HIV positive. And are you sure you're pregnant?"

"That is so stupid," Sina said, taking a swig of her Mexican Jade. "There aren't any symptoms for HIV first of all and I can't get through this weekend on probabilities. I'm three damn weeks late Scott. And there was only one other time I was late. And guess what, I was pregnant?"

"Pregnant!" Scott exclaimed with his brows arched in surprise. "I guess I find out more and more about you as time goes by. You never told me you were ever pregnant."

"But what about our child, Scott? What are we going to do about our child?"

"That's simple. You are too young to be a parent Thomasine. I will give you the money for an abortion."

"Abortion!"

"That's right. I don't want to be a father, and you surely aren't ready to be mother," Scott said. "That's the best thing for all parties involved. You can go on to graduate school and on with your life."

"Maybe that's the best thing for you. But for me and my child. I will make that decision since you have just relinquished your decision making rights with talk of an abortion," Sina said rising up from the table. "Not me, and not my child. Not ever."

Sina spent her last weekend before graduation in her room, in the dark, crying. While all of her other classmates were out partying and celebrating, she separated herself from the rest of the world, taking a breather only to order some take out. She was eating pizza and drinking vodka and lemonade. As she went to pour the vodka into the lemonade she thought twice. *I can't do this. Not to my child. I just can't.* She tuned out the ringing of the phone and the knocks on her door.

Okay, Sina said as she pulled out her typewriter to write the final scene for her Advanced Screenwriting course. *Get yourself out of this rut. The end is in sight.* She took a bite of the pizza she had ordered the night before. "Okay, let's see. How should I end this?" she asked herself. "Should I have a happy ending, a tragic ending or hmmm—a cliffhanger?" She began to type on her electric typewriter. "Oh," she moaned and grabbed her stomach. "I guess I should have put this pizza in the fridge," she said as she got up to go to the bathroom. *I guess I deserve to be sick for eating this day old unrefrigerated pizza.*

She walked in the bathroom, slightly hunched over, and the other women made a speedy exit because they just knew she'd be in there a long time. Needless to say, Sina was pleased with the results.

"Scott," Sina said from the telephone as she looked out the window of her dorm.

"Just where have you been all weekend Sina? I've called, I came by and

I got no answer. I owe you a really big apology. I've really been thinking and it was wrong for me to suggest to you to get an abortion," he said taking a seat on the sofa. "We'll work this out. And I'll be here for you. I promise."

"Scott, I got my period, I got my period," Sina said in a sing-song voice, now realizing that she had been so excited that she had yet to take time to address her condition with certain feminine hygiene products.

"That's great Sina. But I've been doing some thinking. And I would like for us to give our relationship another chance."

"Look Scott," Sina said, thinking about his recent treatment of her. "I've got a script to finish and a graduation party to plan," she said and then paused. "Oh, and Scott," she said smiling, "Have a nice life," she said hanging the phone up.

Graduation day was just about as bizarre as the last few months had been for Sina. Early, the morning before graduation, some jerk pulled the fire alarm. This seemed to be a normal occurrence each semester just prior to the last day of exams. And an excellent opportunity to find out who was creeping. Sina put on her coat and sneakers and grabbed her car keys. She couldn't believe what she saw when she went outside. Freezing rain. In May. And some of the residents came outside in shorts and shower thongs, or worse, no shoes at all. Sina just walked across the street and got in her car until she saw the others walk back into her building. She was even more surprised when she woke up the next morning to move her car and found the campus blanketed with snow. But Thomasine Mintor didn't let that spoil her commencement. Her family was so proud of her. Kelsey, Tommy, Trevaughn, Aunt Carla and Uncle Sandifer, Rachel, and of course Sina's parents came up for her graduation. Scott even came and brought her a card. Everyone was there except one person. "Where's Aunt Mary?" Sina asked Rachel as they walked to the gymnasium for the commencement exercise.

"Her Chicago Bulls are in the playoffs. The way she's acting you'd think she owned the team or something. She said she just couldn't miss the game."

Love Under New
Management

21

A s Thomasine neared Louisville, she made special note to look for the sign leading her to I-65. *Stay in the correct lane so that you don't end up like you did when you came down to find an apartment.* In the summer of 1990, Sina summoned enough courage to drive her new Nissan Stanza to Durham. Her family was hesitant about her driving so far by herself and Tommy even volunteered to go along, but after all Thomasine had endured the past few months, a good long drive was just what she needed. Sina reassured her parents that she would call every time she stopped for gas and food. Her father mapped out the route. "Take 94 to Gary and look for 65. Stay on I-65 through Indiana and when you get near Kentucky look for the signs for I-64 East to Lexington. Make sure you're in the right lane too because one lane stays on 65, one goes to 64 and the other will take you to 71 and you don't want to go there. When you get to Lexington look for 75 South, which will take you to Knoxville. While you're there, stop and call your cousin Trevaughn. Get on I-40 East and that will take you straight to Chapel Hill."

Thomasine listened to her father, but when she got to the bridge over the Ohio River, she was jamming to Tony Toni Tonē's *Feels Good* and the next thing she knew she was headed for Nashville. "Oh, what to do, what to do," Sina said, thinking out loud. She decided to just stay on that route. *I'm sure to see a road to Lexington soon.*

Sina had no problem finding an apartment in southwest Durham. She opted for a two-bedroom townhouse, hoping that she'd get a roommate before classes started. A straight shot down 15-501, from the South Square area to Franklin Street, Sina said as she drove back to her hotel after signing a lease. She was surprised at all of the action on Franklin Street and the UNC campus given that it was summer. Her undergraduate campus did not have this much action in the heart of the semester.

Sina had anxiously awaited her 21st birthday since she was a college freshman. That meant she never had to sneak in another club or bar. Now she'd be able rent cars with some agencies. Now she was an adult. And most of all, for Sina, she could now buy liquor without having to go to one of those neighborhood stores who charged over $5 for a four pack of wine coolers because they knew buyers weren't legal. And that was exactly what she did on her 21st birthday. Sina stopped off in the drugstore on her way to work on her birthday and grabbed a fifth of Absolut Citron, proudly handed the cashier the bottle. The brown-skinned, middle-aged, woman with a grandma figure stared at Thomasine as if to say "I know you can't be any older than 19." She was disappointed when the woman didn't even bother to ask for her license.

Sina had saved that special bottle for the going away party Hope and Rachel had given her. Hope's parents were out of town for the weekend so they partied as hard as Hope would allow. Sina finally got a chance to meet Rachel's Patrick and he had looks to go along with a sweet personality. He and Rachel talked every day, at 9:30, alternating days to save money. One evening his brother got tickets to a St. Louis Cardinals' night game which meant he would be out way past 9:30. Patrick was so considerate that he called Rachel that afternoon to tell her he was going to a game—being a big Sox fan herself, she wished she could have been there with him. But he didn't call to tell her he was going to the game. He called to tell her he would not be at home at 9:30 and he didn't want her to think that he was blowing her off. He wanted her to know that he cared for and respected her. Now is that sweet or what? Patrick was tall, about 6 feet, with skin the color of oak and smooth as velvet. He had knowing eyes and a box haircut. Hank had come along too. It was a good thing because he and Jason paired up against Sina and Rachel to get their butts beat in Spades. Patrick and Hope didn't want to have anything to do with cards, and even less with that bottle of liquor Sina had brought. But just like Tommy said when Sina had a cookout for her 15th birthday and invited as many people, but only Rachel and Hope showed up, "That's just more for me." Even Jason had a little nip.

Rachel and Hope awakened early that morning to see Sina off. And as usual, Rex ran off. The dog must have had some sort of Sina-is-leaving radar in him or something. "Have you heard anything about that position in Kalamazoo yet?" Sina asked Hope as they walked toward her car. Both her car and her father's car were loaded up with Sina's belongings so as much as the Mintors would have liked to offer Hope and Rachel to ride along, they couldn't. Sina had so much baggage.

"I haven't heard anything definite, but my professor back at Harrington said they should have an opening soon. Someone's retiring."

"Just keep me posted," Sina told Hope as she hugged her good bye. "Now ya'll have my phone number?" Sina asked hugging Rachel and practicing a little southern drawl.

"Yes," they said in unison.

"Well, use it," Thomasine said getting into her loaded car and starting the motor. "I expect to hear from you."

Sina was pleased with her apartment, her courses and the ease with which she was able to get around between Chapel Hill and Durham. The heat bothered her though. After attending T.A. orientation and being advised on her class selection and registration procedures, she found herself inside a hot gymnasium with tables all around and fans and water coolers placed strategically throughout. She stood in a long line to register, only to be told that new graduate students were to register at 2PM and not 10 A.M.. Knowing that if she went back to her cool apartment she probably wouldn't come back to register, Sina decided to hang out on campus. She just wouldn't come back. Not in this heat. This campus was much larger than her old one. She was impressed by the buses which ran on a schedule she could set her watch to. Buses to South campus, to the Airport Road lot and one that just ran around the campus in a loop.

When Sina crossed South Road and walked up the stairs between the Student Union and Student Stores she was amazed at the number of students out and about in that area called "The Pit." There were several little folding tables from various organizations, supporting causes ranging from Recycling to Voter Registration and everything else in between. Sina made her way through the maze of student activists, impressed at the level of activity so early in the day and week before classes even started. Here it was Monday, and classes didn't even start until Wednesday. The students had just moved back in the dorms on Sunday, and already, campus was abuzz. "This campus is never dead," she overheard from a short, distinguished looking man with a receding hairline carrying a nylon attache case. It was only ten in the morning but it felt like ninety degrees in the shade. Sina sought refuge in the Davis Library. It was eight stories tall so she figured there would be plenty of space for her to cool off.

Thomasine learned her first rule about UNC libraries really quickly. Always wear rubber soled shoes. As she walked down the aisle beside the stacks looking for a table wearing her sandals, virtually everyone looked at her as if to say, "Could you be a little more quiet." She found an empty table. She did not understand why the library was so occupied before classes even started. People there were deep into books, scholarly journals and folios. Sina sat down and put the tapestry floral attache case her Aunt sent her for graduation on the table and pulled out a pen and her leather portfolio pad. On the first sheet of paper she wrote a list of names, Kelsey, Rachel, and Hope. She had more than three hours to kill and wanted to grab a bite to eat before she went to register because she could tell by the looks of things that it would not be a simple process.

August 27, 1990

Dear Hope,

I love North Carolina and the South. It's just too hot here. I know what you meant when you described it when you first went to Harrington. Would you believe it was so hot that a plastic cassette case melted in my car? It has been 90 or above every day. But the people are so nice and friendly. And since we're on the subject of the South, what is a Pig and Chicken Pickin'? I guess you've heard of it before. When I was invited, I said, "What on earth?" But I guess I'll find out in due time. I understand the Black Graduate Student Organization is having one sometime in September. It should be interesting.

Have you heard anything about that job? I really hope it comes through. You have worked so hard and you're so smart. You really deserve it. I hear the NFL Scouts are really looking at Jason. Once he gets drafted and signs a contract you'll get that ring you deserve. Who knows? Maybe seven carats for the seven years you've been together. What are you doing for your anniversary? If you can last seven years then marriage ought to be a piece of cake. I really want you to have a great job and just a great life. After all the misery I experienced in the last year, and you only know the half of it, I'm seeking my own happiness. And I want to see all of my sisters happy too.

Oh, I almost forgot to tell you about my apartment. I just love it. The community is well landscaped. There is pampas grass. Oh, and birds wake me up every morning in the tree just outside my window. It's 2 bedroom, 1½ baths. The bedrooms and full bath are upstairs. And I bought 2 full sized beds so that you and Rachel will have someplace to stay when you visit. When you come in you're in the dining room, and I got a little dinette set to go in there. Then there's the kitchen and directly across the hall from it is the bathroom. My kitchen came with a dishwasher and a mi-

crowave. And the living room is a nice size. I got a sofa with a floral print in there and a coffee table that I put my stereo on. You
know I have to have my music. I found a church in the yellow
pages too. Actually it was one Daddy suggested because he knows
the pastor, Rev. Anna Grace. She used to be one of his assistants.
The name of the church is Oaks of Righteousness African Christian Church and they have an 8:00 service. I didn't go this Sunday,
then I felt a little guilty. I really should have gone because there
was nothing else for me to do but watch TV. I got cable hooked up
Saturday and I have HBO and Cinemax at least for one month
since the first month is free. So I spent Sunday watching TV and
eating, not because I was hungry, but because it was time for me
to eat. I'll be glad when classes start so I won't be so bored.

I tried to go to Sears at Northgate Mall Saturday to get a dryer
so I can wrap my hair, but I got lost and ended up on the Durham
Freeway. I nearly panicked because I looked up and I didn't see
anything but trees. It was scary because I thought I was on my
way to Greensboro. But then I saw a sign for I-40 to Chapel Hill
and I was all right. That is one thing I don't like, all those trees.
They scare me. Someone could kill somebody and throw them
back in those trees and they will never be found. It gets so dark at
night here too. The roads aren't as well lit as they are in Chicago.

I haven't found a roommate yet, but I don't think I want one.
I really enjoy my solitude. I feel that I'm really starting to know
myself. And too, it would just be so hard trying to get used to
someone else in Gwen's room. Well, I gotta run and grab a bite to
eat before I register. But I promise I will drop this in the mail on
my way home. There's a post office down the street from me.

Sisterly,
Sina

"Excuse me ma'am," a tall man with hazel eyes, peanut butter brown
skin, and a brilliant smile said to Sina. "Do you mind if I sit at this end of
the table?"

"Not at all," Sina said as she folded her letter to Hope and put her belongings in her attache. "I was just leaving."

Hope stared at the boxes surrounding her in her new apartment in
Kalamazoo. "Will this process ever end?" She went to her kitchen to make
tea and grabbed a donut. She set them on her coffee table and sat on the

couch and began to remove items from her box marked AKA. Hope had gotten her kitchen, bedroom and dining room together first, as she felt they were the most important. So far, she liked her new job with Nelson, Ware & Associates. It didn't pay what the New York job paid, but then the cost of living wasn't as high. The one thing Hope had done in the living room was to place pictures of her and Jason, Rachel and Sina on the mantlepiece and hang the portrait of her and Jason on the wall just above the fireplace. Taking a bite out of her crueller, she carefully unwrapped her AKA paraphernalia and organized it by shelf for her AKA corner which would go just beside the fireplace. Jason had picked out a queen-sized bedroom suite for Hope, but practice and the start of football season limited his time there. Hope picked out a cherry dining room table with Queen Anne chairs. And she only wanted the best in kitchenware—Oneida, Mikasa and Circulon. Although she was a little lonely, she had plenty to do before Rachel arrived. After making the living room look a little less like a disaster zone, Hope jotted a list of the other items she needed to buy and how much she wanted to pay for them. She had plans to set up her den as an office with a futon or a sleeper sofa, but since futons really weren't Hope's style, she scratched it off her list. Hope was one who always bought quality items for as little as possible. She was crafty too at the art of negotiation, getting her bedroom suite and dining room furniture for slightly below $1,000. "So what, the four poster bed has a scratch at the bottom of the headboard. No one will see it," she told Jason just before she asked the salesman how much he would take off. "And that scratch on the dresser," she said, examining the floor plan of her apartment and realizing it would be right next to the wall. "How much will you take off for that?" Her mother drove up earlier in the week and when Hope came home from work, there were a sofa, loveseat, coffee and end tables already arranged in the living room. With that done, Hope had the money she needed to buy that computer she wanted so badly. She could make money on the side doing statistical analysis. Once she placed the last box from her living room in her storage closet on the balcony, she heard a knock at the door. "Rachel," she yelled as she waddled through the living room to the front door. She hugged Rachel and offered her one of her French crullers, which Rachel declined. Aunt Mary had fixed her breakfast before. she left Chicago. Besides, Rachel couldn't stand those things.

"Your place is so nice. And you asked me to come here to help decorate. It doesn't look like much else needs to be done."

"I still need to set up the den," Hope said. "Oh, and I need to get some towels and stuff for the kitchen and bathroom. Just let me jump in the shower. And Rachel, make yourself at home."

Rachel sat back on the sofa and inhaled deeply. "Hope's in Kalamazoo, and Sina's got her own crib in NC. I wonder where I'll be this time next year." She picked up the remote control and flipped through the channels. Finding mostly cartoons on, she decided to turn it off. *What's taking Hope so long?* She went into the kitchen and looked in each cabinet for a plastic tumbler for juice but could not find one. Hope didn't have a plastic cup in her apartment, except for that pink and green one in her AKA corner. Rachel reached up into the cabinet and was amazed at how heavy the glass in Hope's cabinet was. The glasses were all the same, just different sizes. "Oh well," Rachel said. "Aunt Mary wouldn't let Hank and me drink out of anything this nice unless it was a special holiday." Rachel was surprised to see how well stocked Hope's refrigerator was. She had orange juice and grapefruit juice, eggs, milk, ketchup, mustard, mayo and three kinds of salad dressings. A well stocked, see-through fruit bin, a package of bacon on the bottom shelf alongside the lunch meat, cheese, and a loaf of bread. On the second shelf, a refrigerated cake and a sweet potato pie. It looked like one of Mrs. Jones' pies. And the top shelf was well stocked with Diet Coke. As if that would really make any difference. Rachel poured her juice and could only imagine what the freezer looked like. She was certain Hope had vanilla ice cream to go with the sweet potato pie. When Rachel poured her juice, she noticed her friend's favorites on the top of the fridge — French Crullers.

As Rachel took her last sip of juice, Hope walked in the living room, "I'm ready," she said. "Let's go." But Rachel didn't know what was in store for them. By the time they had finished shopping Rachel was amazed at how much Hope had bought.

"You must not have a credit limit," Rachel said as they brought in all of the towels, comforters and office supplies Hope had purchased.

"I need these things to set up my apartment. You know, to make it more like a home," she insisted. "By the way, do you think you can stay until Monday afternoon. Just so I won't have to ask the apartment office to let the delivery men in? I want the sleeper sofa here," she said of the area just in front of the window. "The desk goes here, and the file cabinet here. Oh, and remind me to give you a few extra dollars so they will set up the computer. It would take me forever, and besides, Jason can't come see me for a while with his football and all."

"No problem," Rachel said. "Classes don't really start for me until Thursday since I only have Tuesday and Thursday classes. You know we start on Wednesday."

"I know. Jason told me. So are you student teaching this year?"

"Yes. That'll start in a few weeks," Rachel said with a twinkle in her eye thinking about how she would finally be able to get her feet wet in the job she had been pursuing since she was six. "Hope," she began. "Does Sina know you got the job yet?"

"Oh my goodness. I haven't even called her. And she wrote me before I moved from Chicago. She is going to kill me," Hope continued. "Now just where did I put her number."

"I've got it in my phone book," Rachel said sitting down on the couch and opening her purse. "Here it is."

"I bet Sina isn't even home," Hope said. "You know, with it being Saturday night and all."

"Well dial her anyway," Rachel insisted. "At least she'll know you still care."

"Hello," Sina said, anxious that someone was calling her and hoping they weren't trying to sell anything.

"Sina."

"Hope? It's so good to hear from you finally," Sina continued. "What's going on? Did you get the job? How are you and Jason? Have you talked to Rachel lately?" Sina bombarded her with questions.

"Rachel's right here, I'm going to give her this phone and I'll go in my bedroom. And we can have a real three-way. Just hold on a second."

"So how's Carolina treating you," Rachel asked, excited to hear her friend's voice.

"I can't complain. I can't complain at all," Sina said. "What's the weather like in Chicago? You know I'm coming for Fall Break first weekend in October."

"You are?" Rachel said. "I can't wait to see you. Oh, Hope has something to tell you."

"I got the job," Hope said, sounding only mildly excited. "I started at the beginning of the week; oh, and I'm calling you from my new apartment. Rachel's here helping me decorate."

"Ooh," Sina replied. "Tell me all about it."

"It's one bedroom, one bath with a den. It has a fireplace a vaulted ceiling and a skylight."

"I'm scared of you girl."

"It's real nice," Rachel interjected.

"Oh, and it's on the southwestern side of town. I'm not that far from Western Michigan U and Crossroads Mall. Right off I-94."

"And I had no problem finding it," Rachel said. "Oh Hope, did you hear Sina say she'd be here the first weekend in October?"

"Yeah, I will have to come up and check out your apartment. I have a flight Wednesday evening. My prof even canceled class because so many of us are going out of town. And I come back Sunday evening."

"That will be great," Rachel said. "We can drive up Friday afternoon."

"The first weekend in October," Hope said as if she were trying to remember something. "That's Duncan's first home game. You know those scouts will be there looking at Jason. And now that I'm so close, I bought tickets for all of the games."

"Why didn't you just buy season tickets?"

"Because then I couldn't sit with Rachel."

"That's right. My student fees pay for those tickets so I will not buy season tickets."

"I heard that," Sina replied. "Rachel, why don't you pick me up a ticket for that game. It'll be fun."

"I'll do that."

"Say, Sina, how are your classes going? How do you like UNC?" Hope asked.

"It's great. I'm thinking of declaring Performance Studies as my concentration and I'm going to get a certificate in Women's Studies. My cohort goes out every Wednesday after class to this neat little bar and grill in the middle of a street in Carrboro for 25¢ chicken wings and the best lemonade and vodka. And then on Thursday I meet with my Black Women's Graduate Student Support Group."

"I bet in graduate school you need all the support you can get," Rachel interjected. "What I want to know is just how is the Southern comfort?"

"Somehow I knew you'd ask that Rachel," Sina said. "And it's interesting you should ask. Last night I went to the Black Graduate Student Pig and Chicken Pickin' and did the most clumsiest thing. I was so embarrassed."

"What did you do?" Hope asked.

"My question is, what on earth is a pig and chicken pickin'?" Rachel interrupted.

"Here when they barbecue they roast a pig and when it's done, you pick off whatever part you want. They had chicken too which I had. You know I like me some pork, but I thought the chicken was a little more sanitary."

"I'm waiting," Hope said. "I want to know what you did."

"Anyway, I had fixed my plate and picked up my punch when I accidentally bumped into this slim and spilled his plate all over him."

"Oh no," Rachel said.

"Actually it wasn't that bad. Their barbecue sauce is vinegar based and very thin. Now if it had been our barbecue sauce, it would have been one grand mess."

"Well what did he say?" Hope asked.

"All he said, and his name is Kenneth, was, 'I've seen you somewhere before.' And there I was embarrassed, apologizing and everything and he didn't even seem to care. So I went back over to my table with some of my friends from the support group and was minding my own business eating and enjoying my chicken when he came back to my table."

"No," Rachel said.

"And he just said, 'The library. That's where I've seen you before. The library.' And he turned around and left just like that. I guess he was paying me back because when I had written the letter to you Hope, he came to the table where I was and asked if he could share it. And I told him, sure, he could have the whole table, that I was about to leave."

"It all sounds interesting."

"Well I saw him again as I was going to my car. We were on the same bus. Do you believe I have to park my car two miles off campus and take a bus in?"

"And?" Rachel asked as if she were trying to get some juice

"We chatted on the bus and he said he'd like to take me to lunch."

"So?" Hope asked now getting in on it too.

"So, I just got back from lunch and a movie."

"Where'd you go?" Hope asked, as if she were familiar with the Triangle area restaurants.

"What did you see?" Rachel asked simultaneously.

"I met him at a Jazz Cafe in Cary. You know I didn't want him to know where I live yet. You have to be extra careful when you're a single woman living by yourself," Sina responded. "And we saw *Mo' Better Blues*."

"So tell me about Kenneth," Rachel said, almost giddy.

"He's a second year MBA student. That sounds like one intense program too. He's an officer in the Network of Black Graduate Students in the Triangle. It includes UNC, Duke, North Carolina Central, Steeplechase, and N.C. State. He's from a small town called Selma, not in Alabama, right here in North Carolina. He loves Jazz so that gives us plenty to talk about. You know I got my radio start in Jazz."

"So," Rachel started. "Are you going to see him again?"

"I'll put it this way. Just maybe by the time I'm with you in Chicago, he'll know where I live. He wants to go out tomorrow but I told him I have other plans."

"So what are you doing tonight?"

"I'm getting ready to watch *Twin Peaks*. You know that's my show now. Besides I have to get up early for 8 o'clock service."

"Have you joined the choir yet?" Rachel asked. "Because I know they'll be glad to have you."

"No, I go to church because I have to deal with so many different personalities during the week that I just feel like I need to go to the altar and pray. That's pretty much it right now. I don't want to overextend myself either. I'm doing voiceovers on the side and right now that's enough."

"I really don't blame you because I hear grad school can be rough."

"Rough to say the least. I find myself reading articles two and three times before I even discover what they are about. For some of them I have to have a dictionary by my side. But I guess it's just this academic jargon; once I get the hang of it, it won't be a breeze, but it will be more manageable."

"I heard that."

"Look," Sina said. "I'm going to have to go. My show is coming on."

On that beautiful October afternoon the Three Musketeers finally made it to their seats after waiting in line after line of traffic and people to get into the stadium. There were vendors all over selling those green and white pennants, pom pons, T-shirts, caps, and foam #1 hands. Little girls who could barely walk wore Duncan cheerleader uniforms, and posters from a recent *Sun-Times* back page article titled "The Real McCoy," were plastered everywhere.

"We're live at Harding Memorial Stadium on the Duncan University campus for the national broadcast of this explosive match up between the Duncan University Spartans and the Lake Effect State Bobcats. The Spartans are up 21-13. That Jason McCoy is dynamic. He ran for 33 yards to put the Spartans up," the play analyst said over the loudspeaker.

"That's right," the play-by-play announcer said. "He is one hot prospect. Expect to see him in the NFL."

"Now on to the second half."

"So!" Rachel started as she sat from doing the wave with the other fans. "Did you let Kenneth know where you live yet?"

"Yes, but I'm taking things slow, real slow," Sina replied. "I actually wouldn't mind being in — what did you call it? A holding pattern for a while. Because I've crashed and burned too many times already."

"That's right," Hope interjected. "Just take your time. Jason and I have. You don't have to put out for him to hold on."

"Wait a minute," Rachel said startled by what Hope had just disclosed. "You mean you and Jason haven't—you're still a virgin?"

"Sometimes I wish I still was," Sina said. "You know, when I look back, it wasn't worth it. Pregnancy, pregnancy scares, oh and with AIDS. I don't know about you, but I ain't playing no more. My cousin Kelsey lost her college roommate to AIDS. And that is no joke."

"Wow."

"The girl's family just wrote her off. How can a family do that to their own?"

"I can't believe that," said Rachel. "Some families treat their convicted murderers better than that."

"So Kelsey was there by her side until her death," Sina continued. "And now she is starting up her own nonprofit agency for women of color with HIV and AIDS. She calls it Sisterfriends.

"Girl, that Jason can sure run fast," Sina said as she watched Jason elude his defenders to gain a first down. "And he can move. You know I haven't seen him play since high school."

"Yeah," Rachel and Hope, cheered as they heard the others around them.

"What just happened Sina?" Rachel asked.

"Duncan just got a first down."

"Go Duncan, Go Duncan, Go Duncan," Rachel chanted after the fact.

"Yeah, girl, by the looks of things I wouldn't be surprised if you got a ten-carat ring," Sina told Hope while admiring Jason's play. "When he gets drafted in June and signs that contract, don't forget about us little people."

"You all know you'll be my best friends forever," Hope said hugging Rachel and Sina.

"The Spartans are on their 45-yard line. The ball is snapped, McCoy catches it."

"What a beautiful pass," the play analyst interrupted.

"Look at him go, he's on the 40,—the 35—the 30 yard line, and he 's out of bounds."

"Good move on McCoy's part. The Bobcat's Romanizak was right on his heels. And at 280, he looks like he could even put a hurting on the Fridge."

"First down and 10."

"Okay," the analyst said. "If McCoy gets the ball, the game is as good as 27-13. It looks like this will be another Duncan victory."

"Don't you hate when they say that stuff," the short fat man with a stomach that lapped over his belt, turned and said to the trio. "Now he'll probably fumble the ball or be intercepted or something. Just because he said that. I hate commentators. They are always hexing something."

"On the 30 yard line, the Spartan quarterback, Blide, hands the ball off to McCoy. He's on the 25-the 20-the 15," the play-by-by announcer said as the crowd rose to its feet. "At the ten, and he's down, hit by Romanizak."

"That was a pretty hard hit. That Romanizak is pretty fast for his size."

"McCoy's down, he's not getting up."

"Oh, look at his leg. That was one nasty hit. His knee must have been locked when he was hit. He'll be out for the rest of the game."

"By the looks of things—," the play by play announcer said as the trainers and team doctor came onto the field with a wheelchair, "—he'll be out for the rest of the season. You know, knee injuries are the worse. They can end your career."

When Sina and Rachel looked at Hope, tears were flowing down her face.

"I'm sure it's not as bad as it looks," Rachel said, trying to stop the stream.

"And everything will work out just right," Sina said. "You know, Jason is no dummy."

Thomasine turned onto the cul-de-sac and looked for #22. She was so happy to finally get to Hampton to see her cousin Kelsey. She just knew she would have made several trips by now as it was only a 4½ hour drive from Durham. "Here it is," she said as she parked her car in the space marked "V" for visitor and got her bag out the back seat. She walked up the short walkway and rang the doorbell. She hadn't been able to spend any real time with Kelsey since she was small.

"Hey Boo," Kelsey said, hugging her younger cousin. "You're looking good girl. Much better than you did when I came up in May. Korrin, Sina is here."

"I feel a lot better too."

"Let me take your bag and coat," Kelsey's husband Korrin said.

"The turkey's in the oven." Kelsey walked to the living room and sat on the sofa in front of the fireplace. "So little cuz, tell me how things are in NC."

"Well, we have about two weeks to go before finals. But I don't have any exams. Just papers and projects to finish. Got a small paper that's due Monday knocked out of the way. That's why I couldn't leave until this morning. I registered for a class in "Performance Traditions of Women of Color," for the Spring, along with three others. I'm in a support group of

Black Women Graduate Students. We'd be meeting this evening if we had school. It's a good group too, we get-together whenever N.C. Central's theatre department puts on a play and have a potluck and then go to the play as a group."

"Speaking of support groups, did you get your letter of interest in?"

"Sure did, and guess what," Sina said. "I heard the Alumnae chapter is supposed to have a line in the spring. Anyway, school's great and I think it was just what I needed. You know it's like I feel free now."

"You were so burdened down in Wisconsin," Kelsey said, turning to face her cousin. "With the baby and your roommate dying and everything."

"You're right," Sina said, pausing. "You know sometimes I wonder—"

"About your daughter?"

"Yes. I wonder what she looks like, her first words, her favorite foods and games. I don't know, Kelsey. I wonder if I made my decision too hastily."

"I know you will think about her from time to time. She'll always be in your heart. But I think you did the right thing by giving her to a loving family."

"I suppose you're right. But I can't help wondering."

"I'm sure she has a far better life," Kelsey continued. "You were only 19. There was only so much you could provide for her."

"You know, now that I think about it, we both have better lives."

"Yes you have," Kelsey said. "How are your friends Rachel and Hope?"

"Rachel is doing just fine. She's doing her student teaching and she's in love with this grad student named Patrick. I think he's studying counseling."

"Is Hope still with that Jason?" Kelsey asked as she heard the timer go off and walked into the kitchen.

"She sure is. I told you about him getting injured and all didn't I?" Sina said as she followed Kelsey.

"Well no, but Korrin did. He saw the game on TV. He said that he probably wouldn't be back."

"That's what Tommy said too. You know he played football when he was in college up in Iowa," Sina said. "Jason had to have surgery. I think Hope told me it was the anterior cruciate ligament or something like that."

"Sounds serious," Kelsey said taking the turkey out of the oven.

"That is one pretty bird," Sina said. "Do you need my help with anything?"

"Yes," Kelsey responded. "Cia, come on down and set the table," Kelsey called to her stepdaughter.

"Let's see, Here are the serving bowls, if you could just get the food in the bowls and set them on the table it would be a big help.

"So Sina, you've told me all about school. How about some extra curricular activities."

"Well, I'm supplementing my assistantship by doing voiceovers."

"You always had a good set of pipes. And, is there anything else?" Kelsey asked walking over to the sink. "Because I think you're holding out on me."

"Well there is someone special in my life," she said smiling.

"I knew you didn't get that twinkle in your eye and that glow all around you just from school. Tell me about him. And don't leave nothin' out."

"His name is Kenneth Winston. Oh, and Kelsey, he's a slim. He's a second year MBA student."

"Hmmm. Increasing pep."

"Pep?"

"Potential Earning Power."

"We met at the pig and chicken pickin' when I knocked his plate on him," Sina said as she and Kelsey laughed. "And he didn't even get mad."

"Is he good to you."

"Yes he is," Sina said. "He sure is."

"And."

"I'm in love Kelsey," Sina said with a dead serious look in her eye. "And this time it's for real. We have taken things slowly. We spend as much time together as our school schedules will allow, and then we're usually studying or critiquing the other's papers. He's a graduate of Steeplechase you know. This just feels so right. Like it's never felt before."

"I'm so happy for you,"Kelsey said hugging her cousin. "You really deserve that."

"Oh, and we went earlier this month and got HIV tests. We both wanted to be sure before we reached that plateau, if you know what I mean."

"I know that's right. That's nothing to play with."

"Tell me about it. Scott had me scared shitless," Sina said recalling her tumultuous spring. "But Kenneth and I both know we're clean, and we're going to have the test again in May just to be sure," she said smiling from ear-to-ear.

"Hmmm," Kelsey said. "Oh, and that reminds me," she continued as she placed the bird on the dining room table. "I have some good news to share with you," Kelsey was silent as she walked back into the kitchen.

"Well," Sina said. "Don't keep me in the dark."

"Sister Friends received $750,000 in grants, one of them federal."

"That is so wonderful. Now maybe you can get some people in the high schools to teach these kids the reality of HIV."

"From what Lucia's told me, we need to start in the elementary schools," Kelsey said. "But my stepdaughter's gonna wait 'til she's married, isn't that right."

"That's right. I don't want no babies or no death sentence or anything else."

"Smart move," Sina said, patting Lucia on the shoulder.

"Korrin," Kelsey yelled, "dinner's ready. And," Kelsey said looking Sina in the eye and smiling. "I'm three and a half months pregnant." Sina screamed. "The baby's due in May."

"We both have so much to be thankful for," Sina said as Korrin asked them to bow their heads and bless the food.

Addictive Love

22

"T hank you for having us over for Easter dinner," Rachel said to her Aunt Mary as she and Patrick feasted on the dinner of baked ham, green beans, candied yams and rolls.

"This is the best ham I have ever had," Patrick said once he'd chewed and swallowed his forkful. "I hope you taught Rachel your secret?" he added now smiling.

Aunt Mary enjoyed entertaining and had a theme for each group of guests, which is why Rachel was surprised when her Aunt didn't have the house decorated for Easter with little straw baskets filled with goodies for each of her guests. Aunt Mary's house was clean as always. She had even polished the pine dining room table with its autumn blush stain. It went well with the pale yellow walls in the dining room. "Service sure was good," she said pouring herself a glass of iced tea. "Rev. Mintor sure did preach, didn't he?"

"He sure did," Rachel replied. "It was just strange not having Sina here to sing."

"It sure was."

"But she's coming home for a few weeks this summer. She'll even be here for my graduation in June."

"That'll be great," Aunt Mary said. "It will be nice for her to take a little break from school and everything. Now what is she studying, again?"

"Performance studies," Rachel said. "And women's studies too. She is mapping out her thesis proposal right now."

"Already? It seems like she just started."

"The program is only two years."

"Well what does she plan to do with that Performance degree anyway? Does she want to go into acting or something?" Patrick asked, sipping his tea.

"It's actually very interesting. She interviews a group of people in similar circumstances, collects their narratives, and then constructs a performance based on their narratives. She interviewed two women with AIDS at her cousin's nonprofit organization last month for her class."

"It sounds fascinating. But how is she going to make a living from that?"

"I don't know, but she can always teach. And she does have her radio and TV skills too. They can always pay the bills. I hear she is doing quite well with voiceovers."

"That's great."

"I saw Hope and Jason today too?" Aunt Mary continued. "What's Jason going to do now that he can't play ball?"

"Well, he got into law school. Guess where?"

"Where?" Aunt Mary asked.

"Lake Effect State University," Rachel replied. "I hear they have one of the best programs in Sports and Entertainment Law. So he'll be right near Hope."

"I never understood why they gave that school such a dumb name."

"Hope told me that when the administration building was built, it sat on the border between Kalamazoo and Calhoun counties and the county boards had an ongoing battle over what to name it. The builder was drunk or something and made a mistake, built the building right smack dab on the county line. The people in Kalamazoo wanted to call it Kalamazoo State and the people in Battle Creek wanted to call it Calhoun State. Now this debate went on for months and months and they were supposed to open the doors of the University on January 1st of that next year and here it was December 29th and they still didn't have a name."

"So how did they arrive at Lake Effect State?"

"Well, they got a heavy snow fall in the wee hours of the morning on December 30th, one of those snows where an Alberta Clipper came down, and when the cold front was over Lake Michigan, the warmth of the water produced lake effect snow which traveled all of the way to that county line," Rachel explained. "And then the county boards decided to accept Lake Effect State as a happy medium."

"Why didn't they just name it Kalamazoo-Calhoun State?"

"I heard they couldn't decide which name would come first," Rachel said as the three of them laughed.

"Now that's a funny story," Aunt Mary said as she stood up to clear the dinner plates. Rachel observed her aunt's slow and feeble rising and quickly jumped up to help. She took her and Patrick's plates as Aunt Mary started in the kitchen with hers. "Is everything alright?" Rachel asked her aunt. "You look like you've lost weight."

"I don't know Rachel, I guess I need to go to the doctor. Lately, I've been having problems with hemorrhoids and stomach cramps. I'm not regular either. I haven't had as much energy as usual lately. I guess it's just a sign of old age."

"Aunt Mary," Rachel pleaded. "You need to go to the doctor. Promise me you will go to the doctor this week."

"I've got so much to do. I have choir rehearsal, lessons, and I have to take Sister Henderson to the doctor."

"But Aunt Mary, you have to take care of yourself," Rachel said as she sliced the sweet potato pie. "You are the most important person to me. Just promise me you'll go."

"I'll call first thing in the morning."

"So, Aunt Mary," Rachel began, "What do you think of Patrick?"

"Is this the young gentleman who gave you that friendship ring for Christmas?"

"The one and same."

"He seems like such a fine young fellow. And quite handsome too." Aunt Mary responded. "What you and Sina would call a—slender."

"A slim Aunt Mary," Rachel said as she and her aunt walked back into the dining room.

April 17, 1991

Dear Sina,

So much has happened since you were here for Christmas. I guess kind of like what you went through last year. Right now I'm in the waiting room at Duncan University Medical Center. Aunt Mary has colon cancer and she's in surgery right now. Sina I wish you were here. Hank is on his way and Patrick was with me, but he had to leave to take an exam. He is so good Sina. He got up at 4:30 this morning and picked up me and Aunt Mary and brought us here. She had to be here at 6:00. The doctor said the cancer had metastasized, but she thought they could get it all. Your mother was very reassuring. She calls all of the time to check up on Aunt Mary since we found out about the cancer. She may have to have chemotherapy after the surgery.

I'm so scared Sina. I don't know what I'll do if I lose Aunt Mary. I had just accepted a job in St. Louis, but now I don't know if I can take it. Aunt Mary really needs me. Patrick and I are talking about marriage. I was suppose to move to St. Louis after graduation. Hope was right about that holding pattern thing.

Patrick and I recently had that smooth landing and boy was it smooth. I really love him. And sex can be so beautiful when you're both in love. I'm really glad we took our time. I just hope everything works out.

How are things between you and Kenneth? I hope you all are still together. You seemed so happy and looked so good at Christmas. And I think he had a little somethin' somethin' to do with it.

I will probably spend most of my time at Aunt Mary's — except for when I'm on call in the dorm. You can call me there. The other R.A.s have been really good about helping me out since Aunt Mary got sick. Graduation is June 1st. I can't wait to see you again.

Love,
Rachel

"Poor Rachel," Sina said to Kenneth as she finished reading the letter and put it down on her coffee table. "Aunt Mary is such a wonderful person. When Uncle Charlie died 2½ years ago it was really sad, but now — I just hope she will be alright. By the way, Kenneth, when do you start your new job?"

"Around the 17th of June. Why?" he asked, looking up from his book.

"I'm going home for Rachel and Jason's graduation. I'll stay bout two weeks. Want to come along?"

"Sounds like a plan."

"Let's see," Sina said, pulling her Carolina Week-by Week out of her backpack. "If we drove straight through it should only take us about 12½-13 hours or so. Let's plan to leave on the 29th. That way, all of the Memorial Day travelers will be back home. And we can come back around the 13th. That will give you time to rest up before you start that new job." Sina put the calendar back into her bag and walked into the kitchen.

"You know Sina," Kenneth said as he walked behind her. "I've never been to Chicago."

"Oh, then you're in for a real treat," Sina said as she turned on the hot water and squeezed dishwashing liquid into the stream. "And summer is the best time to go. We'll be there for the Blues Fest and the Gospel Fest. Oh yeah, and then there's the Sox and Cubs games."

"And from the look of things, the Bulls are going to be in the playoffs. They have the best record in the Central Division. If they can get past Detroit, they just may go all the way."

"You think so?"

"Definitely. They have a triple threat with Jordan, Pippen and Grant. And that B.J. Armstrong is deadly with his three pointers."

"I guess I've been so buried in my thesis proposal and pledging and everything I hadn't really paid attention."

"Well, by this time next week, the semester will be well over. Do you have any finals?"

"No, just papers," she said, as she rinsed a plate. "I just thought of something."

"What's that?" Kenneth said now standing directly behind Sina.

"This will be like a—I don't know—refresher and celebratory trip. You'll have your M.B.A. And I will have defended my thesis proposal." She shut off the water and turned to kiss Kenneth. "And we will have our second test results back."

They both had very busy schedules and respected each other's time, yet they found themselves at one or the other's apartment at least twice during the week, studying their individual subjects followed by an in-depth study of each other. Thomasine got to see Kenneth's family again at the graduation on Mother's Day. She regretted not being able to spend Mother's Day with her own mother. But Crystal Mintor understood that her daughter was swamped with her thesis project. With her proposal, *Still I Rise: How Acquaintance Rape Survivors Negotiate their Experience and the Impact it has on Future Relationships* defended and having made a quick trip to Hampton to see Kelsey's new son Korrin Jr., Sina was now free for her jaunt to Chicago in Kenneth's new Infiniti M30.

Harding Memorial Stadium was packed for the Spring Commencement exercises. The field had been lined with yellow chrysanthemums in pots wrapped in green foiled paper. The band played a spirited *Pomp and Circumstance* and the procession was the longest Sina and Hope had ever seen. As the guest speaker spoke briefly about college and the development of lasting relationships, he said, "Some of you have met your best friends here at Duncan. Others have met future business partners. Maybe that girl you sat next to in English 101 will be your first child's godparents. Or better yet, maybe that young man who came to your rescue will be your husband." Hope and Sina were amazed when they heard the speaker ask Rachel Louise Curtis and Patrick Stephen Long to stand. The speaker then told the entire audience how they had met and how Patrick wanted to take this opportunity to ask Rachel to be his wife. Cameras followed Patrick as he walked out of the Master's candidates section, found Rachel in her green robe and put a ring on her finger. Aunt Mary, who had gathered up enough strength to come to the commencement, was smiling as a tear trickled from her eye. Crystal held her hand tightly and smiled. "You have done a wonderful job with Rebecca's children," she said as she smiled with pride. "An absolutely wonderful job."

Hope sat still, almost in disbelief and in anticipation. It was so hard to believe that her friend was getting engaged to a man that she'd known for a little more than a year and in anticipation of Jason's proposal. But once the speaker was hooded and seated, she knew this was not her big day.

"Ooh, girl," Thomasine said as she walked into the Anderson's kitchen with Rachel. "That is one nice rock."

"My man has good taste, doesn't he?"

"He sure does. Were you surprised?"

"I was surprised at the way he proposed, especially since he is so private and all. That's the first time he's really kissed me in public, you know on the mouth." Rachel poured Kenneth a glass of lemonade.

"I'm just so sorry I haven't spent much time with you. I've been showing Kenneth around and stuff. That is when I'm not working. I was really lucky getting voiceover jobs. I did my first voiceover for a TV commercial Monday. I may stay a few more days. With the money I'm bringing in I will have no problem buying a plane ticket back."

"That's great Sina. I'm just glad you and Hope were able to come to my graduation. I hated not being able to go to Hope's graduation last year. But Savannah is so far away."

"It sure is," Sina said, grabbing a glass for herself. "Say, have you two set a date yet?"

"Not yet. I really haven't had much time to think about anything but Aunt Mary. I did get to spend some time with Patrick before he left Sunday though. Hope came by and was a big help. Once she gets through this cycle of chemo, then I can give some serious thought to my future."

"Yeah, how is she doing. I hear chemo can be a living hell."

"To say the least. She went in today. And she's always so weak afterward. She just comes home and gets in the bed. I've been with her around the clock."

"You have, and despite that sparkle in your eye, you do look drained. Hank doesn't look so great either."

"It's definitely rough."

"Hmm," Sina said. "I tell you what. Kenneth and I have tickets for the Sox game. But right now we're about gamed out. We've been to game after game. And with all of the sight seeing and everything, we'd just like to cool out for a while. Why don't you and Hank take the tickets?"

"I don't know Sina."

"Take them, I insist. Kenneth and I will stay with Aunt Mary. And if we have any problems, we'll call mom and she'll be right over."

"Are you sure?"

"I'm sure," Sina said, hugging Rachel.

"Thank you so much. I really owe you big time. I'll have to dance at your wedding."

The new Comiskey Park was packed with teenagers, suburban families with children and the usual bleacher bums. It was the bottom of the fourth, the Sox were down three-zip and Rachel found herself suddenly craving nachos with chili. Knowing that most of the vendors who passed through the stands had only hot dogs, pop, and beer, she decided to scope out some nachos. "Do you want anything to eat Hank?" she asked as she put her purse on her shoulder and stood up.

"No. Not right now."

"Well I'll be right back." Rachel made her way past the other fans sitting in her row. As she turned to walk down the aisle, she noticed a slim with much oomph wink at her, but she just passed it off. Making her way to the restroom, before getting in the long line at the concession stand, Rachel felt someone following her. But she figured she was a little paranoid considering all that she was going through. After she bought her nachos with extra cheese and chili and a white pop, she turned and the winker was directly in front of her.

"I can't believe your boyfriend let a woman as beautiful as you out by yourself in such a big crowd. I mean, your fiancee," he added, fixating on that pear shaped 1-carat diamond on her left hand. "If you were my woman, I'd be at your beck and call. I'd be at your service 24-all. I'd wine you and dine, plant you flowers in a line. If you were my woman, I'd be there all the time."

"What a line," Rachel said, walking away.

"You need to give that brotha his walking papers," he yelled to her back. "He needs to come correct."

"The Bulls are on fire," Aunt Mary said from her bedroom to Sina and Kenneth. "I think they're going to do it tonight. They just have to. I've waited the last twenty-five years of my life to see them do it."

"I'm sure they'll win tonight Aunt Mary," Sina replied. "And I bet with this team you'll see another championship the next year, and the year after that, and the year after that."

"I don't know Sina," Aunt Mary said. "This chemo is just killing me. I can hardly eat because I got sores in my mouth and it's so hard for me to swallow. And then just as soon as I get it down, it comes right back up. I'm surprised I still have that good dinner you served me."

"Sina's got that magic touch when it comes to cooking," Kenneth said smiling while momentarily tuning out the game. "That magic touch," he said as he rubbed his stomach.

"You know," Aunt Mary said. "If I were rich, the doctor probably would have had me in gene therapy years ago. Then I wouldn't be in the state I'm in. But I can tell now, it won't be long. Not long at all," she said as the final buzzer rang and the 1990-91 Chicago Bulls made history by winning their first world championship. Aunt Mary grabbed Sina and hugged her just before she began to cry.

"What's all the excitement for?" Rachel asked as she and Hank walked in.

"The Bulls won! The Bulls won."

"That's great," Rachel sat on the bed. "I'm so glad to see you've perked up Aunt Mary. Just don't overdo it. You have to try to keep your strength up."

"I knew they would win," she said. "Charlie was right."

"What do you mean?" Rachel asked with a puzzled look on her face.

"Charlie told me they would win tonight, June 12, 1991. He told me that after they lost Game one here."

"I think we better be going," Sina said to Rachel. "It's getting late, and we want to jet home before the celebration pours out into the streets."

"Good idea." Rachel walked Sina and Kenneth to the door. "Besides, you two have a long trip ahead of you tomorrow, don't you?"

"Kenneth is heading back in the morning, but I'm going to stay about another week. I have a job next week. And maybe I'll get to spend more time with you and Aunt Mary too," Sina said as they approached the front door. "How was the game?"

"Okay. You know the Sox lost. But it was good to get away. Except for this guy who followed me from my seat, waited while I was in the bathroom and then followed me to the concession stand to tell me that if I were his woman he'd wine me and dine me and plant flowers in a straight line'."

"What?" Sina asked. "Did he see your engagement ring?"

"Yes. I guess he thought Hank was my fiancee. And I didn't tell him any different."

"Now that brother was way out of line," Kenneth said. "How's he going to try to hit on someone's future wife with a tired line like that?"

"I just said 'what a line,' and walked away."

"Say," Sina asked as they walked down the walkway. "Have you talked to Patrick lately?"

"Yes. His cousin was shot last night. He died early this morning."

"I'm so sorry to hear that."

"Me too, I really wish I could be there with him. But I can't leave Aunt Mary. I just wouldn't feel right."

"Have funeral arrangements been made yet?"

"I don't think so, but I bet I'll hear from him in the morning."

"Everything will be alright," Sina said as she got into the car.

Kenneth began his journey back to North Carolina after he woke up, showered, and ate a breakfast of salmon cakes and grits Sina had prepared for him. He really liked Sina's cooking. Especially the salmon cakes she seasoned with ginger, garlic, tarragon and red and white pepper. He thought they were good enough to make him almost want to slap his Mama, but he knew better than that. After Kenneth drove off, Sina stripped the sheets from the guest bed, put them in the washer and sat down on the sofa in the basement and fell asleep. Her visit here had been very taxing for her as she had to do all of the sight seeing and work.

"Hello," Sina said somewhat groggily when she was awakened by the telephone.

"Sina I'm scared," Rachel said. "I'm really scared. Aunt Mary keeps talking about Uncle Charlie being right there with her. She's even talking to him, and her mother and father and even my father. She told him he would be so proud of his children and how I'm going to be a teacher and Hank's going to medical school. Could the chemo have made her crazy?"

"Rachel," Sina said. "I'm on my way over. I hear Daddy upstairs piddling around. We're on our way over right now."

Thomasine knew exactly what this meant. She remembers her father telling her about his mother's death in 1964 and how she said his father who died in 1940 told her about things that were about to happen. She recalled that Kelsey was an infant and her parents were on their way to come see about Grandma Mintor when Kelsey got sick and they had to delay the trip for a day. "Jeanne Ilene and her family won't be here for another day, the baby's sick," she told Rev. Mintor. "Your Daddy told me so."

When the Mintors arrived at Aunt Mary's house, Rachel was in the living room with her head in her lap crying hysterically. "Rachel," Rev. Mintor said. "Everything's going to be alright. Just trust and believe. The

Lord will not put any more on you than you can handle," he said embracing her.

"Rev. Mintor, she's talking about all of this beautiful music she's hearing," Rachel said tearfully. "This is it. Isn't it?"

"Let's go pray." Rev. Mintor took Rachel's hand and Sina put her arm around her shoulder. When they reached the bedroom, Hank was sitting on Aunt Mary's bed holding her left hand. Rev. Mintor stood beside Aunt Mary and placed his hand in Aunt Mary's. Thomasine stood beside him and held his hand and Rachel sat on the bed and held Sina's hand and Hank's outstretched hand. "Let us bow our heads. Oh Heavenly Father, whose most infinite wisdom has guided us and directed us thus far. Your omnipresence and unconditional love give us inner peace. And your Heavenly Power in the midst of struggles strengthens our faith and enables us to make it over. Lord, Sister Mary is a dutiful servant of yours with a faith so strong and peace so harmonious that we can all have the calm assurance that Mary will continue to serve you and love you in your Kingdom. Lord, continue to grant her soul peace. Mary is the type of servant, Lord, who, in the midst of her own pain, struggle and tragedy, put service of others ahead of her own cares. She continues to keep on keeping on in spite of, and because she loves You so. And after the tragic loss of her nephew and the suffering of her niece Rebecca, and even despite the agonizing loss of her husband Charlie and her painful illness, she continues to grow in faith. And it is only through Your love, Your wisdom, and Your power that she and all of us are able." Rev. Mintor paused as he felt Aunt Mary squeeze his hand.

"The Lord is my Shepherd, I shall not want," she began. "He maketh me to lie down in green pastures: He leadeth me beside the still waters," the others joined in. "He restoreth my soul: He leadeth me in the paths of righteousness for His name's sake..." they continued. "Surely goodness and mercy shall follow me all the days of my life; and I will dwell in the house of the Lord for ever. Amen."

As Rachel said the 23rd Psalm along with her aunt, brother and the Mintors, she thought about Aunt Mary's life and how full and happy it was. Aunt Mary never worried about a thing, even in the midst of her struggles. She would give a stranger in need her last dollar and not think about it again because she knew that the Lord would provide for her. Rachel also considered the words of the 23rd Psalm. It was because Aunt Mary knew the Lord would provide for her that she could give her last dollar to a stranger. And each and every day, Rachel thought, we walk through the valley of the shadow of death—and because of God's goodness and unconditional love, we are comforted. Goodness and mercy had followed

Aunt Mary all of her life, and it was at this moment Rachel decided she wanted the same.

When Aunt Mary died later that day, Crystal and Rachel's mother came by to help make arrangements. Rachel called Patrick and he was very concerned and disappointed that he could not be there when his future wife was in need, but with the untimely death of his teenage cousin who was like a little brother to him, he felt he needed to stay in St. Louis. He promised though, to come and see Rachel as soon as he could. When Rachel discovered she did not have a dark dress or shoes to wear to the funeral, Sina took her to the mall.

"These will go great with that dress," Sina said, holding up a pair of earrings to Rachel's ear. "What else do you need?"

"Just some hose, and shoes," she said as she paid the cashier for the earrings. Sina recommended off-black hose and black pumps. Rachel always thought Sina had such good taste. "I'm so glad you're going to sing at the funeral," Rachel said as they walked over to the shoe department. "Aunt Mary would really love that."

"You know I owe most of my talent to her," Sina replied smiling. "I had just a smidgen when I first came to Front Street and she taught me basically everything I knew. I owe her greatly," she continued as she held up a shoe and told a shoe selling slim she'd like it in a 9. "I think those will go nicely." Sina sat next to Rachel.

When the salesman came back, he took one giant step backward. "I see he's done it again," he said.

"Who's done what?" Sina asked.

"I just don't understand how a man with a fiancee as beautiful as you could just—I tell you," he said shaking his head. "If you were my woman I'd be there to guard, and if by chance I couldn't I'd bring you a card—"

"You'd wine me and dine me and plant me some dumb flowers in a line too I suppose," Rachel said as if he were annoying her.

"Oh," Sina said laughing.

"So are you getting these shoes for your big engagement party?" He put the shoe on Rachel's right foot. "Or have you had that already?"

"It's for a funeral, okay. My aunt who was like a mother to me just died of cancer and right now I don't have time for no silly games."

"Sorry." He put the other shoe on and was silent.

"Those fit you good girl," Sina said as Rachel walked over to the mirror. "And they don't gap. I hate when I try on shoes and they gap when you walk. That just doesn't look good."

"I'll take them," Rachel said curtly and sat down to take them off.

Rachel put her old shoes back on and she and Sina made their way past the other customers and salespersons. "Look," the salesman said. "I'm sorry. I didn't know," he paused. "But I know what you're going through because my mother died of breast cancer last year. It can be hard losing someone so close, and watching them suffer." He slipped his card into Rachel's hand. "If you ever need to talk, or just someone to yell at give me a call. I'm D. Brown, but my good friends just call me Brothaman."

The funeral was a glorious tribute to Aunt Mary's life. Sina and Hope spent most of the next week with Rachel as she settled Aunt Mary's affairs. Aunt Mary left the house to Rachel and her new car to Hank as well as a generous endowment. Rachel figured she needed it to keep the house up and Hank had his heart set on Duncan University's Medical school. Patrick came to see Rachel when he could which was mostly on weekends. Since he was probationary on his job, that was a wise move. They set their date for July of 1992 which would give them plenty of time find jobs and relocate because one of them obviously had to. Sina sent Rachel a cass-single of Sounds of Blackness *Optimistic* to keep her inspired. And when that didn't work, Rachel picked up the phone and called Brothaman who was always willing and eager to comfort Rachel with moral support, that is until they began to spend time together and found they had similar interests. Before long, Patrick's weekend visits didn't stand a chance to all of that love and support Brothaman gave Rachel. But Rachel loved Patrick and felt that he was the perfect husband for her—the man she wanted to spend the rest of her life with.

And speaking of the rest of your life, Thomasine was down in North Carolina arranging her interviews for her thesis. The Institutional Review for using human subjects in a research study was arduous, but she knew it would be well worth it. The stories of acquaintance rape survivors needed to be told. The statistics said that one in eight college age women experience acquaintance rape and a very small percentage of them report it. She felt that through her performance of their narratives, other women would be uplifted, inspired and empowered. Between the thesis, her upcoming karate belt test, and Kenneth's job, she knew they hadn't been giving their relationship the attention it deserved. That is why she was so happy when Kenneth asked her to dinner at that Jazz cafe in Cary where they had their first date. She knew this was exactly what they needed. And since they hadn't been out in so long and he would be coming to pick her up straight from work, she decided to get her hair done and wear something special.

"You look so beautiful," Kenneth said to Sina who wore a sly, seductive smile. "Beautiful woman and beautiful music," he said of the sweet melody playing over the loudspeakers.

"Thank you Kenneth. It's an early Wynton Marsalis tune from *The All American Hero* album. It's called *Time Will Tell*. I used to play it on my show when I started in radio. It was the first song I played because it's so long. Over twelve minutes and I figured that would give me plenty of time to come up with something to say. I used to be so afraid of going on mic. I had cuing up the records and playing the cart down pat, but once I got past the weather and a PSA, I was almost in panic mode."

"You, in a panic mode?" Kenneth replied. "Now I can't even picture that," he reached across the table for her hand.

"I hate that we really haven't been spending much time together. But with me and this thesis and you and your new job—I guess things are just different for us now—"

"Things are going to be different for us from now on," Kenneth interrupted as Sina felt butterflies in her stomach, recalling how one of her friends in college broke up with her boyfriend. She had set up a candlelight dinner in her dorm room complete with wine and his favorite fruit, strawberries. She had gone to great expense too because strawberries are expensive in central Wisconsin in December. Anyway, after a night of romance and passionate love making which drained the last drop of energy from him, sister girlfriend just kicked him to the curb. Just like that. *But I don't want it to be different* Sina thought, yet somehow the words just wouldn't escape.

"Thomasine Mintor," Kenneth said. "When I first saw you in the library almost a year ago, I knew then that I wanted to have the opportunity to get to know you better. Fate brought us together at the Black Graduate Organization picnic."

"Fate and similarities," Thomasine said laughing. "The mere fact that we're both Black graduate students."

"Well not entirely. You know only 10% of the Black graduate and professional students attended that picnic."

"Really."

"That just means you have a job cut out for you as secretary," he said smiling. "I guess if you had known, you would have thought twice about running."

"That's true," Thomasine said. "But I'm up for the challenge."

"I didn't bring you here to talk about the BGO. But it was a nice little ice breaker," he said, massaging her hands. "I brought you here to talk about something else. Over the past 11 months we've shared so much with each other, learned so much from each other and taught so much to each other. And I'm here to tell you Thomasine Mintor that I love you. And I am confident that over the years," he said as he got down on his knee, "we will continue to share, learn and teach. Thomasine Mintor. Will you marry me?"

Thomasine sat there with tears in her eyes and gazed into Kenneth's eyes. "Kenneth, I'm crying because I'm so happy. I have never been able to share like I've shared with you," she said as she sobbed and thought about the past. "And no man has ever told me he loved me.

"From our first date, through our trip to Chicago—I just feel like you came into my life at the right time and everything is finally working out." He used his napkin to dry her tears.

"Well don't keep a brother in suspense. What is your answer?"

"Yes. Yes I'll marry you. That is if you don't mind me keeping my name," she said smiling.

"We've talked about this before and you know I don't mind."

"It's not a women's thing. It's a family thing. You know I'm the last Mintor. And since my brother is in his mid-thirties with no prospects for marriage, well I understand he hasn't brought anyone home lately, I just feel like I have to preserve the name as long as I can."

"I understand," he said. "And understanding is the key to making marriage last. Now, can I kiss my future wife?"

Eager to get their new life started, Sina and Kenneth set their date for May, just after Sina's graduation.

Back in Kalamazoo, Jason had moved into his dormitory apartment and accepted his duties as Assistant Area Director. That gave him free rent, $200 on his meal card and a small stipend. He was thankful for it too, but he still had to take out student loans to help pay the out-of-state tuition. But sports and entertainment law was a lucrative arena and he was sure to be able to pay the loans back in a heartbeat once he was practicing. Having quickly tired of the cafeteria food, Jason was delighted when Hope asked him over for a romantic candle lit dinner. His heart warmed when he saw the low lights and heard the soft jazz music of Najee flow from the new stereo Sina had persuaded Hope to buy. Then there was this scent, sweet and captivating. The aroma was not overpowering, but permeated the apartment. After the dinner of oysters and Riesling, Jason was in a mood for romance. "Let's dance. We haven't danced together in so long."

With his arms wrapped around her voluptuous body, Hope was ecstatic that she had stopped off at that roadside psychic Mystic. *This Hearts of Gold oil is really working.* Jason just pulled her closer and their bodies pressed together and the sweet aroma and soft music put Jason in a trance.

When Hope blew softly in his ear and ran her hands up and down the length of his backside he desperately wanted more than she had ever offered. He looked her in her eyes and softly said, "I love you," all Hope needed to hear.

He carried her into the bedroom, lay her gently on her bed and began to undress her. He first used his hands and then his nose and his mouth to touch every inch of her body. "For starters," Jason said. "I've waited for this moment for so long. And I promise you, it will be special."

"I know," Hope replied. As Jason dazzled Hope with kisses in places he had never seen before, she spoke softly. "You love me, don't you Jason."

"Yes, Hope. I've loved you for almost eight years now."

"And I love you."

"I know you do," he said continuing to kiss her. "I've felt the warmth of your love for so long."

"You know, Rachel is engaged. And so is Sina, and I know we'll get married someday. But with you in law school right now, you probably have a lot of expenses and can't afford the kind of ring you want to give me."

"That is so true," Jason said pausing to look in her eyes. "But I promise that when I am able, I will get you the most beautiful ring you have ever imagined."

"Guess what," she said as Jason began to rub his bare body against hers.

"What, my queen?"

"I already got it."

"Got what?" Jason asked.

"The ring," Hope reached under her pillow and pulled out the velvet box. "And now that I've got the ring, you can propose to me. We have waited for this moment for seven long years, eleven months and six days. This is the most special moment of my life," she said opening the box to display the 2-carat marquise cut diamond ring. Jason stared open-mouthed. "Rachel has a 1-carat pear and Sina got a 1½-carat trillion. Don't you think I'm worth a 2-carat marquise?"

"You, my queen, are worth this and more,"

"And we both have waited so long for this. All of this," Hope said in a bedroom whisper.

"Yes we have." He took the ring out of the box, slipped it on her left hand ring finger. "We most certainly have."

Don't Want to Be a Fool

23

"Rachel you there?"

"Yeah."

"Hope, you there?" Sina asked.

"Yes."

"Now that I've got you both here, you can tell me which one of you is pregnant," Sina said in a motherly tone. "Because I've been dreaming about fish lately and I know it's not me or Kelsey."

"Can't I even get a hello first?"

"Well hello; now who's pregnant? I know it's one of you two."

"It's me," Rachel replied. "And guess what?"

"What?" Sina and Hope said in unison.

"I got married."

"You got married and you didn't even invite me," Hope replied.

"So Patrick found a job in Chicago?" Sina asked. "That's wonderful."

"Well, it kinda just happened. On Monday we went down to City Hall and got our license and we've been married now for oh a little more than 24 hours."

"I guess you were too busy last night to call and let us know. So where is Patrick working?" Sina asked.

"I didn't marry Patrick," Rachel said. "Brothaman and I have been kickin' it since the summer; I just didn't feel right marrying Patrick."

"Brothaman?" Sina and Hope asked simultaneously.

"Yes, I am now Mrs. David Brown."

"You mean Mrs. Wine and dine plant flowers in a line?"

"What?" Hope asked.

"Yes, she met him at a Sox game last summer. Then we saw him in the mall. He was selling shoes and reciting the corniest lines I ever heard."

"You passed on a counselor with a Master's degree, a future, and a recession proof job for a shoe salesman. Rachel, are you crazy?" Hope asked.

"Brothaman is educated. He's a graphic artist. And he writes the most beautiful poetry. He was just trying to be funny that night. He wrote wonderful vows for our marriage and a poem for me last night called *Your Essence*."

"*Your Essence?*" Sina questioned.

"Yes," Rachel replied. "Your essence is like the ocean, it runs deep and flows wide . . . ," she began.

"Okay," Sina said. "So when is this baby due?"

"In July. We're fixing up Hank's old room for the nursery. Oh, and Brothaman's gonna go into advertising."

"Girl, I just couldn't imagine calling my husband Brothaman," Sina replied. "But advertising is a good field. Competitive as hell, but it's still a good area. Especially for someone creative. Oh, and I have good news."

"What?" Hope asked, "because after all of this I need to hear some good news."

"My paper was accepted for the conference in Sydney."

"Congratulations."

"I'm trying to get funding for the trip right now. I've been to the dean, the provost and even to some community organizations. I'm going to be bogged down with presentations when I get back, but it will be an excellent opportunity for me to share aboriginal culture with some people here. The church here as well as Front Street is helping me, given that I give a presentation to Junior Church when I get back."

"When do you go?" Hope asked.

"March 26th. They say it takes a couple of days to get over the jet lag. You know they are 16 hours ahead. I leave on March 26th and by the time I get there, it will almost be the 28th. My presentation is on the last day, April 1st of all days. I'll probably head back on the 2nd or 3rd because it just doesn't seem worth it to go that far across the world and stay only a few days."

"That sounds like so much fun?" Rachel said.

"Fun? I've got to revise my paper in the midst of trying to finish my thesis."

"How is the project coming?"

"I am really fascinated by it all though. It's really emotional having these women from different places and different backgrounds come together to share their similar experiences."

"It sounds so intriguing," Rachel said. "But why did you pick such a somber topic?

"For a number of reasons," Sina replied. "And it will all come out in my presentation. Both of you have to come down in April for my defense. And you can pick up your bridesmaid dresses and have them altered."

"What colors have you chosen?"

"Red and white of course, and the wedding is going to be the day before graduation—May 9 since all of my family will be here for that as well. Have you and Jason set a date yet?"

"July—but with Rachel's baby due in July, maybe we should change it to October," she said, now smiling. "You know we started going together in October of 1983. We are getting married at Front Street. And I still expect you to sing—Always and Ave Maria."

"You know I'll be happy to sing."

"Look Rachel," Thomasine said, noting that Rachel was not in the conversation. "If you are happy, then I am happy. You know Brothaman better than I do and you know what's best for you. I was just surprised by all you told me, but I guess if I had been better about keeping in touch with you, then this wouldn't have been such a shock."

"I'm more sure about this than I've ever been."

"Well, the good thing is that at least you will already be off for the summer when your baby is born. You want a boy or a girl?"

"A girl, and I'm going to name her Amber."

"That is so pretty. Isn't it, Hope?" Hope who virtually ignoring Rachel.

"Yes it is, but you know I like Hope better."

"Well, I like Amber Thomasine."

"Now don't you two get to fighting over what I'm going to name my child. I don't even know if it will be a girl."

"Okay," Sina replied. "But there's one thing we're certainly not going to fight over."

"What's that?" Hope and Rachel asked.

"The reception we're going to give you when I come home for Christmas. Look, I just heard Kenneth come in, I'm going to have to go."

"Don't you fool around and get pregnant too," Hope said.

"That would be cool," Rachel interjected. "If we were both pregnant at the same time."

"We'll have to plan that sometime, but for right now I'm not having any children for a while. I just want to spend the next few years getting used to married life."

"I heard that," Hope said.

"But I really have to go," Sina said. "I have to get up early in the morning. Kenneth and I are going house hunting."

"Already?"

"That's not an overnight process. My lease is up at the end of February and May will be here before we know it. We surely don't want to be in no apartment. We want to have something that's ours."

"I know that's right," Rachel replied, "especially two professional people like you."

"Well, I better go."

"Bye," Hope and Rachel said in unison.

Sina put the phone on its cradle and walked downstairs to her kitchen and poured herself a glass of vodka with ice and lemon. "Whoa," Kenneth said. "What's got your goat?"

"I just got off the phone with Rachel and Hope," she said as she lifted the glass to her mouth. "And you would not believe what Rachel has gone out and done."

"What?"

"She got married and she's pregnant, but not in that order."

"Well she and Patrick moved up their date. No big deal."

"Here's the clincher. She didn't marry Patrick. She married that Brothaman guy. You know the one from the White Sox game," Sina said gulping.

"No, she didn't."

"Yes she did. They went down to City Hall yesterday."

"Pour me one. Straight, no chaser."

Thomasine and Kenneth woke up bright and early the next morning and met with their realtor who took them to a variety of houses and townhomes. Sina fell in love with a three-bedroom town home near the Park where Kenneth worked. It was spacious and upscale, yet affordable for a couple just starting out. They went back to the realtor's office where she wrote up the contract and Kenneth reluctantly wrote a check for $1,000 from their joint account for the earnest money.

"Are you sure that's the home you want?" Kenneth asked as he drove Sina back to her apartment. "There's not much space for us to grow."

"I think there's plenty of space for us."

"But once you get settled in your job you may decide to have children," he said looking at her while stopped at the light." And we'll outgrow that place in a few years."

"That's something we need to talk about Kenneth," Sina began. "You know I've been working on my thesis all semester."

"Yes, and you know I support you 100% in that. I think it's commendable."

"The research experience for me has been—captivating," Sina said finally thinking of the right word. "Performance Ethnography is not something I thought I'd do, but I'm just—turned on by it."

"That's good honey. You should be passionate about your thesis project."

"And I feel like I must pursue my passion," Sina continued. "So I have decided to apply to a Ph.D. program in Anthropology."

"But I thought we were going to—"

"We'll just have to put off a family for a few more years. That's all."

"But I thought you said you were tired of school," Kenneth said as he parked the car.

"That was before," Thomasine said as she got out of the car and walked up the two steps to her front door.

"I just don't want you to get burned out." Kenneth sat at the dining room table.

"I won't. I should be finished in three years. That will give us time to build a strong foundation," she said, sensing he was slightly salty about her decision. "Being a college professor is ideal for raising a family; three weeks off at Christmas, summers off, flexible schedule. While the children are small, I can teach evening classes while you stay home with them, and while you're at work during the day, I will be home with them. There's not a better profession for me and a family than that," she said standing behind his chair, putting her hands on his shoulders and kissing him on the forehead. "And just because I want to wait a few more years before we have our first child doesn't mean I love you less."

"I know," he said looking up at her. "Oh, my Aunt Bertha from Florida is excited about meeting you at Christmas."

"Kenneth," Sina said like a child who got caught stealing from the cookie jar. "I have to talk to you about that too. There's been a change in plans."

"What?" he said, rising.

"I'm really concerned about Rachel and this Brothaman."

"That's none of your business."

"I know, but I'm her friend. And I did tell her that Hope and I would give her a reception at Christmas."

"Sina, we planned this a long time ago. What am I going to tell my family? They were so looking forward to meeting you."

"Tell them I had a wedding reception to go to. Now I have to try to get a plane ticket," she said suddenly unfazed by his concerns.

"I don't believe this," Kenneth said. He shook his head in utter disbelief at the bombs Sina had just dropped on him.

"Well I did spend Thanksgiving with you and your family," she said as if trying to prove a point. "I'll be back to bring in the new year with you," she said sweetly. "We'll spend Christmases for the rest of our lives together. I love you even more because you're so understanding. After all understanding—"

"—Is the key to making marriage last," Kenneth said mockingly.

"Say, are we still going to the movies?"

"No, we'll have to do that some other time. I've got some business to take care of."

"Kenneth Winston," Sina said, running to the door. "I love you, I love you, I love you."

"Yeah."

Kalamazoo and the campus of Lake Effect State University were blanketed with snow as Jason sat in his torts class on a January morning. The Christmas holiday had come and gone quickly, but not quickly enough for Hope to sashay around Chicago and announce their upcoming October nuptials. And with everyone she told, she held her hand out to show off the two carat diamond. Sina and Rachel wondered how on earth Jason could afford such a big rock, being in law school and even living on campus to cut costs. Hope even wanted to take a finger shot with Rachel's one-carat on the right of her and Sina's carat and a half on her left, but since Rachel gave the ring back to Patrick and in Hope's mind, settled for a simple gold band, she decided against the picture.

Rachel and Brothaman had a beautiful reception, courtesy of Sina and Hope. Sina baked and decorated a red velvet cake which surprised her friends, but since being on her own, she learned that she could cook just about anything. "All you need are the right ingredients, the recipe and a measuring cup and spoon set. You can cook anything you want." Rev. Mintor let them use the Fellowship Hall but was disappointed at not marrying Rachel and her new husband; still, he was supportive. Sina was uncomfortable calling Rachel's husband Brothaman and even more uncomfortable when she met some of his friends who seemed like typical bullshit artists.

Marriage, Jason thought. Such a big word, such a big commitment, the rest of his life, with Hope. Now he did love her, but he thought back to the reception and how joyous, yet bittersweet it seemed. He did want to marry Hope, but right now all of it seemed so confusing, so permanent, so final. Perhaps in nine months the tide would turn and he'd feel more confident about himself, his life and Hope. *Time will tell.* He looked up and his professor was standing directly before him.

"Mr. McCoy, I've already asked you twice. Now what is the answer to the question?"

It was then that Jason remembered where he was and decided to focus solely on the task at hand.

Early one March morning Brothaman looked out the window and watched the snowflakes fall in the glimmering glow descending from the streetlight. He thought about how only a year ago he was a college senior, and one of the most talented artists in his program and a regular contributor to the literary magazine. Now he was a married man with a child on the way. Everything had happened so fast it seemed. When he first saw Rachel that June afternoon, he never dreamed that in less than six short months, she'd be his wife. But he was thankful. Very thankful. *Today is a new day.* This was the day he started a new job in his field; after all, he didn't spend four years in college studying art to become a shoe salesman. He knew that the only way to move forward was to simply take the first step, and his wife and unborn child were the motivation he needed. He looked down at his wife beside him as the first rays of sunlight filtered into the room. She seemed so peaceful. He watched her chest move up and down and listened as she snored. *She is the reason.* He smiled and Rachel began to open her eyes.

"Morning," he said as she sat up.

"Morning," Rachel kissed her husband. "You're wide awake, what were you doing."

"Just sitting here, watching you sleep, listening to you snore, and thinking how lucky I am."

"I do not snore," Rachel protested.

"Yes you do. When you inhale, it sounds like the motor of a buzzsaw. And when you exhale it sounds like you're cutting wood," he said as Rachel frowned. "Like you're cutting wood, but sweetly."

"Are you excited about your new job?"

"You know I am. I am so glad I don't have to put shoes on people's feet anymore. I'm happy too, to finally have a job where my creative juices can flow freely."

"I can't wait until you get home this evening so you can tell me all about it." Rachel made her way to the bathroom.

Brothaman's day started with him running down the stairs at the 95th Street station for a train he missed. When he finally got on, he gave his seat up to a pregnant woman, as he would expect someone to do the same for his wife. After seven stops and guest appearances by children selling fruit bags, newspapers, pantyhose and even a group of rappers who ended their performance with, "And just before, we leave this station, we'd like to ask for a little donation—We take dollars, quarters, pennies, nickels, dimes, bus tokens, transfers, and food stamps . . . " Brothaman was very glad to walk down Michigan Avenue to his job at a new, moderate sized advertising agency.

"Dave, we're happy to have you here on staff with us," his boss told him as he walked him to his work area. "I'd like for you to start out by drawing 50 thumbnail sketches of this water pitcher. Make this baby come to life."

Piece of cake. He began sketching. He thought about how he would be able to provide for his family and how quickly he would rise to the top in this field. He was good and he knew it. From the time he got his first box of crayons when he was three, Brothaman knew he wanted to be an artist. His mother had put him in all kinds of Summer art camps and competitions so that he could hone his craft. That was what he and Rachel had in common; they both knew at a very early age what they would do when they grew up, and they both stood by it. *In a few short weeks I will be able to buy my wife the prettiest ring to go on top of that wedding band.* Brothaman drew feverishly and when he had 50 sketches of the water pitcher from every angle imaginable, he proudly took the sketches to his boss who didn't even look at them, tossed them directly into the circular file. "Welcome to the world of advertising."

He was furious all day. On the train, he refused to give his seat up to anyone, even the little old lady who reminded him of his grandmother. When another group of young rappers got on the train and one of them began beatboxing, Brothaman rapped for them "I think you better, use your brain, and get the hell up off this train."

While that was only a little release for him, he was much calmer by the time he got home to his wife. "Here's the mail honey," he said as he dropped it on the table and went on upstairs.

"When you get settled," Rachel called up the stairs. "I want to hear all about your first day on your job." She sat at the dining room table which no longer had the luster and shine Aunt Mary demanded. It had become a mere drop off point for virtually everything since Brothaman moved in. Rachel went through the mail, "Bills, bills," she said as she looked at the return address on each of the envelopes and placed them on the table. When she got to the very last letter, she noticed it had a North Carolina return address, but it didn't look familiar to her. And it was typed. Sina never typed letters. But she opened it anyway, and to her surprise, it was indeed a letter from Sina.

March 2, 1992

Dear Rachel,

I decided to take a break from transcribing interviews to drop my friend a line and give her my new address. I just moved in this past weekend—you know my lease was up on my apartment. Kenneth is staying with his sister in Cary until we marry. I love this new place. I can't wait for you to see it and I can't wait to see you. You fly in on April 4th right. My defense is scheduled for the 8th. You will love this place. Oh yeah, and Kenneth bought me a puppy, a Golden Retriever I named Sparky. He looks just like Rex. I can't wait to bring him home for a week this summer. Maybe Rex can teach him a thing or two.

Let me tell you about my new place. It's three bedrooms, two full baths. I have a guest room when you first come in the front door. My kitchen is bigger than in my old apartment and the dining room is right beside it. My great room has a fireplace and is 20 X 26. It has a vaulted ceiling and is open to the upstairs. Hell, the master suite has a walk-in closet bigger than the kitchen in my old apartment and I have an office upstairs with a daybed in it. I can't wait to have you and Hope here.

How are you and your husband doing? Did he get that advertising job? I wish him the best of luck. Right now I better get back to my thesis and put some finishing touches on that Australia paper. You know I leave on the 25th— the ticket's cheaper if I leave then. The flight on the 26th sold out of all the economy class tickets and you know I can't afford business or first class. I hope I'm over my jetlag by the time you come.

Take care,
Sina

Thomasine was so engrossed in her thesis that she didn't even hear Kenneth walk up behind her. "Why aren't you ready?"

"Ready for what?" she continued typing.

"You know I have that banquet tonight. You need to be dressed, and your hair is a mess. You're going to have to work wonders. We're due there in the next hour," Kenneth said as Sina turned to face him in his tux.

"Tonight, oh shit, I can't go Kenneth. I have to finish my thesis."

"What?"

"Just go without me."

"I don't believe this," he said. "This is a $50 a plate banquet, I'm getting an award, and at the eleventh hour, you tell me you can't go."

"Look Kenneth," Sina said continuing at her keyboard, "I have my defense in two weeks. I have to finish this tonight, have it copied and to my advisor tomorrow. If I hadn't had to revise the Sydney paper then I could have spent that time on this. But I have to get this done."

"Go put on that dress I bought you. I'm not taking no for an answer."

Sina was surprised by Kenneth's brash tone. "Then, I suppose," Sina said turning to face him, "You're not taking an answer at all because I have to finish this. This is my thesis and if you can't understand that, I'm just sorry."

"You know Sina," Kenneth said angrily, "you never seem to have time for me lately. First it was the Mardi Gras dance, then my parents' anniversary and now this. I wonder if you're going to even show up on May 9th for our wedding or will you be too busy?"

"Now Kenneth, that's not even fair. Two weeks. Two f'in' weeks is all I'm asking you. Just be patient with me. When I defend, I'll be done and I can devote all of my time to you and our wedding."

"Until you start that Ph.D. program, or one of your friends needs you, then it's put little old Kenneth on the backburner and let him simmer while I tend to this or that."

"When you asked me to marry you and when we set this date, we both knew that I had a thesis to write and defend. And you know—understanding is—"

"Yeah, I know," Kenneth said as he stormed out the room.

At 5:13 a.m. Sina typed the final words of her thesis, ran spell and grammar check and printed it. She was surprised that Kenneth didn't come by, but since she moved in the townhouse and he had moved in with his sister in Cary, he didn't come by every day as he had before although he worked just down the street. Sina didn't mind though. She walked into her room and fell fast asleep fully clothed on top of her bed. It was when she had a dream about her former college roommate Gwen that she awakened. She wondered why she was dreaming about Gwen and if she were trying to tell her something. Then she remembered Gwen died exactly two years ago.

With the thesis copied and in the hands of her advisor Abby and two readers, Sina packed her bags and boarded the first of two long flights to Sydney. This was her first conference presentation and an international one at that. But she was up for the mission and was certain she could handle it. Her first trip abroad, she was awake for most of the flight, and if she could sleep, being seated in the center of the economy class area added to her discomfort and anxiety, no matter how many glasses of wine she drank. The fourteen-hour flight gave her a lot of time to think about a lot of things, and maybe Kenneth was justified in complaining about how she had been treating him lately. He had stayed up with her helping her pack and had gotten up before dawn to take her to the airport when he had a full day of work ahead of him. He had to love her and she felt she had to let him know that she truly loved him and get their relationship back on track. She was going to let him know exactly how she felt as soon as she got back to North Carolina.

Arriving in Sydney, Sina was bombarded with the usual questions from the customs: why she was there, where she was visiting and even how she found out about the places. She made her way to her hotel at about midnight on the morning of the 27th , called her parents and Kenneth collect to let them know she had arrived safely, and then dropped off to sleep. The next morning, she had breakfast at McDonald's just across the street from the Furama Hotel and took the monorail to the Sydney Convention Centre at Darling Harbour where she ran into Abby who told her about an aboriginal neighborhood just one stop from the central train station on Eddy Street.

Sina, Abby, and one of Abby's friends from graduate school boarded the train for the Redfern stop. Abby and her friend were looking for art, and luckily, an Aboriginal woman who just happened to be on her way to the Arts Council to submit a grant for children's art classes, took them there and introduced them to Denise and Melba, both from Queensland. These women were like long lost relatives, telling Sina how happy they were to meet her and how rare it was for them to meet black women from the states. With the advent of the International Basketball League, they met many black men but not many black women. They told Sina they wanted to show her around the next day, and Abby, the blue-eyed sister that she was, understood and encouraged Sina to skip her Saturday meetings.

Sina met Denise and Melba at Circular Quay the next morning where they gave her an aboriginal flag. "Red is for the earth, yellow is for the sun and black is for the people," Denise told her. Melba gave her a pair of boomerang earrings and both presented her with a hand-carved boomerang, "So that you'll come back love." Melba told her about her Torres Strait Islander ethnicity as they rode the ferry to Manly to the aquarium. Sina really felt that she was seeing long lost friends as she hugged them goodbye right before they invited her to a night on the town, beginning with a Fijian club and ending with breakfast at a little coffee shop in

Kings Cross. She was warned to be careful because the area was well known for crime. Although everyone was partying and many were drunk, the Aussies were still very polite. She observed as a young man told the other blokes to "move out of the way so the ladies can walk by." This was nothing compared to the crime in Chicago. Sina was thousands of miles away, but she felt as safe as she did at home, even safer than in Durham with all of its trees and curved streets.

Confident and assured, Thomasine presented her paper on the morning of April 1st. Her advisor came to her to congratulate her. "You did a great job with your presentation Sina," her advisor said "I've read your thesis and we need to talk."

"You aren't going to keep me in suspense until we get back to NC are you?"

"Let's get seated first," Abby said walking over to an empty table. "I'll have some of that Blue Mountain coffee, "she said to the waiter. " Sina, did you get a chance to go to the Blue Mountains? They are absolutely beautiful. They are blue because of all the eucalyptus trees. And you have to see the Three Sisters."

"Yes, Denise and Melba told me all about them. I didn't get by there yet but I plan to tomorrow," Sina said with some concern. "But let's talk about my thesis."

"Well, as I've already told you, I read your thesis and I just want to tell you," Abby began as the waiter brought her coffee, "I'm proud of you. You have truly developed into a fine scholar. I can't wait for your performance next week," she said sipping her coffee. "By the way, have you heard from the Anthropology department about your application?"

"Not yet."

"Well you will hear soon, and I'll be extremely surprised if you are not accepted—with funding. You have done such a thorough job with your thesis research."

"You trained me well Abby," Sina said smiling.

"Do you have anything else here?"

"There is a session I want to attend tomorrow," Sina said as she took a sip of water. "But what I really want to do is get back to my fiancee. He has been so understanding through this entire thesis process and I have really shut him out the last few months while I've been busy with this thesis. I just want to get things right again. As soon as possible."

"Why don't you head out today? Surprise him," Abby wore a cunning smile. "I'm sure you'll be happy you did."

"I think there's a flight out at one," Sina said checking her watch. "And it won't take me too long to pack. I think I'll do that. And Abby, thanks for everything."

Sina was one of the first to arrive at Sydney's International Airport and requested an aisle seat this time. She sat in the food court and was pleased that Denise and Melba were able to make it to the airport during their lunch hour to see her off. "You send us a snapshot from your wedding love," Denise told Sina as she hugged her goodbye. "And I think you should really consider going to Cairns for your honeymoon. You and your bloke will love it." Thomasine found her seat and was content that it was in the first row of the economy class seating. She was ecstatic when the flight attendant moved her to the business class seating in order to accommodate a family who wanted to sit together. In twelve and a half short hours, Sina would be calling Kenneth to pick her up from the airport so they could begin their reconciliation. Ravishing thoughts about making up with Kenneth soothed Sina into a seven-hour nap on the plane, this time without the assistance of any of that Hunter Valley wine.

When Thomasine claimed her baggage at Raleigh-Durham International Airport, she tried one last time to reach Kenneth. She had tried his private line at his sister's, his voice mail at work and even the townhouse, figuring he was probably feeding Sparky. Sina hailed a cab and noted the unseasonably cool temperature. They pulled up in front of her townhouse and Sina saw that her car was parked just where she left it. She saw another car that looked vaguely familiar, but thought nothing of it as she rifled through her purse for her key as the cabbie took her bags out of the trunk. Sina held the door open for the cabbie to put her bags by the steps when she heard him say, "Aw shucky ducky. Da brother is wrong." Sina was amazed to see Kenneth naked as a jaybird in front of a roaring fire on the oriental rug, his face planted firmly between the legs of Sophronia Lucas.

"And the brother know he's wrong," Thomasine said walking over to the fireplace. "I asked you to take care of the dog, not be the damn dog," she screamed. "Now for you little missy, just put your clothes back on and just get the hell up out of my house," Sina said walking toward her. "I'm mad, but I can't really be mad at you. You never told me you loved me. You never got down on your knees and asked me to be your wife. And you sure as hell never told me you wanted to have children just like me. Just get out," she said pointing toward the door. "And for you Kenneth Winston. I just want you to get all of your things and get out. Out of my house and out of my life," Sina ran up the stairs to her room with Sparky at her heels.

"Sina, we need to talk about this," Kenneth said banging on her locked bedroom door. "Let me in. I'm worried about you. I don't want you to kill yourself. Let me in."

The last thing Sina said was, "Now that's some funny shit. That you'd think you're worth me ending my life." Sina sat on the comforter with Sparky at her feet and thought about all that had happened, trips together, the proposal, the house hunt and the recent shopping sprees for new furniture. She even thought about how she had rushed back from the other side of the world just to see him and make up. She cried. A quiet stream. Hours passed, morning broke and there she still was, in the middle of her queen-sized bed crying, and a hungry Sparky in her lap. Enough is enough. She fed Sparky on the patio and called Kelsey who said she'd drive down after work. Rachel and Hope said they'd hop on the first plane out of Midway as soon as Hope got to Chicago. She snatched up the rug and tossed it into the fireplace and watched it smolder. The urge to destroy all of their photos taken together gave way to simply cutting Kenneth out. Why rip up perfectly good pictures of herself? Before she took Sparky for a walk, she went to the storage closet and grabbed one of those boxes she used in the move and put everything in it that even hinted at Kenneth. With new energy and resolve, she erased him, from the diploma in the office to his elephant G-string in her lingerie drawer. "I told him to get his shit," she said to Sparky as she attached the leash to his collar.

After an invigorating walk, Sina jumped in the shower, shampooed her hair, unpacked her bag, ironed her red pantsuit, put her hair up in a French roll and polished her nails as she sat under the dryer. She gathered up the box of his things because she just decided to make a detour on the way to the airport. "If he won't get his shit," Sina said as she drove down Highway 54 toward The Park, "then I'll just have to take them to him."

For just a moment, Sina stepped outside of herself. She parked her car in a visitor's space and got the box. She saw several people leaving for lunch appointments as she began to stand pictures of Kenneth up in the border between the grass and the sidewalk. She laid every trinket on the lawn with the exception of the G-string which she hung on the entrance sign. She was just about to take his diploma out when Sophronia came outside for lunch but ran back in to get Kenneth.

"Thomasine," he said with his hands on her shoulders. "What the hell do you think you're doing?"

"I told you to come get your shit, Kenneth. And since you didn't take it with you last night, I'm bringing it to you. Because right about now, you're just a distant memory."

"Sina, we need to talk about this. Once you calm down and think this thing through—"

"There's nothing to talk about."

"Once we sit down and talk, you'll understand—"

"Understand this. It's over. I don't ever want to see you again. If you see me walking down the street, you better cross the street," Sina said as she began to walk away. "And the rest of your stuff is in the box."

"Sina."

"Oh, yeah. I almost forgot. Here's your ring," Sina said taking off her ring.

"No Sina. Keep it."

"What for. I don't want you, I don't want it and I sure as hell don't want anything that will remind me of this year and a half that ended in misery. Take it. It's yours. Oh, and I will keep the townhouse."

"Sina. Just let this blow over," Kenneth said pleading.

"It'll blow over all right. Just like a fart in a whirlwind. Now here," Sina said as she extended her hand to give him the ring.

"I'm not taking it."

"Fine, suit yourself," she said as she drew her arm back and aimed for the fountain in front of the building.

"You better not."

"Better not what?" It made a small splash.

"You bitch," Kenneth said, slapping Sina. "Do you know how much I paid and am still paying for that damn ring." She massaged her right cheek which still smarted from Kenneth's slap.

"Now see, you know I'm not the high drama type, but you have driven me to this," Sina said as she broke out in a zenkutsu dachi and began to give Kenneth a royal South side of Chicago butt whipping—karate style. "It's on now." He remembered that she was testing for her blue belt. She thought about the women she had interviewed for her thesis project and their experiences, and even had driven her to take up karate. Unfortunately for him, Kenneth was every man who had ever violated any woman, those she had interviewed and more. Sina was finally able to let go.

Calling My Name

24

After Sina picked Rachel and Hope up from the airport, she stopped by the ABC store to stock up and then to the mall for lunch and an outfit for the thesis defense. She didn't even let Hope and Rachel unpack their bags. She just told them to throw their bags down and get back in the car. She ran into Naja Adande Washington, one of her sorors and a graduate student at Steeplechase, and told her to stop by for her freedom celebration later that evening. By the time the Three Musketeers got back to the townhouse, Kelsey had arrived.

"It's so cold here," Kelsey giggled as she stood near the fire sipping her Buttery Nipple in Sina's living room. "But that rug got that fire all warm and toasty."

"That man knows good and well he was wrong," Naja said. "Know he wrong. Girlfriend don't you even look back."

"That's right and that Sophronia Lucas ought to be ashamed of herself—first Rodney and now Kenneth. Who's next?" Rachel added. "But he ain't even worth it."

"Now Rachel's absolutely right about that," Hope said. "How does he expect you to trust him now? After you caught him with another woman. I thank God for Jason. He'd never do anything like that," Hope continued as Sina, Kelsey and Rachel erupted in laughter.

"I know one thing," Kelsey said. "I sure wish I could have seen you kick Kenneth's ass out there. Right in front of his co-workers and all. That shit had to be funny as a three dollar bill," they all laughed. "I'm sure it went over big—"Kelsey began.

"Like a turd in a punch bowl," she and Sina said in unison exploding in laughter.

"Trust must be earned" Hope began. "And after eight long years. Actually eight years, five months and—"

"We get the picture," Rachel interrupted.

"You know, she's right. You have to be careful. You really need to take time to get to know him before you marry. Me and my Terence have been together for over four years now."

"That is not true," Kelsey said. "I think you should know in oh, a few months—three or so, if he is someone you would want to spend the rest of your life with. If he isn't, then just give him the ole heave ho. If he is, then move forward."

"Amen," Rachel said giving Kelsey a high five.

"You know," Sina said, finally joining in the conversation. "When a man puts a ring on your finger, somehow he gets the idea that he—I don't know—owns you or something. Like what he says must go or else. Everything was near perfect between us before he put that ring on my finger. Then it was like, 'my plans can't change.' He had a problem with me coming home for Christmas and then he couldn't understand that I couldn't go to his dumb banquet because I had to finish my thesis. Oh, and he really had a problem with me applying to a Ph.D. program instead of having children."

"Have you heard anything yet?" Naja asked.

"You know, I haven't even looked at my mail since I've been back," Sina said walking over to the dining room table. "It looks like I just got bills, I'll have to make sure they send Kenneth's bills to his sister's because he ain't coming up in here to get nothing. And I mean that."

"Even if you have a mean case of dwd," Rachel asked, laughing.

"Dwd ain't even that serious. Not for me to go back there."

"What's dwd?" Hope asked while Kelsey and Naja looked up in the air as if they were trying to decipher Rachel and Sina's code. Kelsey looked at Rachel and Naja looked at Sina and they burst into laughter.

"Here it is," Sina said, holding out an envelope from The Graduate School at UNC-Chapel Hill. "And I can't open it. I'm too scared," she said, as she took a swig of her kamikaze.

"Open it," Rachel and Hope yelled.

"I can't."

"Well give it here," Kelsey snatched it out of Sina's hand. "How you gonna ever know if you don't open it?" She tore the envelope open. Kelsey unfolded the letter and read it with a poker face.

"The verdict?" Sina asked.

"My Boo's gonna get her a Ph.D. in Anthropology."

"You got it going on girl," Naja said and hugged her Soror.

"Congratulations," Hope said.

"I'm so proud of you Sina." Rachel joined the hugfest.

"I feel so free now, like a weight's been lifted off my shoulders. "

"Your ass is drunk as hell, just wait and see how you feel in the morning," Kelsey said.

"This calls for an even bigger celebration," Naja said raising her glass.

"Let's hold off anymore celebrations until I defend this thesis. I have to write my performance and memorize my lines by Wednesday."

"Well, we can help you. That's what we're here for."

"Look, it's getting late. And I have to T.A. in the morning so I better be running." Naja started toward the door. "And since you will have a little free time after your defense, why don't you work with me in Project WIDEN-G one Saturday?"

"That's such a good program," Kelsey offered. "You should do it."

"I'll give it some thought," Sina walked Naja to the door.

"And if you need anything, or just want a shoulder to cry on I'm here," Naja said. "I mean it too. Anytime of the day or night."

"Thank you for everything Naja."

"That's what sorors are for," Naja hugged Sina.

"I just thought about something."

"What's that?" Rachel asked.

"Not only didn't I check my mail, but I didn't check my answering machine either. I could have a message from one of my readers or something," Sina said, walking into the kitchen and pressing the play button on her machine. "These are all those messages I left for Kenneth to pick me up from the airport. Oh, and here are the messages from dumb ass Kenneth. Like I'm going to call him back."

"Girl, if you do, I'll drive right down here and kick your ass."

"I'll kick your ass and I'm six months pregnant," Rachel added.

"Don't even think about it Sina," Hope said. "Because I'll be right behind them."

"This is Mrs. Morris from *Oaks of Righteousness African Christian Church* calling to remind you about your pre-marital counseling session with Rev. Grace at 10:00 tomorrow morning."

"I guess I can cancel that one."

"No Sina," Kelsey said putting her arm on Sina's shoulder. "I think you need to see your minister. She can give you some spiritual insight."

"Isn't this a sight, you're drunk as a skunk and telling me to go get some spiritual insight."

"She's right Sina," Rachel said. "That is exactly what you need."

"It can only help you," Hope began. "And make you stronger."

"I guess you're right," Sina replied. "And I guess that gives me about twelve hours to get sober and clean myself up."

Thomasine stood in the lobby of the big church on Fayetteville Street and peered out through the glass window at the fountain in front of the church. She remembered the first time she attended Oaks of Righteousness. She drove right past it looking for a more traditional church building. When she noticed the street numbers getting smaller and smaller, she realized she must have passed it. She turned around on the campus of North Carolina Central University and headed in the opposite direction. Amazed that the church took up an entire block, Sina turned onto Nash Street to get to the parking lot in the rear of the church she had noticed on her trek back. *Daddy would like this.* The circular drive, reserved parking spaces and land were impressive. "Rev. Grace will see you now," said Mrs. Morris, a middle aged woman with a pleasant smile and friendly disposition, interrupting Sina's reverie. "Come right this way. Rev. Grace's office is on the right."

"Thomasine Mintor," Rev. Grace said giving Sina a big, tight, it's-been-ages-since-I've-seen-you hug. "I'm so glad you finally got around to seeing me. I remember when you were just a baby, back when I interned under your father. You have truly blossomed into a fine young lady."

"Thank you Rev. Grace. I've really been intending to take you to lunch and thank you for that wonderful letter of recommendation you wrote for me — you know for Delta and all, but this thesis has kept me absolutely swamped with work. I defend on Wednesday."

"I know all about thesis defenses and trust me, I understand. But don't even worry about taking me to lunch or anything — it was my pleasure — really. I'm just so proud of you, getting your Masters — "

"I got accepted into a doctoral program too — in Cultural Anthropology at UNC."

"Congratulations. M.A., Ph.D., Mrs. You're getting all your letters now I see," Rev. Grace said brightly. "Now where is this future husband of yours so we can get on with the counseling session. He'll be here shortly, won't he?"

"Actually he won't. There isn't going to be any wedding in May."

"Thomasine, what happened?"

"Let's just say I rushed back from Australia to find him in our new townhouse in front of the fire in — a compromising position with one of his co-workers," Sina said sadly, fighting back the pain.

"No. I'm so sorry."

"So basically I told him to get his stuff and leave — forever."

"You know what all that was about don't you?"

"Well, he felt that I had been ignoring him—working on the thesis and all."

"That's not it at all," Rev. Grace said as she leaned back in her high-back executive style chair. "You don't know."

"Yeah, I was made a big fool of."

"Not at all, Precious," Rev. Grace said recalling one of the many pet names Rev. Mintor had for his baby girl Sina. "Right about now you ought to be on your feet rejoicing and praising the Lord."

"What?"

"Don't you realize that He just delivered a potential problem out of your midst?" Rev. Grace answered. "That ex-fiancee of yours is clearly the fool; and the Lord knew it and revealed it to you before it was too late.

"And remember, that while you can't change your past, you can chart your future—with Jesus Christ. All that old mess with him and anybody else—just rise above it. You don't need that in your life. Don't claim it and it won't be yours. With Jesus, you can rise above the mess and all the rest..."

Sina listened to the words of wisdom from Rev. Grace and as she listened, thought of all she had been through and how free she had felt with her release the previous day. What Rev. Grace said rang true. You can't change your past, but you can take control of your future. Thomasine then realized that her father being a minister would not save her, a notion she had lived with for most of her life. Today she had to take a big step, turn over a new leaf. Today, Thomasine Mintor realized that she would have to seek salvation for herself.

"Say Thomasine," Rev. Grace said with an unsuspecting look on her face. "I remember when you were a little girl back at Peace A.C.C. You sure could sing. Just like a sweet little bird. Do you still sing?"

"Yes Rev. Grace. I sang with the Gospel Ensemble in college back in Wisconsin. We didn't have enough Black students for a choir, but I haven't really sung since then, but I still love to sing."

"Great. Then you can direct the youth choir because the Lord knows, those children need help. Bless their little hearts. And they need someone young like you, someone who's in tune to them and what they're going through. You know things aren't like they used to be. I never had to walk past a metal detector just to get to school. We need to draw more youth in too, because if we don't make an investment in the youth, we won't have a prosperous future."

"You're right Rev. Grace. You're absolutely right. And maybe directing the youth choir is just what I need."

"Great, then you can start next week—right after your defense."

The experimental theater was packed with Sina's friends, professors, women from her support group of Black women graduate students and the women she interviewed. "I Rise," Sina began. "Poet and author Maya Angelou so eloquently wrote these words in a poem about Black people's triumph over oppression," Sina said just before she began to recite the poem *And Still I Rise*. "To win over oppression, in all its guises, we must empower ourselves, just as Deborah, Sarah, Hannah, and Miriam have done. Though from different places and backgrounds, they all share the same horror: acquaintance rape."

"They say that one in eight women have been raped by someone they know," Sarah said taking a seat in a group of four chairs arranged in a semi-circle.

"You know, one in twelve men admits to having forced or attempted to make a woman have sex with him—yet none of these men view themselves as rapists," Deborah said taking a seat beside Sarah. "They just don't get it," she said, shaking her head in disbelief.

"I always thought a rapist was someone who attacked you in a dark alley at gun point," Miriam said walking into the semicircle. "Not someone you know, and trust, and certainly not someone you go out of your way to help."

"It wasn't rape, there was no penetration—I'm still a virgin," Hannah said. "It was prom night and we were all dressed up. He had bought me a corsage and told me I looked really pretty. He took me to dinner after prom. And for a $20 dollar dinner, he told me I must earn my keep. We were sitting in the car, the car his big brother had rented for him. That cost too, he reminded me. And when he discovered that I had my period he just grabbed me by the back of my neck and told me I had to finish what I had started. I begged him not to. I shut my mouth as tight as I could, but he just pinched my neck harder and harder until I had to open my mouth and give in. We were alone. No one was nearby."

"There she goes wearing those short skirts again, my co-workers always said about me." Deborah began standing up and walking into the center of the semicircle. "I was working and going to school. Trying so hard to make it, you know, fulfill my dreams. Then one evening when I didn't have class my boss just bombarded me with work. Top priority. Had to be in New York first thing in the morning and I had to stay until it was finished. That was the bottom line. By the time I took him the final draft, we had to be the only ones on that floor—if not the entire building. I went into his office and he walked me to the door and stood with his back against it. And locked it. He told me about how regal I looked in purple and that it was his favorite color and about the raise I would be getting if I continued to do good work. 'She asked for it; she's nothing but a trouble maker—a Jezebel,' those same women who criticized my short skirts said about me after I filed charges. Less than 50% of acquaintance rape is ever reported," Deborah said, turning to sit down.

"My mother was always silent. 'Now Sarah', my father always told me, 'good little girls are silent.'" Sarah sat in a chair near the center of the circle, holding her arms to her chest. "He was my friend. I met him in Music Appreciation. One Friday night I ran into him at the caf. He had my favorite movie on videotape and told me to stop by. He had wine coolers and herb. He was my buddy. He knew my boyfriend—but we were on the outs. I confided in him. He confided in me. But I can trust him no longer," she said looking at the audience. "And I can no longer trust men."

"I trusted him too," Miriam said walking up to Sarah and putting her hand on her shoulder. "I cared about him. I helped him. I did favors for him. And this is the thanks I got. Acts of goodwill any time of the day or night. My daddy always told me to help others when I could, that I would be blessed through it. My blessing was an unwanted pregnancy," she said beginning to tear up. "A baby I had to give up because the memories were too painful. And he never even knew."

"Well I am the middle child. I have two older brothers and two younger brothers," Deborah said rising, "So my daily life was a fight. A fight for the bathroom, a fight for the phone, a fight for a piece of chicken at dinner time, and a you-better-not-let-her-walk-all-over-you-or-else-we're-gonna-kick-your-butt fight my brothers often threatened when I had a disagreement with another neighborhood girl. And I was conditioned by my brothers to fight for a reason. And like the fights for the bathroom and the piece of chicken were essential to my survival—so was this one."

"It wasn't really rape," Hannah started walking beside Deborah. "I was still a virgin—yet I felt like I had been robbed. If I'd reported it, I would have been laughed out of the police station. A virgin raped—please, they would say. I loved him, and I didn't want to ruin his life, so I continued to see him. But I just put that awful memory out of my mind. Just erased it—poof—it's gone. That's what I had to do to survive."

"I denied it too," Miriam started. "Until I found out I was three months pregnant. Then I became silent. To my parents, to my friends and to myself."

"Silence. It's what I was taught to do," Sarah said, still sitting in her chair. "Women are silent. But silence got me in that situation. It is that silence that caused me not to speak up, not to yell no in his ear. I did say no, I really did, but I didn't yell. If I had hollered, screamed, kicked and fought, just maybe, it wouldn't have happened. But Daddy always said good girls don't make such loud noises. Good girls are quiet."

Thomasine looked around the theater at the faces — fear, rage — and pain. They continued to talk, mostly about how to start anew or starting over, freeing themselves for future relationships.

"Your anger, rise above it," Deborah said as she walked back near her seat in the semi-circle.

"Your fear, rise above it," Hannah said following Deborah.

"Your blame, rise above it," Miriam said walking into the semi-circle.

"Your fear of being alone, inability to trust, and your depression — rise above it all," Sarah said, still in her seat.

"I rise," Deborah said matter-of-factly, taking her seat.

"I rise," Hannah said a pitch higher and slightly louder than Deborah.

"I rise," Miriam said even louder than the other two as she sat down.

"I RISE!!!" Sarah yelled, standing to her feet.

I Give it Back to Thee

25

Thomasine looked around the choir room of Oaks of Righteousness at the empty chairs and the eight teenagers scattered about who comprised the youth choir. "Before we begin rehearsing," she said right after prayer, we are going to establish some ground rules." She walked through the rows of seats. "Number one, we are in the house of the Lord which means we are about some very serious business. You will keep that first and foremost in your mind and treat everything we do with the utmost respect. Number two, rehearsals are important to your performance; therefore, attendance is extremely important. Number three, this is your choir. It will only be as prosperous as you make it. This means," Thomasine said as she walked to the front of the group to face them, "that each of you has an opportunity at each rehearsal to give your input. We are open to new music. If you can get the sheet music, that would be great, but a tape will suffice. And finally, I want each of you to bring someone else next week. I was in the youth choir when I was growing up and it was a wonderful experience. And I hope each of you has an even better experience with this choir than I did," Sina concluded, recalling how she had met Conrad. "Now who is the president?"

"We don't have one."

"I suppose when we get more members we will elect officers," she said taking a seat at the piano. "What songs have you rehearsed?" She decided to just pick up where the former director left off.

"What a Friend we Have in Jesus," Joy, a petite, slender girl with dark chocolate skin and a short bob haircut responded.

"Okay." Sina said. That was the first hymn she learned to play on the piano. "Do you know what key?"

"Key?" Kwame asked.

"Next week I will give you a crash course in music theory. I will teach you how to sight read, but for now let's just go over this song. Okay, who leads this one?" Sina asked as Joy stood and Sina began playing a very spirited *What a Friend.* "I'm going to give an introduction and then your parts," Sina said as she played the last bar and broke the first chord down into soprano, alto, tenor and bass although no bass were present.

"What a friend," Joy sang, but Sina stopped playing.

"Wait a minute. What version of this song have you been singing?"

"The one in the hymnal," another teenager replied.

"You're kidding, right?"

"No. Everything we sang is in the hymnal."

"That explains," Sina began to say of the small number of youth in the choir, but decided it was in her best interest to be silent on this one. "I tell you what. We're going to start with all new music. Let's see. I think we'll start with a new processional. How many of you are familiar with *Come on Children, Let's Sing?*"

Joy raised her hand.

"I'll have to change the key, but I want you to lead it for now since you know it. Okay, the words are," Sina said as she wrote them phonetically on the board and sat back at the piano to begin teaching them their parts. She found that she had to change the key several times and still the choir couldn't seem to find the right pitch and some couldn't stay on beat—with the exception of Joy. Sina had them stand so they could sing from their stomachs but to no avail. She decided then that the next week would be spent listening to a song, analyzing it, feeling it, and learning the basics of music.

On her way out of the church, Sina ran into Rev. Grace. "So how did it go?" she asked.

"Well Rev. Grace," Sina began but decided that since she couldn't say anything nice about them, it was best for her to be silent.

"That bad, huh?"

"Will they be ready for Youth Day the second Sunday in June?"

"Hmm, that's eight weeks away. With some new music, more members and a whole lot of prayer, I guarantee they'll turn the church out. I promise. But it will take some praying. Some serious get-down-on-your-knees-at-the-altar praying."

"I'm not even going to worry," Rev. Grace smiled. "Because I know you can handle it."

Jason sat at the table with a bowl of Muesli to join his fiancee in breakfast. "This dress looks so nice," Hope began as she finished off her second French crueller with white icing. "But I'll probably have to lose a few pounds," she said of the off the shoulder straight white gown with a very tight fitting bodice.

"I'm sure whatever you wear will be beautiful." Jason poured skim milk on his cereal. "And I love you just the way you are."

"But everything has to be perfect. It must be. That's why I suggested we move the date back into the fall because Rachel is pregnant and her baby is due in July."

"What's that got to do with anything?"

"You know they say first babies come two weeks early or two weeks late. That baby would probably be born right on our wedding day—if I hadn't changed it."

"I suppose you're right," Jason said continuing with his cereal.

"And now that Rachel's the Minister of Music at Front Street, I'm sure she'll—"

"Everything's gonna work out all right. Don't worry," Jason said recalling what his Uncle Leroy had told him a month ago when he went to him to talk about his doubts.

"Look Jason, you love her, don't you?"

"Yes I do Uncle Leroy."

"You can trust her, can't you? She wouldn't tip out on you?"

"She wouldn't ever do that."

"She's devoted to you, isn't she?"

"Yes?"

"Well Jason, it's like this. Anytime you face a change in life there is always some apprehension. Remember when you graduated from eighth grade and were headed to Piney Hill. You were nervous about that. And then coming to Lake Effect State U. There was some apprehension because we fear the unfamiliar."

"That's true."

"And this isn't any different," Uncle Leroy continued. "But Hope is a good woman. She'll make a good wife. She could stand to lose a few pounds for her health, but she'll make a real good wife. I just can't understand why it took you so long to propose."

Jason looked at his uncle and thought about that evening with Hope. The evening. "I just had to wait for the right moment. Everything had to be in place first."

"Jason," Hope said shaking his hand and bringing him out of his daydream. "You are excited about our wedding, aren't you?"

"Of course I am. I just wish I were finishing law school next month."

"But you will finish in two short years," Hope said, on her fourth donut. "You'll be the best sports and entertainment lawyer in the Midwest."

"You think so?" Jason took the donut.

"Certainly. The best by far. You know I have faith in you and I trust you," she said, reaching for her breakfast.

"Uh-uh," Jason tossed it in the trash. "If you want to lose weight for that dress, you're going to have to cut back on these. And I have faith and trust you to do it," he said, smiling and remembering why she had been such an important part of his life for so long.

Rachel and her mother Rebecca greeted Front Street members as they began their short excursion around the corner from the church to the place Rachel and Brothaman now called home. "You really played that organ today," Rebecca told Rachel as they walked past the trees that were finally beginning to retain their color and fullness. "Your Aunt would be really proud of you."

"You think so?"

"Definitely. I'm so glad you invited me to your church. Oh, and to dinner."

"I just hope the meal turns out all right."

"I'm sure it will," Rebecca said as they reached the house.

"Have a seat," Rachel said to her mother as she motioned to the sofa. "I baked the chicken last night and I just have to warm it up and the beans; I'll be right back."

Rebecca looked around the living room and observed that it lacked the order and neatness Aunt Mary had attained for so long. Brothaman had his drafting table over in a corner and papers and pencils were scattered all over. Rachel tried to get him to keep his supplies in a box, but it was no use. "So have you heard from Hank?"

"Yes. He called yesterday. He's really looking forward to graduation week after next. I'm so glad that he got into Duncan Medical School. I'll be able to see him all the time," Rachel said walking back into the living room. "Ooh, the baby just moved." She d put her mother's hand on her stomach.

"My first grandchild," Rebecca said smiling. "And I'm sure it will be a girl. That baby's sitting in your stomach just like a watermelon. That means it will be a girl. If it was like a pumpkin, then it would be a boy. But you know, girls are the first born in our family. Look at you and Hank."

"I hope it's a girl. But then I don't know, Hope and Thomasine were fighting over what I should name her. I really like Amber."

"That's pretty."

"Amber Thomasine has a nice ring to it, but Hope would be absolutely livid with me if her name wasn't somewhere in there."

"You don't want to do that then."

"Oh, it just came to me. I think I will name her Amber Rebecca. After you."

"Honey, I never did like my name Rebecca, but I would be honored to have you name your first child after me."

"Amber Rebecca Brown," Rachel said to her husband walking in.

"Amber Rebecca," Brothaman said. "That sounds nice and all, but I think this one's going to be a boy."

"I don't know," Rebecca said.

"We shall see. Honey, do you have something on the stove? It smells like something is burning."

Rachel got up and ran into the kitchen to discover that she had burned the beans. Everyone knows just how bad burnt beans smell. It was probably just as well though because she had taken those string beans straight out of the can and heated them up, no smoked meat, no garlic or onions, or no seasonings. Rachel put the chicken on a serving plate and whipped the potatoes up and made a tossed salad. She couldn't possibly mess that up. She usually went to Mrs. Jones' for Sunday dinner because although Hope was away in Kalamazoo, she still prepared a big meal. That usually gave her and her husband enough food to last through the middle of the week. The rest of the time it was TV dinners and carry-outs. Rachel shoved the brown and serve rolls into the oven and put the mashed potatoes in a serving bowl. She just tilted the pot to the side and the potatoes just slid right into the bowl. She called her mother and husband to the dinner table and carried the food into the dining room.

"What kind of dressing do you like?" Rachel asked her mother.

"Ranch, French or Italian." Rachel went back into the kitchen and opened the refrigerator. Rebecca was surprised that her son-in-law didn't even get up to help her carry the meal into the dining room. She decided that she would have to make more visits to her daughter's because from what she could see right now, Rachel would have quite a job once that baby came.

Rebecca put a forkful of chicken in her mouth. Rachel had cooked that chicken to death being careful of salmonella. Rebecca chewed and chewed and chewed, smiling the entire time. And the longer she chewed the bigger that small piece of chicken seemed to become. "How is it?" Rachel asked.

"It's fine, thank you. But with that baby coming, I want to share some of my recipes."

"Honey, where are the rolls," Brothaman asked, sniffing the air.

"Oh no!" Rachel scrambled from the table to get the burning rolls out of the oven. This got under Rebecca's skin even more.

Thomasine sat in her living room, munching on chocolate chip cookies with Sparky at her feet and listened to a tape of the youth choir's performance. Her prayers had been answered. The choir had grown in size and talent and would grow even more as evidenced by the number of teens who asked about rehearsal after church. She sang along with the tape as Joy soloed on *I'm Available to You*. She had a beautiful voice and she brought members of Oaks of Righteousness to their feet. Just as the guest minister began his sermon, Thomasine heard the phone ring. She walked to the kitchen counter and picked up her cordless.

"Hello," Sina said.

"Hello Princess."

"Daddy."

"I just called to see how church went today."

"The choir was outstanding. I'm really proud of what these young people have done in two short months."

"That shows you that prayer changes things. You know that's our Crew Members for Christ theme this year."

"It surely does. I'm a witness."

"Say Princess, will you be able to come home for the tea this year, you know it's at the end of next week."

"I suppose I could come home, but I'd need to get a ticket quick. And I don't know what I'm going to do with Sparky."

"Bring him. You know how I hate for you to be on the road by yourself. Just get a ticket. I'll pay for it."

"Then I'll come home. Probably on that Friday morning. You know I have to go to choir rehearsal on Thursday nights. I can stay until Wednesday. I need to get some more voice over work."

"That will be wonderful. You know you haven't been home since Christmas. And then you were only here for a week."

"I know Daddy," Sina said putting her feet up on her coffee table. "How did church go today?"

"It was great. Especially because I didn't have to preach. The youth choir sang and Rachel had that organ rocking. Caleb preached. Took his text from *Romans* 12."

"I love that text. And it's so appropriate for today's youth."

"Or the youth of any era. You know we had our own set of struggles too. It was nothing like today, but they were still struggles."

"Did anybody join the church today?"

"Yes, a young man who just got his M.B.A. from the University of Chicago. He used to play at Illinois when he was in college. And he just signed with this new international basketball league. Let's see, his last name starts with an H. You know I'm getting old now and I don't remember like I used to."

"Rodney Harris?"

"That is it. Do you know him?"

"We graduated from Piney Hill together and interned together at the Superstation. I'm glad to know that he's doing well."

"Well to say the least. You know, he's not like those other athletes either. Most of them sign those multimillion dollar contracts and move right out to the suburbs, but not him. He signed with the Windy City Gale Force. I saw him on the news the other night. He does a lot of work with the youth. He's even going to work with the Youth Crew for Christ."

"That's great Daddy, but what about when his season starts. I'm sure they'll have him going all over the world."

"Yes, but he's willing to do what he can while he's here and it's appreciated."

"I suppose you're right. You know, more people my age need to invest some time in mentoring this next generation because they have to deal with things we never even dreamed about."

"That's true Princess. Hey, when you get here next week, you'll get to see Rodney. I'm sure he'll be at the Crew Members for Christ tea."

"That'll be nice Daddy," Sina said trying to be pleasant although she felt her father was meddling. "Look, I better get on the phone and find myself and Sparky a plane ticket."

"Okay Princess, just call me and let me know when to pick you up from the airport."

Thomasine arrived in Chicago and spent the afternoon with Rachel. Sparky was safely locked away in the garage with Rex for the evening and Sina was neatly tucked in her bed and comfortably asleep when the phone rang at 2AM that Saturday morning. The last time someone called her at this ungodly hour she told them off real good but she knew that it could only be bad news with a call coming into her parents' house at this time. Sina sat up in the bed and braced herself for the inevitable as she reached for the phone.

"Sina, my water just broke."

"Oh my God, where is Brothaman?"

"He went out with his friends, you know the baby's not due for another two weeks."

"The baby's due whenever he or she decides to be due. Let's see," Sina said fluctuating in and out of panic mode. "Write your husband a note that I took you to the hospital and pack your phone book so I can call your mother up in Evanston. I'll get mom's car and I'll be by in a jiffy. Just wait by the door. Oh yeah, and make sure you have your keys out so you can lock up the house."

Calm down, Thomasine said to herself as she drove east on 95th Street to pick up Rachel only to turn around and drive west on the same street to get her to the hospital. Since there was absolutely no traffic out, she was able to make it in record time. "How far apart are your contractions?" Sina asked, briefly recalling her delivery.

"About ten minutes," Rachel said as she let out a loud scream.

"It's going to be a long night."

Sina paced the floor, then joined Rachel's mother and Hank in pacing while they waited for Brothaman, who did manage to arrive just in time for the birth of his son Martin. "It's about time," Rebecca said to her son-in-law. "Your wife is in here having a baby and you're out gallivanting all damn night." Feeling gulity and knowing it was in his best interest not to have a confrontation with his mother-in-law, Brothaman just walked on down the hallway to join his wife in the labor room.

Thomasine and Rachel sat in the living room looking out at the leaves which were quickly disappearing from the trees on an early autumn afternoon. "He's really gotten big," Sina said holding a three-month-old Martin. "They just seem to grow so fast." She kissed his forehead as his mother handed her a bottle.

"You know Sina, I love little Martin to death, but I had no idea he would be this much work."

"He has to depend on his parents for everything, absolutely everything. It's a good thing you have a husband because if it were just you, it would seem ten times as tedious," Rachel just smiled at Sina and remained silent. "So Hope is finally getting married."

"Yes, she's waited for this for a long time."

"I know. Remember when we were getting ready for prom. The girl had her dress picked out then. And I hope she changed her selection because that dress is definitely out of style now."

"She changed all right. Have you seen her lately?"

"No, the last time I saw her was at my thesis defense."

"Girlfriend has dropped at least 40 pounds. She's down to a size 12. Some kind of herbal cleansing or something."

"Wow," Sina replied in amazement. "And I'm up to a 12."

"I noticed, but I wasn't going to say anything."

"Thank you. It seems that I just study and eat and go work with the youth."

"Girl, get you a man in your life, he'll knock those pounds off."

"So that's your secret? That would be nice, but right now I don't have time. I have so much to do."

"Well you need to take some time out for yourself. And some way or another get some exercise."

"I'll start exercising. And I'll do it for about two weeks and then something will happen and I'll stop."

"Remember, that all work and no play makes Sina a dull girl."

"Me, dull? Please," Sina responded smiling as she and Rachel heard the doorbell and walked excitedly toward the door.

"Mom," Rachel said hugging her mother. "I guess it is that time already," she said walking back into the living room. "You remember my friend Sina, don't you."

"It's so nice to see you again Mrs. Thorne." Sina held Martin upright to burp him.

"It's good to see you too," Mrs. Thorne replied. "Now how's my little grandbaby doing?"

"He's full as a tick. And now he won't have gas."

"That's good, now he'll sleep on the trip back home. How's grandma's little dumplin' doing?" she said, kissing him.

"Mom is going to keep Martin this weekend since Hope's wedding is going to have me really busy."

"You and me both. I'll probably sleep all the way back to Raleigh-Durham and I'm thankful that Monday is University Day—I don't have any classes since my only class on Mondays is before noon."

As smoothly as Hope's rehearsal dinner went off, the wedding was guaranteed to be perfect. Rachel and Sina had the procedure down pat because they had been hearing about it for the last five years— it was cemented in their minds. And Hope really looked good. She hadn't been this small in years. She wore her hair in a French roll and a form fitting suit to her rehearsal dinner. She even ate really light. Just a salad. But she was in for a surprise once she got to her hotel suite with her attendants.

"My little cousin Hope is getting married," Hope's cousin Charity from Savannah said crying. "You're making me feel so old you know."

"You," Mrs. Jones said. "It's my daughter who's getting married to-morrow," she said as crocodile tears fell from her face.

"Look here," Sina said taking each of them tissues. "I'm not about to have any of this tonight. Now stop that crying and save it for something sad, like Hope and Jason's first football head-shaped baby." They all laughed.

"What's in that basket?" Rachel asked.

"Let's see," Hope took the basket off the desk and set it on the bed. "A satin pillowcase—so that I may have sweet dreams. Bubble bath in a champagne bottle, so that I will smell sweet," she continued. "A silk chemise," she said holding up the ivory gown, "so that I will feel good when I sleep. Oh, and matching slippers so that each of my steps is as if I'm walking on air."

"We see what all you got. What does the note say?"

> Hope,
>   *I am my beloved's, and my beloved is mine...Thou art beautiful, O my love..., the note began. ...How fair and how pleasant art thou, O love, for delights!*
>   *Words from Song of Solomon. Tomorrow, you will make me the happiest man who ever walked this earth.*
>   Jason

"I just have one question," Thomasine said with a sensuously sly look on her face. "If the bubble bath is so that you will smell good tomorrow, what are the soaps and bath towels for?"

"Tomorrow night—Lake Geneva."

"I'm scared of you girl," Rachel said just as they heard a knock at the door.

"I'll get it," Hope said quickly jumping up and running to the door. "Now Jason," she began.

"I'm not Jason," said the tall, dark man with a body he had made a serious investment in. "I'm Diamond Stud,"

"And you sure ain't no dud," Charity said as he closed the door behind him and began dancing. "Hey."

"Cousin Charity, you're a married woman."

"But I'm not," Charity's sister Faith said. She began an exhausting session of bump and grind.

"Go Faith, go Faith," Rachel chanted laughing. "What about you Sina?"

"You leave me out of this girl, you got a husband to go home to tomorrow night. I don't"

After Diamond Stud finished his fulfilling performance that was so moving even Mrs. Jones joined in, sipping champagne and doing a half-gainer into the bean dip, Hope was surprised with an evening of pampering: a massage, facial, manicure and pedicure. This made it possible for her to have the most peaceful night of rest before her big day.

Steven Jones pulled out all the stops for his only daughter's wedding and reception at the biggest hotel downtown. A limousine picked Hope up from the hotel, not just any limo — it was a Jaguar. Fresh flowers adorned Front Street from the last pew to the altar. He even hired a small chamber orchestra to accompany Rachel. Sina and Jason's cousin sang *Always* as beautifully as only the songwriters themselves could have intended. Two-hundred-fifty dined heartily on prime rib or grilled salmon as they patted their feet to the jazz ensemble Mr. Jones hired. Crystal Mintor thought it was a shame though that Hope was going to toss that beautiful fresh bouquet, but it was almost completely intact when Faith caught it.

"Look, you married women," Sina wrote on a note she was planning to put inside the Christmas cards she was sending Rachel and Hope. "I'm dreaming about fish again. And I bet it's you Hope. Because if it's me, then it's an immaculate conception. I'll be in Chicago on the 17th. See you then."

If I Could

26

Sina, Hope, and Rachel spent an enjoyable, memorable holiday together, with Sina fluctuating visits between Rachel's South side home and Hope and Jason's new apartment on the west side of Kalamazoo. They had a den with built-in bookcases on the first floor as large as their master bedroom. It was what they needed since Hope had her accounting work and Jason his law studies. Right beside their den was a living room with a fireplace where a 10 X 13 wedding portrait hung just above the mantlepiece and beside the French glass doors leading to the patio. This apartment had a much larger kitchen and dining room than Hope's one bedroom. They found, however, that their busy schedules—especially since this was tax time—did not allow them to spend the quality time Hope had expected. So they decided to have a date on Friday night—their special evening—when the law books were shut and tucked away in the den and Hope's computer was logged off and the calculator unplugged. They found however that they needed rest more than anything and both fell asleep on the couch watching videos.

"Hope, come on up to bed," Jason said shaking his wife from behind.

"I can't believe," she said groggily, "that we set this time aside to share with each other and spent it sleeping."

"Yes," Jason said laughing. "I suppose that happens in the best of families. Now get up."

"Okay, okay," Jason was fortunate that his wife got up because the trip up the stairs and to the bedroom was not as short as it was in her old apartment.

"Baby, you're going to have to give those donuts a rest."

"You know we all have to have a little something extra to keep us warm in the winter."

"I'll be your little extra," Jason said as they started up the stairs.

"I am so tired." Hope forced each foot to move. "I feel drained."

"I know exactly how you feel. I'm going to have to start a new exercise regimen soon. That always helps with energy."

"Really."

"Definitely. Since I stopped playing football I haven't been real good about working out," he said as he sat on the edge of their bed and put his pajama bottoms on. "But exercise does a lot for your energy level. I was never sick when I exercised daily. Never. But now, I just seem to get cold after cold."

"That's because you sleep without a shirt on," Hope said from the other side of the bed as she put her nightgown on. "You need to keep your chest covered. This is Michigan and we are in the dead of winter."

"I was hoping you'd do the honors." He got into the bed and pulled Hope's head to his chest. "I am so tired, I'm sorry."

"There's no reason to be sorry," Hope said jokingly. "I don't kiss on the first date anyway." Those were the last words Jason heard Hope say as he fell fast asleep. He was awakened by Hope's tossing and turning.

"What's wrong?"

"I don't know, Jason."

"You seem to be really restless lately."

"It's just—"

"Come on, tell me. I'm your husband. You can tell me anything."

"I'm just. You know, I'm an only child," she began, making something that would be short and sweet, long and complex.

"Yes."

"And I always had my own room. You know you are the only person I have ever shared a bed with."

"What's so funny?"

"I was just thinking of how lucky you are. When John and I were small we had to share a bed and John had a bed-wetting problem. It would be cold at night too. And I'd be comfortably asleep. You know after I had rubbed my feet together to get them warm, and then it never failed. He would wet the bed. Finally Momma started waking him up in the middle of the night, taking him in the bathroom and turning on the water so he'd pee," he said as Hope laughed along with him.

"I guess I had prepared myself for the toilet seat and everything else I heard caused conflict in marriage but this sharing a bed thing—it will just take some getting used to."

"Get used to this," Jason said as he pulled her into him.

Taking a break from grading papers, she went to the window, barely able to see through the driving rain. *Will it ever stop?* By the way the baby kicked, Rachel knew she would have her hands full and even thought that the baby might come early. Martin sat on the floor playing with his toys scattered throughout the living room while Brothaman sat at the dining room table and talked on the phone. Brothaman eased the phone on the hook and anxiously walked into the living room tripping and falling over one of Martin's toys. "Rachel darling," he said as he scrambled to his feet while Rachel laughed. "I have good news."

"What is it?"She shifted on the couch and rubbed her full belly.

"I got the job. We're moving to Nashville."

"What?"

"This is the opportunity of a lifetime for me. Martin, come to Daddy," he motioned for Martin who tottered to him. "And they're setting us up in an apartment. Since the baby's not due til late July we won't move until mid-August."

"But what about me? I have to find a new job."

"That will be no problem. You know Special Ed teachers are needed virtually everywhere. You are looking at McCann, Garrett & Burton's new Art Director. I never imagined I would have a job like this just two years after graduation." He and the baby sat on the sofa beside Rachel.

"I suppose you're right."

"And you said you didn't want to raise our children here anyway," Brothaman said, holding Martin up in the air. "And with Hank moving in here, we're getting kind of crowded."

"That's true." She put Brothaman's hand on her abdomen so he could feel the baby move. "I just hate to leave Front Street. That was Aunt Mary's baby for so long."

"With this new baby and adjusting to our new home, I doubt seriously if you have time to play at some church." He put Martin back on the floor.

"Aunt Mary always told me that if you don't use your God given talents you will lose them," she said getting up. "And I do not plan to lose mine." She walked into the kitchen to warm a bottle for Martin. and thought about Aunt Mary's service and generosity, the life she wanted and the mother she wanted to be. She decided then that it was important that she bring her children up in the church as she, Hank, Sina and Hope had been. Front Street had given them a foundation and a strong sense of self. She felt too, that in time, Brothaman would come around and go to church with them. But she knew that it was a choice he would have to make for himself.

After going to Rev. Mintor for advice on the matter, Rachel mailed her resume to the Nashville Metropolitan School System. Rev. Mintor reminded her that although she would be missed at Front Street, she would have the same opportunity to be a dutiful servant for the Lord wherever she lived. He also recommended *Well of Salvation African Christian Church* to her. He knew Rev. Hermann very well and knew he could provide the spiritual leadership she needed. On July 7, 1993, Rachel gave birth to Malcolm. This time Brothaman stayed really close to home because he didn't want to have to face Rebecca Thorne. She had already expressed her concern about Rachel and her precious grandbaby moving ten hours away—especially since she and her daughter were just beginning to really get close. She felt that she had been distant from Rachel and Hank for all of their childhood and needed to make up for lost time.

Thomasine was happy that her friend would be closer to North Carolina. That way, she'd have many opportunities to visit her friend who was like a sister to her and to see her new godson Malcolm. So once again, the three were together in Chicago—to see Rachel off and to celebrate Sina's 24th birthday.

Sina and Hope spent the evening at the grocery store and the meat market. Only the finest cuts of meat and the freshest ingredients for the salads and red velvet cake Thomasine would bake. Back at the Mintors' house, they put the red potatoes on to cook and washed, seasoned and marinated the meat. Thomasine took eggs out, boiled some and left the others out so they could reach room temperature for her cake. It was important to have the freshest butter, eggs, baking soda and buttermilk for her Red Velvet cake. No imitation vanilla for her; only the purest, finest Madagascar Bourbon Vanilla. When Crystal Mintor discovered how Sina liked to bake these cakes, she stocked up on red food color at the dime store. It didn't make sense to her for Thomasine to spend so much money for food coloring at the grocery store, when she could get it for 59¢ at the dime store. Hope cut the celery and onion for the salad and made a base for the punch. After Hope left, Thomasine stayed up half the night finishing off the cake. She had to take her time because she wanted it to be perfect. She had to cream the butter until it was light and fluffy before she added the sugar. Separating the eggs was crucial. She added one yolk at a time and reserved the whites for the last step when she beat them stiff and folded them into the mixture. Mrs. Jones was bringing some of her pies and a few other side items.

When Sina finally woke up the next morning, it was after 11 and she had to get a move on so the food would be ready when her friends arrived. She threw on the shorts she had worn the day before thinking she could hit the shower once the food was on the grill; took the meat that was marinating out of the fridge and went outside to wash the grill. Not finding the grill outside, she went back in the house and pressed the button on the garage door opener and looked where Rex once lived before he had to be euthanized last Fall. Sina was puzzled. Maybe Tommy had it, she thought as she went in the house to call him. After talking to him and her father who told her that the grill was just out there on the weekend because he and her mother had grilled some steaks, Sina checked one more time. She remembered her neighbor, Mrs. Newsome, telling her about the thefts in the neighborhood and how one neighbor went to give his dog some water one day only to reach down to turn on the hose and discover that his water hose and cart were missing. Other neighbors reported missing ladders, lawnmowers, bicycles and even those resin chairs you get at the dime store for $6. One neighbor said someone even tried to steal a stone birdbath from his backyard. Perhaps realizing how heavy it was they just turned it on its side and left it in the yard. *This can not be.* What right did someone have to go in their own neighbor's yards and steal things that people had worked so hard to get? But with crack taking over the country, anything was possible. Rex had managed to ensure that the Mintors kept their worldly possessions. In fact, Rev. Mintor was forced to lie some years before when one day while he was gardening, a derelict remarked that he had not seen Rex in a while and thought that perhaps he was dead. Rev. Mintor indicated that Rex was away for special training, to strengthen his jaws and sharpen his teeth.

Word must have gotten around the community because it seemed that virtually every home on Spruce Street had been hit except the Mintors'. "This type of behavior cannot be tolerated." Sina washed her face, threw on a baseball cap and began her march down the street.

"Mr. Fenceman," Sina began, walking up the steps of the house that had been splattered with red paint from an angry neighbor. "My grill is missing, so I am an unhappy little camper. You see, I was planning to have a birthday celebration today and a going away party for a good friend of mine."

"What it look like?"

"It was round and black. A Happy Cookchef. It had three rust spots on it too where it had tipped over a few times. You know my parents have had that grill since I was in grammar school and now I'm in grad school so it was really old."

"I'on't know nuttin' 'bout it," grunted the short dark man with an extremely bad case of Dunlap's disease.

"Are you sure you haven't seen it?" Sina continued. "Because I noticed a lot of grills beside your house as I walked up. You have a lot of ladders too."

"Why's it evertime sumthin' be missin' you people always comin' down heah? I don't think the neighbas like me."

"I wonder why?" Sina turned to leave.

"Look, now, if ya need a grill, I can sell ya one. I got one with three rust spots and a chip."

"Honestly," Sina said turning around and looking him dead in the eye. "I would not give you the satisfaction of selling something back to me that you know good and well you stole or had stolen."

"I didn't steal nuthin'. I bought that at the flea market."

"The Spruce Street Flea Market I suppose," Sina shot back, shaking her head. "You know, by the looks of things you have one foot in the grave and the other on a banana peel. You are too old for this and you really need to try to get yourself right while you have time. Have you ever thought about where you will spend the afterlife or do you think you're immortal?"

"I ain't immoral." Just then a thin, raggedy, dirty man with hair so matted that it would break even the best clippers, rode up in Fenceman's driveway. He was sitting on the hood of a Pinto in a gangsta lean carrying a ladder which had obviously been stolen from someone's yard.

"Look," Sina told the Pinto man. "I will give you ten dollars to take that ladder back where you got it from because he ain't gonna give you but about five at the most. People work too hard for their things to have you steal them out of their yard."

"I ain't stote nuthin."

"Fine, Mr. Fenceman. Give some serious thought to what I just told you. Oh, and may the blood of Jesus be upon each of you," Thomasine went to call Tommy to pick up a new grill on his way over so they could proceed as planned. She was not about to let some insignificant coward who would rather steal than go to work and earn a living rain on her parade that day.

Hope sat at her kitchen table one late August afternoon sipping on diet Coke and admiring the flowers Jason sent her. She heard the key in the lock. "How was your day?" Jason gave his wife a quick kiss.

"Honey, we need to talk. Are you sure about this graduate program thing," Jason asked as Hope reviewed her admission materials from the Master of Healthcare Administration program at Lake Effect State U. "You have a really good job right now."

"Yes, but there is no opportunity for growth for me there. And you know I've always wanted to be a hospital administrator since I was a little girl—with Daddy being in the pharmaceutical business."

"Don't get me wrong," Jason began. "I know you would make one hell of an administrator. I'm just concerned about your time management, especially when tax season rolls around," he said drinking his orange juice. "We barely spend enough time together as it is."

"We'll be at the same school now, and when you are studying for your law exams, I will be studying too. And besides, I will be at home by 9. I have one class a night Monday through Thursday. No class Friday, so that won't interrupt our weekly date. Who knows, maybe if we don't take a break, I'll get out even earlier."

"I just wish you'd give it some more thought. Maybe wait a year or so. I graduate in May and after I pass the bar and get a job then you could quit your job and go to school during the day."

"Now is the right time. Why should I put off what I can do today until tomorrow?"

As the semester got under way, Hope began to believe that just maybe Jason had been right. Working from 9-5 and rushing off to LESU for her evening courses had taken its toll. Hope no longer had the energy she had had during the summer that inspired her to get up and exercise with Jason each morning. She usually stopped off each evening at the vending machine in the lobby of the Ramsey School of Public Health to get a sweet roll and a Diet Coke to get her through her evening class. Once she got home and unwound, she ordered pizza on Wednesdays to get her through her studies unless Jason had cooked dinner which he did on Tuesday and Thursday—the days he didn't have afternoon classes. They ate the leftovers from Sunday on Monday. So on Wednesdays it was pizza, onion rings and of course, Diet Coke. Thursdays she usually got a little reprieve since she was required to take Principles of Experimental Analysis and was a stats whiz. Although crunching numbers was as easy as taking candy from a baby for Hope, the assignments were tedious and she had found herself finishing much earlier than the other nights. By the time she finished studying for the next evening's class, it was well after midnight and every evening Hope felt obligated to reward herself with dessert. Her favorite was ice cream with Mackinac Island fudge and chocolate-covered peanut butter cups. Of course, ice cream just wasn't ice cream without her toasted coconut. And after she washed the dish to hide the evidence she climbed in bed beside her husband and fell fast asleep. She didn't seem to have as much trouble sleeping now as she did when she was first married. Could it be that she was adjusting to married life and sharing her bed, or maybe that it's much easier to sleep with a full belly?

Thomasine tapped her fingers on the seminar table one Fall afternoon as her classmate told a descriptive tale of his experience in a Holiness church during her *Art of Ethnography* class. The young man was fascinated by the dynamics that took place at *The Purchased House of Prayer*, from the call and response, an African tradition, to the members who became slain in the spirit and those who spoke in tongues. While the African Christian Church was not known for having the same Holy Spirit experience as the Holiness Church, this information was not new or as fascinating to Sina. The word was that the African Christian Church had a similar worship style to the Holiness church until the A.C.C. people got too saditty to shout.

"That was amazing," Dr. Farnandis said with her Birkenstock outfitted feet propped up on the table and her tie-dyed T-Shirt. "And the music," she continued. "The music in the Holiness church is just awesome." Thomasine recalled the concert she required the class to attend at the beginning of the semester which was given in a small country church with natural air conditioning. Sina thought this would give her an opportunity to get some new music for her choir. She arrived on time only to wait thirty minutes before the first group performed. She felt like she would be deaf after the concert because the amplifiers were turned up as high as they could go without giving any whiny feedback. As the groups performed, Sina had looked back at Dr. Farnandis who looked on in wide-eyed wonder.

"Sina, would you like to share some of your ethnographic experiences with us?" Dr. Farnandis asked.

"Well, you may not find my experiences with Project WIDE-NG as intriguing or as fascinating as the Holy Spirit," she began. "But as many of you know, youth are very important to me. They are all we will have to depend on when we are older. And it is important that we invest time in youth which is where Project WIDE-NG comes in. Our aim is to widen, or broaden the horizons of young people and introduce them to things which may not be in their immediate environment. One area of particular interest to me is Communication Apprehension. This happens on several different levels," Sina explained recalling her communication background. "It happens on an interpersonal level and more often in a public communication level. People have a fear of speaking before groups. I recall when I was a T.A. for Public Speaking class and speech delivery dates rolled around, more people went to Student Health on those days than the law allowed," she said as the class members chuckled. "When I took Public Speaking in undergrad there was this one woman in my class who put on a performance whenever she was called on. She would put her head on the desk, sigh and finally drag herself up to the podium, sliding her feet along the way. But enough for my background. I've been working with Project WIDE-NG since April which certainly makes me a participant-observer, and this semester I've instituted recitation of poetry and short speeches. The youth group of about 25, ranging from 5 to 17, select the pieces they recite which is important because it gives them some autonomy. They live in a world where teachers and parents constantly tell them what to do, when to do it, and how to do it, which is important because they do indeed go to these people for direction, but I feel that in this extra-curricular activity, allowing them to select their own literature to recite is effective. It allows them first of all, to pick something of interest to them. And I must mention that they select works which are appropriate to their grade level. I've even heard some original prose. It also teaches them research skills, essential to their future as scholars. Each of our local Project WIDE-NG members goes on to college, many of them on scholarship. The program's other areas include career exploration, SAT preparation, tutorials, self-enhancement workshops just to name a few." Thomasine continued by naming some of the selections the youth had chosen and discussed the speech writing workshops she would initiate in the winter. When Sina finished her presentation, she sat down with a smile as she discovered that she finally had her dissertation proposal.

The flowering of the dogwood trees signaled the arrival of spring in Nashville. Rachel had adjusted quite well to her move. She was able to find a dependable and knowledgeable babysitter for Martin and Malcolm after she became a mid-semester replacement at a Nashville Metro elementary school. Everything seemed to really go her way too because shortly after she arrived in Nashville, she became the organist at *Well of Salvation*. Rev. Mintor was pleased and proud to offer Rachel his highest recommendation because she was a natural and fell right in place at *Front Street* after Aunt Mary's death. Between the children, the school and the church, Brothaman expressed concern about her overextending herself and spending time with the children. But she took them to the church with her virtually every time she went. The members just loved the children and the nursery attendants said they were a joy to care for during the service. Her response to Brothaman was, "you were the one who wanted to move here, I don't ask you to babysit that often; besides you're their Daddy so you really aren't babysitting because what I do is never considered babysitting, and you surely don't complain about that extra thousand that comes in each month from my playing the organ and directing the choir. You should come some time, you might be touched by the experience."

Their lives had become waking up in the morning and arguing over breakfast and about her not staying at home with the children. But Rachel was never a homebody, she had been on the go all her life. In the evening he usually complained about her choir rehearsal or prayer meeting or to the hospital visits to do music therapy for some terminally ill member. She had tired of the arguing which one night nearly escalated to a dish throwing fight. Rachel decided that she was going to do what the Lord led her to do and if Brothaman didn't like it, too bad. It was on this same Friday that she was invited to a co-worker's birthday party at Arny and Ed's Bar & Grill and Brothaman was going to spend the evening with his children.

"Look, I've got to run," Rachel said handing Malcolm to Brothaman. "Oh and he needs to be changed." She touched up her makeup. Brothaman put Malcolm on the blanket on the floor and proceeded to change him and was surprised that Malcolm had not completely finished taking care of his business. "Damn," he said looking at the wet spot that now adorned his dry-cleaned white shirt. "Look Rachel, we really need to talk."

"We can talk later."

"We need to talk now."

"I don't think one evening out with my co-workers is too much to ask," Rachel said putting her purse on her shoulder. "You hardly ever watch your children and I never, and I mean never, complain about your late business dinners and trips. You," she continued pointing at him, "need to spend some quality time with your sons. We will talk in the morning after I come back from children's choir rehearsal. Oh, and you will watch your sons then too."

The walls of Arny and Ed's were adorned with antique farming tools and advertisements for products which hadn't been manufactured in at least fifty years. The wooden dance floor was surrounded by round tables with chairs that looked like they had been overvarnished and those awful red and white gingham tablecloths. While the decor didn't excite Rachel, the country/western music suited her fancy. Besides the church, one good point about her move to Nashville was that she could turn on several radio stations and find country music that Sina couldn't understand why she loved.

"Come on Rachel," urged Beulah Jean Rayford, her co-worker who was celebrating a birthday. "Let me teach you the *Six Shooter*."

"No, I think I'll pass," Rachel said, observing that there were no African-Americans on the dance floor.

She sat and watched and talked to Beulah Jean's mother as the music changed and the dance of the moment became the *Texas Waltz*. "They just look like they're having so much fun up there line dancing," Rachel said to Beulah Jean's mother.

"You should try it honey. Useta do myself 'til I fell and broke my hip last year."

"I don't know. I like country music and all, but I'm a city girl," The music changed once again and the dancers began doing the *Electric Slide*. "Now I can get with this," she said as she got up and joined the others on the dance floor.

"So you finally decided to join us." They half-turned, sashayed to the right for three counts and grapevined to the left.

"Now this," Rachel said as they took two steps back, "I know. That six shooter I don't know. But it really looked like such fun." The record ended and the music changed once again. Rachel had started off the dance floor when Beulah Jean grabbed her hand.

"Girl, you gotta learn the *Boot Scootin' Boogie*. Right heel front, cross over left, back out front, feet together," she instructed. Rachel hadn't had that much fun in a long time.

"Guess what Rachel?" Sina asked when she called Rachel one late April evening.

"What?" Rachel asked.

"I'm ABD."

"ABD?"

"That's right. I've completed all of my courses, exams and defended my dissertation proposal. I've done all but the dissertation."

"That's great."

"And if things go smoothly, I should be getting ready to graduate about this time next year."

"You and Hope. But Lake Effect is on quarters so she will probably graduate in June. You know Jason's graduating from law school in June."

"Wow, it seems like he just started."

"Him, it seems like you just started your doctorate and already you've finished your classes and everything, wow," Rachel said dryly.

"What's up Rachel? You don't sound like your usual cheerful self."

"So much has happened in the last month. Brothaman lost his job. Said he was set up and something about you have to understand the plight of a blackman."

"Oh no, I'm so sorry to hear that."

"So he went back to Chicago because he felt that was a better market for him in his field. He's staying in the house with Hank."

"Oh my goodness. Has he found a job yet?"

"No."

"You must really be catching it with those two babies by yourself."

"They have a great babysitter. Sister Gates is retired. She raised 7 children and 2 of her grandchildren after her youngest daughter was killed. She is great with kids and the boys just love her."

"I'm going to come and see you. Maybe I can drive over around the end of next week. I really need to get away because the last few months have been absolutely intense with the comps and the proposal and everything. I was determined to have that proposal defended before the start of the Fall semester."

"You know Sina," Rachel said giving Malcolm a bottle, "you shouldn't push yourself like that. Why couldn't you wait and take the exams over the summer?"

"Because summertime is research time for the faculty. And my advisor, Abby is going away to do research all summer as is Dr. Farnandis — she's going to Brazil. And I'm really glad it's over. I can spend the summer going through the institutional review. You know you have to do that whenever you use human subjects."

"Well, I'm glad you're coming. We can go to Arny's and Ed's for karaoke night and line dancing night."

"I can get with the karaoke, you know I'm a diva. But line dancing. Rachel, Black folk don't country line dance."

"They do too!" Rachel insisted. "You always see at least one Black couple on TNN line dancing. Besides, it's fun. You might like it."

"I seriously doubt it. You know I never understood why you like that country music being a city girl and all. But I still love you," Sina said as Malcolm started crying again.

"Look, I'ma have to run, but congratulations and I'm really looking forward to seeing you. I'm sure it will be a slice."

"Bye girl."

Jason's graduation from Law School was a joyous occasion that just had to be accompanied by a grand slam party given by his wife and her mother. And the only thing that was missing was one of Sina's Red Velvet cakes. Uncle Leroy came too and reminded Jason how proud he was of him and asked him to work with him a few days a week in his heating and cooling business. "You know just until I find someone else." Jason thought about all that Uncle Leroy had done for him and felt obligated to work for him even though he really needed to spend the time studying for the bar which was no joke.

"So how do you think you did?" Hope asked after Jason's final day of the excruciating exam.

"I'm just glad it's over—I hope anyway," Jason said, relieved that he had completed the exam, but lacking confidence that he had passed. "And if I didn't pass—"

"Didn't pass?" Hope asked. "You need to think positive."

"I don't know, Hope, maybe I should have spent the time I did working with Uncle Leroy studying for the exam, but we do need the money and Uncle Leroy does pay me well. You know, with you in school you weren't able to take on the income tax work like last year. And we can't have our cupboards bare."

"That's the truth."

"Look," Jason said touching Hope's now extremely plump arm with his hand. "I'm going to Chicago for a few weeks to work with Uncle Leroy. He's really having a rough time finding another technician."

"What about John, can't he help?"

"That brother of mine has no mechanical skills whatever. He doesn't know the difference between a wrench and a channel lock. Uncle Leroy really needs me, we need the money and I need the work to take my mind off the test. Maybe by then I will have the results back. And you can come up on weekends too."

"I've got something to take your mind off the test," Hope said.

You Gotta Be

27

Almost there," Sina said as she reached back to pet Sparky on the head. She looked all around her and saw nothing but open fields. She had actually looked forward to getting to this part of her trip. She hated driving through the mountains and had anxiously awaited reaching Indiana which meant flat, solid ground. No *Falling Rock Zones* in that state. But for the last three or so hours she had quickly tired of looking at the open fields on either side of the Interstate. A quick jaunt through Indy gave her a brief respite, but she was soon back to staring at those open fields. "About another hour and a half or so." Since her book on tape had finally run out, she turned the radio on.

"Next up, music by Martha Rudy, a hot new band out of Chi-town. Only on The Eye."

Listening to the funky bass line, she was reminded of her 25th birthday when she, Hope and Rachel had gone to a small club on the North side of Chicago to hear live music. "A reprieve from hip-hop" is what Hope had called it. Actually Rachel and Sina were surprised that Hope was daring enough to venture North to hear new music. With Rachel and Sina's strong musical background, they were lovers of all good music. Hope's musical taste, however, was limited to R & B ballads and mellow jazz. After her visit to Rachel in Nashville, Sina had even acquired a liking for Country/Western music—not a penchant, but a liking nonetheless. Still, she couldn't get with the country line dancing.

After paying the minimal cover charge, the trio selected a table near the rear of the bar so as not to be overwhelmed by the amplification of the music. "What would you like to drink?" asked the short, red-headed waitress wearing a tee-shirt and demin shorts.

"I'll have a Screwdriver," Rachel responded.

"And I'll have a Singapore Sling," Hope said as the waitress made note.

"And I'll have a Ginger Ale," Sina said smiling.

"Ginger Ale?" Rachel asked, puzzled.

"Yes a Ginger Ale."

"But it's your birthday and you should have a drink," Hope responded. "Besides, I'm paying."

"I don't drink much anymore."

"Miss Omicron Obsession and wop?"

"What's wop?" Hope asked.

"You heard me right. I have a glass of wine every now and then, but as for the shot every day and under the table drinking—it's just not me anymore."

"But what is wop?"

"When I was in undergrad, whenever we had a party, wop was served. It was made from Orange Kool-Aid, cheap orange flavored wine, and whatever other kind of liquor available. Mixed together in one big cooler with lots of ice," Sina said, as she moved her head to the beat of the music.

"Sounds interesting," Hope replied.

"About interesting enough to wop you over the head. That's what it did to me."

"Oh Rachel that was your first taste of alcohol—next to that glass of wine Jamal gave you on *that* night."

"True, but still," Rachel said as the waitress brought the trio their drinks.

"You know what?" Sina began. "This is a first."

"A first what?"

"This is our first outing that did not include a meal at a restaurant."

"That is so true," Rachel said giggling.

"I used to come here all the time when I was at Duncan," Rachel began. "I like it because of the variety of music and people," Rachel continued as a girl with purple hair and earrings on her nose and eyebrows walked by.

"Variety is the spice of life." Thomasine got up to dance.

"I'll be right back," Hope said, leaving Rachel at the table alone as she went to the bathroom. It was as if someone had been watching the trio, just waiting for the right opportunity to strike because just when Hope was out of view, a tall, well built man with a jheri curl, wearing royal blue rayon shirt and pants and a big rope chain, sat next to Rachel. Rachel observed his gold nugget ring as he extended a handshake and the huge Mercedes-Benz emblem hanging from his rope chain. The music was so noisy that she didn't hear him when he gave his name and she was pretty certain he hadn't heard hers. He wasn't nearly as observant as she because although she wore a wedding ring, he proceeded to tell her how much he knew about women and asked about her deepest, darkest sexual fantasy. Rachel wondered if she had heard him correctly.

"Since you profess to know so much about women," Rachel said looking him in the eye with a dead serious why-don't-you-leave-me- the-f— alone look, "why don't you tell me?"

"Most women's deepest, darkest fantasy is to be in a public place, doing something with a whole lot of people around. But nobody knows what they are doing," which of course sent Rachel laughing in stitches.

Hope came out of the stall in the ladies' room after waiting in a short line and proceeded to wash her hands and comb her hair when a tall, thin blonde who obviously had a lip implant complimented her on her orange lipstick. "That's a great color. Can I wear some?" the woman asked just as Hope was about to go into her purse to freshen up her lipstick.

"I didn't bring it with me," Hope responded to the woman's boldness. "But it is Jazz Orange by Flori Roberts. Maybe you can pick some up when you're at the mall again." She completely ignored the sexual connotation in the woman's request and was actually offended by it. Both Hope and Sina made their way back to the table as Rachel's unwanted guest was leaving.

"What's up with homeboy?" Sina asked. "Looking like he's straight from '88 with that rayon, rope chain and golden nugget jewelry. Doesn't he know that was played out at least five years ago?"

"Just some weirdo who asked about my deepest, darkest sexual fantasy."

"Didn't he see your ring?" Hope asked.

"He didn't even care. He could have watched your husband leave your side and still would have come over here," The waitress returned to clear the glasses and take more orders.

"A Cape-codder," Rachel replied.

"A Long Island Iced Tea," Hope said.

"I'll have a White Zinfandel," Sina said, finally joining her friends in their indulgence. "I guess I can have one glass of wine on my 25th Birthday."

"I don't see how you can drink wine."

"I don't see how you can mix liquors. Besides, wine has less alcohol and alcohol is full of calories and I'm really trying to lose weight. You know I'm up two sizes since college."

"Grad school will put the weight on," Hope said. "I know I have gained at least twenty pounds," giving her friends only half truth. Since Jason had been in Chicago most of the summer working with his Uncle Leroy's

Heating and Cooling company, the kitchen had once again become Hope's favorite room.

"So how's your love life?" Rachel asked Sina trying to change the subject quickly as the alternative band Martha Rudy was introduced.

"Right now," Sina said as she started to applaud. "I have a hot date with my dissertation."

Hope sat in her living room watching a videotape of Oprah discussing the marathon she had recently run. Oprah had dropped the pounds and looked good. Hope stopped for a minute as she wrestled to become comfortable on her sofa and looked at herself. She was uncomfortable, miserable and craved ice cream. Struggling to get up from the sofa, all she could think about was that Moose Tracks Ice Cream. "Oprah could lose that weight because she wasn't in graduate school. When you're in grad school it's easy to gain weight, even Sina said so." Hope attempted to rationalize her craving and scooped out four tablespoon sized scoops. She wobbled her way back to the sofa and put the first spoonful in her mouth. Her eyes rolled back in her head as she savored the taste of the Mackinac Island fudge and miniature peanut butter cups. A true delight! By the end of Oprah's show, Hope had made her way into the kitchen once more to fix herself another dish of Moose Tracks.

"Hi honey," Jason said, making his way into the front door with his tool belt over his shoulder. "With it cooling off, things got kind of slow and Uncle Leroy doesn't need me as much."

"You got some mail from the State Board of Law Examiners, I didn't open it, but I'm so excited. Soon you won't have to work for Uncle Leroy anymore and you can open your practice and we can buy a house and start a family." She paused for another spoonful.

"Don't get your hopes up just yet." Jason put his tool belt on the floor and sat beside his wife.

"Well, open it already."

"Okay.".

"Well."

"I guess I can take it again in February. I didn't pass this time. But most people have to take it more than once."

"Well I really didn't expect this. You're too smart to flunk the Bar Exam. Maybe you need to study before taking it again now that you have an idea of what it's composed of. And since you don't work for Uncle Leroy, anymore you have plenty of time to prepare for the next bar exam. Beginning now. And from now on, don't let me or anyone interfere with your studies. Because I want you to pass this test. Not because I want you to make big money, but because I want you to fulfill your dream."

"Well I thought I was prepared already, but I see that I fell short, so I'll have to find out just where I went wrong."

"Get busy. With school starting next week, you'll have no interference from me."

One evening when Hope came home from her Quality and Utilization Management class, Jason was sitting in the den at his desk writing on a legal pad. "I'm so proud of you," Hope said as she walked up behind her husband. "I'm sure you'll pass the bar this time," she said looking down at the writing on the pad. "McCoy Heating and Cooling?"

"Yes. I have good news. I'm starting my own Heating and Cooling company. You know I've worked with Uncle Leroy since I was about 13 and I know the business well. It will be cold here before you know it."

"Heating and cooling? You're not a blue collar worker. You're a professional. And I did not wait for you to go through law school so you could fix furnaces."

"Well Hope," Jason said turning to face her. "I'm sorry if you don't think the heating and cooling business is honorable enough for me, but I do have to keep a roof over our head, food in the fridge, help you with tuition and pay off my student loans. So until I can do better, you'll just have to accept this. And besides, I'll be studying at night."

"I guess you don't have the ambition I thought you had. Lately you seem to be willing to settle for less."

"So then I suppose, that must be why I married you, I wanted to settle for less—but right about now you look like more, much much more," he said snatching his jacket and hat and making his way to the door. "And it shows."

After Jason's abrupt departure, Hope found herself once again peering into the freezer for her delectable ice cream. "I'll show him all right." She sprinkled toasted coconut and sliced a piece of her mother's caramel cake.

"And they lived happily ever after," Rachel read to her boys. "The end." She put the book on the shelf and kissed each of her sleeping sons goodnight. Exhausted after playing at two services that morning and a funeral in the afternoon, she managed to gather enough strength to cook dinner for her and the boys. She would have loved to have gone out, but with Brothaman recently starting his new job as a copywriter—a great demotion from Art Director, Rachel felt it best to conserve every penny she could. She was happy she would be off the next day—Columbus Day, so she could catch up on her rest and spend some time with Martin and Malcolm. Relaxing in a hot bath, she wished her husband had been there to massage her with warm oil and make love to her, but had to accept the reality that that would not happen. She had finished her bath when the phone rang.

"Hello," Rachel said in a sexy voice, hoping it was Brothaman.

"Sis, we need to have a heart-to-heart about your husband."

"What's up?" Hank sounded serious.

"I had to put him out."

"You did what?"

"He always gave me a sob story about how he had to send you and the boys money and couldn't pay his share of the electric or gas bill. And I gave him the benefit of the doubt."

"What? He never sent me any money."

"That's because he's been spending it on his other lover."

"Another woman?"

"Much, much worse," Hank said, pausing. "Cocaine. And if I were you, I wouldn't even want him around the boys because I would be afraid of what might happen."

"I can't believe this."

"I came back from my rotation in Peoria early. He wasn't expecting me until next week and he was having a big cocaine party right here in Aunt Mary's house. I saw him snorting with my own two eyes."

"Oh my God!"

"And that Conrad was over here too, so you know nothing good could have been happening."

"Hank," Rachel began, fighting back tears. "Thank you for telling me."

"Personally I think you ought to divorce him, kick Brothaman right to the curb. He can't keep a job. He's had three in the last six months and he's sure to lose this one soon. He moved you and the boys to Nashville only to lose his job in nine months and give you some bullshit ass line about 'you have to understand the plight of a black man.' Plight of a black man my ass. Those same friends of his who showed their ass at your reception were there Friday night. One of them was dealing drugs over this phone. People were calling here all day yesterday wanting to buy, and I may have the number changed tomorrow. What if the neighbors had called the police about the noise? They would have walked right up in here just like he had people walking in and out. And we would have probably lost the house. He is not worth it. He needs help, and he has to seek it for himself. But in the meantime I think you should file for legal separation. I'm sure mom would help you with any legal fees because she wants the best for you and the boys. He doesn't take care of them. Did he even send them birthday gifts or go to see them? You know, that's probably why he lost his cushy job in Nashville. Probably didn't pass a drug test or maybe he even got caught using. And he didn't even think about what this would do to you and the boys. He's selfish, no-good and you and the boys don't need him. But then, he hasn't even been there," Hank said, still fuming from his discovery.

"Oh God!" She felt her world crashing around her.

"So what are you going to do, sis?"

"I'm going to talk to him about it."

"Oh come on, he's just going to beat around the bush and say that I blew things out of proportion. He's always got a story."

"Look Hank, you call me up and drop this bomb on me and expect me to just be able to cut my husband off just like that. Without talking to him or anything."

"You don't really even have a husband. On a full-time basis that is. Brothaman Brown is just your part-time husband. And your sons don't need him. They need a full-time father." Rachel thought about all of the late meetings lasting into the wee hours of the morning and overnight business trips. "Just give some thought to what I said," Hank told his sister. "And don't let it get you down because it doesn't have to be your problem."

Thomasine stood on her patio grilling chicken as the warm May Carolina sun gave Martin and Malcolm a nice little place to stretch their young legs. The winter had come and gone and Sina's hot date with her dissertation ended as she defended in early April and submitted two copies and a check to the graduate school to insure she would get her diploma come May 14. Rachel and Hope came down early to help her celebrate and the Mintors were due to arrive later that day. Sina thought about taking her friends to her favorite restaurant on Franklin Street or to *Shrimp Boats*, but after the scene Hope caused in the *Krisp & Tasty* shop earlier that morning, she thought it best to slip off to *Harris Teeter* for chicken and deli salads. "So Hope," Sina said as she sat down next to her friends on her patio furniture. "Did Jason pass the bar this time? Or has he heard yet?"

"He missed the deadline for filing. He was running around cleaning furnaces and stuff and clearly missed the December 15 late filing deadline. But I made damn sure he filed this time, before March 1. I'm not gonna let him miss it. No, no, no. And he's gonna pass this time too so we can move on with our lives."

"That will be so nice. You'll be a hospital administrator and he'll be a sports and entertainment lawyer. Just invite little ole me to your Bloom-field Hills housewarming. And I promise I won't drop any crumbs on the floor of your mansion."

"Don't worry about that," Rachel said laughing. "Because I'm sure Hope will have a maid to sweep up the crumbs behind you. Say Sina, do you have any job leads?"

"I made the short list and interviewed for a tenure-track position at Steeplechase. Two other candidates were interviewed. I heard from Naja who heard from a student in the Anthro. department that one of the candidates went to Yale. The other one finished in December at Harvard— and she was a Steeplechase undergrad so she will probably get the position. I guess there goes my house."

"Your house?"

"Yes. They're building at a new subdivision called River Run Estates. I picked out a floor plan and bought the lot and everything. But if I don't get this job, I don't know what I will do. I really want to stay here in North Carolina, but I don't know."

"You're building a house, just for you?"

"Yes. I need more space. Mom and Dad are helping me with the down payment too as a graduation gift. You know I have kids from the choir and Project WIDE-NG come over and spend the night sometimes. Hold on a second." Sina went into the house for a folder.

"I can't believe she's going to buy a house," Hope said. "What does she need with a house by herself?"

"I think Sina has worked very hard and if she can afford it, she should have it. And you should be happy for her. Shoot, if I had the money, I'd have one in Nashville."

"You already got one in Chicago. All I know is that Jason McCoy better pass that damn bar exam in July and stop wasting his time with that stupid ass heating and cooling business."

"Hope, I'm shocked," Rachel replied. "I've never heard you use such harsh language before."

"Well, Sina," Hope asked when she returned. "Just what are you going to do with your townhouse?"

"If things work out all right, I should be out of here by the end of August. And I'll rent this place out to graduate students. Here are the floor plans. There is a two-car garage with a bonus room just over it. That's where I'll have my office/exercise room. I do plan to lose all this graduate school weight. The Bonus room is huge so there will be plenty of space for my computer desk, filing cabinet, book cases and a treadmill. I of course will have the Master Bedroom which has a garden tub and two walk-in closets. That will give me plenty of space for those hats I've started to wear to church. Oh, and I want to eventually put a baby grand in the living room. I have a dining room and a kitchen with an island. I've always wanted a kitchen with an island. And the family room has a fireplace. With all of that space, I have no excuse for not keeping it neat. And there will be plenty of space for you to stay when you come to visit."

"That is so nice," Rachel replied. "And just who do you plan to share this space with? Because I think you're holding out on us. That dissertation is done. So who's your new hot date? And will we get to meet him this weekend?"

"My hot date is now a book proposal which will really help my career," Sina said as she heard the phone ring. "I'll be right back—don't let the food burn."

"You know I'd never do that," Hope retorted. Sina went in to her living room and searched frantically for her cordless phone.

"Hello, this is Dr. Nestor, Chair of the Anthropology department at Steeplechase."

"Yes, Dr. Nestor. It's so nice to hear from you."

"I'll make this short and sweet. I'm calling to offer you the joint position in Anthropology and Women's Studies." He explained the starting salary, benefits package, computer, research start-up costs, graduate assistant, and availability of travel funds. "We were very impressed by your research presentation and are willing to do whatever it takes to have Dr. Thomasine Mintor as a member of our department here at Steeplechase. You will make such a good fit."

"Dr. Nestor, I am very interested, but I'd like to take a few days or so to think about it?"

"Let me put it this way, Thomasine, how much would it take to woo you over to the Park?"

The two negotiated because Abby had schooled Sina well in the art of academic job offers. "Counter their offer immediately, and ask about benefits, course reductions for the first semester or year, the amount of time before you can take a sabbatical, retirement plans, etc. And whatever you do Sina, do not settle."

268 Trevy A. McDonald

"Well, Dr. Nestor, you are talking to the Anthropology and Women's Studies Department's newest faculty member," Thomasine said smiling but thinking of calling the builder to tell him to move ahead with her new home. "And I must say I am quite honored to have an opportunity to become a part of Steeplechase University's legacy of excellence."

"Great Dr. Mintor. I'll have the contract ready first thing Monday morning."

"I'll see you then, at nine," Thomasine said. "And thank you." She ran out to her patio dancing and singing. "I got the Steeplechase job."

"Congratulations."

"I guess I'll have to call the builder and tell him to get started."

"Is the food ready yet?" Hope was anxious to change the subject.

"It'll be ready in a little while. You want to make sure the chicken is good and done. I don't want any of you to get sick from salmonella."

"So how is Brothaman?"

"Okay, I suppose. He's going to rehab."

"I think you need to leave him," Hope said. "Because drugs are nothing to play with."

"I think if he's willing to go to rehab and try to get his life straight, then you should give him a chance." Sina said, more forgiving than Hope. "But he needs to do it for himself. And I don't blame Hank for kicking him out. He was way out of line moving those people in and having parties in the house when Hank was away doing rotations."

"I don't blame Hank either. You know after all these years he had to have the phone number changed because of all the people calling to buy drugs. But I believe in my husband. He can overcome this and I know that he will. He didn't get in this state overnight, and I don't expect him to get through it overnight."

"That's right," Sina replied.

"And you could always get a quarter of a million-dollar life insurance policy on him," Hope interrupted.

"But always remember this too shall pass," Sina said, ignoring Hope's snide remark, as she removed the food from the grill.

The Mintors arrived later that day and piled into Sina's home. On Saturday, Sina had a graduation party at D.A.D.H. which was attended by her advisor Abby, who was quite pleased that Sina had accepted the Steeplechase position. Like Sina, she was a joint faculty member sharing her time between the Communication Department and the Anthropology Department Naja and several of the Project WIDE-NG members also attended as well as Rev. Grace and members of the youth choir. Kelsey and Trevaughn even came in for the weekend. They were all so proud of Sina, but her parents were the proudest. They were disappointed though that they didn't get to see her march across the stage because on the morning of May 14, 1995 there was an eighty percent chance for thunderstorms. Suddenly it dawned on Sina that she was graduating—getting her Ph.D. at about 3 A.M. the morning of her graduation. She just lay in bed and thought about all that had happened to her since high school. *I've made it.* Hope slept very peacefully having finished a slug of Sina's sheet cake before bed.

Sina got up at five, took a bath and began cooking breakfast because she knew her family and guests would have a very long day ahead of them. They all loaded up in Sina's and the Mintor's cars and headed to Chapel Hill. Traffic wasn't as bad as Sina expected, but then she left so early because she wanted to make sure she was there in plenty of time to line up to march. She posed for pictures with her guests before she headed off to find Gate 10 outside of Kenan Stadium. She then found her other sorors and support group members and cohorts in the College of Arts and Sciences. She had one of the finest gowns too, no econo robe for her. She rush ordered her gown from a Bible bookstore and found a seamstress to sew her doctoral bars on the sleeves. With her black gown, six-cornered hat with the gold tassel and her Delta kente stole, Sina stood out. And it was very easy for her to spot her brother Tommy because he was sitting there with his bright green shirt just snapping pictures. Thomasine stood alongside the other graduates earning doctorates while the graduating seniors marched in an ocean of Carolina blue playing leap frog, touch football and doing somersaults. Sina didn't pay them any attention though because she was marching across that stage. Or so she thought. With nearly 4800 graduates it would have taken days to call all of the names so only those earning Ph.D.'s actually got to march across the stage. After hearing a very moving and inspiring speech by one of her sorors who was a college president, Sina sat with bated breath as the chancellor and provost began to present the honorary doctorates. Then it happened. Rev. Mintor himself had never seen the sky darken so fast. Sina saw that both the chancellor and the provost seemed worried about the clouds. Then the sky opened up. Sina had given her umbrella to her mother, so she and her friends ran under a tarp. It was no use. Sina heard the chancellor quickly confer all of the degrees for all of the graduates and end the commencement exercises. She was disappointed, but perked up slightly when she heard him tell all of the Ph.D. candidates to come into the field house so their names could be called.

The summer of 1995 was one the Midwest will never forget. The sweltering heat had caused hundreds of deaths in Chicago alone. The heat was unbearable. More intense than what Sina had experienced in Durham or what Hope had endured in Savannah. But for Jason McCoy, it meant big business. It seemed that people waited until it got hot to consider getting their A/C's serviced, which was just fine to Jason. That meant that he'd make even more money. He had spent money advertising an early bird special prior to June 15 for an A/C Clean and Check. But when people waited to get their A/Cs serviced, that meant he usually had to charge them for a service call. He had hired a few other men to work with him and transferred his business line to Hope's direct line at work. She was home in the evenings too now that she had finished her M.H.A. program at Lake Effect State. Before they knew it, the end of July had rolled around. Hope hadn't found a job yet in her new field. And Jason worked around the clock. He usually started at about 6:30 in the morning so that he could get to people before they left for work, and made his last service call at 11:00 at night. He was one hard-working brother. And Hope really shouldn't have complained. But she did nothing but complain when he overslept for the Bar that Saturday morning.

"I can't believe that you did this. What about us? What about our dreams?"

"What about all that money I paid to register for the test?"

"That too, it's all wasted!"

"Well, I can make that money back easily?"

"But you can't make the kind of money you would as a lawyer."

"You know Hope, I've been thinking. Maybe I need a little vacation from all the rigor. Not that working with my hands doesn't require thought, but it doesn't require the same type of thought. The heating and cooling business is more — visual. It's easier for me to detect what's wrong because I can see it. I'm only 26. I have my J.D. and I have the rest of my life to pass the Bar.

"And what if I had taken the Michigan Bar and you got a job offer you just couldn't refuse in Arizona or somewhere. I'd be in the same boat I'm in now."

"But what about our house and children? Even Sina's buying a house now that she got that Steeplechase job."

"So that's what all this is about. What Sina's doing. I know you've always competed with her, but I thought by now you'd have outgrown it."

"Sina has nothing to do with this. This is about us. I am sick and tired of living in this apartment. I want us to get a house and have some children."

"Two bedrooms, two baths with a den, fireplace, eat-in kitchen, dining room, patio and balcony are not shabby at all. And as for children, we really need to wait until we are both settled. You have plenty of time. It's not like you're having hot flashes," Jason said.

"I want more, and I will not—" Hope began getting ready to say settle but stopped abruptly remembering how she was now very careful to use that word. "I just want us to progress Jason, that's all."

"We will," Jason said, wrapping his muscular arms around Hope. "You just have to be patient, that's all. Everything will work out."

Sina rolled out of bed when her alarm sounded at 6 A.M., put on her exercise clothing and walking shoes and grabbed Sparky's leash. He liked their new River Run Estates home which gave him ample space to romp and roam. There was even a cute Chocolate lab next door that he kind of had a thing for. She put her keys around her neck, keyed in her PIN code on her home security system and went out back to greet Sparky. "Time for our walk," she said attaching a leather leash to his collar. Sparky loved the morning walks and wagged his tail all the way. When Sina returned from walking her dog around the subdivision, armed with a sheet of old newspaper and a plastic bag for anything Sparky decided to leave on the journey, she usually came in to her freshly brewed coffee, washed her hands and fixed Sparky's food and fresh water. When she came back in, she washed her hands again and sat down to her coffee and newspaper before her aerobics work out or toning and conditioning session. Thomasine was determined to get her 18-year-old figure back and was really working hard at it. She was amazed when she looked back at pictures from her recent graduation and saw that she had gained 40 pounds since college graduation, but that's exactly what late night eating and going right to sleep will do. After hitting the shower Sina ate a hearty breakfast and headed to either her home office, the library or her office at Steeplechase if it were one of her teaching days. Just when Sina had adjusted to her schedule, the semester was over and she had to do it all again. But since she had the same teaching days as in the Fall semester, the adjustment wasn't difficult at all. It was just getting used to teaching an afternoon class in the anthropology department and running across campus that would have gotten to Sina had she not begun her exercise routine. Sina seemed to mail out tons of queries and completed proposals for her book on *U.S. Women of Color* in the Fall semester, but she had yet to hear from any of them. Right now she had to get ready for a women's studies conference in Nashville. She was also looking forward to seeing Rachel and the boys. She tried to support them as much as she could because the Brothaman situation had yet to improve. She hadn't been able to catch up with Rachel lately but knew that Rachel would be happy to see her. First she had a presentation to prepare and papers to copy. Oh, and she also had to review the papers she had to respond to, put Sparky in the kennel, stop the newspaper and buy timers for her lights. Sina had her work cut out for her.

Rachel had just finished singing to her boys and tucking them in when she heard a loud knock at the door one Friday evening in late March. "Who is it?"she asked as she looked through the peephole and didn't recognize the faces.

"Uncle Jasper and Aunt Ernestine," they hollered back. "We were just in town, just passing through, and Brothaman told us to stop by whenever we—" they continued as Rachel opened the door.

"Come on in and have a seat," Rachel said deciding to be hospitable to her husband's relatives.

"It's so nice to finally meet you," Uncle Jasper said hugging Rachel as if she were a long lost relative of his. "Got any cold chicken in the fridge."

"No. I didn't cook today."

"So what you like t' cook?" Uncle Jasper asked. He picked up some papers from Rachel's coffee table. "So you play church music huh? Isn't that nice 'Stine?" Jasper said to his wife who seemed to be in an explorer's mode, just looking around Rachel's kitchen, going in every drawer and cabinet as if on inspection.

"Yeah, Jasper. Dat's mighty nice," she drawled.

"Actually, I don't like to cook much. I keep my meals simple."

"Girl, you gone have to learn how to cook if you want dem boys to grow up strong. And I'll teachya," she said taking pots out from underneath the stove. "Chile," she said looking in the refrigerator. "You ain't gots no food in dis fridge. Alls you gots is some milk and some bread. You gots to get you some food."

"I do need to go grocery shopping in the morning. So what brings you to Nashville?"

"Just passing through. And that nephew of mine tole me I could stay with his wife and kids. Said you'd be happy to have us."

"I would, but we don't have much space, but I'd be happy to," Rachel began as Jasper got up to get some bags.

"Now my nephew would be quite mad if his wife didn't find it in her very gen'ous heart to let his favorite uncle stay the night when passing through."

"Where your sheets at?" 'Stine called from the bedroom. "Because I'se gots to sleep on me some clean sheets. And hurry because after all that driving up, I'm ti-ed."

Rachel could not believe the recalcitrance of this woman. Being a gracious host, she allowed the intrusion. She made the bed and slept on the couch. Her weekend consisted of cooking fried chicken, fried fish, greens, string beans, black-eyed peas, candied yams, etc, etc. Hope's mother's kind of cooking, all under the guise of teaching Rachel to cook. Aunt 'Stine shouted orders from the living room where she sat on her duff and watched TV. "More salt here, a pinch of sugar there," she would say. And Rachel thought the weekend was bad, but it was just beginning. After these people sat up in Rachel's living room all day and watched TV she found herself rushing home to fix her and the boys dinner to watch them eat most of it. By the time she met Sina for lunch on Tuesday afternoon, she had had just about all she could take.

"They what?" Sina asked over a lunch of Chicken Kiev, wild rice and steamed carrots. "See, they would have to go. To go through your stuff like that and comment about the money you make at the church. I'd go in there and tell them to, Lord forgive me, unass that couch and get to stepping because that is outrageous. You agreed to let them stay the night, and they've been there now for four nights. I'll get rid of them if you want me to. No problem whatsoever. And guess what? I'm free 'til tomorrow morning so what time should I come by?"

Rachel rushed back to her school somewhat relieved, yet she wondered just what Sina had up her sleeve. But she just sat, joyously teaching music to her students and anxiously awaited Sina's plan. After picking the boys up from the sitter, Rachel swung by the Holiday Inn Crowne Plaza to pick up Sina who was waiting in the lobby for her. "What next?" Rachel asked.

"I'm taking you guys to dinner. Drive to your favorite restaurant. My treat."

"How's Cajun?"

"Sounds good to me."

"Let's head to Rollins'"

"You're driving and I will eat wherever you take me."

Rollins' had been a staple in Nashville for over ten years and in Sina's estimation had some of the best crawfish cakes she had ever eaten. Rachel chose the Charleston Chicken and the boys had kid's meals of fried shrimp and french fries. Sina pulled out all the stops too, splitting an appetizer of hot crab dip with Rachel and topping things off with key lime pie. It was the best meal Rachel had in a long time, but she was still curious about what Sina was up to.

On the way home from the restaurant, Sina insisted that Rachel stop by the grocery store. Sina was in and out quickly with a small shopping bag. When they arrived to Rachel's apartment, Jasper and 'Stine were livid. "Where you been all day chile? We been waiting for you, we hongry?" 'Stine drawled.

"Some people do have to work you know," Sina said, sizing them down.

"And who dis Miss Missy wit' an attitude?" Jasper questioned.

"This is my best friend Dr. Thomasine Mintor, she's in town for a conference?"

"Say Doc," 'Stine said slipping her shoe off. "You thank you can look at my bunions?"

"I'm not a podiatrist. I'm an anthropologist."

"Oh, she one of dem ant doctors 'Stine."

"Sina, I mean Dr. Mintor is a college professor. She teaches anthropology at Steeplechase University."

"Oh, excuse me," 'Stine dragged out while rolling her neck. "So ya thank ya too good for Black college, gots to go to da man fo' yo' money huh?"

"First of all I don't think I'm too good for anything," Sina said taking a seat in the chair. "My parents didn't raise me that way. The way I see it, whether I'm at a Black college or a white college, I'll be able to mentor someone. But getting back to how my parents raised me, they didn't raise me to be rude, overbearing or lazy. And not to wear out my welcome," Sina hoped they'd get the message.

"Yeah, she work fo' da man. Dat Steeplechase. Dose folk thank dey all poo poo la la and stuff," Jasper said, moving his shoulders from side to side.

" So you have a problem with the man."

"Yeah. And I ain't trying to have nothing to do wit' him or his money."

Sina burst out in laughter as she got up to go to the kitchen and fix Aunt 'Stine and Uncle Jasper's plates. "What's so funny?" Jasper asked.

"It is simply hilarious to me that you'd sit here and talk about me working for the man. You know Rachel works for the man too. And you ate all the food bought with the money she made from the man. Slept on the sheets that the money from the man bought and watched the cable TV that was paid for by money from the man."

"Huh, she all saddity and stuff," 'Stine retorted. "Rachel, what you cooking fa dinner."

"I'm not hungry tonight. Sina took me out to a very nice Cajun restaurant and the boys and I are full. I'm getting ready to get them out of the tub now."

"But what about us?"

"I'm fixing your dinner," Sina said.

"Yeah, Sina's a good cook," Rachel hollered from the bathroom. "She can really hook up some fish and spaghetti."

"Well all right. Dat's what I'm talking 'bout." Uncle Jasper said as Sina put the bread in the microwave and rinsed and dried Rachel's finest china. When the timer on the microwave went off, Sina cut the pita bread into quarters and placed them on the plate alongside the other delicacies she had picked up from the deli. Lucky for Sina it was Mediterranean night. "Dinner's ready." They mozied on from the living room to the dining room to the candlelit table.

"We sho is hongry," 'Stine said walking to the table in a rocking motion from all of her weight.

"Look 'Stine," Jasper said sitting down. "She dun fixed da plates up all nice and stuff. I guess she ain't too bad after all. Got da collards rolled up all nice and stuff."

"They aren't collards," Sina said spreading some hummus on a pita wedge for herself. "They're stuffed grape leaves." 'Stine spat. "But they're good for you."

"She got us some garlic spread too for this fancy bread," Jasper said spreading some on his pita bread and putting it in his mouth. "This some mighty funny tasting garlic spread."

"It's called hummus—made from ground chick peas."

"And what is this red stuff?" 'Stine asked.

"Smoked salmon."

"Oh, I likes me some salmon—especially in croquets wit' a liddle cheese in the middle."

"Dis shit is raw," Jasper said spitting it out. "You tryin' to kill us?"

"It is not raw, it is smoked salmon, but I guess you aren't used to that huh?"

"You need to heat this up. Cuz I ain't never had no cold greens and fish."

"It is supposed to be served cool, and since I'm popping popcorn now, you can't use the microwave." Sina snatched a bag of popcorn out of Rachel's cabinet.

They didn't even get as far as the tabouli before deciding it was time to go. Sina knew if there was one thing that could run these freeloaders out of town, it was a cold, exotic dinner.

Thomasine managed to find time to see Rachel once more after the conference started Wednesday morning. And it got her to thinking. They were really growing up. There was a time when they knew they'd see each other in November, December, March and all summer. But things were different now. Here it was 1996, and they were all approaching 27. It dawned on Sina that they were no longer teenagers, but closer to thirty than they ever imagined. Sina thought too about how her tastes had changed, in clothes, movies, and especially music. She found herself trying to watch *The Big 80s* and *8-Track Flashback* on VH-1 every chance she got and noticed that she was listening to radio stations with music menus from the 70s and 80s, now called oldies. She wasn't prepared to hear music from her college days referred to as oldies. She was listening to Jazz quite often and was thankful that North Carolina Central University turned on WNCU—a 50,000 watt jazz station. It had come right in time with her change in tastes.

When Sina landed in Raleigh-Durham International Airport she grabbed her garment bag and briefcase and waited outside for the shuttle to take her to her car. She stopped by her office at Steeplechase since it was on the way from the airport to check her mail and pick up any papers her students may have slid under the door.

"Good morning Dr. Mintor," Julia, the departmental secretary in women's studies said as Sina closed the door.

"Good morning Julia."

"How was the conference?"

"It was great. But now that it's over, I just have to start getting ready for the next one."

"Does the process ever end?"

"I think so, but that's not until you become full professor, which is a long way off for me," Sina said chuckling as she walked over to her mailbox and grabbed the envelopes she figured held rejection letters quite similar to those she had previously received. "I'm going to run," Sina said, stuffing the letters in her briefcase. "But you have a nice weekend Julia."

"You do the same Dr. Mintor."

Sina rushed in her office and grabbed the papers she would start grading on the weekend. Sparky was so excited to see her when she got him out of the kennel that he nearly knocked her over. She was surprised too because usually when she brought him home, he ran straight to his water pail to dilute the drugs from the vet that made him less hyper. After putting him in the backyard, Sina sat at her desk in her office/exercise room and went through the publisher's letters. "Rejection," she said as she scanned the first. "More rejection," she said placing the next one on top of the previous. By the time she reached the fifth and final letter she started "Rej—contract." Sina read the letter again."They want to publish my book," she said, smiling.

Crossroads

28

 efore I hand back your papers," Thomasine told her Performance Traditions of Women of Color students, "I'd like to remind groups four and one that your performances are next week. Okay, Charlotte," Sina said, handing the student her paper, "Meredith, Carol, Bob, Herb, Nikol. If I indicated in my comments for you to come see me, you need to do so A.S.A.P." She continued passing back the papers.

"Dr. Mintor, are you going to your office now?"

"Yes Nikol," Sina said, gathering her books in her arms and turning off the lights in the experimental theater. "What's up?"

"You wanted to see me. I really worked so hard on this paper." They walked down the hallway for the short trip to Sina's office.

"I'm sure you did," Sina said unlocking her door. "Have a seat."

"It's just that I think it is a good paper."

"If you turn the page and read my comments Nikol, you will see what I think about your paper," Sina said. She showed no emotion.

"You think it's," Nikol began. "An outstanding paper."

"Yes Nikol. I was quite impressed with your paper." Sina put her books on her shelf and walked to her chair. "I asked you to come by because, though you are but a sophomore, I want to encourage you early to start thinking about graduate school. Your writing is exemplary, and your analysis," Sina began using her hands to find the right words. "Your analysis is phenomenal. I know you want to be an anchor woman, but you can always go to graduate school and end up teaching future anchor women and men, and who knows, maybe you can have your own show. But before we get to all of that, I want you to keep up the good work and give serious thought to pursuing a graduate degree. I'd be happy to help you find a program, and it's never too early to start looking for funding."

"Wow," Nikol said smiling. "I guess Project WIDE-NG really helped me."

"I'm sure Project WIDE-NG played a role, but there was something that you had to have inside first. You are an intelligent young lady and I know you will succeed at whatever you do. Our students aren't encouraged to go to grad school as much as they should be, but I want you to think about it. You could even take the GRE next year for practice if you want. I'm sure you will do well in a graduate program, and who knows, maybe in the next seven years, I will have a new colleague — Dr. Nikol Stringer."

"Thank you Dr. Mintor." Nikol stood up. "Thank you for everything."

"There's no need to thank me for telling the truth," Sina said smiling.

"Are you leaving soon? Because I'll walk out with you. You know it's not safe up here at night."

"No, I'll be fine, I have to look over some papers for mailing tomorrow morning, and I'll call campus security to escort me to my car. But thank you." Nikol walked out of her office into a stream of students just leaving another evening class.

Sina spent the next hour reviewing her application for the post-doc at Harvard and the study abroad research grant she wanted so badly. She started at the bottom of each page to check for misspellings then read through each application once more. She didn't want a misplaced comma or an "of" instead of an "on" to keep her from getting one of the awards. Finding no errors, she put each application in a separate envelope, typed address labels, and called campus security. She stopped off in the Department office and left the envelopes in the outgoing mail stack while she waited for security.

Despite his busy schedule, Hank had managed to find time to decorate the house for Christmas just as Aunt Mary used to. Martin and Malcolm sat around the tree playing with their toys and Hope and Sina sat with Rachel at the kitchen table. "My girl Sina has got a book out," Rachel said. "You go girl."

"Look on the dedication page."

"To my sisters Rachel and Hope," Hope read. "How nice."

"Had a tough time deciding whose name should go first so I flipped a coin."

"So how does it feel to have your name in print?"

"Like it's time for me to start working on another proposal. You know I really need to publish my dissertation, but after working on it day and night, I'm not quite ready to even look at it again yet."

"I heard that. You had a love affair with that thing," Rachel said laughing. "Now I think you should do something with your thesis. That was heavy."

"I'm not ready to open that wound again either, but I know I'll have to do it sooner or later."

"Rachel," Hope began asking as she sipped her egg nog. "Has Brothaman been by here to see the boys yet?"

"Not yet, but he called earlier today and said he would stop by later. He has to wait until Hank goes to work because Hank warned him to never step foot in this house again."

"Why don't you take the boys to him?" Sina asked.

"In all this snow and stuff, it's easier for him to come here. Besides, he said his furnace isn't working."

"Don't even say anything about furnaces. Do you know right now Jason and Uncle Leroy are installing a furnace at my mother-in-law's house? On Christmas day!"

"She has to have some heat too, that is, unless you are going to let her and your nieces and John and his wife come to your mother's house."

"I guess you're right."

"So have you made a decision about what you're going to do Rachel?"

"I'm giving him until the spring, and if he isn't clean, then I'm filing for divorce."

"Did you get that life insurance policy?" Hope asked. "Because if you did, you can probably just ride it out and get paid soon."

"That is such an awful thought Hope," Sina said. "That is an absolutely awful thing for you to say about your godson's father."

"He hasn't done a thing for her so I think a quarter of a million is worth all of the misery he put her through. And the way this problem has escalated, his days are probably numbered. It will be no time before he goes down."

"He can still change. I did, didn't I?"

"But you didn't have a drug problem."

"I had plenty of problems you didn't even know about. And I know that with God's power, people can change."

"Time will tell," Hope said using Sina's favorite line. "Well I have made a decision," Hope said abruptly, changing the subject.

"What's that?"

"That maybe it is not meant for Jason and me to stay in Michigan, so starting the first of the year, I am going to apply for any health care administration job in financial management I can find—in the US that is."

"How does Jason feel about that?"

"I haven't discussed it with him yet. But when I get the job, I'm sure he'll come along."

"Are you sure?"

"Yes I'm sure. He even said that maybe he couldn't pass the Michigan Bar because we were supposed to go somewhere else. So who knows?" Hope said as Hank came down and told Rachel he was heading to work.

"Hospitals are usually the busiest on holidays too," Sina said.

"Yes, and I'm in the ER tonight."

"Boys, say goodbye to your Uncle Hank."

"Bye Uncle Hank," Martin said. "And if you see Santa Claus, tell him me and Malcolm said thank you."

"Okay," Hank said smiling at his young nephews. He walked toward the back door to the garage.

Hank hadn't been gone long before the doorbell rang. "I wonder who this could be," Rachel said as she walked through the lattice of toys her sons had spread across the living room. "Hey Baby," Brothaman said kissing Rachel as he walked in the door. "Look boys." He had two baseball mits, a right handed one for Martin and a left handed one for Malcolm. "Oh, I didn't know you had company. I waited until I saw Hank drive off."

"We were just leaving," Sina said. "Weren't we Hope?" Hope sat still at the table, didn't move a muscle. "I need you to take me home, I gotta get there; you know the Bulls are playing shortly."

"Call your parents and tell them to tape it."

"I don't watch taped games. Now be a good friend and take me home."

"Okay," Hope said reluctantly, finally getting the message as Sina tossed her her coat.

"Look Rachel," Sina said hugging her. "I'll give you a call before I head back to Durham, okay."

"Thanks for everything. Oh, and I'll tell you what I think of the book, but I'm sure it's good," Rachel said walking her friends to the door.

"It was nice of you to bring the boys baseball mitts," Rachel said, breaking the ice.

"Yes, you know that's where we met," Brothaman said taking off his jacket. "At a White Sox game. And you know our decision to go to that game on that day changed our lives forever."

Rachel smiled as she remembered how she met her husband and all of the good times she had with him. "But I didn't just get something for the boys." He picked up his jacket and produced a Swiss watch. "You know I got a new job. Graphic design at one of the biggest advertising agencies downtown. And we can finally get back on track. I just bought a car. It's not new but it's dependable." He put the watch on her wrist. "If things go well, I'll be Art Director there by the summer, and after school is out in June you and the boys can move back up here and we'll buy a house in Beverly Hills.

"Rachel, I am so thankful that you stood by me, believed in me, and now that I've gone through rehab, I'm a new person. You know I've been clean for six months now," he said looking up to the left. "And it is all because of you," he said now looking at her. "And the boys." He slid his arms beneath hers and pulled her close. With his head bent to her neck, Brothaman dropped a trail of kisses up the length of her neck, to the side of her face, up to her forehead and back down. Rachel forgot about the divorce. It was clear to her that he had changed, she was certain they would work things out. Taking her hand in his, he told the boys to play real nice and led Rachel upstairs. It had been so long since Rachel had felt her husband's touch, his massage, his caress. She savored every moment. Brothaman put his sons to bed before he left, ensuring that he'd be gone long before Hank returned.

"I can't believe your mother kept this old furnace for so long," Uncle Leroy said as he disconnected the gas line. "This thing has to be at least 30 years old."

"At the least," Jason said. "And I think we're going to need some help getting this out and loading it on the truck. "Hey Johnny," Jason yelled for his brother. "He may not be mechanical, but he is strong."

"And it will definitely take his help to get this thing up the stairs and out the door."

"I know that's right," Jason pushed the old furnace out from the wall.

"Say Jason," Uncle Leroy said pausing. "Have you taken that test again?"

"You know I failed it last February, so I didn't even bother to take it in July."

"Why don't you try the Illinois Bar?" Uncle Leroy asked, putting his tools in his box. He had to have his tools neatly organized at all times and never wanted to mix his with anybody else's. Not even his nephew's. "Say, I just installed a furnace for this woman who teaches a review course. Said she's having one in the spring. That's the slow season and just maybe you can take it then."

"I'll give it some thought."

"Oh, and I'm sure Hope would have better luck finding a job with all the hospitals here."

"You're probably right, but let's not even say anything to her about this until I pass the test."

"Bet," Uncle Leroy said as he bumped his fist with Jason's. "Johnny! If you want some heat, you'll get yourself down here right away."

The new year rang in and Rachel managed to spend a little more time with her husband—when he wasn't working—before heading back to Nashville. She had such a good feeling about him, and his rehabilitation. A Special Ed conference brought her and the boys to Chicago for the Dr. Martin Luther King, Jr. holiday weekend. "I can't believe you left your sons with that man all night," Hank told his sister as she packed her bags early one morning when he was getting off work. "And to think you'd let them stay down on that end of town."

"Since you don't want my husband in this house," Rachel said shutting her suitcase, "he has to stay somewhere else. And he doesn't want to spend an arm and a leg for rent because the less he spends, the more he can save for our house in Beverly Hills."

"Yeah, right. The only way you'll get a house in Beverly is if you win the lottery."

"Anyway, I'll call you when the boys and I get to Nashville."

"You be careful going down there and by all means, drive safely. Don't speed."

"I'll be very careful." Rachel hugged her brother.

On a normal Monday morning, it would have taken Rachel three times as long to get to Brothaman's apartment, but it was a holiday and the roads were clear. *I just hope I don't run into any bad weather along the way to Nashville.* Rachel walked up to the front door of her husband's building. Little did she know a major storm was already brewing. As she approached Brothaman's door, she caught a whiff of smoke just outside his apartment and frantically banged on the door, just before Martin came yelling, "Help. Fire." And Rachel couldn't believe what she saw. Her babies were trying to cook.

"Where is your father?" she asked as she put the fire out.

"He's sleep," Malcolm said as Rachel observed that he had his shoes on the wrong feet.

"Well I'll just have to wake him up." Rachel stomped in the direction of his room.

When Rachel finally hit the road after stopping and buying her sons some breakfast, all she could think of was how happy she was that she had listened to Hope's advice. That annual premium made finances lean for her and the boys. As Rachel drove, she thought about Aunt Mary and her death and how she decided she wanted to live her life. Once again, the devil jumped in and tested Rachel's faith. After nearly losing her children in a fire that would have been full force had she gotten caught in traffic on the Ryan, Rachel decided to cut her ties with Brothaman. For the last two and a half years they had been going in circles. Around and around, never stopping at the same point.

Rachel managed to get back in the swing of things and planned to give Jason a call for legal advice when she just didn't feel herself. She attributed it all to that she had been through in the last month. She watched her sons playing. Martin picked up a pencil with his left hand and wrote his name on a picture. "Here Mommy," he said handing the page from his coloring book to Rachel with his left hand. "I almost stayed inside all the lines too."

"Very good Martin," Rachel said kissing her son on his forehead.

"I drew you a picture Mommy," Malcolm said handing Rachel his masterpiece with his right hand. Martin looked just like Rachel, and Malcolm looked just like Brothaman and they were both cute. Rachel smiled and felt she owed it to her sons to pay her doctor a visit. She had to stay healthy for them. She was all they had.

Rachel's follow-up visit to the doctor put her in a depression induced sleep. She tried to ascribe her melancholy to winter's lack of sunlight, but knew it had been caused by something greater and more personal. "Mommy, telephone," Martin said. "It's T-Sina."

"Okay baby."

"Rachel, I hope you're sitting down because I have bad news."

"I'm lying down. Besides nothing could be worse than what I found out today."

"So you already know?"

"Know what?"

"Tommy called and told me Brothaman was arrested for possession today. Since it was his first offense, he'll probably get 150 hours of community service. Apparently he ran a red light, was stopped and then searched. The police found a stolen watch on him—possession of lost or stolen merchandise is a misdemeanor. I'm so sorry to be the bearer of such bad news. I guess Hope was right."

"Yes, she and Hank were. I just wish I'd listened."

"You sound really bad. Are you sick? Have you been to the doctor lately?"

"I just came back from the doctor."

"She must have you on some strong antibiotics or something."

"The only thing she prescribed was prenatal vitamins," Rachel said crying. "I'm pregnant, due in September—"

"Oh Rachel," Sina said softly.

"Not only did that sorry husband of mine give me another baby for Christmas, he also gave me genital warts."

"Oh my God! I'm so sorry Rachel. What are you going to do?"

"All I know right now is that I'm filing for divorce. Beyond that I just don't know."

"Well you're going to have to make some plans, and soon," Thomasine said pausing. "And remember—I'm here. You can call me any time of the day or night—collect if you need to. I'm here. Now you get some rest, and take good care of yourself and the boys."

"I told her, but she just wouldn't listen," Hope said when she called Sina from Kalamazoo. "I knew from the beginning that Brothaman was no good; she should have stayed with Patrick."

"Look Hope," Sina said leaning back on her sofa. "I am not going to sit here and listen to you talk about how you told Rachel so. She doesn't need to hear I told you so right now. What she needs is a friend and that is what you need to be for her. What's done is done. She needs your support now, and if you can't give that to her, then she's better off not hearing from you at all."

"I suppose you're right," Hope said, reconsidering her words. "I'm going to be in Nashville in two weeks for an interview. Maybe I'll take her to lunch or something."

"Good. She'll really appreciate it. It would be great too if you and Jason moved to Nashville."

"It will be nice for me and Jason to move on with our lives, but I don't want to get him all ready to move and stuff until I get an offer, so let's not say anything to him about it."

"That's so silly Hope. Jason knows when you interview for a job, there's no guarantee you'll get it."

"Well as far as he knows, I'm going to Nashville for Nelson, Ware & Associates."

"Your secret's safe with me."

"So how is your love life. Now that your book is published?"

"I got the postdoc at Harvard. I'm holding off on making a decision until I hear about the Study Abroad Grant."

"Harvard's not bad at all."

"But if I can go to Australia for two years—."

"Look, I have to go. Jason and I have a date tonight."

Birds of paradise and other tropical flowers adorned the floral arrangement in the lobby of the posh hotel where Hope was staying. When Rachel walked up that afternoon it seemed to her that Hope was even larger than she remembered. "Hope," Rachel said as she extended her arms to hug her friend. "It's so nice to see you. And that is one nice hairstyle you have," Rachel added looking for something to compliment her on.

"I noticed a cute little restaurant just down the hallway, and I'm starving. I haven't eaten since breakfast," Hope added as Rachel looked up at the clock and observed that it was only 12:15.

"I'm so glad you finally came to Nashville. Oh, and the boys told me to give you these," Rachel said of the folded pictures in her purse. "Martin colored this for you. He is really getting better with his coloring too. And Malcolm drew this. He is quite an artist."

"These are masterpieces. Two first available," she told the hostess.

"Right this way ma'am."

"How have you been, really?" Hope asked Rachel as they sat down.

"About as best as can be expected," Rachel said scooting her chair in.

"I was so sorry to hear about your miscarriage," Hope said adding another, "really," which made her seem less than sincere.

"You know as shocked and dismayed and confused as I was when I found out I was pregnant, I was upset when the doctor told me my daughter was not developing properly. I knew though, that it was best to terminate the pregnancy. But with God's help, I've managed to put much of this behind me. You were right about my husband. I only wish Sina hadn't pulled you off so fast that night. Then it probably would have never happened."

"May I take your order?"

"I'd like the rotisserie chicken with corn and mashed potatoes, sweet tea and peach cobbler with vanilla ice cream," Hope said immediately.

"Would ya like a quarter or a half?"

"A half."

"And for you ma'am."

"I'd like the French onion soup and a salad, a pitcher of water with lemon slices on the side," Rachel said.

"Eating light, are we?"

"I'm used to just eating a sandwich for lunch so this is a real treat. How are things with you and Jason?"

"To be honest, they haven't been great lately," Hope started in her usual loud voice. "When we first got married, he was in law school and I was working and going to school and we spent very little time together. Now that he's doing the heating and cooling thing, we spend even less time together."

"But once he passes the bar things will get better, you'll spend more time together when you work the same hours."

"Maybe, but I don't think Jason thinks I'm—"

"What Hope?"

"Jason doesn't think I'm sexy anymore."

"Why would you think that?"

"We hardly ever sleep in the same bed, let alone make love. It all started back when he failed the bar the first time. And if we sleep in the same bed, he comes to bed long after I'm asleep and gets up in the morning to exercise before I get up."

"Why don't you try getting up early and exercising too? It'll give you a chance to spend some time together."

"I don't know. It's like he doesn't even know me either, if you know what I mean."

"No," Rachel said sipping her water and glancing over at a blonde southern belle who gave Rachel a why-is-she-talking-so-loud-look. "Please explain."

"The last time we made love, Jason wasn't quite in—the right place. He was kind of in between two folds of skin and he didn't even know," Hope said at broadcast volume level. Once again Rachel looked at the woman now in stitches. "And I was too ashamed to tell him. I don't know what to do." She put her head down on the table.

Rachel just could not believe Hope. The most intimate thing she ever shared with her, she made it known to half of the restaurant. As solemn a look as Rachel had on her face, she was snickering inside.

"Don't go in the water!" Sina yelled to Martin and Malcolm as they ran with Sparky along the sands of Long Beach where Sina had a time share in a condominium. "I really wish Hope could be here." She walked along-side Rachel who carried a blanket and a bag with snacks and sun screen.

"If things work out for her, she and Jason can live on the beach."

"Yeah, it would be nice if she got the job in Virginia Beach. Then I could see her more often. I try to get up and see Kelsey a couple of times a year. It's just too bad that I won't be here for a while now."

"So you made your decision?" Rachel said as she stopped. "How's this spot?"

"As good as any I suppose. I've decided to go to Australia for two years."

"That's wonderful Sina, you know I'm going to miss you."

"Girl get you a computer and we can talk every day," Sina said sitting down. "You know what? You can use my desktop. I'm not lugging that thing across the sea with me. And you know about how much my parents will use it if I take it to Chicago. Shoot, when we get back to Durham I'll send it to you and we can start e-mailing right away."

"Thank you."

"If you chat with me every day just maybe you won't miss me as much," Sina said putting her straw hat on. "But these two years will go by so fast. Just look at how fast the last ten years have gone by."

"That's true."

"You know, I can't believe Martin is already five years old. It seems like just yesterday you were calling me to tell me your water had broken."

"And you stayed so calm. You are always so cool and calm. Shoot, you were even kind of calm when you had to dump Kenneth."

"After all I had been through, that was really minor."

"Both you and I."

"It seems like Hope never goes through anything."

"Oh she does, she just doesn't tell us like we tell each other. When she came to Nashville a couple of months ago, she was telling me that things aren't going too well between her and Jason." Rachel said, almost snickering.

"That's too bad. I feel sorry for her. It's like she's put all of her eggs in one basket with Jason. You know Jason is cool and all, but for the last fourteen years he has been her one and only. And I just couldn't imagine that," Sina said going into her small cooler for something cold to drink. "Hey, look at Martin. He's really growing tall."

"Yes he is, he certainly is, just like his daddy," Rachel said looking at her oldest son who was the spitting image of her, but didn't act like her or Brothaman.

"Have you heard from Brothaman?"

"He completed his community service last month. But he's out of my life. I have filed for divorce and the sooner it comes through, the better."

"Goodbye and good riddance is probably your best bet," Sina said taking a sip of her juice. "If Hope were here, she would probably tell you to drag it out just in case something happens so you could collect on that dumb insurance policy she told you to get."

"I don't think it's so dumb."

"Don't tell me you got it."

"A quarter of a mil. For the boys—if anything happens," Rachel said, staring out at the water.

"I know that's a morbid thought, but my goodness Rachel, you're off in another world."

"I've had a lot on my mind lately."

"I bet you have with this Brothaman deal, the pregnancy, the miscarriage, and—"

"Patrick."

"What about Patrick?"

"I never told you about the night we broke up."

"No, but I didn't expect for you to share those details with me."

"Well, I felt really bad because Patrick was such a sweet man and Brothaman and I had hit it off really well. And although I hadn't really done anything—I thought about it, but decided that I just couldn't marry Patrick. It wouldn't have been fair to him. I felt so damn guilty. Like I had been dishonest to him, so I thought it was best if I just broke it off. You know, give him his ring back and everything."

"That's understandable."

"And I didn't want to do it over the phone either."

"That wouldn't have been a good idea. That's the coward's way out."

"So one weekend when he came up around the end of September I told him that I couldn't marry him and it would be best if we just broke things off."

"Oh and you feel bad about hurting him?"

"Well that and—anyway I didn't want to be cold and heartless so I wished him well and hugged him one last time. Then he begged me to make love to him, just one last time. We were in the house alone so, to make a long story short, now that I think about it, I believe that was the night Martin was conceived. He is more and more like Patrick every day. He's left handed just like Patrick and curls his upper lip when he smiles just like Patrick. I watch him play with Malcolm and I see more and more of Patrick in him."

"Come again," Sina said now in shock by this revelation.

"Sina, I think Martin is Patrick's son. But I thought I couldn't get pregnant that night, it was two weeks after my period."

"Rachel, that's when you get pregnant, you ovulate around the middle of your cycle," Sina said just shaking her head in disbelief. "When was the last time you talked to Patrick?"

"That night. He probably doesn't want to have anything to do with me ever again."

"Rachel, you have to tell him about Martin. Have him take a DNA test or something. He has already missed out on so much of Martin's life. His birth. Even Brothaman almost missed that. His first steps. Shoot girl, if you don't hurry up and move on this, Patrick may miss out on his son's first day of school. The least that you can do is tell Patrick what you've just told me because he deserves to know."

"I kind of got the courage one day, one of those days when I felt things could get no worse. I picked up the phone and called his number and the old woman who answered said no Patrick lived there. Said she had had that number for two years. He's probably married and has a family of his own by now."

"But you won't know until you try to find out. More than anything, Rachel, you owe it to Martin. Patrick really loved you; and for all I know, he may still love you, or he may hate your guts, but he needs to know that he has a five-year-old son."

"But how? I don't have his number. I don't even know where he lives now."

"Let's see. Is he the type to have an unpublished number?"

"He was very private, but always listed his number in the Duncan Directory and the Chicago White Pages when he was in grad school. And he always used his full name."

"Well we can get on the internet and look him up. We'll find all of the Patrick Stephen Longs across this nation and call them all up because this is important."

"You're right," Rachel said. Martin and Malcolm ran up to Rachel and Sina.

"Mommy I'm hungry."

"T-Sina fixed you some sandwiches." The boys cleaned their hands and Sina gave them their lunch.

"You know," Sina began, petting Sparky whose sad eyes watching the boys eat told Sina that if she didn't give him something soon, he would probably start drooling. "I wish I had children."

"What? Ms. Hot Date with my dissertation, book or grant proposal."

"Yes, I think I'm tired of being by myself. Now don't get me wrong, I love the kids in the choir and in Project WIDE-NG and even my students, but it's not the same."

"It's not too late for you to start. You aren't even 28."

"I know, it's just that my parents are getting older and seeing Daddy with Korrin last summer at the family reunion made me feel like I was— I don't know, denying him grandchildren. And since almost all of my grandparents died before I was even thought of, it is very important that my children get to know their grandparents. You know Daddy will be 73 next year and mom will be 71 in September."

"Girl, I didn't know your parents were that old."

"Sometimes I think I shouldn't have given my daughter up for adoption. But I just had to. I just couldn't bear—it was just the best decision. But I think about her every day. She'll be nine next month."

"Why don't you try to find her? She should know about you."

"I don't think that's a good idea. It would just totally disrupt her life. What if her adoptive parents haven't even told her she was adopted? It could ruin her life. If she decides to look for me, well that will be different."

Shaking Free

29

Thomasine had finally arrived in Chicago and Sparky was happy to finally be free of the confining back seat of Sina's car. He had to be thankful though, that she had made a trip home earlier in the summer to bring some of her belongings. If she hadn't, he really would have been cramped. The fourteen hour drive didn't seem as long with all the reminiscing over the last ten years about the lives of herself and her two closest friends. She would have made it in about twelve, but having to stop and walk Sparky managed to put a few hours on the trip. Sina was lucky that her trip was not made longer by heavy traffic or accidents.

"Princess," Rev. Mintor said as he helped Sina unload her car. "I'm so glad you're home. You know I don't like you out on the road at night by yourself."

"I know, but Daddy, you know I'm never alone."

"I know." Tommy and Jesse walked up. "You must be exhausted."

"I am. You know, I'm not 18 anymore. Seems like I was just full of energy then."

"Now you know how I feel," Tommy said teasing his sister.

"I sure do, I remember just before Rachel, Hope and I went away to college you told us we made you feel old. And now we are all there. Or I will be there in a few minutes," Sina said looking at her watch.

"Oh," Tommy said patting Sina on her shoulder. "You have about another hour—you didn't change your watch to Central time yet." Tommy took Sina's suitcase out of the car. "Look, we'll unload your car and put everything in the basement. You just go in and get some sleep."

"I think I'll take you up on that. Just give Sparky some water."

"I'll take care of that," Crystal said as she started out of the side door.

"Mama," Sina said hugging her mother. "I'm tired."

"Well, your room is ready for you. Just go on in and hop in the bed. We'll talk in the morning."

Sina went right in, took her sleep shirt out of the dresser drawer, brushed her teeth, tied her head, and slept for almost as many hours as she had spent driving to Chicago the previous day. She would have slept longer if not for Tommy. He stopped at the house with another one of his favorite Sina birthday cakes, a white layer cake with pineapple filling between the first and second layers and raspberry filling between the second and third layers with butter cream frosting. Tommy always ordered the cake from his favorite bakery, but Sina didn't find it too appetizing. She would have preferred an atomic cake. What Sina thought was a mosquito was Tommy in a playful mood, rubbing a string of thread on her face.

"Look, you need to get up. It's after 1:30. I've never seen anyone sleep half of their birthday away."

"That's right," Sina said smiling as she got out of bed and put on her robe. "I guess I was really tired. Now where are my slippers. Oh no, did Daddy feed Sparky."

"Fed him and walked him this morning."

"I see he's adapted well," Sina said as she began walking down the hallway.

"Who, Daddy or Sparky?"

"I guess the both of them," she said, smiling as she reached the kitchen.

"What's up with all of those donuts?"

"You didn't eat any of them did you?"

"Just one of the pineapple, why?"

"Good. That baker's dozen is Hope's, and I need to get them to her."

"I wouldn't want to mess with Hope and her donuts after what she did in NC," Tommy said laughing. "Well aren't you going to open the fridge?"

"It's that nasty old cake you like so much isn't it."

"Go on, cut it."

"Okay big brother." Sina walked across the room to get a knife.

"Don't forget the waxed paper either while you're over there."

"Okay, okay. These ten years have gone by so fast," Sina said walking back to the table. "Class reunion already."

"Cut a piece for Jesse too," Tommy said. "This is our dessert for lunch."

"You watch that cake and those donuts, because at your age, your metabolism is probably shot," Sina said trying to get her brother back for waking her.

"Yeah, you may have lost that weight from grad school but you watch out because it can creep up on you just like it crept up on me. I'ma have to run, but Happy 28th Birthday little sister."

"Thanks."

"And have fun tonight."

294 Trevy A. McDonald

"I'm sure I will." Sina walked downstairs and began to sort through her belongings, putting the Australia stuff in the laundry area and taking the other items to her room. After she had hung her finer clothing in the closet and put the others in her dresser drawer, she found her favorite bath oil, ran the tub and got in. The hot water soothed her body, stiff from sitting in the same position for hours upon hours the previous day. As much as she dreaded getting to this age, Sina looked forward to the reunion. She didn't feel 28. Not like she thought it would feel. She couldn't complain though because she was certainly too blessed to stay stressed.

After she was lotioned, perfumed, and dressed, Sina called Rachel to confirm their plans for the evening. "What's up girl? I called you at about 11 but your father said you were sleeping, that you had gotten in late."

"Yeah, I got in just before midnight."

"Well Happy Birthday."

"Thank you. Are we still on for tonight?"

"I'm afraid not."

"What's going on?"

"It's Hope," Rachel said almost whispering. "She really needs you right now."

"Is she there?"

"Yeah, she's sitting in the kitchen wallowing in self-pity."

"Okay, I'll come right over." Sina untied the scarf from around her head.

"Could you get some perch? You know I love your perch."

"Yes, I'll stop by the store on my way over. Say, do you have any hamburger?"

"Yeah, why?" Rachel asked.

"Just put it in a skillet and cut up some celery, green pepper and onion so that part will be ready when I get there. We're going to have a traditional Friday evening Chicago style dinner — fish, spaghetti and cole slaw."

"Sounds great, I have everything to make the spaghetti and I can do at least that much. Please excuse me for a moment," Rachel said as she told the boys to go out back with their Uncle Hank and play. "I have some cabbage and carrots too."

"Good, get Hope to grating. Maybe it will get her mind off whatever's got her so upset. If that doesn't, I have something that definitely will."

"Consider it done," Rachel said.

"I'll be there shortly," Sina grabbed her spices.

When Sina parked her car in front of Aunt Mary's house Malcolm's ball rolled out into the front yard. "T-Sina," he yelled. "Martin, T-Sina is here."

"Come give me a big hug. Did you miss me?" she asked as she knelt and hugged the boys.

"Yes," Martin said. "T-Sina, can you take us to the beach."

"No, T-Sina. I want to go and get some ice cream," Malcolm said.

"How about if we go to the zoo on Monday? How does that sound?"

"Yeah," Martin and Malcolm said giving Sina a five one at a time.

"Could you do your T-Sina a favor?"

"Yes."

"Carry this bag," she said, handing Martin the bag with the fish. "And this bag," she said, handing Malcolm the one with the vegetables and spices, "into the house and then you can go right back out and play."

"Okay T-Sina."

Thomasine walked back to her car to get Hope's package off the back seat when she felt somebody behind her. She turned around immediately and was greeted by none other than Conrad. "Thomasine Mintor, just how has life been treating you?" he asked reaching out to hug her.

"Do not touch me."

"Well excuse me, but I just thought I'd come by and say hi to you."

"It has certainly taken you a long time. What," Sina said as she counted on her fingers, "nearly ten years. But I've forgiven you. By the grace of God, I've forgiven you."

"What are you talking about?" Conrad asked, puzzled.

"That night... Conrad I *begged* you to take me to Rachel's party when you pulled off the outer drive. I *pleaded with you not to...* And I have lived with that pain far too long!" Thomasine said as a tear trickled down her face. "Conrad, I said no. I told you I wasn't ready, but you just ignored me and did exactly what you wanted, then left me to deal with the consequences."

Conrad stood still with his head bowed and mouth open. He couldn't even look Sina in the eye.

"And I was in denial for so long. I denied that you raped me, I denied that you didn't love me, and I denied as long as I could that I was pregnant because I just couldn't believe that you would do such a thing to me. Why Conrad? Why did you rob me of the most precious thing I ever had? You just took it and left me standing in the wind. Do you know that somewhere out there we have a daughter who will be nine in five short days?" Sina said as a girl of about two years walked up to Conrad.

"Daddy, Mommy said to tell you dinner is ready."

"Okay sweetie," Conrad picked her up. "Thomasine, I'm so sorry. I was young, I was high that night and—there is really no excuse for what I did to you, so there is no use in me standing here trying to—God has forgiven me, you have forgiven me, but I know I'll have to answer for it."

"What you did to me was horrible Conrad, but I could no longer let a grudge I was holding against you keep me imprisoned. I sought my freedom, because that haunted me for years. But God has been so good to me that I couldn't let what you did to me go with me to my grave. So while I absolutely despise what you did to me and while I never wish it on my worst enemy, I have managed to find it in my heart to forgive you."

"What my mother always said must be true then," Conrad said, unable to find the right words to apologize to Sina after all this time. "Through Christ all things are possible."

"That is the ultimate truth." Sina took the box of donuts off the back seat. "Goodbye Conrad."

As Thomasine walked into the kitchen she felt like her feet never even touched the ground. After all these years, she finally had her catharsis. She thought it would come after the birth—but it didn't. The thesis was therapeutic but it did not do the same thing for her that finally confronting Conrad did. And she was as glad as Conrad was lucky that it came after Sina was saved. Had it come any earlier, she might have killed him, but because of God's unconditional love, Sina now realized that justice will be served—whether in this life or the next and she was confident that she would rather serve hers here than to take it to the next level.

"Hope," Sina said, "I brought you a little something. Some donuts from *Krisp & Tasty*." Sina placed the box on the table in front of Hope. "And I managed to keep Sparky out of them for 13 hours too."

"I don't want any damn donuts," Hope said crying. "Jason has left me and a damn donut will not bring him back."

"Oh, Hope, I'm so sorry," Sina said shocked.

"I gave him fourteen years of my life. I've been with him half of my damn life, and he tells me he's leaving me."

"Just like that?" Sina asked as she picked up where Hope left off with the grating of the cabbage. "I can't believe this is happening to you. You all were together for so long and appeared to be so happy and so together," Sina said before she realized she had been in North Carolina for the last seven years and had actually seen very little of them since they married. "Did you suspect that he was going to leave you? Were there any signs?"

"He had been coming to Chicago quite a bit. He took the bar here and he told me he was moving here to take a job."

"Well maybe you can move here and get marriage counseling."

"He's moving in with his mother."

"So he's a mama's boy. You should have seen signs of that."

"And he said it just isn't working. We don't communicate, we don't do anything together and we don't have anything in common."

"I just can't believe that he would do that to you," Rachel said as she walked back into the dining room. "Why did he even ask you to marry him in the first place?"

"I don't know," Hope said. "Maybe I rushed him."

"Rushed him?" Sina replied now cutting up the onions for the slaw and becoming teary eyed. "It took him nearly eight years to propose."

"But he wasn't ready and I knew that. I just wanted to be engaged like you and Rachel."

"If he wasn't ready, then why did he buy you that ring?"

Hope looked down at the two carat marquise diamond ring and gold wedding band and big tears welled up in her eyes.

"We're not going to have any more of that. He's not worth one of your tears. And I should know because I've been through it."

"You and me both. Remember Kenneth Winston? " Thomasine said walking over to console her friend. "Boy, I wish I still drank, because with the way my day is going, I could use a good stiff one." Thomasine began to cry.

"I could use one too." Rachel joined her friends. "But we're not going to spend our evening sitting around here in misery over some no-good men. Sina's going to go in that kitchen and fry that perch. I'm going to finish the slaw and we strong Black women are going to get our groove and grub on." Rachel stepped into the living room and turned on Hank's stereo.

Thomasine busied herself with heating the grease while she washed, seasoned and breaded the fish. Perch was Sina and Rachel's favorite and they had to have spaghetti and cole slaw to go along with it. And of course white bread. Sina stood at the stove and watched the fish fry to golden perfection. It was virtually brown when Sina heard one of her favorite songs from yesteryear on the radio. She took the fish out and placed it on a plate she had lined with a paper towel to drain the grease. Rachel had made the slaw and set it in the refrigerator and the spaghetti should have been seasoned to perfection now that it had simmered with bay leaves.

"All right now," Sina said as she walked in the living room dancing and singing to *Got to Be Real.* "Hey now." Sina tilted her head to mimic a trumpeter which made Hope chuckle. "Now this is my song," Sina said when

Phyllis Hyman's *You Know How to Love Me* came on. She danced and pranced around the living room, doing a forward moonwalk during the chorus with Rachel as her back up singer and musician hitting a few keys on the piano every now and then in sync with the sound from the speakers. Sina gyrated her hips from side to side as she sang the second verse and walked around in front of Hope like she was working a crowd. When Sina sang the last notes of the song and the DJ segued into a song Sina absolutely hated, she was applauded by her audience.

"Bravo, Bravo," Rodney said as he clapped his hands. "A magnificent performance Sina."

And anyone who knew Sina really well knew that she was a diva and just ate up what he said.

"You think so?"

"Oh yes. I think you should take your show on the road," he said smiling. "And make sure you take some of that perch because Hank, the boys and I really enjoyed it. They will both go over big."

"I don't believe," Sina started as she considered picking up something and throwing it at him and Hank. "I ought to make you go to the store and buy me some more fish. But I didn't want fish anyway. I think I want an Italian Beef."

"And I want a polish," Rachel said. "Let's go to Fred and Jack's."

"Oh, and you two can continue to watch the boys. Come on Hope because I'm sure all that laughing you just did worked up an appetite."

Hope got her purse and followed Sina and Rachel out of the house.

"So how long have Hank and Rodney been buddies?" Sina asked Rachel.

"Since Rodney asked Hank to come in and talk to Junior Church about careers in medicine. I see Rodney quite frequently when I come to Chicago," Rachel said as they got into Sina's car. "So Sina, you will be going to Australia in a few weeks huh?"

"Sure will," Sina checked her mirrors and signaled before pulling from the curb.

"You've always been such a safe driver Sina."

"Aren't you afraid to go so far away from home for so long?" Hope asked.

"Not really, I'm looking forward to it. The last time I was there, there was this tall dark man kinda looking me up and down when I was at a Fijian club, but I was so into Kenneth then I didn't even look back. Not long anyway. I looked long enough though to see that he was cute. But that's not what I'm really going there for. I'm going there to do research. You two will have to come and see me next year."

"I suppose we could. If Rachel could get someone to look after the boys we could surely come. By the looks of things," Hope said as a tear trickled down her face, "We'll all be single women again."

"Well I can't wait to get my freedom from Brothaman," Rachel said as Thomasine headed north towards 83rd Street. "Then I can sort of close that chapter of my life."

"I know that's right. Say, Rachel, did you get in touch with Patrick yet?"

"Not yet. I did look up all the Patrick Longs on the internet like you told me and there were over 100, 10 Patrick S. Longs. I got in touch with just about all of them, except for one who lives just south of me. I know I called at least two or three times but all I got was a voice mail."

"Did the voice sound familiar?" Sina turned west on 83rd Street.

"It was some voice mail standard voice. So yes the voice sounded familiar, but it was like that on my voice mail."

"But you are going to call again when you get back aren't you?"

"Yes Sina," Rachel turned onto Vincennes.

"Do you have everything you need for the reunion dinner tomorrow?"

"Yes."

"And you Hope?"

"I'm not going."

"That's what you think," Sina replied.

"You have to go Hope; you were the valedictorian."

"I just can't, not after this breakup."

"Well he could have waited until after the reunion," Rachel said.

"He said he was tired of pretending and could not just play along any more."

"Wow," Sina said as she pulled up into the parking lot of Fred and Jacks.

"Look Hope," Rachel said. "You are not the first one to go through this and you won't be the last. Look at all Sina and I have been through."

"Yeah, look at all the mind games that have been played on me the last ten years. And Kenneth was a doozey. After him, I decided I just needed to be by myself for a while. And in the last five years I've learned a lot about myself. Maybe you just need some time to yourself—some space. But I don't think that should keep you from going to the reunion tomorrow."

"That's right sister girlfriend. Hold your head high and don't even give Jason the satisfaction—because what he did was foul," Rachel said as they got out of Sina's car and walked toward Fred and Jack's.

Under Your Spell

30

The day had finally come. Sina wore her favorite red evening gown and was pleased that in two years, she was able to knock off most of those Ph.D. pounds. But it took hard work and that was exactly what she and so many of her classmates from Piney Hill's Class of 1987 had done. There were doctors, lawyers, teachers, accountants, social workers, professional athletes and jacks of all trades parading around the room meeting and greeting friends they hadn't seen in ten years. Some people hadn't changed at all in ten years. "Oh, I'm so happy to see you," a woman Sina recalled as Loretha Jackson said as she walked up and embraced Rachel in a bear hug just before she stepped back, looked down at Rachel's name tag and said quite insincerely, "Rachel," just before she walked away. These people acted the same, looked the same, dressed the same as at the prom and even wore their hair the same.

Then there were others, like Thomasine, who believed that she looked even better than she had ten years ago. And of course there were those who had aged without grace. "Is that Maximilian Tate?" Sina whispered to Rachel as a bald, fat man walked toward the trio.

"Rachel, it's so nice to see you," the man said as he reached out with his stubby hand to shake hers. "Do you remember me? I'm Maximilian Tate."

"Oh Max," Rachel said shaking his hand. "It's so nice to see you again after all these years." Sina stood behind Max and made faces that nearly caused Rachel to laugh so hard she had a stitch in her side.

"I see time hasn't been as kind to some," Hope said as Max walked away.

"Hey," Sina said. "Will you ladies excuse me for a moment?" She turned toward the ladies' room. She was in the mirror washing her hands first and then freshening up her makeup when a very pregnant Sophronia Lucas-Winston waddled in. "Hello Thomasine. You know, Kenneth and I are having our second child."

"Kenneth really did want children. When we were engaged, he wanted us to start a family right away. But you know what?"

"What?"

"If you and Kenneth are happy, then I'm happy for you. You see, God has a master plan for each of our lives and I am so happy that my life has gone according to His plans, not mine." Sina put on her Dangerously Red lipstick and walked out. *My goodness, I ran into Sam yesterday in the store, Conrad at Aunt Mary's and now I have to see Kenneth. Is this a reunion of ghosts from each of my past relationships or what?* Thomasine was so deep in thought that she didn't even see Rodney until she had bumped into him.

"Look Sina. I'm sorry about eating your fish last night but what can I say? I was starving. I hadn't eaten since breakfast. But it was good."

"Don't worry about it. I wanted an Italian Beef. Really," she said as they walked back toward the ballroom. "In the next few weeks I'm going to try to have all of my Chicago favorites because that's going to be all she wrote for the next two years."

"Why, you can come here from North Carolina anytime you get ready. You know, your father is always talking about you. Always."

"I could come from North Carolina, but not from Australia. That's where I'm going for the next two years."

"That's so far away." *There's Nothing Better than Love* was playing.

"I know, but I'm going there to do research. But you probably don't want me to bore you with the details."

"That sounds interesting, I'd love to hear all about it. You know I've been to Australia a few times."

"Well I'm sure my father will fill you in on everything. He has a tendency to do that," she said as the song reached the first chorus. "You know, I used to really love this song."

"Would you like to dance?"

"Sure," Thomasine said as Rodney took her hand and led her to the dance floor. "I'd love to."

Hope and Rachel stood along the wall chit chatting and Hope became quiet when something caught Rachel's attention. Rachel stood still with a look that could kill in her eyes. When Hope turned around, she saw Jason. "Hello Hope."

"Hello Jason."

"How are you?"

"How do you expect her to be?" Rachel interrupted. "I can't believe your nerve," she continued as Jason just put his head down. "Hope is a good woman, and she loved you for so long. Waited forever for you to marry her and just like that you tell her you're leaving. And you aren't willing to even try to work things out."

"I do love Hope, but both she and I know this marriage was over a long time ago. Probably before it even started. And we can't go on pretending any longer." He turned to Hope.

"If you've been pretending so long, then why did you even ask her to marry you and buy her that ring in the first place?"

"I didn't buy that engagement ring; Hope did. I never actually asked her to marry. It was just a given that we would get married," Jason said just before he walked off.

"Oh Hope," Rachel said. "I'm so sorry. I had no idea."

Thomasine's hot dates with dissertations and books over the last few years had made her forget how it felt to be touched by a man, especially one with so much oomph. With Rodney's hand on the small of her back for just a minute, she thought she'd lose it but the feeling had to end as the song was fading and Rachel was tapping on her shoulder. "It's Hope," Rachel said to Sina. "She just can't take it any longer so we're leaving."

"But I can't leave yet," Sina said shifting her eyes in the direction of Rodney. She felt that after five years of being dateless, she deserved to have just a little fun tonight.

"I can take you home Thomasine," Rodney said.

"Are you sure?"

"Yes. It's no problem at all."

"I'll call you when I get in and see how Hope is doing."

"You do that," Rachel said smiling as Rodney took Sina's hand and continued dancing midway through Freddie Jackson's *Have You Ever Loved Somebody?* He sang softly in Thomasine's ear and Thomasine returned the favor when *Old Friend* was played.

Thomasine looked up at the stars which dotted the sky as she and Rodney rode south on the Ryan in his convertible Mercedes SL500R and *Dindi* from *A Twist of Jobim* played from the CD player. "It was great seeing so many of our classmates," Rodney said.

"It was great seeing some, not so great seeing others, to be honest," Sina replied.

"It really brought back some memories seeing some of those people," Rodney turned briefly to face Sina. "Remember the time when Al started that Dick Tracy Crimestoppers club."

"Yes, and I actually joined. My code name was Sweetie Pie."

"Mine was Sugar Cane."

"*Blue Interlude*," they said in unison.

"You must be a jazz aficionado. I really love that CD. It's one of my favorites by Wynton Marsalis," Thomasine said.

"I have it at home myself," Rodney responded as the midnight air encompassed them.

"How about the time Ted set off smoke bombs in the cafeteria?" Sina asked.

"He was always into some devilment. You know he started most of the food fights during seventh period lunch our senior year."

"That's right; we used to eat together."

"We sure did, and then all of a sudden you didn't speak to me anymore. And I never understood why. We were talking and everything and then you just cut me off," Rodney said as they passed the 87th Street exit. "For the last ten years I've wondered why, so please don't keep me in suspense any longer. Because I really like you."

"I'll answer that plain and simple. Sophronia Lucas. She threw the two of you up in my face every chance she got."

"There wasn't anything going on between us other than me taking her to the prom. And that was only after you cut me off. It was just that one night and I dropped her conniving butt off at home after the prom and I never took her out again."

"Rumors were all over Piney Hill about you and Sophronia at that time. What did you expect me to believe?"

"Well, why didn't you ask me? You shouldn't have stopped speaking to me. I was approachable."

Thomasine thought about the words she had exchanged with Sophronia in the ladies' room earlier that evening. "Just maybe the time wasn't right. Then."

"Maybe so," Rodney responded as he exited the Dan Ryan at 95th.

"But you don't have to worry about Sophronia anymore. She's happily married."

"She sure is, to my ex-fiancé. I certainly hope she's happy."

"I'm sorry to hear that, I wasn't aware of that. When did that happen?"

"About five years ago, just six weeks before our wedding date I came back from a conference in Australia to find—let's just say that Kenneth and Sophronia were in a very compromising position on my living room floor."

"Oh my. I know you were shocked."

"Not nearly as shocked as he was when I threw the engagement ring he refused to take back into the fountain in front of the company where he works. This was of course after I left his things that he refused to take with him there also,"

"What did he do?"

"Something I never expected. He slapped me."

"Oh, no."

"But I was testing for my blue belt so I handled things. By the way, you need to make a left turn at the next light."

"Tae Kwon Do or Karate?"

"Karate."

"I studied Tae Kwon Do. You didn't hurt him too badly did you?"

"I don't know, because I never looked back. But if I did hurt him, it wasn't nearly as bad as he hurt me."

"I know that's right. How could he do that to you?"

"Turn right at the next corner," Thomasine said continuing to direct Rodney to her parent's home. "I don't know. But I just chalked it up to being God's way of showing me in the eleventh hour that he was not the one for me. And I'm really thankful for that."

"Which house?"

"The one with the porch light on. Daddy has always left that light on for me—for the last ten years," Thomasine said as they slowed and turned into the driveway.

"I had a nice time," Rodney said. Thomasine began to open the door. "I'll get that for you." Rodney jumped out of his car, walked around the back and opened the door for Thomasine.

"Thank you Rodney. I had a nice time too"

"I'm glad," he said smiling as he walked her to the door. "I was afraid you'd hold a grudge about the fish—you know after the high school thing."

"Shut up Sparky, it's me." Sparky whimpered and wagged his tail. "That's my dog—he's a little overprotective of me."

"What kind is he?"

"Golden Retriever—five years old."

"I have a three-year-old Black lab."

"It seems that we have a lot in common. Jazz, martial arts, dogs, what else?"

"There's only one way to find out."

"How's that?"

"Will I see you again? A group of us are going to Ted James' church tomorrow. The service starts at 11:00. *Grace and Mercy Tabernacle* on Stony Island."

"I'll be there. Lord knows my friend Hope needs a healing," Thomasine said looking at her watch. "It's late, I better run. Goodnight."

"Goodnight Thomasine," Rodney said as he kissed her cheek. "I look forward to seeing you tomorrow."

The small church was packed, with members of Piney Hill's Class of '87 sprinkled throughout. The choir rocked the house with *Order My Steps*. Rachel and her sons, Hope and Thomasine sat side by side and Rodney joined Sina on her right. They were all amazed when Rev. James asked all other clergy to join him in the pulpit and none other than Conrad walked up. "Hank told me he was a minister," Rachel said. "But I just didn't believe it."

"Stranger things have happened," Thomasine said. After the offering had been collected, all visiting ministers and other guests had been acknowledged, and the choir prepared to sing their sermonic selection *The Battle is Not Yours*. An usher entered the pulpit and gave Rev. James a note which sent him literally running out of the pulpit leaving the note in his trail. Conrad picked up the note, and following the choir selection, he approached the podium.

"It is always a pleasure to enter the House of the Lord," Conrad began. "I first bring you greetings, and I have some news to share—good and bad. The bad news, as you may already be aware, is that Rev. James will not be with you this morning. The good news however, is that his wife is in labor with their first child. And this morning I will deliver the message. Now I'll leave it up to you to determine whether that is good or bad news," he said as the congregation chuckled.

"Bad news," Hope whispered to Rachel and Sina.

"But the mere fact that each of us is here today is a blessing. This means that God has brought you from a mighty long way and you need to thank Him for it. You need to be on your feet rejoicing in the Lord if you are here this morning. Thank God for seeing you here safely. Thank the Lord for food and shelter," he started as the organist backed him up with a series of chords. "If you are in your right mind you need to praise Him because that is truly a blessing in this day and age. Praise Him for waking you up this morning. Praise Him for a restful night of sleep. Praise Him for this beautiful day," Conrad continued as members of the congregation rose to their feet. "But most of all, praise Him for loving each and every one of you unconditionally and for His most precious and perfect gift—His Son

Jesus Christ," Conrad said as the organist began playing *Praise Him*. When the choir finished and the congregation settled down, Conrad prayed briefly asking God to cast Conrad aside and bring the preacher and His inspired words out so that someone's life could be changed. He then turned the congregation's attention to *Psalm* 46.

"The topic for your hearing this morning is *God Will Fight Your Battles*," Conrad said finally beginning his sermon. "There are some battles in this life that you just can't fight alone no matter how high and mighty you may think you are. Doctors, lawyers, teachers, preachers—we all need a little help from the Lord every now and then. You sit at work all day, and your boss is just breathing down your neck, pressuring you beyond imagination. Work is a battlefield. You sit at home—at your dinner table eating with the kids and creditors keep your phone ringing and ringing because you've overextended yourself while trying to make ends meet. Finances are a battlefield. You've done all that you can do, yet you find yourself sleeping in separate bedrooms. Somebody in here right now, is sleeping in the guest room or on the couch. Not talking to each other. Just seeing each other in passing and uttering an insincere hello or how are you doing here and there. Your home is a battlefield. Home situation just all messed up—all mixed up. And you can't seem to understand why. Glory to God," Conrad said as a smile lightened his face. He began recounting the journey of Moses and the Israelites into the Promised Land with their wanderings in the desert and defeats at Heshbon and Bashan. He then turned their attention to *Deuteronomy* 3:21-22 where Moses says "At that time I commanded Joshua: 'You have seen with your own eyes all that the Lord your God has done to these two kings. The Lord will do the same to all the kingdoms over there where you are going. Do not be afraid of them; the Lord, your God Himself will fight for you.' He didn't say that a lawyer would fight for you, no, no, no. He didn't say that a spouse or a friend would fight for you. Naw, no, no, no. He said that the Lord, your God Himself, will fight for you. Now you may ask yourself," Conrad continued as he walked the pulpit. "What must I do in order for God to fight my battle? Turning your attention back to *Psalm* 46- 'God is our refuge and strength, an ever-present help in trouble.' That first verse tells us that it is through God's strength and power that we can get through all of these battles, and valleys and ruts we find ourselves in. But we must take them to Him in prayer. God is not a temporary retreat—but an eternal refuge. Just go to Him and as the next verse tells us—do not fear, because God and God alone has the ability to save. Second, God is a sustainer. Look at verses 4 and 5. The psalmist discusses a river whose streams make glad the city of

God. Rivers at that time, sustained people's lives by making agriculture possible. Jerusalem didn't have a river. But they had something much much better. God. And as long as God lived among the people, the city was invincible. If God is with you, and truly in your heart you too will be invincible because you have the most sophisticated security system ever created. And even millions of dollars can't buy the Great Protector. You just ask. Just ask and you will have protection greater than you ever imagined. Finally," Conrad said wiping his brow, "You must wait on the Lord. Verse 10 says Be still and know that I am God. Repeat that with me."

"Be still and know that I am God," the congregation and ministers said in unison.

"Again."

"Be still and know that I am God."

"Now say it like you really mean it."

"Be still and know that I am God!"

"The psalmist didn't tell us to be still until we got tired, or to be still until we got hungry or to be still just for as long as we want to be still, but the psalmist tells us 'Be still and know that I am God; I will be exalted among the nations, I will be exalted in the earth.' We need to honor Him and His power and His ability to step in, not when we may want Him to, but when the time is right.

"If you feel like you're losing, ask God to fight your battle. If you feel like things just can't get any worse, ask God to fight your battle. If you feel like you're overwhelmed by insurmountable odds, go to God. For if you trust and believe that He will step in right on time, He will fight your battle. The doors of the church are open," Conrad said, stepping down out of the pulpit as the choir sang *Just When I Need Him Most*.

Thomasine and Rachel were in tears by the end of the sermon which had touched so many. They were amazed and shocked, but even more when Hope stood up, made her way past Sina and Rodney, and walked up to the front of the church to rededicate her life to Christ. After the doxology and benediction, the members and visitors formed a line to greet the ministers and their families. "That was really one uplifting sermon," Rodney told Conrad as he shook his hand.

"You delivered the inspired Word of God so eloquently," Sina said to Conrad as she and Rodney walked out of the door.

"So," Thomasine began. "Will I see you at the picnic this afternoon?"

"I'm afraid not. We have a team meeting this afternoon. But how about tomorrow. I thought maybe we could go out on my boat."

"Eeww. I'm afraid not. I promised Rachel's sons I would take them to the zoo tomorrow morning since that will be the last time I see them for so long."

"Do you mind if I tag along?"

"Are you sure? They can be little monsters sometimes."

"Look, I spent the afternoon with them Friday. I'm sure."

Now this will be a test Sina thought as Rachel, Hope, Malcolm, and Martin walked up to the car.

Hope's mother provided the picnic eats for the Three Musketeers and Martin and Malcolm so although they were not doing the traditional Sunday supper, they had a meal to remember. Dan Ryan Woods was filled with the 30 and under crowd and the under went all of the way to a few weeks old. "I don't know why that girl wanted to bring that newborn baby out here—she can't be anymore than two weeks old," Hope commented.

"Shoot, if I had a baby just a few weeks old I'd probably be in myself, knowing me. Just sitting back chilling, being waited on hand and foot," Sina said.

"Well it isn't always that simple," Rachel said as she watched her sons play ball just a few feet away. "It's like you're locked in a prison and any time you can get out, you take advantage of."

"Well that's something I won't know about for a long time," Sina commented. "Because I don't anticipate having any children in the next 2 or 3 years."

"Me neither now," Hope replied. "You know, I've been thinking today."

"That's a good sign," Rachel interrupted laughing.

"And what I always imagined marriage would be like with Jason never really happened. It was never like I thought it would be."

"That's why it's best not to imagine things. We put so many limitations on ourselves when we do that. And after all I've been through, I'm not going to try to be that specific with the future."

"I heard that," Rachel said as Sophronia, Kenneth and Kenneth Jr. walked by. "Did you see that?"

"I saw that last night. It's no biggie."

"That girl always wanted your men Sina and I could never figure out why," Rachel said as Sina started laughing. "What's so funny?"

"It's just that Rodney and I had a long talk last night and Sophronia was the subject. It seems that she was really a schemer. He swore to me that there was nothing going on between him and Sophronia in high school, it was all some game she was playing."

"No," Hope said interrupting.

"He said he only took her to the prom because I turned him down."

"Wow," Rachel said. "I wonder what would have happened if she hadn't interrupted."

"Honestly, I think I would have probably been married to Kenneth which I'm certain would not be at all like I'd imagined. So actually, I'm blessed that she did stick her nose in."

"Well all I've got to say," Hope said. "Is what goes around, comes around."

"You know, although she caused me to go through some very trying times—and I do think it's fair to say that, I don't wish any bad or ill luck on her. Because I'm confident that God will take care of it all."

"He sure will," Hope said. "Just turn it over to Him."

"I know that's right."

"You know, just maybe Jason and I weren't supposed to get married. I really pushed the issue and in our nearly five years of marriage, we were only close to being partners for about a year and a half. When the honeymoon was over, so was the marriage."

"At least your marriage wasn't over before it even started. You know, Brothaman and I weren't equally yoked. So it was destined to fail."

"Say," Sina said, fixing herself a plate of Mrs. Jones' fried chicken, "has he been in contact with the boys since you've been here?"

"Not at all. And you're taking them to the zoo tomorrow, right Sina?"

"Yes, Rodney and I are taking them to the zoo."

"Whatsup with that?"

"You know what I'm about to say."

"Time will tell," Rachel said smiling.

"But you don't have much time before you leave for Australia."

"This is true," Thomasine said biting into her chicken wing. "You know this is the last time we'll all be together for a long time."

"And by then we will all be single women again," Hope said.

"I know I can't wait for my emancipation day," Rachel added.

"If I were you, I wouldn't be in such a big rush. Anything could happen."

"I know but I just want to close this chapter of my life. Take my name back."

"I know that's right," Sina said as she finished chewing a spoonful of potato salad. "You know it's funny."

"What's funny?" Hope asked.

"Remember how there were all these cliques when we were in high school—"

"The Gucci girls, the Guess girls, the Coach girls," Rachel began.

"The Louis Vuitton girls," Sina added.

"Oh and don't forget that group who wore those black leather riding boots. Half of them probably never saw a real horse before either," Hope added laughing.

"Oh yes, how could you forget that group. Remember that time we had a half-day and those thuggish girls came from Crouch High and took Sophronia's leather coat."

"And the boots off her feet," Thomasine added. "I will never forget about that."

"Well what about them?"

"They were so cliquish and seemed so close in school, but look around now. It seems that we have remained the closest in all these years."

"And we've all been successful too."

"I think that was due in part to us being close."

"I think so too," Thomasine said as she went to the picnic basket for dessert. "We have been such a great support system for each other."

Rodney and Sina stood on the front porch of Aunt Mary's house, hand in hand, waiting for someone to open the door. Hank had planters with petunias and impatiens on each side of the porch beside the banister. When Aunt Mary was alive, she often won the neighborhood's yard of the month award. While Hank's efforts were not ribbon awarding, they did brighten up the home. Just before Rachel opened the door, Rodney leaned to kiss Sina. "So Rodney and Sina," Rachel said interrupting a private moment. "Are you sure you want to take my boys to the zoo? I mean are you ready for this? They can be overwhelming sometimes."

"You know how many challenges I've faced in the last ten years. This one will be a piece of cake."

"Boys, did you wash your hands and face," Rachel hollered up the stairs to her sons.

"Who could be coming here this time of morning on a Monday?"

"It's probably Jehovah's Witnesses," Rodney said. "They usually come to this neighborhood on Mondays."

"Well there's one thing I have always truly admired about them."

"What's that?" Rachel said, walking to the door.

"Their willingness and dedication to witness."

When Rachel opened the door expecting to simply give some money for publications, she was surprised to see a thin, frail Brothaman. "Rachel," he said as he leaned forward to kiss her. "I came to get the boys. You know, and spend some time with them."

Rachel took a step back because she did not intend to have this man who nearly caused the death of her sons kiss her. "Well your time is up," Rachel said looking him dead in the eye. "We have been here since Thursday and this is the first time you have even contacted us. I don't think so. We get on a plane this afternoon."

"Well, I'll have them back by then," Brothaman said as the boys walked down the stairs.

"I don't want to go with him," Martin said, crying. "I want to go to the zoo with T-Sina."

"It's all right baby," Rachel said pulling her son to her leg and caressing the top of his head. "You and Malcolm will go to the zoo with your T-Sina and Mr. Harris. And when you come back, then we will get back on the plane and go back home to Nashville. There is no change in plans."

"Rachel," Brothaman said, "These are my sons and I want to spend some time with them."

"The last time you said you wanted to spend some time with them you didn't. You just did your thing and left them to take care of themselves. They are children—just 4 and 5 years old. And right now," Rachel said as Rodney who felt this argument was going to escalate into a serious fight, stepped in between them. "They are going to the zoo with Sina and Rodney."

"Look man," Rodney said putting his hand on Brothaman's shoulder, "Let's go outside and have a talk. You know, cool off."

"Don't tell me what to do," Brothaman said, pushing Rodney's hand off his.

"Look man, I'm not trying to tell you what to do," Rodney said calmly. "But I think in the best interest of everyone here, we should go out and have a talk. It'll just take a minute."

"I'll go when I get good and ready," Brothaman said looking up at Rodney's 6'5" frame. "And now, I'm ready." They walked out the door.

"Boys go upstairs and brush your teeth really good," Rachel told her sons. "You know milk can really make your breath stink." The boys ran upstairs just before their mother began crying. "Sina. I hate for the boys to see him that way. I'm so embarrassed."

"You have nothing to be embarrassed about. None of this is your fault. And I don't think you should internalize Brothaman's choices. My only concern is, will you be safe here after we leave?"

"Hank is due home anytime now."

"Well, all I know is that Brothaman better jet before Hank gets back. And I'll call Tommy and see if he can make sure this area is patrolled while we're gone. Because I'm really concerned. He's real hyped up now."

Lincoln Park Zoo hadn't changed a great deal since Thomasine last visited, which was before she had ever met Rachel or Hope. The ladies' room was still next to the Lion House and that stench lingered. The boys had seen the apes, lions, and reptiles and they were now headed to the petting zoo. "Sina," Rodney started. "Why isn't a beautiful, intelligent and generous woman like you married?"

"That's a good question. But it's primarily by choice. If I just wanted to be married, I could have been married a long time ago. I was nearly married a long time ago. But actually I'm glad I'm still single. How about you?"

"Now Sina, you haven't completely answered my question."

"Okay, to be honest I guess I've built up walls—on the North, South, East and West."

"I know what you mean. I meet so many women who are only interested in my money."

"Why doesn't that surprise me?"

"You know the type who want me to buy them a car or who want to move into my house."

"You mean the webes."

"Webes?"

"Yeah, as in webe living in your house, webe driving your car, webe eating all your food."

"Exactly," Rodney said laughing.

"It amazes me that there are people who think that's all there is to life."

"I know. Just completely shallow. No emotion, no spirituality—"

"No depth."

"None whatsoever. The type who just live for the day, but do nothing to promote or improve the future."

"Yes indeed. That's why I enjoy working with youth so much. Letting them know there's so much more out there than what they see in their immediate world."

"Me too." Rodney put his arm around Sina's shoulder. "You know that's something else we have in common."

"And I'm sure there's more," Thomasine said as Malcolm and Martin walked out of the petting zoo.

"T-Sina and Uncle Rodney," Martin said as Thomasine silently questioned Martin's reference to Rodney. "We got to pet the goats and the pony."

"That must have been fun," Rodney said with a glimmer of light in his eye.

"Yes," Malcolm said. "And when I go home I'ma tell Mommy to get me a pony."

"Well I don't know about that," Sina began explaining to Malcolm. "If you had a pony then you would have to have a lot of land for it to run and play in—"

"So just maybe you can't have one right now, but you can have one in the future."

"Yes, maybe you will." Sina took her anti-bacterial wipes out of her purse and wiped the boys' hands thoroughly. That was what she liked so much about Rodney. He wasn't afraid to dream big like her and he made an investment in the future through his work with youth. She took Malcolm's hand and Rodney took Martin's hand and they continued to walk arm in arm through the zoo.

"You all look like such a happy family," a septuagenarian woman with a bumpy, lumpy shape and silver-blue hair told them. "It's so good in this day and age to see such togetherness like you all have." Rodney and Sina didn't want to rain on her parade so they didn't tell her the truth.

"We might just make a very happy family one day," Rodney said as they continued toward the exit.

"Your middle name must be Joshua."

"How did you know?"

"Because the walls are tumbling down," Sina said smiling.

Hope took a look around her apartment at the empty spaces Jason's departure had left. Her trip back to Kalamazoo seemed longer than it did that time she and Jason had to drive back in a snowstorm. She thought she had begun to come to terms with his leaving, but it didn't really hit home until she was back at the apartment. She took a seat on the couch and looked around the living room at their wedding portrait just above the mantlepiece. Tears welled up in Hope's eyes as she realized that she would now have to get used to sleeping alone again, right after she had become accustomed to sharing her bed. *Alone again.* Hope got up and decided to check her messages. She went into the den which no longer held Jason's law books, and pulled out the telephone message pad she had purchased when Jason started the Heating and Cooling company. A tear dropped from her eye as she pressed the button on her machine and began to write down her messages. "Hope Jones-McCoy, this is Rona Hunter from Centura Health in Virginia Beach. I was calling because we would like for you to come out sometime next week for a second interview. Please give me a call at (757)555-3900, X 3452," Hope wrote diligently and listened for her next message which was from Rachel asking her to call and let her know she had made it safely. Hope called Ms. Hunter back and made arrangements to fly to Virginia Beach later in the week and then called Rachel who told her she was there whenever she needed to talk, particularly since she knew exactly what she was going through. She even suggested that Hope consider getting counseling because the dissolution of her marriage had to be her biggest loss.

The next week and a half just zoomed by like a Florida snowfall. Here it was Sina's last night in Chicago for the next two years. She and Rodney had managed to visit all of her favorite restaurants including Harold's, Woo Woo's, Docks, Michelangelo's, the polish stand and her favorite place for ribs and hot links—Dem Bones. They had become attached to their pet names for each other—Sweetie Pie and Sugar Cane. All of Sina's things which hadn't been shipped were packed and she had said her good-byes to Hope when Rachel returned her call.

"Whats'up girl?"

"Just getting ready to leave,"

"You weren't going to sleep were you?"

"No, I have a date tonight."

"With Rodney?"

"Of course. Rachel, I'm in love. It seems that all I ever do is think about Rodney. We have been together every day since I came to Chicago. Remember he and Hank ate all the perch."

"Yeah."

"He even took me to his mother's house for dinner Sunday."

"Meeting his mom—that sounds serious," Rachel replied. "So have you all done it yet?"

"Rachel," Thomasine said. "Now you know good and well that would be a sure-fire way for me to crash and burn—and I don't intend to do that. Not this time."

"Sina, Sina. Just how do you exercise such discipline. You were dateless since Kenneth."

"Now Rachel, I didn't say I hadn't thought about it, I just didn't act on it," Sina said giggling. "But we have done so much together. I went out on his boat, we walked our dogs on the lakefront, he even came by and helped me pack."

"That's so nice."

"But so much for me, what about you? Have you gotten in touch with Patrick yet?"

"No, I keep calling but all I get is voice mail. He must be on vacation or something because I got Beulah to drive me down there the other day and there were no signs of life."

"What will you do if he's not the one?"

"I guess I'll hire a private eye because what you said was right. He really needs to know, and I'll just deal with whatever happens. It can't be any worse than what I've already had to deal with."

"That sounds like a move," Thomasine said, looking out of the window. "Look Rachel, I'm going to have to go. Rodney's here. But I'll send you an e-mail the minute I get it set up down under."

"You do that."

"And I'll be in touch. I promise."

"Okay."

"Ciao."

"Hold on a second. Martin and Malcolm just got out of the tub, they need to say goodbye to you."

"Okay."

"Goodbye T-Sina," Martin said.

"Bye Martin. I want you to be a good boy, and do everything your mother tells you to do."

"Okay T-Sina. Tell Uncle Rodney I said bye too." Sina wondered again what was up with this Uncle Rodney thing and why Martin was so obsessed with it.

"But he's not going with me. You just may see him when you come to Chicago again if the Gale Force is not playing an away game."

"Okay, Malcolm wants to talk to you."

"Bye T-Sina."

"Bye Malcolm. You be a good boy, okay, and maybe I'll send you and Martin some boomerangs from Australia."

"Okay T-Sina."

"Look," Rachel said. "I'm going to make that call as soon as I put the boys to bed."

"You do that. And I'll be in touch as soon as I can. And as always, I'm here for you."

"I know. Now you can't keep Rodney waiting much longer."

"Do you mean that literally or figuratively?"

"You better go."

Sina and Rodney found themselves in an intimate restaurant in the North Loop that featured great jazz. They sat on the roof deck and enjoyed the gentle breeze. The waitress had taken their dinner orders of grilled salmon with string beans cooked in smoked turkey and wild rice and Rodney ordered a bottle of champagne. "So what's next?" Sina asked Rodney.

"You tell me."

"When I came to Chicago two weeks ago I never dreamed I would have such a wonderful time. Rodney, I think our chance meeting was destined. And I'll always wonder what would have been if I didn't have to go to Australia."

"You're not gone just yet," he said, reaching for Sina's hand.

"I know, but it's just that when we're getting so close, when everything is finally falling in place for me—"

"Something else seems to come up and inter—"

"Throw a boomerang in my plans." Sina said as she and Rodney took turns completing each other's sentences.

"The good thing about a boomerang, though is that it always returns," he said as he took a sip of champagne.

"That's true," Sina continued. "But it's like I've finally resolved some things and now I'm ready to move to another level—with you. Which has really been a long time coming."

"Why is that?" Rodney asked as their meal was set on the table.

"I decided a long time ago not to settle. I want all or nothing," she said putting a forkful of salmon in her mouth. "Casual sex has never been my thing—"

"Mine neither. But some of my colleagues in the International League really play roulette. Different women in every city. And some of them still think they are so invincible. But my life is worth far more than playing a little game of connect the women between cities."

"I heard that," Sina said continuing as the music over the loudspeaker changed to Ramsey Lewis' *Love's Gotta Hold*. "But finally I feel like I am able to give my all, to you." Rodney leaned across the table to kiss her.

"Thomasine Mintor, I love you."

Rachel sat on her sofa in the living room with her favorite Nancy Wilson tape playing in the background, giving her the courage to make the call in spite of the butterflies in her stomach. "Hello," the deep voice said on the other end of the line.

"Is this the Patrick Long who went to Duncan University?" Rachel asked.

"No Patrick Long here. I think you got the wrong number ma'am."

"Sorry, I must have misdialed." Rachel said as she depressed the switchhook so that she could try once again. Her heart beat faster and faster as she dialed that final number and checked and rechecked each digit as she dialed.

"Hello," the voice was familiar.

"Hello." Rachel thought her heart would leap from her chest. "Is this the Patrick Long who went to Duncan University?"

"Yes it is, and I sent in my alumni dues last week."

"Patrick," Rachel said slowly. "This is Rachel."

"Hello Rachel," Patrick said with no emotion. "How have you been?"

"Oh," Rachel sighed. "I've been doing pretty good," she said as she heard her call waiting signal. "I'm sorry Patrick. Could you hold on a second?"

"Sure," he said. "No problem."

"Hello," Rachel said after she depressed the switchhook.

"Rachel," her mother said. "I've got some news about your father."

Rachel remembered that she had a very important task to complete. "Can I call you back Mom? I'm on a very important call and if I don't do this now, I just may never."

"Okay honey. Call me back as soon as you get off the phone."

"Patrick. Thank you for waiting. That was my mother."

"Well, I'll let you get back to her."

"No, I have something very important to tell you. I just don't know how."

"Just tell me," Patrick responded when Rachel's call waiting signal beeped again.

"I don't believe this. My phone hasn't rung all day," Rachel started. "I should have canceled the call waiting. Could you hold on again?"

"Sure Rachel, it's no problem. I'm not doing anything else."

"Rachel, are you sitting down," Hank said as Rachel began to say hello.

"What is it Hank?" Rachel said now annoyed by all of the interruptions.

"It's about Brothaman."

Thomasine looked all around her. And as she heard that her plane to LAX was boarding and hugged her parents and brother goodbye she was a bit disgusted. She couldn't believe that Rodney had broken his promise to meet her at the airport. It was his last chance to see her and since he decided not to show, Sina knew just what that meant. *Actions speak louder than words.* She took her seat and was so sorry she had poured out so much of herself and given so much of herself to Rodney. She just chalked it all up to her bad luck—that Thomasine kiss of death.

Rodney was startled to see how late it was when he finally woke up. He had trouble falling asleep all night, thinking about Thomasine, and when he finally got to sleep Thomasine was probably getting up to catch her morning flight. He honked the horn at the gapers on the Ryan and found himself driving on the shoulder trying to get to O'Hare in time. When he finally made it to the Kennedy, he decided to test the performance of his car when he was pulled over by a trooper as he approached the O'Hare Airport exit.

"I can't believe this." The trooper walked over and began the ritual all too familiar to Black men in expensive cars.

"What's a person like you doing driving a car like this?" the trooper asked, looking under the seats.

"Just who are people like me? Graduates of U of I? University of Chicago MBAs? Professional basketball players? Or Black males? Because when you look at me, that's all you see."

The trooper remained silent and wrote Rodney's ticket.

"You see that plane up there?" Rodney said, pointing upward. "The woman I love is on that plane and she's going away for two long years, so yes, I was speeding so that I wouldn't miss her, but the rest of this isn't necessary. Could you just give me my ticket so that I can figure out what I can do now that I've missed the plane?" Rodney got back in his car with his ticket in hand and added, "Oh, and my attorney will be in touch."

Rodney looked frantically through his glove compartment for his passport. "Yes," he said as he checked to see if his visa was current. He found a space in Parking Lot C, took the elevator to the tunnel as fans stopped him for autographs. He kept moving forward and scrawled his name on whatever was handed to him. "I would love to talk to you," he said to the young boys, "but I'm running late for a plane."

When he got to the American Airlines ticket counter, he was dismayed by the long line, even in first class. He finally made it to the front of the line. "I need a one-way ticket to LAX."

"All we have available sir is a center seat in row 29. And it's boarding now, Gate H5."

"I'll take it." He handed the woman his American Express Platinum card. "What time will that put me in LAX?"

"It's due to arrive at 12:37. Do you have any baggage to check?"

"No," he said taking his ticket and charge card and running toward the metal detectors.

When Rodney got into that cramped seat and the plane reached its cruising altitude, he called his travel agent. "Christina," he said. "I need a one way ticket on Quantas flight number 8 out of LAX to Sydney. Preferably business class. And I will need a ground transport to get me to the international terminal."

"That flight leaves at 1," Christina said. "And business class is all full. What time are you due to arrive in LAX?"

"12:37."

"You can't make that Rodney. You have to be at the gate at least by 12:00."

"Please see what you can do for me. I really, really need to be on that plane."

"I'll see, but I can't make any promises."

After that long flight made bearable by an in-flight movie, Thomasine looked around the gate area one last time before boarding her Quantas flight, wondering if she were wrong for doubting Rodney. No such luck. Sina had gotten comfortable in her aisle seat in Business Class where she flew last time. She found economy class to be a good deal, but too confining. Sina met the person sitting next to her, took off her shoes and put on those terry cloth socks Quantas provided for each passenger. She looked at her watch and completely gave up hope of seeing Rodney. It was one o'-clock and she would be pulling away from the gate any second now.

"Welcome aboard Quantas flight number 8 with non-stop service to Sydney. We were due to leave at 1:00 but there will be a slight delay. Due to inclement weather on the east coast, we have some passengers who are currently on their way to the gate. It should be about a 30 minute delay, so just sit back and relax. Our flight attendants are serving Hunter Valley wine and you may listen to the in-flight music while you wait. As soon as they have all boarded, we will begin our flight."

Thomasine plugged in her headphones and pressed the button on the arm rest until she found the jazz channel and listened to music from Art Porter and Pete Escovedo. The song *Lake Shore Drive* just reminded her of the last few weeks with Rodney and she teared up. She watched as the East Coast passengers boarded. No sign of Rodney.

"As soon as all of the passengers are seated and all carry-on luggage has been properly stored under the seat in front of you or in the overhead storage bin, we will begin our flight. If you will turn your attention to the monitors, you can follow our journey to Sydney. The flight will be 14 hours and we will show you three movies and—" the pilot said as Sina tuned him out and reflected on the years. He continued, and as the plane took off, she could see that they were now over water.

"Now that we have reached our cruising altitude, dinner will be served. And we have some very special desserts in business and first class." Sina continued her reverie, "In Business Class, we have a little slice of Sweetie Pie," he said as Sina patted her feet and shook her head to Pete Escovedo's *Boomerang*. "And in First Class, we have Sugar Cane."

The End?